A

SHADOW THREAT

NEW YORK TIMES #1 BESTSELLER **TONY LEE** WRITING AS
JACK GATLAND

Hooded Man MEDIA

INSPIRATION • PRODUCTION • PUBLICATION

Published by Hooded Man Media.

Cover design by L1graphics

First Edition: June 2025

PRAISE FOR JACK GATLAND

'Fast-paced and action packed, Jack Gatland's thrillers always deliver a punch.'

'This is one of those books that will keep you up past your bedtime, as each chapter lures you into reading just one more.'

'This book was excellent! A great plot which kept you guessing until the end.'

'Couldn't put it down, fast paced with twists and turns.'

'The story was captivating, good plot, twists you never saw and really likeable characters. Can't wait for the next one!'

'Totally addictive. Thoroughly recommend.'

'Moves at a fast pace and carries you along with it.'

'Just couldn't put this book down, from the first page to the last one it kept you wondering what would happen next.'

LIQUIDATE THE PROFITS

FOLDED HANDS

Declan Walsh. Ellie Reckless. Tom Marlowe. Liam Harper.
Ryder Waites. Damian Lucas.

Discover the worlds of Jack Gatland and Tony Lee in their
VIP Reader's Club!! And gain two EXCLUSIVE PREQUELS,
completely free to anyone who joins!

Join at http://bit.ly/jackgatlandVIP

Also by Jack Gatland

COUNTER ATTACK

STEALTH STRIKE

BROAD SWORD

ROGUE SIGNAL

SNIPER ALLEY

SHADOW THREAT

SENTRY POINT

ELLIE RECKLESS BOOKS

PAINT THE DEAD

STEAL THE GOLD

HUNT THE PREY

FIND THE LADY

BURN THE DEBT

TAKE THE KING

LIAM HARPER BOOKS

FINAL STRIKE

BLOOD RIDGE

TRACK SHIFT

SEBASTIAN SILVER BOOKS

SILVER AND THE SUNDAY CYPHER

DAMIAN LUCAS BOOKS

THE LIONHEART CURSE

STANDALONE BOOKS

THE BOARDROOM

As Tony Lee

For Mum, who inspired me to write.

For Tracy, who inspires me to write.

For Alan, who read these until the end.

CONTENTS

PROLOGUE

THREE YEARS AGO

When it came to booking hitmen, The Broker was like no other. While others were like managers or agents, taking percentages for death, The Broker was a *savant*, doing it for the love, for the challenge, for the body count. He didn't need his percentages; with a generational wealth that people had no idea about, The Broker lived a comfortable life. He could've stopped tomorrow, and the lavishness of his life wouldn't have changed. In addition to that, if he did this, nobody would ever see him again, because bar a few people from a life long ago, nobody knew The Broker's real name.

All they knew was that he was rich and did this for fun– and that The Broker had his own ways of making money. Perhaps his hits, when he arranged them, provided him with an income *outside* of the agency fee. It didn't matter. Either way, when you wanted a hit placed on someone special, and you didn't want to miss, you went to The Broker.

And that's what had happened here; a French ambassador had been a naughty boy, caught selling secrets to the British. MI5, MI6, it didn't matter who it was, and if he was being brutally honest, The Broker didn't care what had happened or why the man needed to die. All he cared about was making sure that he could match the perfect killer to the task.

The Broker had a list, you see; names and numbers of killers across the globe, although the names were all likely fake and the numbers were dark web contact bases, mainly through message boards or internet chats. No hitman–no self-respecting hitman, anyway, would ever give a phone number, even a burner.

That way lay madness.

The problem was nobody seemed to want to take the hit on. He'd started speaking to some of his usual people but found that MI5–or perhaps MI6–were doing their best to call in every favour they could to *stop* this happening.

And so The Broker had been forced to turn to alternative hitmen, going "off name", rather than risking his own reputation, becoming even more of a ghost than he had before, speaking to *similar* ghosts, including the man he was currently waiting to speak to, now sitting alone at a table in a piazza in Rome. He sat across from the Pantheon, the sun beating down on his head and he'd wanted to go into the shade, but the message had been clear. His contact wanted to see him in the open before he made himself visible.

The Broker understood the caution. This was a life of secrets and lies, he was desperate and on a time crunch, and the man on the other end of the message chat was someone that The Broker had never dealt with before.

Which meant, of course, that the man had never dealt with The Broker.

There was no trust created yet. But, after this hit, there would be. Maybe he'd even give his name, but most of the hitmen he dealt with only learnt properly of The Broker when they'd fulfilled three or even four hits. Most times never.

He'd done what he was requested to do and on arrival had sat down at the table, ordered two flat whites with oat milk, a Diet Coke and a pastry–a particular one requested by the potential asset. The Broker assumed this was the equivalent of wearing a red rose, or placing a particular newspaper on the table, and when the server returned, an elderly man with the expression of somebody who'd been asked to do something but didn't have a clue why, he had a smartphone in his hand.

'I've been told to give this to you,' he mumbled, his accent Italian, his English impeccable.

'You were told, or you were paid?' The Broker asked, almost amused by the reluctance here.

'I was paid one hundred euros to give this phone to you,' the server admitted, dismissively. 'I don't know why I was given it, or why you need it, and I'd prefer if you weren't at this table after your call. My boss doesn't like mafioso.'

The Broker smiled at this.

'I'll do what I damn well want,' he muttered. 'And I'm not mafioso, tell your boss. They wish they were *me*.'

The server shrugged and walked off, returning into the cafe, and The Broker looked down at the phone. His first instinct was to turn it on, check through the records, see if there was a message, but as he went to do so, it buzzed with a new call.

He answered on the second ring.

'It's very hot and I'm getting tired,' he grumbled irritably.

'If you remember, Mister Bones, I'm the one offering you a job, not the other way round.'

'You can't be too sure,' the voice replied. It was the first time that The Broker had heard the voice of Mister Bones, and there was a slight Scandinavian hint to it. 'After all, you know my name, but all I know about you is that you have a job for me.'

'I don't speak to people over the phone,' The Broker snapped. 'I speak to them face to face.'

'But you have seen my face,' Mister Bones replied. 'I just gave you the phone.'

At this, The Broker looked back at the cafe, half rising from his chair.

'The old man?' he asked.

There was a chuckle.

'Indeed,' he said. 'I gave you the phone, walked back into the building, and right now I'm watching you from a back room.'

'And how are you exactly doing that?'

'I have a sniper rifle on a nearby roof with a remote camera attached to it,' Mister Bones continued. 'It's currently aimed directly at your head.'

The Broker fought every urge to continue upwards to a standing position, in case his head was to explode.

So that's why he was told to sit outside.

'Look,' he said, 'I don't know what you've been told, but this is a business opportunity, nothing more.'

'And I look forward to talking business. But currently we're in a stalemate.'

'And how do you reckon that?'

'I'm here to do a job, but you won't talk to me unless I'm

facing you,' Mister Bones replied calmly. 'I, however, never speak to my clients face to face.'

'I understand you did the Dakota job.'

'I did.'

'That was well done.' The Broker tried to peer through the cafe's glass to see if he could see this mysterious, elderly server again. There was still a part, deep down that believed Mister Bones was lying to him, and that the old man was simply nothing more than an old man.

'Don't damn me with faint praise,' Mister Bones murmured softly. 'It was an adequate job.'

'Was it you who worked with *TransPharma*?'

'It was.'

'Impressive, again,' The Broker continued. 'I heard they needed it completely plausible but fast, and then two of their board were fatally struck down with unknown illnesses.'

'I don't like to speak ill of the dead, but they really shouldn't have tried the Salmon Mousse.'

The Broker wasn't sure if Mister Bones was mocking him or not with the *Monty Python* line.

'You want a French diplomat removed, I believe,' Mister Bones said now, and The Broker frowned.

'How did you know that?'

'I have my ways. I also know that many of the usual people out there have been scared off by the authorities, Intelligence Agencies or by men in black suits from going anywhere near this.'

'Yes,' The Broker admitted. 'I do find myself in a bit of a fix.'

'And so you come to me, hoping I can save the day,' Mister Bones continued. 'Well, I'd love to help you, but unfortunately I don't want to.'

'Wait,' The Broker shouted quickly, desperation visible in his voice. 'If you weren't going to take the job, why have this meeting?'

'I wanted to see if you'd blink,' Mister Bones replied calmly. 'Nothing more. I was curious to see the man who wanted people dead. I don't need your job in the same way that I don't need the money *for* the job, so thank you for your time. The lunch is on me and I wish you all the best. You really should try the pastry. It's to die for.'

'What would it take for you to do this?'

There was a pause and The Broker couldn't help but smile. *Everyone had their price, and it seemed he'd just found Mister Bones's weak spot.*

'A million in cryptocurrency,' he said down the line. 'I'd have full choice on how he dies. I'm aware it's a short time frame and I'd make sure it was done this week. But my name would not be mentioned.'

'But what if I wanted to work with you again?'

'I never work twice for the same person.'

'But I'm an important man, I could—'

'I don't want to know who you are, because it means nothing to me,' Mister Bones continued. 'Once the job is done, and the money is in my cold wallet, I'll never think of you again.'

The Broker looked into the cafe and saw the old man staring at him through the window.

'That's not your face, is it?' he asked. 'You said you'd seen me face to face, but ...'

'You're right, I lied. I wasn't the man who served you. Maybe I was the tourist who asked you for directions as you entered the square, maybe I was the officer you avoided when I approached you,' Mister Bones replied with the slightest of chuckles. 'But I did see you face to face. I didn't say which face I'd wear when I saw you. I wear many identities. It's the best way to get close to people when they don't realise that I'm there.'

'So, this is all a big game of make believe for you?' The Broker snapped angrily. 'You were never going to take the job?'

'No, I was never going to show you my true identity,' Mister Bones replied, and his tone was one of boredom, of resignation—a man already tired of the conversation. 'Send me the details and I'll do it for you. Or don't, and I won't. But it sounds to me like you need a friend right now.'

The Broker knew he didn't have much of a choice, and so he nodded, allowing the motion to be seen.

'You'll have it by the end of the day,' he said. 'I can arrange the cryptocurrency to whatever wallet you want, and all I want to see is a dead body within a week.'

'Do you really want to see that?' Mister Bones asked. 'Because many of my victims are never seen again.'

'As long as he's gone, that's all my clients care,' The Broker admitted. He went to continue, but then realised that the phone was dead, and looking into the cafe, he saw the man was gone.

Had he been the elderly server after all?

Quickly, he rose from his table, hurrying into the building. The server he'd seen standing at the window was no longer there, and as he looked around, he saw that the door to the back was ajar. Sprinting through, he saw a small kitchen with two chefs currently shouting at each other in Italian. The Broker didn't have time to speak to them, and so carried on through, the door taking him out into an alley behind the cafe, and away from the piazza.

There, tossed to the side, was a white-haired wig.

The Broker looked up and down the alley with the faintest of smiles now.

'Okay, Mister Bones,' he said softly. 'Let's see how well you do.'

SIX DAYS LATER, THE BROKER SAT IN HIS RENTED STUDY, THE large floor-to-ceiling windows tinted against the glare of the Rome afternoon sun. Even though this wasn't his property, he still found he was at peace here. In the short time he'd been in Rome this had become his sanctuary, the walls lined with leather-bound books he'd never read, the furniture just uncomfortable enough to remind visitors they weren't welcome to linger.

Maybe he'd buy the place when he was finished.

He'd spent the day monitoring the usual channels, tracking other potential contracts, frustrated that his reputation had taken a hit over the French ambassador situation.

Four refusals. *Four.* That had never happened before, and when he'd offered the contract to Mister Bones, he'd been desperate, something he'd not felt in many years.

The television murmured in the background, cycling through international news stories he barely registered until a familiar name caught his attention.

'... French diplomat Jean-Pierre Moreau has died in what authorities are calling a tragic skiing accident in the Alps—'

The Broker's head snapped up; his attention fully captured. He reached for the remote, increasing the volume as the news anchor continued.

'Moreau, fifty-two, was skiing alone on an advanced slope

when witnesses say he appeared to lose control and went off course, skiing over the edge of a sharp ravine. Rescue teams found his body several hours later, and officials report that while Moreau was an experienced skier, fresh snowfall and poor visibility may have contributed to the accident.'

The screen showed footage of emergency vehicles with flashing lights, their blue and red streaks cutting through the white backdrop of the mountain. A photo of Moreau appeared–distinguished, silver-haired, with the polished and likely artificial poise of a career diplomat.

'Moreau had recently been appointed as special envoy to several Eastern European nations during last week's NATO summit and was scheduled to begin diplomatic duties next week. French President—'

The Broker muted the television, a slow smile spreading across his face. He knew accidents. He'd arranged many of them over the years. This had none of the markers of a genuine mishap.

No, this was elegant. Professional. The body found but no foul play suspected.

The kind of work that didn't trigger investigations or diplomatic incidents.

His laptop buzzed, and he opened up a window in a dark-web browser to see a new message. It was his client, likely seeing the same new report.

Problem solved. Payment incoming. Our gratitude.

The Broker placed the laptop screen back down, walked to his private bar, and poured himself a single malt, savouring the burn as he considered Mister Bones. The man–whoever he was behind that ridiculous codename–had delivered precisely what was needed. More impressively, he'd done it without leaving a trace of suspicion, although he'd need to check this, as there could be information not passed to the press. However, the story seemed plausible. An advanced slope, poor visibility. An experienced skier makes one mistake ... who would question it? Moreau had been skiing alone and this had obviously been planned that way. Perhaps Mister Bones had tampered with the equipment, or introduced some subtle factor to ensure the diplomat would lose control at the right moment.

Or perhaps he'd just pushed the man off the mountain.

Either way, the job was done, cleanly.

For someone who claimed not to care about reputation, Mister Bones had certainly protected his own. And, by extension, The Broker's.

Deciding to congratulate his freelancer, The Broker returned to the laptop, and his secure terminal. The dark-web forum loaded, its interface deliberately archaic, designed to be navigable only by those who already knew their way around. Once more, he navigated to a private channel, one that couldn't be traced back to either of them, and began composing a message.

The Alpine incident was elegantly handled. Your
approach shows refinement often lacking in this industry.
I respect our previous arrangement, but exceptional
talent deserves exceptional opportunity. I have another
situation that might interest you. Payment is being placed
into your agreed cold wallet for this finished job,
either way.

He hit send and waited. Normally, there would be an

automatic confirmation that the message had been delivered to the recipient's inbox.

Instead, a red error message flashed across his screen:

RECIPIENT NOT FOUND

The Broker frowned, checked the destination address, and tried again.

RECIPIENT NOT FOUND

He leaned back in his chair, staring at the error message. It wasn't a network issue–the system was functioning perfectly–the account simply didn't exist any more. No forwarding address, no alternate contact method. Only a cold wallet for the fee, and those things were impossible to track.

Mister Bones had disappeared as completely as if he'd never existed.

There was a second message though; not from Mister Bones, but from an old friend, someone from before the days The Broker became, well, The Broker. He opened it up and read the words. There were only four.

Gregorovich captured. Believed dead.

The Broker closed the channel, logged out of the forum, but not before he erased all traces of his own presence there. He rose, walking to the window, swirling the remaining whisky in his glass as he looked out over the ancient city.

Gregorovich was dead. It wasn't what he had hoped to hear, but such were the ways of the shadows.

'I don't work twice for the same person,' he murmured,

recalling Mister Bones's words. The man had meant it literally. Once the job was done, he'd not only walked away, he'd erased all possibility of contact. It was a clean approach. Professional. And incredibly frustrating.

The Broker prided himself on his network of killers, but Mister Bones was now a ghost in his system, an asset he couldn't access again. And something about that–about a hitman he couldn't control–irritated him more than he cared to admit.

'Well played, Mister Bones,' he muttered to the empty room, raising his glass in silent acknowledgment. 'Well played indeed.'

1

TOOTHACHE

IF HE WAS BEING BRUTALLY HONEST WITH HIMSELF, THERE WERE only a few things that could make Tom Marlowe flinch. The steel grip of a sharp blade at his throat, perhaps, or the red dot of a laser sight visible on his chest. But as Doctor Chopra's drill whined against his molar, Marlowe found himself clutching the armrests of the dental chair with white knuckles as he stared up at the light above.

'Almost there, Mister Ripley,' murmured the dentist, his voice muffled behind his surgical mask. 'Just a bit more cleaning before we place the temporary filling.'

Marlowe nodded slightly, trying not to focus on the metallic taste in his mouth or the persistent ache that had plagued him for three days.

'Five, six, okay, seven, eight, fine.'

Marlowe went to reply open-mouthed, asking what the dentist meant, but realised Doctor Chopra was checking his teeth on either side, passing information to the nurse sat at the computer beside the surgery's window. Instead, he tried to shut his eyes and ignore the burning smell the friction had caused, doing his best not to liken this to the torture scene in *Marathon Man.*

For the last two months after Mount Rushmore his tooth had been troubling him, probably from a crown dislodged during his fight on the top of Washington's forehead, and now after all that, here he was, taken down by something as mundane as a toothache.

The drill stopped and Marlowe exhaled through his nose, grateful for the brief respite.

'You've got quite the cavity here,' Doctor Chopra observed, peering into his mouth with an angled mirror. 'You've been taking care of them, but there's trauma to the jaw. Have you taken up a martial art or anything?'

Marlowe made a noncommittal sound. The last few months hadn't exactly left much time for dental care. Between dodging CIA operatives, dealing with the fallout from Rushmore, and rebuilding his operation with Trix, flossing regularly had been low on his priority list–and he'd spent more time being punched in the mouth than cleaning it.

'This tooth will need a crown eventually,' Doctor Chopra continued, selecting another instrument from his tray. 'I'll place a temporary filling today, but you should come back in a few weeks for the permanent work.'

As the dentist worked, Marlowe studied the man–after all, while stuck in this chair, it was either Doctor Chopra or the light shining into his eyes he could study right now. Mid-fifties, Indian and with a slow, methodical precision in his movements that spoke of decades of experience, Chopra's Canary Wharf practice catered to London's elite: diplomats, business executives, politicians, that sort of thing. Its slightly out-of-town location meant it was also a place for spies, and ex-spies–it was the kind of dentist where political discretion was paramount and the clientele never sat in waiting rooms together, which meant you could come and go with no fear of being confronted.

Unless, of course, they were waiting outside.

'You have interesting dentition, Thomas,' Doctor Chopra remarked as he filled the cavity. 'You have previous trauma to your left incisors. Some kind of accident?'

Marlowe gave a short nod, recalling a particularly unpleasant encounter in Berlin where the butt of a Makarov pistol had left more than just cosmetic damage.

'I treat several boxers,' Doctor Chopra said conversationally. 'Amateur and professional. Though most of my patients are in less ... physical professions.'

The dentist adjusted the overhead light, continuing his work.

'Last week I had a cabinet minister in this very chair. Poor man was terrified of the drill. Funny how people who make decisions affecting millions can be reduced to trembling by a simple dental procedure.'

Marlowe made a noise that might have been agreement.

'And before that, a Russian businessman–though between us, I suspect "businessman" might be a generous description,' Doctor Chopra chuckled softly. 'He paid in cash. Always a bit suspicious, that.'

The dentist continued chatting and Marlowe half-listened, more focused on the dull pain in his jaw despite the local anaesthetic.

'There we are,' Doctor Chopra said at last, removing his instruments. 'Temporary filling is in place. Rinse please.'

Marlowe leant forward, swirling a mouthful of pink-coloured water in his mouth before spitting it out, noting the larger than expected amount of blood emerging.

'How does that feel?'

Sitting back, Marlowe ran his tongue over the tooth.

'Better. Bit sensitive still.'

'That's normal. The nerve is inflamed, but it should settle down in a day or two.' Doctor Chopra removed his mask, revealing a neatly trimmed silver beard. 'If the pain persists or increases, call my office immediately. We might be looking at an infection that could require root canal treatment.'

Marlowe nodded, working his jaw as he sat up in the chair.

'I notice from your patient form that you travel frequently,' Doctor Chopra said, already at the side desk, making notes in Marlowe's "Thomas Ripley" file. 'Any trips planned in the near future?'

'Nothing immediate,' Marlowe replied cautiously.

'Good. I'd advise against air travel for at least a week. Pressure changes can be problematic with dental work. When would be a good time to schedule you for the crown? My calendar fills quickly, but I could fit you in next Thursday afternoon.'

'I'll need to check my own schedule. I'll call your receptionist.'

After leaving the surgery room, Marlowe settled his bill with the receptionist–an eye-watering sum that made him grateful for the war chest he and Trix maintained–and stepped out into Canary Wharf. The February air was sharp with cold, a light drizzle turning the pavements slick, and he turned up the collar of his coat against the chill, scanning the street out of habit.

Nothing unusual. Just the normal flow of Canary Wharf bankers and lawyers.

Marlowe's mouth and upper lip still felt numb, the aftermath of the injection distorting his speech slightly when he'd spoken back in the dentist. He decided against hailing a cab, preferring to walk towards the DLR station while his face regained some sensation.

His phone vibrated in his pocket.

Trix.

'All sorted?' her voice came through, crisp and direct.

'Temporary filling,' Marlowe replied, keeping his voice low as he walked–although he was sure it didn't sound like the words he spoke. 'Need to go back for a crown.'

'I'm sorry, did you say *memphorary fiffing?*' Trix said, and he could hear the smirk in her voice. 'Is someone trying to strangle you? Are you having a stroke? Wait ... did the big bad dentist hurt you?'

'Very funny,' Marlowe mumbled. 'Numb mouth. Any progress?'

Her tone shifted to business immediately.

'I've been analysing the data from Rushmore. The algorithms used have similarities to programs used by hedge funds for high-frequency trading. I'm trying to trace their origin.'

'Steele?'

'Nothing direct yet, but I'm following the money trail through shell companies in The Caymans and Singapore. Some of these paths were created years ago, well before Steele got involved, which is surprising.'

Marlowe dodged a woman pushing a pram, mindful of the slippery pavement, and turned onto one of the bridges crossing onto West India Quay, taking an indirect route towards the DLR station.

'It's also possible that the stock manipulation was just phase one,' Trix continued. 'The real target could have been currencies or commodities.'

Marlowe paused at the other side of the bridge; his tooth was beginning to throb again as the anaesthetic wore off.

'Get back to the church,' he said. 'I'll meet you there in an hour. We need to go through everything again.'

'I'll tell you what, as I didn't understand a bloody word you just said, I'll meet you back at the crypt, yeah?' Trix was almost laughing at Marlowe's discomfort now. 'Don't take too many painkillers–I need you sharp.'

The line went dead, and Marlowe pocketed his phone. The mention of the church's crypt–his converted home and base of operations–brought a mixture of comfort and unease for some reason. After returning from America, he'd been relieved to find his secret crypt beneath the church untouched, even though the main living area had required significant repairs after his last confrontation with assassins. He was wondering though how much longer it would stay as secret as he hoped.

Somewhere out there, St John Steele was pulling strings, and St John Steele knew exactly where Tom Marlowe lived.

THE CONVERTED CHURCH STOOD ON A QUIET WEST LONDON street, its Gothic revival architecture blending into the cityscape. From the outside, it appeared to be a simple conversion–one of many former churches transformed into residential spaces across London. Marlowe had purchased it a couple of years ago through a shell company MI5 had then provided, valuing both its structural integrity and the secret it concealed beneath.

Marlowe entered through the back door, disabling and reactivating the security system as he did so. Inside, the primary space had been transformed into a functional living area; the central nave housed a sparsely furnished lounge, while a mezzanine level contained his bedroom, overlooking the entire space. The altar area had been converted into a kitchen that Marlowe rarely used, preferring the simplicity of takeaway or the microwave meals Trix occasionally brought, but the true heart of his operation lay beneath. Behind a concealed doorway under the stairs, a second, steep, stone staircase led down to what had once been the church's crypt, one never placed on modern maps for some unknown reason. This underground sanctum housed their command centre; a series of workstations and servers that Trix had built after they left the Service together.

He entered the crypt, immediately registering Trix's presence by the soft glow of monitors and the faint smell of coffee that perpetually surrounded her workspace.

'That took longer than an hour,' Trix called from behind them.

'Detoured to pick up supplies,' Marlowe replied, holding up a pharmacy bag. 'Extra strength ibuprofen.'

'How's the tooth?'

'Hurts like hell, but at least it means I'm not talking like I'm punch drunk.'

'Shame.' Trix emerged from her workstation, giving him a critical once-over. Her blonde hair was pulled back in her usual practical ponytail, dark circles under her eyes betraying too many late nights analysing data.

'You look terrible,' she observed.

'Thanks for that,' Marlowe said dryly, resisting the urge to reply back with his own opinion of Trix's current state. 'What have you found?'

Trix led him to the main display where multiple screens showed financial data, geographical maps, and surveillance footage.

'I've been digging into the algorithms Steele was using for market manipulation,' she said, pulling up a series of charts. 'This is what I've reconstructed of Operation Quicksilver's financial structure. Cold War slush funds diverted into black budgets, then fragmented across dozens of accounts. Steele mapped it all, reconnected the pieces.'

'For what purpose?'

'Control.' Trix highlighted several nodes on the diagram. 'Each of these represents a leverage point in the global financial system. Together, they don't just predict market movements–they can cause them.'

'So, Steele wasn't just after the money?' Marlowe studied the diagram.

'No. He wanted the architecture, the system itself. The ability to trigger financial crises at will.' Trix's expression was grim. 'It's economic warfare on a scale we've never seen before.'

'Any idea where he is now?'

Trix shook her head.

'Off the grid since Rushmore. My contacts at GCHQ haven't picked up anything. Last confirmed sighting was in Hong Kong, but that trail went cold weeks ago.'

Marlowe paced the length of the workstation, trying to ignore the persistent throbbing in his jaw.

'He'll resurface,' he said finally. 'He always does. In the meantime, we need to focus on dismantling what's left of his network.'

'There's something else ...' Trix hesitated, then pulled up a message on one of the screens. 'Frank Maguire's been trying to get hold of you again.'

Marlowe frowned.

'What does he want?'

'Not sure, but he's been talking to some of our mutual contacts in MI5. Says he has information you need to hear.'

'About?'

'He wouldn't say. Just that it's urgent and relates to "unfinished business from America".'

Marlowe's frown deepened. Frank Maguire–Essex crime boss and occasional ally now seemed to be a perpetual complication. Their relationship had always been complex, particularly after Maguire discovered Marlowe's true identity behind the "Kieran Lachlan" criminal persona he'd maintained for years. Marlowe had learnt that Maguire had been an MI5 and MI6 asset, and Maguire had been the one who sent Marlowe to Vegas to fulfil a favour; one that almost ended up with Marlowe being killed.

'Set up a meeting,' Marlowe decided. 'Neutral location, usual whatever protocols he'll understand.'

Trix nodded, already typing out a message.

'I'll arrange it for tomorrow afternoon. Camden or Southwark?'

'Camden. Less CCTV, although it's a coin toss these days.'

He moved to the small kitchenette they'd installed in one

corner of the crypt, filling the kettle and tearing open the paper bag, removing a couple of painkillers from the package inside. The tooth was really bothering him now, a persistent ache that seemed to radiate through his jaw as he dry-swallowed a couple.

'Did your dentist say anything about why it hurts so much?' Trix called over her shoulder.

'Inflamed nerve. Said it would settle.'

'Let me know if it doesn't. I know someone who can prescribe something stronger.'

'Your contact list gets more extensive by the day.'

'Just because I spend most of my time with computers doesn't mean I don't have a social life,' Trix replied, her attention back on her screens. 'Besides, after Vegas, we agreed to expand our network.'

She had a point. They'd been too isolated before, too dependent on official channels that could be compromised or cut off. The CIA detention after Rizzo had been a wake-up call. Without their backup identities and Sasha Bordeaux's unexpected assistance, they might still be in black sites, answering questions about everything that'd happened. Marlowe had even expected Bordeaux to keep him there deliberately, but it seemed she'd cut him some slack for once.

'Oh, I also gained some movement on the Quicksilver data from Rushmore,' Trix said, almost as an afterthought. 'A lot was lost when I locked down their systems, and Rizzo's people managed to scrub the most sensitive material before the authorities took control of the facility.'

She pulled up another window, showing fragmented code.

'However, I've recovered pieces of their trading algorithm and parts of what looks like a broader operational plan.

There are references to something called "Tower Protocol"–some kind of purchase, or a side project for Steele.'

'Any indication of what it involves?'

'Not yet. But there are recurring references to London, specifically the financial district,' Trix glanced up at him. 'I think Steele always intended to bring the operation back here, so maybe he's found himself a supervillain lair.'

'Makes sense,' Marlowe nodded. 'This is where he has the most connections, the most influence. The Rushmore operation might have been proof of concept, but London would be the main event.'

He moved closer to the screens, studying the fragmented data.

'Keep digging. If Steele's planning something in London, we need to know what and when.'

'Already on it. I've set up monitoring systems for unusual market activity and flagged certain trading patterns.'

Trix hesitated.

'There's one more thing. While you were at the dentist, I got a message from Curtis.'

Marlowe raised an eyebrow.

'MI5 reaching out? That's unlike them.'

'He also wants to meet. Says it's about "the aftermath of Katherine Saito's death".'

Marlowe's expression hardened at the mention of Saito. His former colleague, friend even, betrayed and manipulated by Steele, and shot dead before his eyes at Harrington House.

Another debt to settle.

'When and where?'

'Rochester, tomorrow morning. Says he'll be there on "personal business" to maintain deniability if anyone's watching.'

'Rochester means the cathedral,' Marlowe mused. 'Curtis always did have a flair for the dramatic.'

'Want me to come with you?'

Marlowe considered it, then shook his head.

'Better if you stay here, continue the analysis. The sooner we understand what Steele is planning, the better chance we have of stopping it.'

'It's been two months, Tom. If we haven't found it by now, we might never find it,' Trix replied, turning back to her screens. 'Just be careful. Curtis may be MI5, but that doesn't mean he's on our side.'

'No one's on our side,' Marlowe replied, his voice flat. 'Not even our bloody allies, it seems. That's why we work alone...'

He trailed off at a raise of Trix's eyebrow at this.

'Okay, mostly work alone,' he smiled.

Mount Rushmore had been a victory, of sorts. Rizzo was dead. Bassett—or Cross, or whatever his real name had been—had joined him. The immediate threat had been neutralised. But Steele remained, and with him the spectre of what might be coming next.

'We should upgrade the perimeter sensors,' he said, still staring at the footage. 'The northwest corner has a three-second blind spot during the camera rotation.'

Trix glanced up from her work.

'Already ordered the parts. Should arrive tomorrow.'

She studied him for a moment.

'You're tense. More than usual. Tooth, still?'

'Just a feeling,' Marlowe rolled his shoulders, realising she was right. 'It's too quiet. Steele's gone to ground, but he's not the type to accept defeat. As you said, it's been two months. The bastard's planning something.'

'And we'll be ready when he makes his move,' Trix assured him. 'We know what we're facing now.'

But do we?

Steele had proven himself a master of misdirection. The operation in Vegas had been full of false leads and hidden agendas. What appeared to be the objective might have been just another layer of deception.

Walking over to the "workshop" area of the crypt, Marlowe accessed their arsenal; handguns, ammunition, tactical gear, all the usual things you'd find in an underground base's hidden armoury, finding comfort in the routine. The crypt had been his salvation more than once, allowing him to disappear when enemies came calling. If needed, he could survive down here for weeks, with stored water, food, and independent power systems, just like his mother had taught him when she created her own bunker in their Epping home.

Yeah, not exactly the usual upbringing.

A thought coming to his mind, he pulled out his phone, opened his reminders app, and sent a brief message to himself, a reminder for something to ask Curtis the next day– nothing major, just a simple request to check Doctor Chopra's client list against certain databases.

Paranoia? Perhaps. But paranoia had kept him alive this long.

'What is it?' Trix asked, noticing his expression.

'My dentist,' Marlowe replied, showing her the message he'd written himself. 'Can't explain it, he seemed a little … odd.'

Trix raised an eyebrow.

'Interesting coincidence, you ending up in his chair.'

'There are no coincidences,' Marlowe placed the phone away. 'He was on the trusted list, so I went there. But there was something ... I dunno. Probably the pain making me twitchy.'

'Want me to dig deeper? I can go faster than Curtis's best people on a good day.'

Marlowe hesitated, then nodded.

'Discreetly. If he *is* connected to intelligence services, I don't want to trigger any alerts. And I don't want to become some other operative's asset.'

'Please,' Trix scoffed. She turned back to her workstation, fingers flying over the keyboard as she opened new search windows. 'I'll set up some passive monitoring, see what comes through without actively probing.'

'Good.' Marlowe moved towards the stairs in the crypt's corner. 'This tooth kept me up all night, so I need to rest before Camden tomorrow, especially if I'm going from there to bloody Rochester. Wake me if anything urgent comes through.'

'Always do,' Trix replied, already absorbed in her work.

Bypassing the bed for the sofa in the main living area upstairs, Marlowe laid back and stared at the ceiling of the one-time church, the ancient stonework visible even in the dim light.

His jaw still ached; a persistent, dull throb that seemed to have spread across his face, so Marlowe closed his eyes, forcing his mind to quieten. Tomorrow would bring Frank Maguire and whatever "urgent information" the crime boss claimed to have. Before that it was Rochester and Curtis with news about Saito's death.

Pieces moving on a chessboard he couldn't fully see. And

somewhere in the shadows, St John Steele was waiting, planning his next move.

Marlowe touched his jaw gingerly, feeling the slight swelling around the treated tooth. *It was a vulnerability, a weakness that needed to be addressed.*

As he drifted towards sleep, one thought remained clear. *Just like the storm that was surely coming.*

2

ROCHESTER

ROCHESTER CASTLE, ON THE BANKS OF THE RIVER MEDWAY, loomed against the morning sky, its ancient stonework strangely colourful against the grey winter skyline, while outside the castle walls the cathedral seemed to wait patiently for its turn in the spotlight. Marlowe believed it was the oldest cathedral in England, dating back to the seventh century and, as such, it stood as a testament to endurance over the centuries–surviving war, plague and the relentless march of time. In a way, Marlowe appreciated the irony as he approached the massive wooden doors. Few places better symbolised persistence in the face of overwhelming odds. It had even been an important place for faith when Rochester Castle itself was part of the Bloody Barons' War that led to the Magna Carta.

He arrived an hour early, a habit born from years in the field. Marlowe hadn't been here since a school trip in his teenage years, and he wanted to make sure he knew the terrain–identify exits, establish sight lines–the fundamentals of survival that had become second nature since his time in the Royal Marines. His tooth still ached, but the pain had now settled into a faint, dull throb, flaring occasionally into sharp jabs that made him wince.

The cathedral was getting busy at this hour; a handful of visitors were scattered amongst the pews and as Marlowe moved through the nave, the fan vaulting overhead created small, almost moving patterns of light and shadow across the stone floor. As he paced around the interior, Marlowe paused at each side chapel and each alcove, building a mental map of the cathedral's inside. There were at least four ways out, including the main West Door, the North Door which provided wheelchair access, and the South Door near the adapted restrooms. Added to this, there were a multitude of hiding places among the ancient tombs and chapels if everything went wrong.

Near where the choir would usually perform, a man sat alone, staring up at the stained-glass window. Curtis hadn't changed since the last time Marlowe had seen him: slim, in his fifties, and currently the section chief of MI5's London office. Alex Curtis was behind a desk now, following a gunshot wound at Westminster a year or two earlier, but he still had the watchful eyes of someone who'd spent a lot of time in the field. He'd hunted Marlowe, and he'd befriended Marlowe, but now, for some reason, he wanted to chat with Marlowe.

He didn't acknowledge Marlowe's approach, though—even though Marlowe knew he'd been spotted the moment he entered the cathedral.

'Enjoying the architecture?' Marlowe asked, sliding into the pew beside him.

'More the history,' Curtis replied, still staring up at the stained-glass window. 'This cathedral saw the Norman

Conquest, the Black Death, two world wars and a dozen squabbles here and there. Makes our current troubles seem rather trivial by comparison.'

He turned and looked at Marlowe.

'Of course, Katherine Saito might not think so.'

Marlowe stiffened. He knew Saito had been a friend of Curtis. But he also knew that Curtis had been briefed on what had happened–especially on how Saito had sided with St John Steele.

'Are you here to talk about her death?'

'Yes, but mainly the fact her killer remains at large,' Curtis replied coldly.

'I know,' Marlowe muttered. 'I was there when Steele shot her through the window, remember? That is ... I guess it was Steele. I only have his word to go on, and the fact that he left me a message.'

'Oh, it was Steele.' Curtis handed him a slim manila folder. 'Ballistics matched a custom rifle registered to one of his aliases. But that's not why I wanted to speak with you.'

Marlowe opened the folder. Inside was a single photograph of a Hong Kong cemetery with a fresh grave–a simple headstone at the end. Katherine Saito's name and dates were clearly visible on it, and he stared at the picture for a long moment before he closed the folder.

'What am I supposed to do with this?'

'There was a memorial service yesterday. Internal only. No family.'

'I wasn't aware she had any.'

'She didn't. Not officially.' Curtis shifted in his seat, glancing around the cathedral. 'But someone sent flowers. Expensive arrangement. Card just simply said, "Forgiven. S.".'

'Steele,' Marlowe murmured. 'Arrogant bastard. Or it's

somebody else–the letter S could mean a dozen different things. Maybe it was someone from her own family–the Saitos–forgiving her for whatever happened, but maybe we just think it was Steele?'

Curtis checked his watch.

'She was buried in Hong Kong. The flowers were delivered from a shop nearby, paid for with cryptocurrency. Trail ends there.'

'Could be Steele covering his tracks,' Marlowe considered. 'Or someone trying to draw him out. Either way, it suggests that whatever Quicksilver was, it's not over.'

Curtis leant closer.

'The problem is, we don't really know what Quicksilver actually was. All references to it have been scrubbed from our systems. Katherine said it was a 1990s operation–government funds diverted, some by the CIA, some by MI5 and MI6, while the rest was hidden.'

'Steele was trying to recover it through something called Stone Blind.'

'Well, yes,' Curtis looked directly at Marlowe now. 'We gathered that much from your previous debriefing, but we need more. We need to know what Steele was planning to do with those funds once he recovered them.'

'And you think if I knew that, I'd be sitting here with you?' Marlowe felt a flare of irritation. 'Steele wants to recreate Orchid in its glory again. He wants to destroy the world. He's hanging out with billionaires. Who knows what he wants to bloody do with those funds?'

'I think you know more than you shared,' Curtis said, levelly. 'You were at Rushmore. You saw the operation first-hand.'

'What I saw in Mount Rushmore was a madman trying to

manipulate global markets using sporting events as cover,'
Marlowe snapped. 'Gabriel Rizzo is dead, and the facility was
shut down. What more do you want?'

'The truth,' Curtis said simply. 'We both know Steele's out
there, and the next time he surfaces, it won't be in America.
It'll be here, on our turf.'

For once, Marlowe couldn't argue with that. Whatever
Steele was planning, the UK capital was going to be central to it.

'Look, what's MI5's interest in this?' he asked. 'Last I
checked, financial crimes still fell under other jurisdictions.'

'If it was just financial crimes, you'd be right,' Curtis
glanced around again, as if checking for other people watching, then lowered his voice. 'We think Steele's been recruiting
inside the intelligence community. Quite a few mid-level
analysts have gone missing in the last month. But their access
codes were used after their disappearances.'

'You've got a mole problem.'

'More–we have a systematic infiltration problem. And it's
not just us. It's MI6, GCHQ, even the Defence Intelligence
Staff. Someone's building a shadow intelligence apparatus.'

Marlowe leant back on the pew staring at Curtis.

'It's not the first time, either,' he said. 'MI5 was infiltrated
by Orchid. That was proven with Vic Saeed, Kate Maybury,
even Oliver Casey, or rather *he* infiltrated MI6, didn't he?
Maybe these new disappearances are just other former
Orchid members returning to Daddy. After all, Steele was the
Arbitrator for the High Council before he went rogue.'

'We've been monitoring what's left of that organisation,'
Curtis admitted. 'Its fragmentation makes it difficult to track.
Sonia Shida's group seems focused on rebuilding internal
structures. Steele's "new kid", as Trix Preston likes to call it,

has withdrawn from most operations. The rest is in disarray. If Steele's recruiting, Orchid's scattered membership would provide him with fertile ground.'

'I need access to Saito's files–personal and professional. Whatever she was working on before she died.'

Curtis shook his head.

'That's impossible, I'm afraid. Her digital footprint's been wiped, and not by us. All we have is what was recovered from her laptop after Harrington House, and most of that was encrypted beyond our ability to crack.'

'I thought Trix had it?' Marlowe frowned.

'She does,' Curtis looked uncomfortable. 'We've ... kind of been working with her.'

Marlowe's eyes widened slightly.

'Trix is returning to MI5?'

'More a case that we'd like her to come back,' Curtis admitted. 'But whatever Stockholm Syndrome issue she has for you is causing issues there.'

'Look,' Marlowe said, half-rising from the pew. 'I get you needed to talk to me about this, but why here? Why now? We could have done this at any point. I could have come into Thames House, I could have—'

'I wanted to talk to you outside of the building,' Curtis replied. 'You've pointed out there could be a mole in our organisation, and there was something else we needed to discuss. The flowers in Hong Kong weren't the only thing that was passed across.'

'How do you mean?'

Curtis rummaged in his pocket and pulled out what looked like a business card at first glance. As Marlowe took it and stared at it, he realised it was actually some kind of plastic mounting that was shaped like a business card, with a USB attached into it. On it was one word.

$MARLOWE

'I don't understand,' he said.

'This was also with the message in the flower envelope,' Curtis replied. 'We're guessing it's a gift for you. Check the back.'

Marlowe turned it over.

To be given to the man bearing this name.

'Okay,' he said. 'So there's something on here I'm supposed to see, I'm guessing. And I'm also guessing you guys have picked through it and worked out what it is?'

'Actually, we haven't,' Curtis shrugged. 'We can't get into it. The encryption is so high that even the best at MI5 and GCHQ are unable to crack it, as it's a code they've not seen before. We were hoping Trix might have a look, as she might have seen the basecode at some point–or perhaps there's something connected to you, which opens it instead?'

Marlowe examined the case.

'Have you X-rayed it?'

'Of course, and there's definitely something inside it. We don't want to touch it, however, until we know what it is,' Curtis said. 'If it's something that helps you–or helps me, by default–we don't really want to cause a screw-up.'

A group of tourists entered the cathedral, their voices echoing in the vast space. Both men fell silent, watching as the group moved slowly through the nave, cameras flashing despite the signs prohibiting photography.

'Walk with me,' Curtis said, standing abruptly. 'I find I need some air.'

―――――――

OUTSIDE, THE MORNING HAD WARMED SLIGHTLY, THOUGH A brisk wind cut through Marlowe's leather jacket. They crossed the cathedral grounds towards the ancient castle ruins that overlooked the Medway River.

'I've been authorised to offer you a contract,' Curtis said once they were away from the cathedral crowds. 'Help us track Steele, figure out what he's planning, stop it before it happens. Generous compensation, full support, no questions about your methods.'

'Sounds too good to be true.'

'It probably is,' Curtis admitted. 'There are factions within the service that aren't happy about bringing you back in.'

'Emilia Wintergreen, perhaps?'

'She's definitely one. For an old mentor she's certainly soured on you following whatever happened in Berlin.'

'She tried to burn me, off books,' Marlowe almost smiled. Berlin had been a disaster, but the end result had also been necessary. 'I don't work for anyone any more because of that. Not MI5, not MI6, not the bloody CIA ... I've found independence suits me.'

'And yet, here you are, still hunting Steele and still trying to fix a defunct secret society. Why not do it with resources behind you?'

'Because resources come with strings. And I've had enough puppet masters to last a lifetime,' Marlowe replied tersely, deciding not to mention the fact that the Vegas heist, among other things had provided Marlowe and Trix with a very healthy war chest.

They reached the castle, its ancient stone walls rising stark against the sky. A few tourists wandered the grounds, but the place was relatively quiet, mainly because the castle wasn't an exciting looking one like Windsor Castle, more a beefy, four-sided fortress. Marlowe had known this castle since he was a child, though; it'd been used on the cover of *Legend* by Clannad.

Strange to see it in the day, though.

'Think about it,' Curtis urged. 'The offer remains open. Keep me informed of what you find. That's all. No reports, no surveillance, no handler. Just … professional courtesy.'

It was a reasonable request, but Marlowe had learned the hard way that reasonable requests often led to unreasonable demands.

'I'll consider it,' he said finally.

Curtis extended his hand. Marlowe hesitated, then shook it briefly. With a final nod, Curtis departed, heading back towards the cathedral, and likely his confused family who were wondering why he had to disappear during their holiday.

Marlowe remained by the castle wall, watching until the MI5 section head disappeared from view, before pulling out his phone to check the time. If he left now, he could catch the next train back to London and be in Camden shortly before lunch.

As he moved towards the path leading to town, though, Marlowe noticed a man sitting on a bench, apparently absorbed in a paperback novel. Ordinary enough, except he'd been concentrated intently on it since he'd first seen him and the pages hadn't been turned, which meant it was either a massively engrossing page of text, or an amateur mistake by someone trying to watch him. Marlowe adjusted course, heading back towards the cathedral instead of the main footpath, testing his suspicion.

The man closed his book and stood, stretching casually before following in the same direction. Definitely surveillance, but sloppy. *Intentionally so? A distraction, perhaps, meant to draw attention while something else happened?*

His instincts prickled. He scanned the area more carefully, noting a second man leaning against the wall near the entrance to the cathedral. This one looked more professional–alert posture despite the casual stance, eyes constantly moving, scanning the surroundings. Military training, possibly.

Shit, Marlowe thought to himself. *This isn't ending well. What have I got myself into this time?*

3

ASSASSINS

MARLOWE MAINTAINED HIS PACE, MOVING BACK TOWARDS THE cathedral. The eleven a.m. service would start soon; tourists and worshippers were arriving. Crowds meant witnesses, which might deter whatever these men had planned.

But they also meant collateral damage if things went wrong.

He entered through the same side door he'd left with Curtis minutes earlier, nodding politely to an elderly woman arranging flowers near the entrance. Inside, Marlowe moved quickly towards the north transept, past the pew he'd sat with Curtis and towards where a narrow doorway led to the tower stairs. From the tower, he could get a better view of who was following him and plan his next move.

As he reached the doorway, a verger approached, key ring jangling at his belt.

'May I help you, sir?'

'Just admiring the architecture,' Marlowe replied smoothly. 'Is the tower open to visitors?'

'Not until twelve, I'm afraid.' The verger smiled apologetically. 'Health and safety regulations. Need a staff member present.'

Marlowe glanced over his shoulder, spotting the man from the bench entering the cathedral.

'I understand completely. Perhaps you could make an exception? I'm actually writing an article on medieval bell towers, and my mother-in-law rings the quarters in Essex. I'd make it worth your while, as I'm catching the next train back.'

The verger hesitated, clearly torn between rules, monetary gain and helpfulness, obviously deciding to help Marlowe as the key now entered the lock with the verger giving the slightest of smiles. However, before he could respond, Marlowe's instincts screamed *danger*. He spun around just as the second man emerged from behind a pillar, moving with the purposeful grace of a predator; his strong side hand held a very nasty looking Karambit, the distinctive Southeast Asia weapon favoured by half a dozen special forces groups around the world, as well as a busload of professional killers.

The verger's eyes widened in alarm, but before he could shout a warning, Marlowe pushed him through the tower doorway and slammed it shut, turning the ancient key that still sat in the lock.

'Sorry,' he muttered through the wooden door. 'Call the police, please.'

The knife-wielder approached, tourists now scattering as they noticed the blade. Behind him, the man from the bench advanced as well, holding a thin wire with round handles on either end – a garrote.

Professional hit team, then. Not local talent.

'Gentlemen,' Marlowe said loudly, backing towards the

nave, the ring of keys in his hand, 'this is hardly the place. God is watching and he won't be happy.'

Neither man spoke, but they did respond. The knife-wielder feinted left, then lunged right, the Karambit slashing towards Marlowe's jugular. Marlowe dropped beneath the attack and pivoted, the blade missing him by inches, and countered with a sharp jab to the man's kidney, using the keys as a knuckle duster. His attacker barely flinched, immediately spinning for another strike, and across the nave a woman screamed as she saw the knife.

Good. Witnesses meant the attackers would be forced to retreat or risk capture. Hopefully.

The second man circled behind Marlowe, trying to flank him; Marlowe backed against a stone pillar, keeping both attackers in view. His tooth chose that moment to deliver a sharp jab of pain, momentarily distracting him and the knife-wielder seized the opportunity, closing the distance with blinding speed.

Marlowe twisted away, but not fast enough. The Karambit sliced through his jacket sleeve, drawing a line of fire across his forearm.

First blood.

He hissed through his teeth, retreating further down the nave.

'Who sent you?' he demanded, though he expected no answer.

True to form, neither man spoke. Around them, cathedral staff were ushering visitors towards the exits. Alarms would be raised soon, police summoned. The attackers would have minutes at most.

Marlowe's hand found a heavy brass candlestick on a nearby table, and he hurled it at the second attacker before charging the knife-wielder, using the moment of confusion to close distance. He drove his shoulder into the man's chest, slamming him against a pillar, and the knife-wielder grunted–the first sound either attacker had made–but maintained his grip on the Karambit, slashing wildly.

Marlowe countered with a vicious uppercut, the keys still gripped tight, and poking through the gaps between his fingers like Wolverine's claws from the *X-Men*, a vicious punch that snapped the man's head back, following with a knee to the groin. Professional or not, some vulnerabilities were universal. The knife-wielder doubled over and Marlowe seized the opportunity to twist the Karambit from his grip.

Before he could turn the knife on the second attacker, he was on him, the garrote now replaced with an expandable steel baton, and all hell had broken loose. Twenty-six inches of solid steel whistled through the air toward Marlowe's head. He raised his arm to block but failed to be in close enough to soften the blow that caught his bleeding forearm. As pain exploded up the damaged arm, he managed to keep hold of the Karambit, slashing at the baton-wielder. The man retreated a step, reassessing, and his expression once more showed Marlowe these weren't amateurs – they fought with a harsh economy of movement that came from years of training. Yet they didn't fight as a seamless team - they hadn't worked together before, Marlowe guessed.

Individual contractors brought together for a single job.

Or deciding to split the payout, perhaps.

The knife-wielder had recovered and was circling again, now armed with a small folding knife, likely his backup, as police sirens could be heard wailing in the distance. Time was running out–for all of them.

'Whatever they're paying you for this,' Marlowe said, 'it's not enough.'

The baton-wielder charged, weapon raised for a devastating blow–but Marlowe sidestepped, using the man's momentum to send him crashing into the same wooden pew Marlowe and Curtis had sat in earlier. The knife-wielder attacked simultaneously from the other side though, folding blade aimed at Marlowe's kidney. Marlowe twisted, the knife scoring another line across his back rather than plunging into his vitals, and he countered with the stolen Karambit, opening a shallow cut across the attacker's cheek.

The sound of running footsteps echoed from the cathedral entrance–cathedral security arriving, and soon, police. The knife-wielder exchanged a quick glance with his partner, some silent communication passing between them.

'Who sent you?' Marlowe demanded again, pressing his temporary advantage.

The baton-wielder smiled thinly, the first expression he'd shown.

'Twelve million,' he said, his voice soft with an accent Marlowe couldn't quite place. 'Highest bounty I've ever gone for.'

Movement to his left–the knifeman again, again moving with obvious skill. Marlowe turned to face him, but it was a feint. The real attack came from behind, the baton-wielder moving in. Marlowe sensed rather than saw the attack, dropping to one knee as the baton swept through the space where his head had been. He spun, slashing with the Karambit, catching the man across the thigh. The baton-wielder stumbled, cursing in what sounded like Romanian.

The knife-wielder closed in, exploiting Marlowe's momentary distraction. His blade flashed in the dim light, driving Marlowe back against the pillar again. They grappled briefly, Marlowe's greater weight countered by the other man's surprising strength, Marlowe cursing as the Karambit slipped from his grasp, clattering to the stone floor.

No time to grab it. Get the hell out of here.

Unarmed except for his ancient keys-shaped knuckle-duster, he ran towards a narrow staircase he'd spotted earlier. If he could reach higher ground, he might gain an advantage.

The knife-wielder, momentarily surprised by Marlowe's decision to run, followed, while behind him, the baton-wielder, limping but still mobile, moved to cut off Marlowe's escape route.

Marlowe reached the staircase and took the steps two at a time, the knife-wielder close behind. The stone stairs wound upwards in a tight spiral, eventually reaching a wooden door. Marlowe prayed he had the right key as he slammed it into the lock–no movement. He tried a second, and still the door stayed solidly closed. He tried a third and almost cried out with happiness as it gave a click and unlocked the door, Marlowe emerged onto a gallery overlooking the main nave. From here, Marlowe could see cathedral security and the first police officers entering below. He considered locking the door behind him, but there wasn't enough time; the knife-wielder now paused at the top of the stairs, assessing the situation. His expression remained impassive, but Marlowe could sense the calculation behind his eyes. The odds were shifting. Too many witnesses, and too little time.

'It's over,' Marlowe said. 'More police will be here soon. You should tell me who sent you while you still can.'

Instead of answering, the man charged, his backup knife aimed at Marlowe's throat in what could easily have been a killing strike. Marlowe caught his wrist, using the man's momentum to swing him towards the gallery's stone balustrade. They struggled briefly before Marlowe delivered a vicious Glasgow Kiss, a head butt that momentarily stunned his attacker.

Taking advantage of the moment, Marlowe pried the knife from the man's grip and reversed it, pressing the blade against his throat.

'Last chance,' he said. 'Who's behind the contract?'

The man's eyes, cold and calculating, met his without fear.

'There are more coming. Many more.'

Before Marlowe could press further, a shout from below distracted him; police were pointing up at the gallery. The moment's distraction was all his opponent needed, and he drove his elbow into Marlowe's injured arm, breaking his grip, then vaulted over the balustrade.

Marlowe lunged to catch him, expecting to see the man plummet to the stone floor below, but instead, the attacker had caught a hanging banner, using it to slow his descent before dropping the last few feet and rolling to absorb the impact. Even as police converged, he was sprinting towards a side exit, his partner already gone.

Marlowe considered his options rapidly. Following would mean navigating police, explaining his presence, his injuries and the fight. Valuable time lost and the attackers would be long gone.

Better to slip away now, gather information, plan his next move.

Using the ring of keys once more, he descended via the opposite staircase, emerging near the choir stalls as police focused on the main exit where his attacker had fled. Moving quickly but without drawing attention, Marlowe used the keys one last time, unlocking and passing through a service door that led to the cathedral grounds.

His arm throbbed where the Karambit had sliced him, blood seeping through his coat sleeve. Not life-threatening, but it needed attention. More concerning were the implications of the attack.

Professional hitters.

A twelve-million bounty.

More coming.

Keeping to the shadows of the cathedral wall, Marlowe pulled out his phone. Trix answered on the first ring.

'Where are you?' she demanded. 'I'm seeing the Rochester police chatter go mental. Did Curtis screw you over?'

'No. Had some unexpected company,' Marlowe kept his voice low. 'Professional hit team. At least two, possibly more.'

'Are you hurt?'

'Superficial. Nothing critical,' Marlowe scanned the increased police activity. 'I need a new exit plan; the train station's not an option any more.'

'Forget the train,' Trix decided, and Marlowe could already hear the keys tapping as she spoke. 'There's a *Zippy Car* location near the High Street. You know, the ones you book online, use and then drop off? I've already booked it for you under one of your secondary identities. Details incoming.'

His phone buzzed with a text–car information and address, and the access code to get in and unlock the car key safe.

'You're a miracle worker,' Marlowe said.

'Just practical. Can you make it there without bleeding all over Rochester?'

'I'll manage,' Marlowe glanced towards the cathedral

entrance, where more police were arriving. 'I need to move now. Things are getting busy here.'

The line went dead. Marlowe pocketed the phone, taking a moment to bind his forearm with a handkerchief before making his way through the cathedral grounds. He kept to the perimeter, using shrubbery and ancient tombstones for cover until he reached a service gate that led to a quiet side street where, forty yards down he could see a Nissan Micra with the *Zippy Car* branding placed all over it. Amusingly, this car was as far from "nondescript" as you could get, and in a way this helped Marlowe–no right-thinking assassin would use such a car to escape a police dragnet.

Good job I'm not right-thinking, then.

As the police widened their search towards Rochester Castle, Marlowe tapped in a seven-digit code, opened the door to the car and climbed in. A few minutes later, he was driving south out of Rochester, taking secondary roads rather than the more direct A2 as a cautionary measure, while his mind raced with implications.

Professional assassins in Rochester and surveillance at the church felt too coordinated, too precise to be coincidence.

Someone had put serious resources into finding and eliminating him.

He just hoped to God it wasn't Curtis and MI5, as that would *really* suck.

4

PIN PRICK

THE *ZIPPY CAR*'S HEATER HAD FINALLY KICKED IN BY THE TIME Marlowe reached the outskirts of London, the warmth easing some of the stiffness in his wounded arm. The bleeding had stopped, but the dried blood made his sleeve stick to the wound, and every time he moved, the pain reminded him how close he'd come to something far worse.

Twice during the drive back, he'd pulled over–once to check he wasn't being followed, and once to buy some wipes and basic wound dressings from a petrol station's shop. Trix had messaged several times demanding updates, but he kept his responses to the bare minimum. Some conversations needed to happen face to face, especially given what he was beginning to suspect.

The hit had been too precise, too coordinated. His attackers had known exactly where he'd be, and when. The only people who knew about his meeting with Curtis were Trix and Curtis himself, and maybe MI5, if Curtis had logged it. Marlowe trusted Trix implicitly, so the choice was obvious; MI5 was a leaky sieve, and either their operational security had been compromised or someone was feeding information to whoever wanted him dead.

He abandoned the *Zippy Car* in one of the designated spots near Camden, and continued on foot, scanning for dangers. He'd originally planned to go back to the apartment and clean up, but now he wanted to speak to Frank Maguire as quickly as possible; it couldn't be a coincidence that Maguire wanted to pass information at the same time people wanted to kill him.

Although people always wanted to kill him, it seemed.

The market buzzed with its usual mix of tourists and locals, the February chill doing little to thin the crowds. Trix had provided Marlowe a location and setting provided by Maguire, and his choice of meeting place had initially surprised Marlowe–too public, too exposed–but, after Rochester he understood the logic.

Safety in crowds.

Multiple exit routes.

Witnesses who would complicate any attack.

Popping into one of the many pubs that lined the main street of Camden Town, he passed through into the men's toilets, locking himself in a stall to properly assess his injuries. The knife wound on his arm was ugly but superficial, a clean slice that had hit nothing vital. He wiped at it with some antiseptic wipes, wincing at the sting, then applied a proper dressing. His back ached where the second knife had caught him, but his jacket had absorbed most of the attack. He couldn't immediately reach that, though, so he'd have to deal with it later. Then, as cleaned up as he could be, and doing his best to hide the cuts in the jacket, he left and headed north, towards Camden Lock Market.

THE MEETING POINT WAS A CRAFT BEER STALL ON THE UPPER level of the market, overlooking the canal, and Marlowe arrived five minutes early, positioning himself at a corner table that gave him views of both the stairs and the canal-side walkway. Out of habit, he mentally logged the CCTV blind spots and the bottlenecks where someone might stage an ambush–these were potential defensive positions, and right now, Marlowe was feeling very defensive.

Frank Maguire arrived precisely on time. The Essex crime boss moved with the confident bulk of a man accustomed to being feared, his long black coat flapping slightly in the February wind. He'd aged a little in the two months since Marlowe had last seen him; more grey in his close-cropped hair, deeper lines around his eyes. Maguire spotted Marlowe immediately, and something flashed across his face; not surprise, Marlowe noted, but confirmation.

'Christ,' Maguire said as he slid into the seat opposite. 'You look like you've been through the wars.'

'Rough morning,' Marlowe replied, keeping his voice low. 'Someone wants me dead. Twelve-million-dollars' worth of wanting, according to my new friends in Rochester Cathedral.'

Maguire's eyes narrowed.

'So, they found you already,' he said. It wasn't a question. 'That was faster than I expected.'

'You knew,' Marlowe said flatly. 'That's why you wanted to meet.'

Maguire glanced around, then leant across the table.

'That's the thing. No one seems to know who put out the hit, or if they do, they're not talking. It's all being handled through someone called "The Broker"; some kind of middleman for high-end contracts.'

'I know The Broker,' Marlowe nodded. 'Last saw him at an auction in Punta Cana.'

'Exotic,' Maguire gave a faint smile. 'Well, he apparently has a client with a serious hard-on for you.'

'Who told you?'

'Pauline Faulkner,' Maguire replied, waving for a server. 'Sorry, dry throat. Need a drink.'

There was a pause as Maguire ordered a craft beer, and Marlowe considered Faulkner. He'd also met her before, when his father had hired an unqualified assassin to kill him, mainly as a message to get him to come and visit. Faulkner had been blunt, calm and very professional—she'd even offered him a job. Marlowe added her to the list of people he'd be visiting soon. But, as he did so, his mind flashed to the USB card Curtis had given him, with its single word: $MARLOWE.

A connection was forming, and he didn't like where it led.

'Tell me everything you know,' he said, his voice hardening.

Maguire sipped at his beer before continuing.

'It's not just a standard contract. This one has rules—weird ones. The total bounty is twelve million, but it decreases with each fatally failed attempt.'

'Encouraging competition and urgency,' Marlowe observed. 'Creating a race.'

'In a way, but it's a bloody strange one. They fail? No discount,' Maguire nodded. 'But if you, as in *you*, Tom, kill the assassin, that's a point to you, and the bounty is halved. Twelve becomes six, and then six becomes three, and on and on.'

'So what, I kill assassins and wait the clock out until they decide it's not worth bothering?'

'Pretty much,' Maguire shrugged. 'I'm guessing someone took a pop at you. But my sources still say it's twelve million, so I guess you let them live?'

Marlowe nodded.

'Well, good for you. But that's not the strangest part. The whole thing's being run through some kind of cryptocurrency. They're calling it "Marlowe Coin". The bounty, the rules, the whole setup is managed through these digital tokens. It's like someone turned killing you into a bloody game.'

'And you're telling me this out of the goodness of your heart?' Marlowe asked, unable to keep the scepticism from his voice.

Maguire leant back, his expression hardening.

'Look, Marlowe, I won't pretend we're friends. But we've done business, even if it wasn't under your real name. You've been straight with me when others wouldn't. And besides, I've got my own operation to think about. Whatever shitstorm is coming your way, I don't want it landing on my doorstep.'

There was logic to that, Marlowe had to admit. Maguire was a pragmatist above all else.

'What else do you know about this contract?' Marlowe pressed. 'Any clues about who might be behind it?'

'Nothing concrete,' Maguire replied, lowering his voice further. 'But it's big money, Marlowe. The kind that doesn't come from your average grudge. You've pissed off someone with deep pockets.'

'I can think of a few candidates.'

'I can tell you this much—whoever's bankrolling it isn't local. Pauline looked into it when she heard The Broker was getting the payday–the money's moving through offshore accounts, digital currencies, the works. Professional setup.'

'International, then.'

'Looks that way,' Maguire nodded. 'And these aren't street thugs they're sending after you. Pauline recognised names, people she uses. Top-notch assassins.'

Marlowe thought of the knife-wielder at the cathedral: his precision, his training, the cold calculation in his eyes.

Not your average hitman.

'Any names?' he asked. 'Anyone specific I should be watching for?'

'No specific names, just that they're bringing in talent from all over. Eastern Europe, Asia, America. Best in the business.'

'Wonderful,' Marlowe said dryly.

'There's one more thing,' Maguire said, leaning closer. 'They seem to know your movements. Not just general patterns, I'm talking specifics. Times, locations, the works.'

A chill ran down Marlowe's spine. That explained Rochester but raised far more troubling questions. *How were they tracking him?*

'Any idea how?'

'That's what I can't figure,' Maguire admitted. 'But this Marlowe Coin thing ... there's something weird about it. From what I've heard, the people buying and then holding these coins somehow get information about your whereabouts. The more coins they hold, the more detailed the intel.'

'Cryptocurrency doesn't work that way.' Marlowe frowned.

'I'm just telling you what I've heard,' Maguire shrugged. 'I'm not exactly a tech expert. But something's giving these hitmen an edge. Watch your back, Marlowe. And if I were you, I'd stay the hell away from anywhere predictable for a while.'

'Bit late for that advice,' Marlowe replied grimly, rising from his chair. 'Stay safe, Frank.'

'You too, "Kieran",' Maguire grinned for the first time, using the name Marlowe had first met him under.

As he descended the stairs, though, Marlowe noticed a man in a dark jacket pause mid-step, his gaze fixing on Marlowe with sudden intensity. Their eyes met briefly–enough for Marlowe to register the cold, professional assessment in the stranger's gaze–before the man turned abruptly, moving back up the stairs.

Another one already? A guard of Maguire's perhaps?

Marlowe changed direction, pushing through the crowded market floor rather than taking the main exit. The man in the dark jacket had reappeared, maintaining distance but definitely tailing him. And now there was a second–a woman with short blonde hair, moving parallel to Marlowe's path on the opposite side of the market.

Coordinated surveillance. Professional.

Marlowe continued moving, taking an abrupt turn down a narrow passage between stalls that led towards the market's western exit. His followers adjusted course to match him, maintaining visual contact without closing the gap. They weren't making a move yet–just tracking, and likely either waiting for a better opportunity or for additional support to arrive. He needed to lose them before they decided to act.

The western exit led to a quieter street–fewer witnesses who might be caught in a crossfire. Marlowe turned left, then immediately ducked into a narrow alley between buildings. Twenty metres ahead, the alley opened onto another street with heavier foot traffic. If he could reach it before his pursuers rounded the corner ...

Footsteps splashed in the puddles behind him–they'd moved faster than expected.

Marlowe broke into a run, ignoring the pain in his arm. He reached the end of the alley and emerged onto the busier street, immediately merging with a group of tourists huddled under umbrellas. The blonde woman appeared at the alley's mouth seconds later, scanning the street, but her gaze swept over Marlowe's group and continued on.

She hadn't made him yet.

Using the tourists as cover, Marlowe moved towards a bus stop where a double-decker bus was just pulling in. Using a pay-as-you-go "burner" credit card for contactless scanning, he boarded quickly, moving to the upper deck and taking a seat at the back, where he could watch the street below, and the bus pulled away before any of his followers could expand their search to include it.

Marlowe knew this was a temporary reprieve, but nothing more. They'd lost him for now, but the fact they'd found him so quickly during his meeting with Maguire was deeply troubling. If they could track him with that precision, nowhere was truly safe.

And how were they doing it?

He needed to get back to Trix, to the crypt, scan his clothing, see if he had a tracker on him, to figure out what the hell was happening. But he couldn't risk leading them directly there. Better to take a circuitous route, use multiple transport changes, and find somewhere to completely change his clothes, ensure he was clean before returning to base.

His phone buzzed again. This time, he answered.

'Where are you?' Trix demanded. 'I've been trying to reach you for an hour.'

'Camden, but not for long,' Marlowe replied quietly, mindful of the other passengers. 'Was in the Market, so signal was probably iffy. Had my meeting with Maguire, though. Got some interesting news.'

'Let me guess–someone wants you dead?'

'How did you know?'

Trix's voice was grim.

'Because I've been digging since your call from Rochester. The dark net is buzzing about something called "Marlowe Coin". A cryptocurrency specifically designed around a bounty on your head.'

Marlowe glanced around the bus, ensuring no one was listening too closely.

'Maguire told me something similar. Twelve-million-dollar bounty that halves with each failed attempt, but only if I kill my attacker ... like a sodding gladiator.'

'It's worse than that,' Trix replied. 'I've been monitoring blockchain activity–this isn't just a payment system. There's something else embedded in the protocol, some kind of tracking mechanism. I don't understand how it works yet, but the holders of these coins seem to be getting real-time data, updated every thirty minutes, about your movements.'

A chill ran through Marlowe despite the overheated interior.

'That explains a lot.'

'Where are you going now?'

'Taking a scenic route back. I picked up some tails after meeting Maguire–professional types. Lost them for now, but I need to make sure I'm clean before returning.'

'Take two showers, just to be sure, yeah? And Tom ... be

careful. This isn't a normal contract. Someone's turned hunting you into a spectator sport.'

'Comforting thought,' Marlowe muttered. 'I'll be back in a couple of hours. Have the medical kit ready–I also picked up a souvenir in Rochester.'

IT TOOK MARLOWE NEARLY THREE HOURS TO RETURN TO HIS church-based apartment, using a combination of buses, underground trains, taxis and on-foot segments to create a near-impossible trail to follow. He changed his appearance twice–once donning a baseball cap and glasses purchased from a tourist shop and later swapping his blood-stained jacket for a cheap bomber jacket bought at a charity shop. Only when he was absolutely certain he wasn't being followed did he approach the church, entering through the rarely used back door that opened into what had once been the vestry, heading immediately downstairs.

The crypt was ablaze with light and activity, multiple screens displaying data streams and security camera footage; Trix sat at her self-built workstation, her fingers flying over the keyboard. She spun in her chair as he entered, her eyes immediately taking in his dishevelled appearance and the exhaustion etched on his face.

'You look worse than you sounded,' she observed, rising from her chair. 'Medical kit's on the side table. Want me to help?'

'I've got it,' Marlowe replied, shrugging off the bomber jacket and moving to the small sink in the corner. 'What have you found?'

Trix returned to her screens, pulling up a complex display of data analytics that looked completely alien to Marlowe.

'This Marlowe Altcoin is unlike anything I've seen before,' she said, highlighting sections of code. 'It's a cryptocurrency, but it's built on a modified Ethereum platform, with custom protocols embedded in the smart contracts. Whoever designed this is a genuine expert: cutting-edge cryptography, sophisticated multi-signature requirements, the works.'

'In English, please,' Marlowe winced as he cleaned his wound, applying fresh antiseptic.

'It's a highly specialised cryptocurrency created for one purpose–tracking and killing you,' Trix said bluntly. 'The total supply is likely in the millions, *billions* maybe, each theoretically worth a percentage of a dollar. When someone attempts to claim the bounty and fails, half the coins are "burned"–permanently removed from circulation–reducing the total amount available and massively raising the price.'

'Creating urgency,' Marlowe nodded, recalling Maguire's explanation. 'Is it out there, or invite only?'

'Oh, it's being traded out there,' Trix nodded. 'Most of the small buyers are crypto day traders, seeing something that's rising. Once you burn the first half, they'll leap on it like crazy.'

'Which means everyone holding these coins makes money every time I defeat an assassin,' Marlowe growled. 'But how is it tracking me?'

Trix's expression was troubled.

'That's where it gets weird. The blockchain itself seems to receive location data from some external source–a device, a tracker, something physical. I can see the data being processed, but I can't identify the source. It blips every thirty minutes, gives the location and then turns off. Which means unless you're scanning the moment it blips ...'

'You'll never find it,' Marlowe paused in the middle of applying a fresh bandage. 'Where does it say I am now?'

'I just see the data code, not the result. Last time it beeped was ten minutes ago, before you got here. I'd need to get into the system to see more. Buy in with the coin, perhaps.'

'Could it be something implanted?' Marlowe asked carefully.

'Possibly,' Trix frowned. 'But it would need to be sophisticated–GPS enabled, consistent power source, secure transmission capabilities. And someone would have needed physical access to you to plant it.'

'I haven't exactly been living in isolation,' Marlowe pointed out, finishing with his bandage and rolling down his sleeve.

'True,' Trix conceded. 'But I've been monitoring your regular haunts, your contacts–nothing unusual stands out.'

'Apart from the bloody dentist.'

'Unless you're about to rip out a filling, we should wait until the next blip, see where you glow on a scanner,' Trix replied, holding a hand scanner up. 'But that means you'd give this location.'

'They know where I live already,' Marlowe considered this. 'That won't be a new realisation, especially if this is Steele screwing around. They'll think I was upstairs and escaped. I can take the bump.'

Marlowe reached into his pocket and produced the USB "business card".

'Curtis passed this to me in Rochester. Said it was recovered with flowers sent to Saito's grave in Hong Kong,' he explained. 'Message on it just says "$MARLOWE", same as this cryptocurrency, with an order to pass it to me.'

'And you're only giving this to me now?'

'I was a bit distracted by people trying to kill me,' Marlowe replied dryly, handing her the device. 'Curtis said they couldn't crack it.'

Trix examined the USB carefully, turning it over in her hands.

'MI5 couldn't crack it? Interesting.'

'Or so Curtis claims.'

'Well, let's see what we're dealing with,' Trix said, moving to a standalone computer system that wasn't connected to their network. 'Better safe than sorry.'

She unclipped and inserted the USB part of the card, and the screen immediately filled with lines of encryption prompts and security protocols. Trix's fingers darted over the keyboard, navigating through the security barriers, humming to herself as she did so.

'Sophisticated,' she muttered. 'Multiple authentication layers, biometric verification requests ... wait, there's something else here.'

Marlowe moved to the computer, studying the screen. A small circular depression was slightly visible on the underside of the USB card–something he hadn't noticed before.

'It's asking for DNA authentication,' Trix said. 'Old school but effective.'

Marlowe examined the depression.

'Blood?'

'Looks that way. Press your thumb there but be careful–it'll probably have a needle.'

Marlowe pressed his thumb against the circular depression. He felt a sharp prick, followed by a warm sensation as the device drew a small sample of his blood. The computer screen flashed for several seconds, then displayed a simple message:

IDENTITY CONFIRMED: THOMAS MARLOWE
WELCOME TO THE GAME: 1,000,000 COINS ARE NOW IN
YOUR ACCOUNT

The screen changed, displaying a stylised logo–a silhouette of a man's head with a target superimposed over it, and beneath it the word "$MARLOWE" in glowing text.

Trix leaned forward, studying the display.

'It's an access portal to the Marlowe Coin network. Someone's given you a front-row seat to your own assassination contract.'

'But why?' Marlowe asked, baffled. 'Why would someone put a hit on me, then give me access to information about it?'

'To watch you squirm?' Trix suggested grimly. 'Or maybe it's part of the game. The hunter versus the hunted–more entertaining if the target knows what's coming.'

As they watched, the screen displayed a world map with a glowing dot over London, slowly pulsing. Next to it, a sidebar showed statistics: the current bounty of twelve million dollars, the number of registered hunters, counting currently as fifteen, and a countdown clock reading seventy-two hours.

'A deadline,' Marlowe observed. 'That's new.'

'This is sick,' Trix said, disgust clear in her voice. 'Someone's turned your life into entertainment.'

'Or a test,' Marlowe said thoughtfully. 'Rochester might have been the first attempt, but it felt like ... an assessment. Like they were gauging my reactions, my capabilities.'

'Well, whatever this is, we need to shut it down,' Trix said firmly. 'And figure out how they're tracking you so precisely.'

Marlowe nodded, his jaw throbbing again as if to emphasise the point.

'The pulsing dot–that's me?'

'Looks like it,' Trix confirmed. 'But it's only showing your general location–London. Not your specific position in the city.'

'So, the participants get more precise information?'

'Probably,' Trix agreed. 'The more coins they hold, the more detailed the tracking data they receive, perhaps, every thirty minutes.'

Marlowe stared at the digital representation of the price on his head. Someone had gone to enormous lengths to orchestrate his death: the cryptocurrency, the tracking, the competitive structure, the countdown. This wasn't a simple hit; it was an elaborate production. His mind was racing with possibilities, none of them pleasant.

'I'd better be ready,' he said as he moved to the weapons locker, pulling out a CZ 75 and two full, spare 16 round magazines. Thumbing the magazine release on the CZ, he confirmed that one was full as well. He next racked the slide, catching the chambered round as it ejected, then did a quick visual inspection before slapping the mag home, cycling a round into the chamber and dropping the hammer with the decocker. 'If a dozen or so professional killers know where to find me, I'm not taking any chances.'

'We should move to one of the backup locations,' Trix suggested. 'If they get a general fix on you here—'

She paused as Marlowe's phone buzzed. He pulled it out, skimming the message.

'Curtis. Says he needs to meet immediately. Claims he's found a direct link between Saito's death and Marlowe Coin.'

'Convenient timing.'

'My thoughts exactly.'

'It's a trap.'

'Probably,' Marlowe agreed, reading the message again. 'But if there's even a chance he has actionable intelligence ...'

'Send me instead,' Trix suggested. 'I'm not the one with a target on my back.'

'And you're not the one Curtis asked to meet,' Marlowe countered. 'Besides, you're the only one who can crack that code. I need you on that USB to see if there's a way to find the people who have connections to the tracker. Curtis wants to meet in thirty minutes, which means I won't be here when the tracker pings. And it also doesn't give our friends much time to prepare an elaborate ambush. You'll be safer here than anywhere else.'

Trix spun in her chair to face him directly.

'And if it's a ploy to separate us?'

'Then they'll find that "divide and conquer" isn't as easy as it sounds,' Marlowe replied with a smile.

Moving to a storage locker, Marlowe handed Trix a small radio with an earpiece attachment.

'Take this. Dedicated channel, short-range but secure. Check-in every ten minutes. If I miss two consecutive check-ins, communications are jammed or the church is compromised, head to somewhere safe and unknown, and wait seventy-two hours.'

'Why that long?'

'Because according to that site, everything's over by four p.m. Friday afternoon.'

Trix took the radio, slipping the earpiece in.

'And if you're compromised?'

'Then I'm already dead,' Marlowe said flatly, 'and you need to disappear. Take everything we've learned about Marlowe Coin and go deep, understand?'

She nodded once; her expression grim.

'Ten-minute intervals. Don't be late.'

He moved to the stairs, looking back at her. For a moment, he considered scrapping the entire plan, staying put, fortifying their position together. But that was defensive thinking. Reactive. And the only way to end this was to be proactive.

'Be careful,' Trix said, her voice softer than usual.

'Always am,' Marlowe replied with a half-smile that didn't reach his eyes. 'Don't forget to lock up behind me.'

5

HOME INVASION

THE LATE FEBRUARY AFTERNOON WAS BITTERLY COLD, A LIGHT fog rolling in from the south which reduced visibility–both an advantage and a complication. Marlowe moved through the one-time graveyard at the church's perimeter, staying close to the ancient headstones for cover. No obvious surveillance, but that meant little these days. Professionals wouldn't be easy to spot.

Curtis had suggested a meeting in Holland Park–public enough to discourage direct action, private enough for a discreet conversation. Thirty minutes by foot, less by tube, but Marlowe wouldn't risk the underground.

As he walked, Marlowe considered the implications of Curtis's message. If genuine, it meant MI5 had uncovered something significant–perhaps the identity of whoever had set up Marlowe Coin, likely Steele, or how the tracking system functioned. But the timing remained suspect and was too convenient by half.

He reached a newsagent's, casually browsing the magazines while checking reflections in the store's security mirrors. Nothing obvious. He made his check-in with Trix, receiving confirmation that all remained quiet at the church. At some point soon, there'd be a blip, though, and people would be on him.

Time to move.

Moving on, Marlowe took a circuitous path through back streets, doubling back occasionally, pausing to examine window displays while scanning for followers. He was approaching a small square with a central garden when he noticed it—the faintest irregularity in the pattern of pedestrians. A man in a dark coat had appeared at the same corner twice in the last ten minutes, moving at a casual pace that matched Marlowe's own meandering route too perfectly.

Professional. Patient. Waiting for the right moment. Possibly since the last blip, as there was no way he'd have made it here so fast.

Marlowe turned abruptly into a narrow passage between buildings. No surveillance cameras here, and limited escape routes—a deliberate choice. If someone was following, better to confront them in a controlled environment of his choosing than wait for them to pick their moment. The passage opened onto a small courtyard with three exits: one back to the street he'd left, one to another alley, and one through an archway that led to a busier road. Marlowe positioned himself against the wall beside the entrance he'd used, drawing his CZ from a concealed appendix holster.

And waited.

The man in the dark coat appeared moments later, moving with the cautious pace of someone expecting a trap but confident in their ability to handle it. He was mid-forties, with the hard eyes and watchful demeanour of ex-military or intelligence, now operating in the private sector. One hand was inside his coat–almost certainly gripping a weapon.

Marlowe stepped forward, pressing the CZ into the side of the man's ribs before he could react. The man froze, instantly assessing his options, but not surprised at the appearance. His hand remained inside his coat.

'Both hands where I can see them,' Marlowe instructed. 'Slowly.'

The man complied, bringing his hands out to his sides. No weapon visible, which worried Marlowe more than if he'd been holding a gun. It meant he was confident enough to enter a potentially hostile situation unarmed.

'Who sent you?' Marlowe demanded.

The man's expression remained neutral.

'No one "sent" me, Marlowe. I'm an independent contractor, same as yourself.'

'Hunting the bounty?'

'Observing,' the man corrected. 'Gathering intelligence. The actual killing comes later, when I've properly assessed the situation.'

'Thorough,' Marlowe acknowledged. 'But not thorough enough, or we wouldn't be having this conversation.'

The man's mouth twitched in what might have been the ghost of a smile.

'Professional courtesy. I could have remained undetected if I'd chosen to. This is merely ... an introduction.'

Marlowe pressed the gun harder into the man's ribs.

'I'm not particularly interested in making new friends right now.'

'That's unfortunate,' the man replied calmly. 'Because I think you'll find my friendship extremely valuable in the coming hours.'

'Is that so?'

'You've already survived two attempts on your life. The price hasn't dropped yet, though. You're not killing assassins. When you start, it *will* drop. But eventually, someone will succeed.'

'Unless I find who's behind this first,' Marlowe countered.

The man shrugged slightly.

'A possibility, certainly. But have you considered that perhaps the game itself is more important than who designed it? This isn't just a contract. It's a competition. A performance. And like any good performance, the audience is as important as the actors.'

'Who's the audience?'

The man's eyes revealed nothing.

'That's the right question. Not who created this, but who's watching. Who benefits from seeing Thomas Marlowe hunted through the streets of London?'

Marlowe's radio crackled in his ear, breaking his concentration for a split second–enough for the man to move. His left hand shot out, striking Marlowe's wounded arm. Pain exploded in his entire arm, and his grip on the CZ weakened.

The man twisted away, ducking beneath Marlowe's line of fire. Not fleeing, but repositioning. This wasn't an escape attempt–it was a calculated shift in the power dynamic.

'I didn't come here to fight you,' the man said, now several paces distant. 'Merely to introduce myself and deliver a message.'

'What message?' Marlowe demanded, the CZ levelled again despite the throbbing in his arm.

'Curtis isn't meeting you in Holland Park. He's been detained for questioning by an internal MI5 review board since noon today, brought back from holiday pretty much right after you met. Someone is using his credentials to lure you away from your base.'

The radio crackled again, more insistently. Trix's voice, breaking protocol.

'Tom, we have a situation. Multiple hostiles appr—'

Static. Then silence.

Marlowe's blood went cold.

'What the hell have you done?'

'Not me,' the man said, backing towards one exit. 'I'm merely the distraction. The real action is happening elsewhere. Good luck, Marlowe. I look forward to our next meeting. By the way, the name's *Passive*. Not my real one, of course. And the next time we meet, I won't be keeping to it.'

This stated, the man known as Passive turned and sprinted through the archway, disappearing into the street beyond.

Marlowe didn't pursue. Instead, he pressed the radio transmit button.

'Trix? Trix, respond!'

Nothing but static.

Not again.

He tried again, changing frequencies. Still nothing. It had to be professional, localised jamming, centred on the church. The timing, the strategy–all of it designed to separate him from Trix at the crucial moment.

He'd walked right into it.

Marlowe began running, no longer concerned with stealth or surveillance. Speed was all that mattered now. The church was fifteen minutes away at a dead sprint–but an eternity when seconds counted.

He stopped as the figure emerged into the alleyway,

blocking his way, hands outstretched, showing he was unarmed.

'Hello, Tom,' St John Steele smiled. 'Long time no see. No need for the weapon, you don't want to shoot me.'

'Trust me, St John, I *really* want to shoot you,' Marlowe muttered.

'Emotionally, you're fractured. I get that,' Steele nodded. 'But if I don't call in by the time your tracker beeps, you'll be in an even bigger world of hurt than you think you are now.'

Marlowe sighed. He knew Steele wouldn't have turned up here without a backup plan.

'The man I just met was one of yours?'

'He was,' Steele confirmed. 'The interesting thing about Passive is that he always meets up with his target first. I knew that I'd just follow him, and eventually he'd find you.'

'You could have just come to my church,' Marlowe suggested.

'Ah, but to do that,' Steele replied calmly, 'would mean you would be *there,* and I need you away.'

Marlowe felt a coldness creep up his spine.

'Trix Preston is perfectly safe if she manages to get out in time,' Steele shrugged. 'I don't like you having an advantage, Marlowe. Home base gives you that. I need you on the run. Cornered, a fox without a den.'

'Why don't you just kill me? Why all this stupidity, this game, this competition–whatever it is–this bloody coin?'

'Marlowe, this isn't just revenge,' Steele said, horrified. 'No, we're making money. We're rocketing up the altcoin ratings. The Marlowe coin is a sure seller.'

He buffed his nails against his jacket as he continued.

'You see, I've got a friend. You know him. Ciaran. Always talked to me about how huge cryptocurrency was going to be.

Had a bagful himself until you and your friend removed it from him.'

Marlowe mentally stored aside the information. Ciaran Winston had been involved in this, it seemed.

'Maybe I should have killed him rather than let him run.'

'Oh, he was working on this *way* before you last saw him,' Steele said. 'Even if you'd killed him, this would still have continued. A billion Marlowe coins were minted–or mined– or whatever you call them. Mining sounds quite like a physical action, but it's all done on ...'

He waggled his hand in the air.

'Well, somewhere. And while you're alive, those coins go up in price, just like stocks and shares. The more coins you buy, the more you can get involved in the game. Of course, the relevant people gained the coins when they were minimal, multiple fractions of a cent in cost. Now you'll be happy to know, you're almost *at* a cent. That's ten million dollars.'

'Doesn't sound much, considering the fact you're offering a twelve-million-dollar reward for me.'

'Absolutely,' Steele smiled. 'But, by the end of the day, we'll be up to three cents. Thirty million. By tomorrow, who knows? Fifty million. A hundred million. A quarter of a billion. Look at Bitcoin five years ago. You could buy one for nine thousand dollars. Now you have to pay almost ninety thousand dollars, as of right now. Imagine what the Marlowe coin will be worth once we start burning some of our stock. Every time you kill someone and the hit is halved, scarcity will build. Interest will build. Money will be made. A week from now? I'll have billions, and it'll all be thanks to you.'

Marlowe shook his head.

'So, this is how you're regaining your money that we took

from you in Rushmore,' he said. 'All those plans you had with Project Quicksilver and all you're doing is a crypto scam.'

Steele's face smiled, but his eyes held no humour.

'The problem with Quicksilver, Marlowe, was I was relying on the Americans and the British to have placed in money without taking it back out.'

He shook his head.

'The Government screwed me, Marlowe. So, it's time for me to take it back against "the man".'

'I don't know how to explain this to you,' Marlowe replied calmly. 'But in this case, *you* are "the man".'

Steele smiled.

'Have you checked your little business card yet?'

'If you're asking whether I've given blood to your cause, then yes. I didn't really have time to look at it, though, before you called me for this bullshit meeting.'

'Then you won't know I've given you a gift, Thomas. A million Marlowe coins, as a "thank you" for your part in this,' Steele spoke as if he was giving a great gift. 'Currently, they're worth ten thousand dollars, but it will go up. As I make my millions, you'll make your hundreds of thousands, and who knows, maybe make something even bigger from this. But it also allows you to play the game.'

'So what, the more coins you get, the better you learn where I am?' Marlowe shook his head. 'This is quite basic even for you.'

'Oh, it's not so basic at all,' Steele shook his head. 'We're going to have fun, Tom. You see, I have some very rich people who have bought in, who really hate you, and who expect to make money from your death. And in the process, the more money that is spent, well, you get certain privileges, like maybe a secondary tracker blip given every fifteen minutes for your favourite hunter—'

'They have favourites?'

'Of course. I've specifically invited a selection of assassins, people I've trusted or, my agent trusts.'

'The Broker.'

Steele shrugged.

'He was good to me in Punta Cana; I felt bad he lost money. And, if I'm being honest, I've realised lately that one of my past "lives" specifically affected his. So, this is an opportunity for him to regain a healthy credit, and for me to repay a debt. But my subscribers, shall we say, the people who are waiting to see you die–more coins equal bigger bonuses.'

Steele shifted on his spot.

'They pay a certain amount, then the next assassin will have a bodycam on, so they'll be able to watch you die in live action. Maybe another one wants to see you killed with an axe. Pay enough money, the assassin will use one. It's reality TV, in the form of an execution, Thomas. And I'll sit in the studio watching on the monitors, as you make me billions while the Marlowe coin rises and rises.'

He looked away, as if envisioning his glorious moment.

'And then at some point, you'll die, and people will start to sell, but by that point it'll be too late–the pump and dump will be over. I'll have made my money, my organisation will be powered again and it'll all be because of you.'

'And if I kill the assassins?' Marlowe asked. 'If I reduce it by half, repeatedly, to the point it becomes pointless and nobody wants to go for me for the money?'

'I still win,' Steele smiled. 'And so do you, Marlowe, because not only will you be alive, but your coins will be worth money. And you will be a valued asset of the new

Orchid. I wonder what your friends in that ancient bag of bones that still claim it's the *original* Orchid will feel about that.'

He turned now, walking away from Marlowe.

'You should contact your friend,' he said, 'and then you should start running. But that'll be the last time you can. Once we start playing properly, anyone who helps you? Well, they become fodder for the gaming mechanics. Oh—'

He paused, looking back with a smile as he held up his phone.

'I've just had a notice on my phone. Your tracker's just pinged again, told me where you are. Right here, exactly where you should be.'

With that, St John Steele walked off. For a moment Marlowe considered shooting him in the back, ending Steele once and for all, but he knew that would be foolish; Steele would have prepared for that. Instead, he felt his jaw.

Was the tracker in his bloody tooth? Either way, it was thirty minutes until he pinged again.

Marlowe started off in the other direction at a sprint.

TRIX WAS RUNNING A DIAGNOSTIC ON THE WEST ENTRANCE sensors when the first alarm triggered. Motion detection on the church's roof–a single figure moving across the slate tiles. She switched to a camera feed, catching a glimpse of black tactical gear before the figure disappeared from view. It looked professional; not coming in hot but executing a careful infiltration.

She opened the security control panel, activating additional measures. Electromagnets sealed all exterior doors.

Reinforced shutters descended over windows–these had been installed a few months back, after a sniper had tried to take Marlowe out through a stained-glass window. The crypt entrance, already secure and hidden from the outside world, engaged its secondary locks.

'Tom?' she spoke into the radio. 'We have movement on the roof. Single operative, looks like advance recon.'

Static answered her. She tried again, adjusting the frequency. Nothing–all communications jammed. That meant a coordinated team, not a lone operator. And if they were jamming transmissions, they knew exactly what they were targeting.

The perimeter alarm triggered again. Three more signatures, approaching from different directions: east entrance, west window, rear utility access. Surrounding the building, cutting off escape routes.

Trix moved quickly, gathering essential equipment: laptop, hard drives, weapons. The go-plan here had always dictated scorched earth–nothing left behind that could be used against them. She initiated the first stage, wiping servers, corrupting data stores, making sure the offsite backups were hidden. Only her personal equipment would remain intact, and only because she needed it to continue their investigation.

The security feed showed the first breach attempt–shaped charges placed precisely on the east entrance lock mechanism. These weren't common assassins; they were breaching specialists, equipped for rapid, surgical entry.

No time left. She gathered her go-bag, already packed for emergencies, and moved to the crypt's secondary exit–a maintenance shaft that connected to the London Underground, a disused tunnel they'd used several times before.

The first explosion rocked the brickwork, the sound muffled by stone and distance but unmistakable. *Front entrance breached.* The others would likely follow in sequence. It was standard tactical procedure: multiple entry points, overwhelming force.

The second explosion came as she was moving into the tunnels. Then the third, almost immediately after. They were inside now, sweeping through the church's main level. The crypt was still hidden, and there was every chance they'd miss it, but there was also every chance they'd find it fast. She had minutes, perhaps less. Enough time if she hurried.

The tunnel that led into the train tunnels was narrow, barely wide enough for her shoulders, descending into darkness. The air was damp, heavy with the scent of earth and old stone, and she activated a small LED light on her watch, illuminating just enough to navigate by. The space widened slightly here, allowing her to move more freely. She checked her watch–three minutes since the first breach. Not enough distance yet. She needed to keep moving.

Keep moving. Focus on the objective. Don't look back.

Through her earpiece, connected to a microphone in the kitchen, angry voices could be heard.

'Clear! Target not present! Check for hidden exits!'

She needed more distance, more time.

The underground tunnel branched ahead, one path continuing straight, the other curving left towards what should be the river, based on her mental map. She chose left, moving faster now despite the confined space.

An exit grating should be coming up–a century-old ventilation access point that emerged in what was now a small park. From there, she could disappear into London's crowded streets, activate her emergency protocols, establish a new base of operations.

Light glinted ahead–the grating. Trix moved towards it, already reaching for the tools that would allow her to open it from the inside.

Her earpiece crackled suddenly, startling her in the confined space. A voice broke through the static–Marlowe's voice, distorted but recognisable.

'... Trix? Trix, respond!'

She pressed the transmit button.

'Church compromised. Full tactical team, professional equipment. I'm exiting via the choo-choo system. Don't try to return. They're waiting for you.'

No response this time. The jamming was reasserting itself, or she'd moved out of range. Either way, the message was delivered. Marlowe would know to stay away ... with a little luck.

Trix reached the grating, examining it carefully before attempting to open it. She saw no signs of tampering or surveillance, so she applied pressure to the ancient mechanism, feeling it resist briefly before giving way with a rusty groan. Cool air rushed in, carrying with it the scents of the city. She pushed the grating up and outward, creating an opening just large enough to slip through.

The small park was deserted, and Trix emerged cautiously, scanning for threats before fully committing to the surface. She secured the grating behind her, making it appear undisturbed, then moved quickly towards the park's exit. In the distance she could see flickers of flames in the sky, hear sirens already approaching.

The bastards had set fire to the church.

Damn, I hope they didn't reach the crypt.

Slinging her go-bag over her shoulder, Trix disappeared into the streets, just another Londoner hurrying home on a cold February evening. Her laptop contained everything they'd learned about Rushmore, Quicksilver, everything about Steele's "New Kid" branch, and of course the recent Marlowe Coin. Her memory held the rest: security protocols, contact methods, fallback plans.

She'd find somewhere safe. Then they'd regroup, reassess, plan their next move.

Assuming they both survived that long.

MARLOWE ARRIVED AT THE ONE-TIME CHURCH TO FIND IT IN flames, emergency vehicles surrounding the perimeter, firefighters battling the blaze that had already consumed part of the roof. Police were establishing a cordon, keeping bystanders at a safe distance.

No tactical teams were visible, no signs of the professional hit squad that had breached the building; they'd accomplished their objective and withdrawn, leaving chaos in their wake.

Marlowe checked his watch. The blip would have given a different location, so maybe they'd decided to give up here.

Or maybe this was a message. Smoke the fox from the den, so the hunt could be more fun.

He melted into the crowd of onlookers, watching from a distance. He knew Trix was following procedure, making her way to an unknown safe house. As soon as she had something for him, she'd put out a contact on one of the various message boards they used, they'd rendezvous and compare notes, plan their next move.

But until then, he was on his own.

Marlowe turned away from the burning church, from the home and base he'd established, unsure of how deep the damage went. The game had escalated. The rules were clear now. No safe havens, no respite, nowhere to hide.

Fine. Let them watch. Let them think they had the advantage.

Thomas Marlowe had survived worse. He'd been hunted before, cornered before, stripped of resources before. And he was still walking, while countless enemies were in the ground.

St John Steele was about to learn a painful lesson, one he should have known before ... that sometimes the prey becomes the predator.

And Thomas Marlowe was very, *very* good at hunting.

6

EXTRACTION

Marlowe took a circuitous route back to Canary Wharf, switching transport modes three times and doubling back twice to ensure he wasn't followed. The tracker he now believed was in his tooth had likely pinged as he passed through Chelsea, and wouldn't ping for another twenty minutes, which gave him just enough time for what he needed to do, while his jaw throbbed with a dull, persistent ache, as if to remind him of the potential betrayal housed within.

The surgical precision of it almost impressed him. A tracking device small enough to fit in during a filling, yet powerful enough to broadcast a location every thirty minutes; no wonder the assassins kept finding him. The question was whether Doctor Chopra was directly involved or merely an unwitting accomplice in Steele's elaborate game.

Doctor Chopra's practice occupied the ground floor of a one-time Victorian Wharf building, halfway down the street

from West India Quay. The brass plaque beside the door
caught the lamplight:

DR. R. CHOPRA, DENTAL SURGERY
BY APPOINTMENT ONLY.

Marlowe observed the building for five minutes from the
shelter of a doorway across the street, noting the security
camera above the entrance, the magnetic lock on the door,
and the discreet alarm panel just visible through the frosted
glass. There were lights inside, but no movement; Doctor
Chopra had likely gone home for the day, like any
respectable dentist would, without knowledge his patient was
being hunted by assassins.

Or perhaps he'd fled, knowing what was coming.

The security system was high end but standard–the kind
that relied on monitoring centres rather than direct police
response. Marlowe moved to the rear of the building, finding
the service entrance used for deliveries. The lock here was
less sophisticated; a simple reinforced door with a cylindrical
deadbolt. He removed a set of lockpicks from his pocket and
worked quickly in the dim light of the service alley, aware
that any minute now his location would once again be
broadcast.

The lock clicked open after forty seconds of manipulation–not his personal best, but respectable, given the
circumstances–and Marlowe slipped inside, gently closing
the door behind him. The alarm system gave a soft warning
beep as he did so, indicating he had thirty seconds to enter
the disarm code. He ignored it, moving instead to the electrical panel on the wall. One quick snip of wires later, and
the system fell silent–though this would likely trigger a

notification at the monitoring service. Of course, if it did, he still had maybe fifteen minutes before someone responded. More than enough time for what he needed to do.

Moving through the darkened corridor, Marlowe navigated to the main treatment room. The space was meticulously clean, with all the equipment neatly arranged, and the surfaces gleaming in the faint light filtering through the windows. He found the light switch for a small desk lamp rather than the overheads, providing just enough illumination to work without attracting attention from outside.

The filing cabinet yielded nothing of interest–Doctor Chopra appeared to keep most records digitally. Marlowe moved to the computer, powering it up, watching the screen glow to life.

Password protected, of course.

He tried the obvious combinations–"dentist," "chopra," variations of the practice name–to no avail, and cursed under his breath. *He needed Trix for this kind of work.*

The sound of a key in the front-door lock froze him in place.

Marlowe killed the desk lamp, drawing his CZ 75 from its holster, and positioned himself behind the door. Footsteps approached–a single person, moving with the confident familiarity of someone who belonged here. The door swung open, and a figure was silhouetted against the dim glow from the street.

Doctor Chopra himself, returning for something forgotten–or perhaps responding to the silent alarm trigger.

Marlowe pressed the barrel of the CZ against the dentist's neck before he could turn around.

'Don't move. Don't call out. Just close the door slowly.'

Doctor Chopra tensed but complied, easing the door shut.

'Mister Ripley,' he said, voice remarkably steady. 'I had a feeling you might return.'

'Lights,' Marlowe instructed. 'Just the desk lamp. Keep your hands where I can see them.'

The dentist moved carefully to the desk, switching on the small lamp that cast the room in a soft, localised glow.

'I assume this isn't about the tooth requiring adjustment?' Doctor Chopra asked with remarkable composure.

'The tooth is adjusting me, it seems,' Marlowe replied, keeping the CZ trained on the dentist. 'What did you put in it, Doctor?'

Doctor Chopra's eyes flickered; the first crack in his professional demeanour.

'I don't know what you mean.'

'Let's not waste time,' Marlowe said. 'I have about twelve minutes before security responds to that silent alarm, and about five before every mercenary in a square mile starts coming here. You have even less before I lose patience. The tracking device in my filling–who paid you to install it?'

Finally, the dentist's shoulders slumped slightly.

'It wasn't meant to harm you.'

'Tell that to the assassins following the signal,' Marlowe countered.

'Assassins?' Doctor Chopra's surprise seemed genuine. 'I was told it was for your protection.'

'By whom?'

'A man,' Doctor Chopra replied, his voice lower now. 'He didn't give a name. British, well-spoken, expensive suit. Said he represented a government agency. Showed me identification–MI5, he claimed.'

'Description,' Marlowe pressed.

'Mid-fifties, thin, aristocratic features. Grey at the temples.'

Curtis? Steele? Both fit the general description.

'He said you were under protection,' Doctor Chopra continued. 'That you were valuable to national security but had a habit of going off-grid when you shouldn't. The device was just for emergencies, to locate you if you were compromised.'

'And you believed that?'

'He paid me fifty thousand pounds,' Doctor Chopra said simply. 'In cash. And he knew things–about my practice, my clients, my situation with the tax authorities. Things he shouldn't have known.'

Blackmail and bribery, then. Effective combination.

'When did he approach you?'

'A couple of weeks back. Said you would likely come in for treatment soon–which you did.'

'The device,' Marlowe said, his patience waning. 'How does it work? How is it powered?'

'I don't know how these things—'

'They must have said something!'

Doctor Chopra paused, eyes wide, nodding.

'The woman who gave it to me—'

'Woman?'

'The man didn't come back. When the woman came, she showed me what I had to put in.'

'What did she look like?'

'Black woman, late thirties, tall, short hair. Bit like Grace Jones.'

It didn't ring any new bells in Marlowe's mind. *Steele had found some new friends, it seemed.*

'Go on.'

'She said it was a passive RFID transmitter with satellite capabilities. No battery–it's kinetic, harvests energy through motion. Your jaw movements generate enough power for a short burst transmission every thirty minutes,' Doctor Chopra's clinical detachment was returning as he explained the technology. 'It's cutting-edge stuff. Spy grade. That's why I thought I was helping.'

'And how do I remove it?'

'You don't,' Doctor Chopra said flatly. 'Not without proper equipment. It's fused with the filling, so, trying to extract it yourself would likely damage the nerve and possibly fracture the tooth structure.'

'What about EMP?'

'It would have to be at the exact millisecond of the pulse,' Chopra replied. 'As I said, the kinetic power only bursts every thirty minutes. I mean, you could try…'

Marlowe gestured towards the dental chair with his CZ.

'Sounds like I'd just be waiting for trouble,' he said. 'Luckily, it's fortunate I have a dentist on hand.'

Doctor Chopra paled.

'I can't just—'

'You can, and you will,' Marlowe insisted. 'Consider it warranty service.'

The dentist hesitated, then nodded reluctantly.

'I'll need to take an X-ray first, to confirm the exact position.'

'Do it quickly.'

Doctor Chopra moved to the X-ray machine, preparing it with care, despite the gun pointed at him. Marlowe kept his distance, watching every movement closely.

'Place your head here,' Doctor Chopra instructed, indicating the positioning device. 'It'll just take a moment.'

Marlowe hesitated, then complied, keeping the CZ at his side, ready to raise it if needed. The machine hummed briefly, capturing the image of Marlowe's dental work, and Doctor Chopra moved to a computer screen, bringing up the digital X-ray.

'There,' he said, pointing to a small dark shape embedded in Marlowe's right upper molar. 'You can see it there–the slightly denser material within the structure.'

Marlowe studied the image. The tracker was tiny, barely distinguishable from the rest of the dental work.

'How long to remove it?'

'Thirty minutes, minimum,' Doctor Chopra replied. 'I'd need to drill through the crown, extract the device without damaging the underlying tooth, then place a temporary filling.'

Too long. Marlowe checked his watch. The security response would arrive within minutes.

'We don't have thirty minutes,' he said. 'Simplified version?'

'I ... could drill into the filling and destroy the device,' Doctor Chopra suggested reluctantly. 'It would leave the tooth vulnerable, but it would stop the transmissions immediately.'

'Do it,' Marlowe ordered, moving towards the dental chair. To the side, Doctor Chopra began preparing his equipment with the calm manner of a medical professional, despite the circumstances, laying out a drill, various picks, and a small mirror.

'No anaesthetic,' Marlowe instructed. 'We don't have time.'

'It will be extremely painful,' Doctor Chopra warned.

'I've had worse.'

The dentist nodded, powering up the drill. The high-pitched whine filled the room as Marlowe settled into the chair, keeping the CZ visible on his lap.

Looks like it's bloody Marathon Man after all, then.

'Open, please,' Doctor Chopra said, reverting to his professional manner. Marlowe almost laughed at this, but instead, he opened his mouth, bracing himself for the pain that was to come. The drill approached his tooth–

The glass shattered inward, spraying fragments across the room. Doctor Chopra jerked backward, the drill falling from his hand as a red mist erupted from his throat. He collapsed to the floor, eyes wide with shock, hands clutching at the wound that had torn open his carotid artery.

Marlowe was already moving, rolling from the chair as a second shot punched into the upholstery where his head had been moments before. The sniper had a clear line of sight through the broken window.

Shit. Looks like the beacon went off. Or he'd been followed. Or they'd been watching Chopra, maybe.

He crawled behind the dental cabinet, taking cover as another shot splintered the wood near his shoulder. Doctor Chopra lay motionless on the floor, blood pooling beneath him, eyes staring sightlessly at the ceiling.

Marlowe assessed his options quickly. The front entrance was likely covered. The rear exit would take him through narrow corridors with limited cover. The window offered immediate escape but would expose him to the sniper.

Muffled footsteps in the corridor outside the treatment room told him the sniper had a partner already inside the building.

Coordinated team—one to flush him out, one to take the shot when he fled.

The door handle turned. Marlowe raised the CZ, aiming at chest height. The door burst open, and a figure charged in, weapon raised. Marlowe double tapped, catching the intruder with two rounds to centre mass. The impact drove them backward, but he saw there was a vest, and it absorbed the shots.

Body armour—these weren't amateurs. The next opportunity, if there was one, would be a triple tap, with the third round to the head.

The assassin recovered quickly, returning fire, and bullets thudded into the cabinet as Marlowe ducked lower. He counted shots—a three-round burst from what sounded like an HK MP5 compact submachine gun.

'Nowhere to run, Marlowe,' a voice called—male, American accent. 'Building's surrounded. Might as well make it easy on yourself.'

'Where's the fun in that?' Marlowe replied, using the opponent's voice to pinpoint the shooter's position. He fired again, two quick shots aimed at the doorway, forcing the assassin back into the corridor. The brief respite gave Marlowe time to glance at Doctor Chopra's body. The X-ray was still displayed on the screen, showing exactly where the tracker was embedded in his tooth.

No time for careful dental surgery now.

Movement at the window—the sniper was repositioning. Marlowe needed to get out and do it fast. He grabbed the drill Doctor Chopra had dropped, examining it quickly.

It was still functional; it'd have to do.

The assassin in the corridor fired another burst, keeping Marlowe pinned down. The angle of the shots suggested he was trying to work his way further into the room, aiming to flank Marlowe's position. Instead of moving further in, however, Marlowe unclasped the dragon-headed catch on his wrist, unwinding the metre-long steel defence chain that had saved his life more times than he could count. With his left hand he swung the chain in a tight arc, flicking it out to its full length, while keeping the CZ ready in his right.

He heard the soft scuff of a boot on the floor to his right– the assassin was almost in position to get a clear shot. Marlowe waited until the last possible moment, then launched the chain in a vicious arc towards the sound.

The weighted end caught the assassin across the face with a satisfying crack. The man staggered backward with a yelp of pain, his weapon discharging wildly into the ceiling as Marlowe surged forward, driving his shoulder into the assassin's midsection, wincing as he felt his arm's earlier wound open again.

They crashed into the corridor, grappling for control. The assassin was skilled, instantly shifting his balance to compensate for Marlowe's greater weight. A knife appeared in his hand–a combat blade, professionally wielded. Marlowe caught the man's wrist as the knife descended towards his throat, using the momentum to slam the assassin's hand against the wall. The blade clattered to the floor, but the likely American assassin responded with a vicious knee to Marlowe's ribs.

Pain bloomed in Marlowe's side as he rolled with the impact, creating distance. The assassin reached for a backup weapon–a compact pistol holstered at his ankle. Marlowe was faster, though. The CZ barked twice, and this time he aimed for the head.

The assassin dropped, lifeless before he hit the floor.

The sniper would have heard the shots; Marlowe needed to move now. Having dropped it during the fight, he once more grabbed the drill.

No time for precision.

He propped his CZ within reach, powered up the drill, and grimaced as he brought it to his mouth, watching in the mirror as he did so.

The pain as the drill bit into his filling was explosive–white-hot agony that radiated through his jaw and into his skull. Marlowe forced himself to continue, using the X-ray image on the screen beside as a guide to where the tracker was embedded. Blood filled his mouth as the drill penetrated the material, catching the gum as he clumsily tried to keep the tip steady, and the taste of burned enamel and metal–both from the blood and the disintegrating tracker–made him gag, but he kept going, ignoring the fire that seemed to consume the right side of his face.

Thirty seconds of excruciating pain later, he was reasonably certain the device was destroyed. Marlowe spat a mixture of blood, saliva, and dental material into the sink, rinsing his mouth with water from the tap.

No pink cups of liquid this time.

The window exploded inward as the sniper, realising Marlowe had moved, tried to get a clear shot into the second treatment room. Bullets shattered equipment around him as Marlowe dived for cover again, retrieving his CZ and chain. His mouth was aflame, blood still flowing freely, but with luck the tracker was neutralised, and that gave him a fighting chance of escape.

Marlowe crawled to the door, listening carefully. There was no sound of movement in the corridor–the sniper was waiting for him to break cover. The magnetic lock on the exterior doors would have reset by now, meaning the front entrance was likely secure again. That left the rear exit as his best option.

If only his mouth wasn't on fire.

Fire. Of course.

Marlowe lunged for the fire alarm on the wall, smashing the glass with the butt of his gun. The piercing wail of the alarm filled the building instantly, and seconds later, the sprinkler system activated, drenching everything in a cascade of water. Under cover of the artificial downpour, Marlowe darted from the treatment room, staying low as he moved towards the rear of the building. The sniper's visibility would be compromised by the water and the darkness, while the alarm would bring legitimate emergency services, adding to whatever local security was already on its way, complicating the assassin's escape. Small advantages, but Marlowe would take what he could get.

Taking a moment to re-clasp the chain around his wrist and reholster the CZ, Marlowe exited into the shadows, blood still trickling from his damaged tooth. He'd claimed a kill–the bounty would now be six million instead of twelve. A small victory, but it would force Steele to adjust his plans.

However, as he went to run deeper into the Wharf, a round from a sniper rifle nicked the ground beside him–the sniper was firing wild now, it seemed. He wasn't sure what to do next, but it didn't matter; it had already been made up for him, as a black Audi A4 screeched to a halt beside him.

'Get in!' The driver, a familiar-yet-surprising new addition yelled, and Marlowe didn't need a second offer, diving into the back as another bullet spanged against the side, with Detective Inspector James Morris driving off away from the building at speed.

Marlowe collapsed into the back seat, wheezing from the exertion.

'How the hell...' he started.

'We had a call—when guns are fired, that usually happens,' Detective Sergeant Louisa Wilcott said as she looked around from the passenger seat. ' Good to see you again ... Mister Lachlan.'

Marlowe fought back a groan. He'd forgotten the last time he'd seen Morris and Wilcott, they'd assumed he was an Irish bomb maker named Kieran Lachlan. They also assumed he was working with Frank Maguire, was part of the criminal underworld, and by now had pretty much worked out he was, as his legend claimed, part of the "real" IRA–a terrorist.

He may have leaped from the frying pan into the fire here.

'I'm not Kieran Lachlan,' Marlowe said, using his proper accent rather than the Irish one he'd used the last time he met them. 'I know that I'd said I was when we last spoke, but—'

'But you're actually some kind of spook,' Morris said, still driving. 'Yeah, we guessed that when the people in black suits turned up a few days after you left and told us to shut up and forget you.'

Marlowe frowned.

'You had a D-notice?'

'Is that a "do not talk about this shit" notice? Then yes,' Morris said, and Marlowe could tell he was unimpressed. 'All I know is we weren't told your name or anything, just that you're some kind of shit-hot ex-spy, who we had to be thankful for, rather than arresting.'

'Yeah, sorry about that,' Marlowe replied. He genuinely

was sorry. 'If it makes you feel any better, I didn't know that Frank Maguire was working for MI5 either.'

'Maguire works for MI5?' Wilcott shook her head. 'Christ, is there anybody there who doesn't work for your bloody security service?'

'Technically me,' Marlowe replied with a smile. 'I left a few months back. My name's Tom Marlowe, by the way. I used to work for MI5. If you want more information on me, you can contact Alexander Curtis at Thames House. He's Section Head, and he'll vouch for me. Well, at least I hope he will.'

'So, he's not the one trying to kill you right now?' Morris asked with a smile.

'No,' Marlowe shook his head. 'That would be a whole gang of assassins who think they're part of some kind of reality TV show.'

'Of course they are,' Morris shook his head as they turned right, heading towards Limehouse. 'First time we met you, you were blowing up a building. Now everybody on the planet wants you dead. Do you ever have a holiday?'

Marlowe smiled.

'Who's to say this isn't one?' he asked, then shut his eyes as the pain in his mouth wrenched through his jaw.

'Can we not go to the police station, though?' he moaned softly. 'I really need an emergency dentist to fix this tooth.'

7

GO-BAGS

'THIS MIGHT HURT,' THE MAN SAID, HUNCHED OVER MARLOWE with a dental pick in one hand and what looked like a small soldering iron in the other. 'Actually, scratch that. This will definitely hurt.'

Marlowe gripped the arms of the chair as the dentist–if you could call him that–probed the broken tooth where the tracker had been before Marlowe had mangled it earlier that evening. Well, more mangled his tooth, but it did the same thing. They were in the back room of a chiropractic clinic in Limehouse, the dentist in question a Ukrainian man with nicotine-stained fingers and a perpetual scowl. Morris had made a phone call, pulled in a favour, and now Marlowe was being treated by a man who, from what he could gather from the whispered conversation, occasionally helped remove bullets from people who couldn't go to hospital–but Morris wasn't supposed to *know* that, of course.

Amusingly, it was the complete opposite of what Marlowe had thought of Morris the first time they'd met; back then every action was methodical, and everything about him was organised and calm, right down to the way he'd aligned his pen parallel to the folder's edge as he tried to interview Marlowe.

Now it seemed he was more comfortable in the trenches than Marlowe had considered.

'You did good job destroying tracker,' the dentist muttered with a worrying knowledge of what trackers were. 'But tooth is, how you say ... *shit* now. I can make temporary crown, last maybe three, four days. Then you need proper dentist.'

'Just make it functional,' Marlowe replied, his words slightly slurred from the local anaesthetic that was only partially numbing the throbbing pain.

Across the room, Morris leant against a filing cabinet, watching the procedure with undisguised distaste, while Wilcott had taken up position by the window, keeping an eye on the street below.

'Clear so far,' Wilcott reported. 'But we should move soon.'

The dentist worked quickly, cleaning the damaged tooth, placing a temporary filling, and crafting a crown from some kind of resin material that hardened under UV light. When he finally stepped back, Marlowe ran his tongue over the repair.

It was rough, uncomfortable, but intact.

'Four hundred pounds,' the dentist said, already cleaning his instruments.

Morris raised an eyebrow but reached for his wallet. Marlowe stopped him.

'I'll cover it,' he said, pulling out several folded notes from an inner pocket of his jacket, one of the few items he still had on him. 'It's the least I can do.'

The dentist counted the money, nodded once, and disappeared through a back door without another word.

'You know, Marlowe,' Morris said as Marlowe rose from the chair, testing his jaw, 'when I arrested you two months ago, I didn't think we'd end up here. Life takes some strange turns.'

'You have no idea,' Marlowe replied, moving towards the window where Wilcott stood. 'I appreciate the assist, but you need to distance yourselves from me. These people aren't amateurs.'

'So we gathered from the dead bodies in the dental clinic,' Wilcott remarked dryly. 'The on-scene guys are going into great detail about it right now. I'm guessing that was your last dentist. You need to stop killing them.'

'A sniper killed the dentist,' Marlowe replied, still pressing at his numb lip. 'I killed the assassin that came in after.'

'Who was following you because of some kind of spy tracker in your tooth,' Morris nodded. 'What, MI5 run out of cyanide capsules?'

'The Met's going mental about it, and they'll have questions,' Wilcott finished.

'Tell the Met police what you saw,' Marlowe said. 'Just leave out the part where you drove me away. Say you've been looking for me, that's why you've been out of touch.'

He paused, wincing at a sudden trauma pang from the tooth.

'I need a favour, though.'

Morris gave him a wary look.

'What sort of favour?'

'A ride to Bermondsey. Industrial estate off Jamaica Road.'

'That's it?' Morris seemed surprised. 'Not weapons, not diplomatic immunity, just a lift?'

'Just a lift,' Marlowe confirmed. 'I have resources, but I can't access them if I'm dead in the back of a taxi.'

Morris and Wilcott exchanged a look, probably wondering whether this was higher than their pay grade. Finally, Morris nodded.

'Bermondsey it is. But after that, we're done. I've got a kid who needs his dad to come home at night.'

'Fair,' Marlowe replied, understanding completely.

They took the back stairs down to the street where Morris had parked the Audi. The night was fully settled now, a fine drizzle falling over London, blurring the streetlights into hazy halos, and perfect weather for disappearing. Marlowe took the back seat again, staying low as Morris pulled away from the kerb.

'If anyone asks about my involvement,' Marlowe said as they drove, 'contact Alexander Curtis at Thames House. Section head for Counter-Intelligence. If he's unreachable, try Emilia Wintergreen.'

Morris glanced at him in the rearview mirror. 'Emilia Wintergreen? Wasn't she married to Detective Superintendent Monroe?'

'You know Monroe?' Marlowe was surprised.

'We have mutuals, and I've seen him work.'

Marlowe grinned.

'He's my uncle,' he said. 'Wintergreen's kind of an aunt. Although I used to work for her, too. Tell her I sent you. She doesn't like me much, but she respects the rules. She'll keep you clean.'

'Christ,' Morris muttered. 'I'm starting to regret not arresting you properly when I had the chance.'

'If it helps, I'm regretting a lot of choices myself,' Marlow chuckled, before another wince silenced him.

THE DRIVE TO BERMONDSEY TOOK TWENTY MINUTES IN THE light evening traffic. Morris maintained a careful route, avoiding major intersections where CCTV coverage was heaviest, Wilcott watching out of the passenger window. Marlowe had watched the thirty-minute timer come and go, relaxing when ninjas didn't swoop out of the sky to attack. Eventually, they pulled into the industrial estate–a collection of warehouses and storage units built in the eighties, most now repurposed into artisan workshops and small business units.

'Unit 14B,' Marlowe instructed. 'Far end, past the blue shipping container.'

Morris parked on the gravel path outside a nondescript roll-up door, the unit number barely visible in the faded paint. Marlowe surveyed the area carefully before stepping out of the car; the industrial estate was quiet at this hour, just a single light visible in one of the distant units where someone was working late.

'Wait here,' he told Morris before approaching the unit. Reaching down to the side of the door and pulling back the rubber seal, he poked around under it until he produced a small key, connected to the back with a magnet, and, after resealing the side seal, unlocked the heavy padlock securing the door.

The metal door rattled as Marlowe raised it just enough to duck underneath. Inside, the unit was empty except for a stack of plastic storage containers in one corner, and he moved directly to them, opening the third one down, revealing a black holdall nestled among what appeared to be Christmas decorations.

Marlowe checked the contents quickly–cash in three currencies, a clean and unused burner phone, a SIG with ammunition, and a set of documents for an identity that wasn't linked to either MI5 or Orchid. Everything still in place. It'd been here a while, too; recently he'd started to favour the CZ 75; the fact this was still his old, favoured gun showed he needed to keep up to date on these. He zipped the bag closed and returned to the car, sliding into the back seat with the holdall clutched against his chest.

'Got what you needed?' Wilcott asked, eyeing the bag with professional curiosity.

'First part,' Marlowe replied. 'There's one more stop, if you're willing.'

'Where?' Morris sighed.

'Aldgate. Office building on Minories.'

'And then we're done?'

'Then we're done, and I disappear. You'll never have to see me again.'

Morris put the car in gear.

'Promises, promises.'

THEY DROVE IN SILENCE FOR SEVERAL MINUTES, EACH LOST IN their own thoughts. Finally, Wilcott broke the quiet.

'This whole thing–professional assassins, tracking devices in teeth–this isn't usual for you, is it? I mean, it feels a little personal.'

'It is,' Marlowe acknowledged. 'Someone I crossed is retaliating. With interest.'

'And the bounty?' Morris asked. 'Is it eye wateringly high?'

'Started at twelve million dollars,' Marlowe said. 'Every time I kill one of them, it drops by half.'

Morris let out a low whistle.

'So, they have an incentive to work fast.'

'That's the idea.'

'But maybe *not* tell us you have to kill anyone, yeah?'

Marlowe smiled and said nothing. The rest of the journey passed in silence, and they approached Aldgate from the south, circling around to avoid the cameras at the main intersection. The office building on Minories was a bland sixties construction, scheduled for demolition to make way for yet another glass-and-steel monstrosity. Most of the tenants had already vacated, leaving it largely empty.

'What I need is on the third floor,' Marlowe directed as Morris parked across the street. 'This one I need to do alone. If I'm not back in ten minutes, leave.'

'Are you sure?' Wilcott asked, turning to look at him directly. 'We can back you up.'

'Better if you don't,' Marlowe said. 'Plausible deniability. For both our sakes.'

He exited the car, the holdall slung over his shoulder and crossed to the building. The security guard station was empty–budget cuts meant coverage only during business hours, so Marlowe used a keycard from a pocket in the holdall to access the service entrance, then took the stairs to the third floor.

The corridor was dim, with emergency lighting casting everything in a greenish glow. Marlowe moved confidently to a door on the right-hand side.

307 – Penrose Accounting

This time he quickly used his lock picks to gain entry. Inside, the office was stripped bare–empty desks, naked walls with lighter patches where pictures had once hung, abandoned ethernet cables dangling from the ceiling. The building was due to be demolished in a couple of months, and Marlowe had intended to come here before then anyway, but he hadn't expected it to be in such a manner. Barely looking at the office itself, he moved directly to a partition wall at the back of the main office space, running his fingers along the edge until he found what he was looking for–a small, almost imperceptible seam in the plasterboard. Stepping back, he placed the holdall down and then used the sole of his booted foot to kick hard at the wall, smashing through it. Three more kicks and his vandalism was complete, his actions revealing a shallow space between the partition and the building's exterior wall.

Inside was another holdall, identical to the first, placed in and plastered over when he first took a lease here, two years back.

Marlowe extracted it carefully, then checked this bag too– this was more specialised equipment, including what looked like theatrical makeup supplies, encrypted communication devices and another set of credentials. He poured the contents of the second bag into the first, making sure he had everything, and now with the bulkier holdall over his shoulder, he tossed the discarded holdall to the side and closed the door behind him, not bothering to relock it–he wouldn't be returning, after all–and exited the building via the stairwell, making his way back to the street.

Morris and Wilcott were waiting exactly where he'd left them, the engine still running.

'Got what you needed?' Morris asked as Marlowe slid into the back seat with his bulkier bag.

'Last piece,' Marlowe confirmed. 'Now I need a drop-off point. Somewhere public, with multiple exit routes.'

'Liverpool Street Station?' Wilcott suggested.

'Perfect.'

Morris pulled away from the kerb, heading east towards the station.

'What happens next for you?'

'I keep moving,' Marlowe said simply. 'Set up somewhere they can't find me. Figure out who's pulling the strings and cut them off. The assassins are just tools. It's the people paying to watch that I need to find.'

'Paying to watch?' Morris frowned.

'It's a game to them,' Marlowe explained, his voice cold. 'Entertainment. Rich people betting on how and when I'll die, trading digital tokens tied to my survival. The longer I last, the more money changes hands.'

'Christ,' Morris muttered. 'And I thought I'd seen it all.'

THEY REACHED LIVERPOOL STREET STATION FIFTEEN MINUTES later. Morris pulled into a loading bay, killing the engine.

'This is where we part ways,' Marlowe said, gathering the holdall. 'If anyone asks, you never saw me.'

'What about the case?' Wilcott asked. 'The dead assassin, the shooter who killed Chopra?'

'Hand it over to Curtis and MI5,' Marlowe suggested. 'He'll bury it so deep you'll never see it again. Hell, you might even get a promotion as a thank you.'

Morris turned in his seat, meeting Marlowe's eyes directly.

'For what it's worth, I hope you make it. And nail these bastards to the wall when you do.'

'That's the plan,' Marlowe replied, opening the door. 'Thanks for the assist.'

'Kieran Lachlan and Thomas Marlowe,' Morris shook his head. 'Two ghosts I never want to see again.'

Marlowe smiled faintly.

'With any luck, you won't.'

He stepped out of the car, the holdall heavy in his hands, and disappeared into the late-night crowd entering the station without looking back. Inside, he navigated through the concourse, eyes constantly scanning for threats, and made his way to the Underground.

HE TOOK THE CENTRAL LINE TWO STOPS, TRANSFERRED TO THE Northern, then exited once more at Camden Town. Another ten minutes of careful counter-surveillance–doubling back, entering shops only to exit immediately through different doors–until he was confident he wasn't being followed. Only then did he hail a taxi, giving an address in Kentish Town.

Twenty minutes later, Marlowe paid in cash and walked the final three blocks to his destination–an unremarkable apartment building on a quiet residential street. Six floors, no doorman, and knackered-looking security cameras that hadn't worked properly in years.

He entered using a key from the holdall, taking the stairs rather than the lift to the fourth floor. Apartment 404 was at the end of the corridor, a worn welcome mat outside the only indication someone lived there.

The same key opened the door.

Inside, the apartment was spartan but functional–basic furniture, neutral decor, nothing that would draw attention or be remembered. It had been leased five years ago through a shell company linked to his mother's maiden name; the rent paid annually in advance through an automated bank transfer. As far as the neighbours knew, it belonged to a quiet consultant who travelled frequently for work. Both Marshall Kirk and Marlowe had used the location, the latter more while the church was being renovated, so there was enough footfall to stop anyone thinking it was a fine place to squat.

Marlowe secured the door–reinforced frame, three separate locks, with a discreet alarm system more sophisticated than anything in the building–and almost by habit did a methodical sweep of the space. No signs of entry, everything exactly as he'd left it months ago, during his last need for a fully deniable location. Only then did he allow himself to relax slightly, setting the holdall on the kitchen counter and rolling his shoulders to ease the tension that had built there.

The kitchen was stocked with non-perishables: canned goods, rice, pasta, and protein bars. The freezer held several meals vacuum-sealed and dated from the last time he'd been here a few months back; enough to survive without leaving for at least a week. Marlowe opened the holdall and extracted the burner phone, the battery separate from the device, as per protocol. He assembled it, powered it up, and dialled a number from memory.

Three rings, then an answer:

'Marshall Kirk.'

'It's me,' Marlowe said simply.

'Didn't expect to hear from you. Thought you were off the books these days. Buggering around in Vegas or something?' Marshall's voice was warm, relaxed. 'Let me guess, you're in shit and you need my help?'

'Why would you think that?'

'Because you're always in shit and you need my help. Also, your name's been bouncing around the usual places and not in a good way.'

'Well, I am, and I do. But not in the usual manner. I need the kit. The special one.'

Another pause.

'That serious?'

'Deadly. I've got hitmen after me so I don't want to bring you or Tessa in.'

'Hitmen don't scare us,' Marshall laughed. 'But it's your monkey, your circus. Usual drop?'

'No. Too hot. I'm at the flat.'

'Twelve hours?'

'Make it six if you can.'

'I'll see what I can do,' Marshall replied. 'Watch yourself, Tom. Word is there's a bounty on your head, making waves.'

'I know. Six million.'

'Was twelve this morning.'

'I've been busy.'

The call ended there. Marlowe disassembled the phone, removing the battery and SIM card. He'd dispose of them separately later.

Moving to the bathroom, he studied his reflection in the mirror. The temporary crown was holding, but his face showed the strain of the day—lines deeper than usual around his eyes, a smear of dried blood on his collar where the late-Doctor Chopra's carotid spray had caught him.

He showered, washing away the blood and sweat, careful to keep the bandages on his arm dry where the blade had cut him in Rochester. The hot water eased some of the tension from his muscles, but his mind remained sharp, already cataloguing threats, and planning countermeasures.

Clean and dressed in fresh clothes from a drawer in the bedroom, but annoyed that one of his favourite jumpers was missing, likely "borrowed" the last time Marshall Kirk was here, Marlowe returned to the holdall. He extracted the pistol–a SIG, not his preferred CZ but serviceable– checking condition and action before loading it and placing it on the bedside table next to the CZ he'd taken from the crypt. From the second drawer, he removed a leather case, setting it aside for later. The money he divided, taking some "moving around" funds for the moment, and then he reviewed the documents carefully, refreshing himself on the details of identities he hadn't used in years.

Finally, from the bottom of the bag, he removed a secure tablet. Unlike standard commercial devices, this one had been heavily modified over the years, mainly from when Trix first joined MI5's Section D on Prime Minister Charles Baker's request–secure boot loader, encrypted storage, air-gapped design that made remote access impossible. It powered on with a fingerprint scan and retinal verification.

At least this one didn't need blood.

Marlowe opened a secure browser, went to an unmoni-tored and long-dead IRC message board for the TV show *Red Dwarf* and composed a short text. Once done, he pressed send, and watched it turn into random text and ASCII code, before being posted, likely seen by anyone else as spam. It was one of dozens of pre-arranged locations he and Trix had established for emergencies. If she was alive, if she was free, and if she was monitoring their emergency channels, she would receive it and know he was safe. And hopefully, reply to confirm she was too.

Marlowe moved to the window, carefully staying to the side of the frame as he surveyed the street below. It seemed quiet, normal. No suspicious vehicles, no loiterers, no apparent surveillance. For the moment, he was safe; the tracker destroyed, his location unknown, his next moves a mystery to anyone trying to hunt him. Marlowe touched his jaw, feeling the unfamiliar contours of the temporary crown.

The Broker had just lost an asset. Steele had just lost his persistent tracker. And the viewers of their sick entertainment had just lost their sure thing.

The game had shifted. The rules remained the same, but the assassins would be working harder now, growing desperate as the bounty decreased. And somewhere in London, Trix was either in hiding herself or trying to unravel the Marlowe Coin mystery from her end.

Good. Let them scramble. Let them worry. Let them wonder.

Thomas Marlowe had been hunted before, had been cornered before, had been written off before. And yet, he was still standing, while graves were filled with those who had underestimated him.

If they wanted a show, he'd give them one they'd never forget.

8

DIGITAL NOMAD

THE BACKLIT SCREEN OF TRIX PRESTON'S LAPTOP CAST A BLUE glow across her face as she hunched over the keyboard, fingers moving across it frantically. Around her, the small room–little more than a converted storage closet in the back of an internet cafe in Shoreditch–was cluttered with borrowed equipment: two additional laptops, an array of external hard drives, and a nest of cables connecting everything together.

She'd been here for over eleven hours now, ever since navigating the tunnels beneath London to escape the church. The cafe was owned by a former GCHQ analyst who asked no questions and looked the other way when paying customers needed privacy and a hard-wired connection that couldn't be easily tracked.

It also helped when they owed her a massive favour too.

The connection wasn't as secure as her equipment in the crypt had been, but it was clean, anonymous and paid for in cash. She was sleep-deprived and muttering to herself, taking a sip from a now-cold cup of coffee, while on the screen, lines of code scrolled past as she worked through encrypted "onion" layers of the dark web, following digital breadcrumbs that had led her to the new, exciting altcoin she now knew as $MARLOWE. Targeted, sophisticated, and explicitly designed around the hunt for Thomas Marlowe.

Its architecture was hauntingly familiar.

'No,' she whispered, as recognition dawned. 'No, no, no ...'

The coding signatures, the specific encryption methods, the elegant way the tracking data was embedded within the blockchain–she'd seen them before. In code she'd helped debug. In projects she'd reviewed. In work done by someone she'd trusted.

Ciaran Winston.

Several months ago, she'd discovered in Berlin that Ciaran–her then boyfriend–had been working for Steele all along. Worse, he'd been feeding information directly to Steele about her and Marlowe's operations. As if that betrayal wasn't enough, she'd also learned he had another girlfriend the entire time. And now here was his digital fingerprint, all over a cryptocurrency designed to track and kill Marlowe.

'You absolute bastard,' she hissed, fingers flying across the keyboard as she dug deeper into the code. It was definitely Ciaran's work–she could practically hear his voice in the programming comments, see his personality in the clunky and slightly overcomplicated solutions to simple problems.

The blockchain itself was brilliantly constructed; each transaction, each transfer of the Marlowe Coin between wallets contained encrypted metadata that updated the tracking information. The more coins you held, the more detailed tracking data you received. And with each assassination attempt that Marlowe survived, a percentage of unsold and unreleased coins were automatically "burnt"–permanently removed from circulation–driving up the value of those remaining, creating artificial scarcity and urgency. Classic market manipulation.

Trix opened another window on the screen; this one connected to a private auction site hidden behind multiple VPNs and proxy servers. She'd discovered it three hours earlier, after following transaction patterns from the largest Marlowe Coin wallets. The screen refreshed, displaying what appeared to be a high-end auction house interface ... except instead of art or antiques, the listings showed options like "Weapon Restrictions", "Location Parameters", and "Viewing Packages".

The site's current active auction read:

Current Hit–$6 Million Dollars

Good, she thought to herself. *Marlowe's fighting back.* She'd expected as much when she saw the police chatter over the gunfight at a dentist's in Canary Wharf. However, there was another line.

Exclusive POV Package – Live Feed from Next Attempt
Current bid: 250,000 $MARLOWE

Trix felt sick as she watched the bids increase in real-time. Wealthy individuals, identified only by wallet addresses, were literally bidding for the privilege of watching Marlowe's attempted murder through a live video feed. They weren't just spectators–they were paying participants, shaping the conditions of the hunt.

A notification popped up on her second laptop–the one running continuous searches through financial databases, tracking the movement of funds associated with known Steele operations. A match had been found.

She switched screens, scanning the report quickly. A series of transactions from offshore accounts linked to Steele had been traced to a digital wallet that had purchased a quarter of the Marlowe Coin total at its initial offering. The wallet was registered to a shell company based in The Cayman Islands but, after two hours of digging, she now saw the beneficial ownership documents listed a familiar name:

Phoenix Elite Consulting, Ltd.

Pho3nix Elit3 had been Ciaran's name on the *Crime City* server.

'Got you,' Trix whispered. Ciaran wasn't just the creator of the code–he was a major investor in the scheme itself. He stood to make millions if the coin's value continued to rise as designed.

She switched back to her main screen, digging deeper into the tracking mechanism itself. According to the transactions she could decode, the system had been receiving regular location pings from Marlowe every thirty minutes for the past several hours, but the last successful ping had been over eight hours ago, from a location in Canary Wharf. After that–nothing. Dead air.

Likely, this was where he disabled the tracker somehow. Or was it something worse?

Trix pushed the thought aside. If Marlowe was dead, the entire Marlowe Coin system would have registered it. The final "kill confirmation" would have triggered massive, automated transactions. That the system was in limbo suggested Marlowe had somehow gone dark.

Which meant he was still alive. Still fighting.

She needed to contact him, but their usual communication channels were compromised, and Trix had lost her access device in the church attack. She'd need to build a new one from scratch.

She began compiling components from her borrowed equipment, cannibalising what she needed–a specific network card, modified firmware, custom encryption protocols. As she worked, she kept one eye on the auction site. The bidding for the live feed package had surpassed half a million $MARLOWE. At current exchange rates, that was moving towards a hundred grand–just to watch Marlowe die.

Another listing caught her attention:

Location Spotter's Fee: $MARLOWE

Clicking through, she found a bounty offered to anyone who could provide verified information on Marlowe's current whereabouts, now that the tracker had gone silent. The cryptocurrency itself had adapted to the loss of the primary tracking mechanism, now incentivising human intelligence instead.

The system was learning, evolving. Just as Ciaran had probably designed it to do.

A dark thought occurred to Trix. If the code was Ciaran's, and if the tracking mechanism had been compromised, then Steele would almost certainly turn to Ciaran to find a way to fix it. This snitch network was likely his first plan. Which meant ...

She quickly opened a new search window, running Ciaran's known identities–well, at least known to her, even if the authorities weren't aware of several of them–through transportation databases. A result appeared almost immediately; he'd arrived at Heathrow from Zurich six hours earlier. Immigration records showed he'd entered the UK on his British passport, which made sense, as technically, although maybe on a few observation lists now, Ciaran wasn't wanted for anything currently.

Ciaran was in London.

Trix felt a cold certainty settle over her. This wasn't just business for Ciaran–it was personal. His ego wouldn't allow for his perfect system to be defeated, especially not by Marlowe, whom he'd always resented, so he'd come back to make sure it worked in his favour.

Maybe she could use this? Perhaps she could create an AI algorithm that spat fake leads at Ciaran's system, gumming it up? That'd be amusing, even if she wouldn't have the satisfaction of seeing his stupid face.

Trix grinned darkly as she searched for any messages left in their digital dead drop.

Nothing. No contact from Marlowe.

She hadn't really expected anything–he would be focused on survival, not communication–but the confirmation of his silence still sent a pang through her chest. Still, undeterred, she checked the usual haunts, the *Red Dwarf* message boards–

There. Random code sent a few hours earlier. Good. She couldn't decrypt and reply, though. Not until she rebuilt something to do just that–she just had to hope right now he was safe.

A chime from her second laptop pulled her attention back to the auction site. The bidding for the live feed package had closed, selling for 750,000 $MARLOWE to a wallet identified only by a string of numbers and letters. The question was though, how would they find him now the tracker was dead?

She dived back into the blockchain, analysing the most recent transactions for clues. The metadata was increasingly encrypted, but she could still extract fragments–enough to piece together that specific assassins had been assigned to monitor locations Marlowe was known to frequent.

They were falling back on traditional surveillance.

But there was something else–a new data structure being embedded in the latest blocks. Something that looked like ...

Face recognition parameters, she thought, the realisation hitting her. *They're hijacking public CCTV networks.* London had one of the highest concentrations of surveillance cameras in the world. If Steele had tapped into that network, to run Marlowe's biometric data through it in real-time, he wouldn't need the physical tracker any more.

Trix opened another window on her main laptop, accessing a backdoor into London's traffic monitoring system. It wasn't supposed to use facial recognition–official policy prohibited it–but the capability existed in the hardware, just waiting to be activated.

And someone *had* activated it. The cameras were now processing facial data against a specific template, searching for a specific person.

Marlowe.

She needed to warn him. *But how?* Their digital message drop would only work if he accessed it, and there was no guarantee he would or could.

She needed another approach.

Started typing her own message into the *Red Dwarf* server. She couldn't use the encryption, but she could still warn Marlowe.

L1sterRawx

Looking for info on Victorian service tunnels near St.
Dunstan's. Friend mentioned access point might be
flooded after recent work by new kids and Thames Water.
Anyone checked recently?

St. Dunstan's was their code for trouble. Thames Water referred to Steele, due to his status as an ex-MI5 and MI6 agent, the offices both sides of the Thames. And the "new kids" line was on the nose a little, but she wasn't being subtle any more. The rest was window dressing. This sent, she then returned to monitoring the Marlowe Coin transactions. The currency's value had spiked in the past hour, climbing almost forty per cent on the news that "technical issues" with the tracking system had been resolved. Investors were pouring in, betting that the next attempt would succeed where others had failed.

Trix rubbed her eyes, fatigue catching up with her. She needed rest, but there wasn't time. Not when Marlowe was out there, being hunted, while she sat here relatively safe.

Her custom messenger pinged, a message appearing on her monitoring system. A financial alert she'd set up months ago, after Ciaran betrayed them, had triggered–a significant transaction from one of Ciaran's known accounts to a secure server farm in East London.

The address was familiar. It was one of his old working locations, a place he'd talked about once, bragging about the military-grade security and zero-logging policies.

He'd entered London and gone somewhere he knew, it seemed.

Trix made a decision. She needed more than what she

could access remotely; she needed direct access to whatever Ciaran was setting up. And that meant moving, exposing herself, taking risks. It was her turn to do what she did best–follow the digital trails, unmask the hunters, and turn their own system against them, but for once while standing in the open.

And starting with Ciaran sodding Winston.

Trix shouldered her backpack and slipped out of the small room, nodding a thanks to the cafe owner as she passed. Outside, London's early morning light was just breaking over the buildings. She pulled her hood up against the drizzle and disappeared into the awakening city, another ghost in a metropolis of eight million souls.

A digital ghost with a very specific haunt in mind.

THE BROKER HAD ALWAYS PREFERRED BREAKFAST AT *CECCONI'S* in Mayfair when he was in London; the restaurant's discreet alcoves allowed for private conversation, while the clientele–a mix of hedge fund managers, art dealers and visiting dignitaries–provided perfect camouflage for a man whose business was usually involving death.

He was halfway through his Eggs Benedict when his phone vibrated against the crisp white tablecloth of his table. This was surprising as only five people had this number, and none of them called without good reason.

'I'm eating,' he said by way of greeting, dabbing at his mouth with a napkin as he accepted the call. St John Steele's face appeared on the screen; the background deliberately blurred to obscure his location.

'Things are slowing and I don't like it,' Steele replied, the connection clear enough that he might have been sitting at the table. 'The value of the coin isn't rising as we projected, and we only have two days or so left.'

'Market forces, nothing more. The commodity proved more ... resilient than anticipated.' The Broker signalled discreetly for more coffee.

'The commodity? He's bloody disappeared,' Steele's voice sharpened. 'The tracker went dark yesterday. Your professionals are floundering without it.'

'Well, perhaps you shouldn't have paid him a visit. It spooked him. The asset you provided us implemented alternative measures, though.'

'CCTV recognition? That's primitive. And the facial match percentage we're getting is too low for reliable targeting.'

The Broker suppressed a rather theatrical sigh.

'You look tired, St John,' he observed. 'Take a nap.'

Steele's expression remained impassive.

'One assassin dead, another in police custody. The tracker no longer working ... this isn't the efficiency I expected.'

'I'm merely coordinating the hunters,' The Broker reminded him. 'Your cryptocurrency system is the payment structure. I can't control your boy's resilience. Or your hacker's self-proclaimed ability.'

'The drop from twelve to six million was anticipated,' Steele said. 'But if we don't see results soon, the investors will lose confidence.'

The Broker took a sip of his fresh coffee.

'The best are still in the game, Steele. The Swede has been spotted near Camden. Rostov's people are watching transport hubs. Passive is yet to move in. And I've reached out to specialists.'

'What specialists?'

'People who hunt ghosts for a living,' The Broker allowed himself a thin smile. 'When a target goes dark, you need hunters with specific skills.'

'I need results,' Steele snapped irritably. 'The next attempt needs to be successful, or at least cinematically engaging. The whales are getting restless. They paid for a show.'

'And they'll get one. Quality entertainment requires proper—'

The Broker fell silent as a figure approached his table. Tall, lean, in his fifties or early sixties with the measured movements of a man who looked to calculate every step. His face was forgettable–the kind that would blend into any crowd, that witnesses would struggle to describe hours later, his beard silver. Only his eyes stood out, pale blue, unnervingly steady, and obviously contact lenses.

'Excuse me,' the man breathed. 'I believe you have a vacancy.'

The Broker stared at the newcomer, frowning. The accent was Nordic but deliberately muted, the suit expensive but not ostentatious, the hands manicured but with calluses that spoke of practical use. Everything about him was controlled, deliberate.

And strangely familiar.

'I'm in a meeting,' The Broker replied, gesturing to his phone.

'So I see,' the man glanced at the screen, where Steele was watching with undisguised interest. 'Hello, Mister Steele. I didn't realise this was a conference call.'

'Who is this?'

The Broker felt a chill down his spine at the words; few

people could recognise Steele on sight, fewer still would dare acknowledge him directly.

'I think I'm exactly who you both need right now,' the man replied, pulling out a chair and sitting uninvited. Something in his posture, his arrogance, even, triggered a memory. The Broker studied him closer ...

'We've met before,' The Broker said, realisation dawning.

'Rome. Three years ago,' the man inclined his head slightly. 'A short conversation in a piazza, and then a French diplomat with an unfortunate skiing accident.'

'Mister Bones,' The Broker breathed. 'You disappeared afterward. Went completely dark.'

'Well, as I told you, I never work twice for the same client,' Mister Bones shrugged. 'But exceptions can be made in ... extraordinary circumstances.'

On the phone, Steele leaned closer to his camera.

'What extraordinary circumstances?'

'Your current target,' Mister Bones rested his forearms on the table, hands loosely clasped. 'Thomas Marlowe. I have a personal interest.'

'The contract is open to all qualified operatives in the industry,' The Broker said carefully. 'Though the price has been reduced. Six million dollars now.'

'I'm aware,' Mister Bones replied.

Steele's voice cut in from the phone.

'If you're so well-informed, you know the tracker has been compromised. We're relying on facial recognition, but that's not brilliant.'

'Which is precisely why you need someone like me,' Mister Bones replied casually. 'I don't rely on technology to find my targets. I understand them. Predict them. Become them, in a sense.'

The Broker had heard similar claims from a dozen assassins over the years, most of them now dead or imprisoned. But there was something about Mister Bones that rang true–a cold certainty that went beyond the professional confidence sitting in front of him.

'You have history with Marlowe?' he probed.

A flicker of something crossed Mister Bones' face before vanishing.

'We've crossed paths,' he said simply. 'He disrupted an operation that cost me considerably. Professional pride demands ... resolution.'

The Broker exchanged a glance with Steele on the screen. Personal motivation was always a double-edged sword; it provided determination, but it could also cloud judgment.

'The rules are specific,' The Broker said. 'Confirmed kill only. No collateral damage that triggers an official investigation. And your methods must be ... cinematic.'

'Cinematic?' Mister Bones raised an eyebrow.

'We have investors who've paid for certain entertainment value,' Steele explained. 'The more dramatic the attempt, the higher the currency trades. Can you accommodate that requirement?'

'I can be theatrical when necessary,' Mister Bones waved off an approaching server.

'And if you fail?'

'I don't fail.'

From the phone, Steele made a sound that might have been a laugh.

'Everyone says that. Yet Marlowe remains inconveniently alive.'

'Previous hunters didn't understand their prey,' Mister

Bones replied. 'I do. I know how he thinks, how he moves. Where he'll go when cornered.'

'Timeline?' The Broker asked.

'Twenty-four hours for location and confirmation. Another twenty-four for execution.'

'That's longer than our investors would prefer.'

'Quality requires patience,' Mister Bones sat back in the chair. 'Unless you'd prefer another rushed attempt with a botched and newsworthy failure?'

The Broker considered this. *Perhaps a more measured approach was warranted.*

'Thirty hours is the most we can give, and we'll need progress updates. Our investors expect that, at least.'

'You'll have location confirmation,' Mister Bones nodded. 'After that, I work alone. No observation, no interference.'

'Unacceptable,' Steele cut in from the phone. 'The participants have paid for access—'

'They've paid for results,' Mister Bones countered. 'I can provide those. But I won't have amateurs watching over my shoulder during the approach.'

The Broker raised a hand, forestalling Steele's objection.

'A compromise, then. No direct observation during your hunt, but the final confrontation must be captured. Our technical team can provide suitable equipment.'

Mister Bones appeared to consider this.

'Acceptable, but I choose the location for the kill. Somewhere with controlled access points and minimal civilian presence.'

'That can be arranged,' The Broker agreed.

'Then we have a deal.' Mister Bones extended his hand. The Broker hesitated only a moment before shaking it.

'I'll add you to the verified hunter list and Hargrove will

explain the details in *The Monarch*, at your earliest convenience,' he said as he sat back. 'The competition structure doesn't allow for deposits or guarantees, as I'm sure you understand.'

'Of course,' Mister Bones replied. 'Though I'll need access credentials for the tracking data. This wallet address will suffice.'

He slid a card across the table. As The Broker took the card, the restaurant's maître d' approached their table, looking nervous.

'Sir,' he murmured to The Broker, 'there's a gentleman insisting on joining you. I explained you were in a private meeting, but he was ... persuasive.'

'Another?' The Broker frowned.

'He didn't give a name. Only this.' The maître d' handed over a plain business card, blank save for a small, engraved shovel.

The Broker's expression changed as he looked at it.

'Oh. Send him over.'

The newcomer approached unhurriedly. Tall and slim, with silver-peppered brown hair and a face that bore the marks of hard experience–the left side pockmarked and scarred, as if from a close encounter with fire or acid at some point in his past–he wore a dark-blue linen blazer over a white shirt, tan trousers completing the ensemble. But what drew attention were his eyes, hidden behind photochromic lenses that darkened in the restaurant's bright interior.

Mister Bones studied the newcomer calmly, but The Broker could sense a sudden tension between the two men– like apex predators unexpectedly sharing the same territory.

'Mister Bones,' The Broker said, 'meet The Gravedigger.'

The Gravedigger inclined his head slightly, the ghost of a smile playing at the corner of his mouth.

'I believe we've met before,' he said to Mister Bones. 'Though under different circumstances.'

'I doubt it,' Mister Bones replied coolly. 'I tend to remember faces.'

'Ah, but how well do you remember your own? After all, you wear new faces every time you meet a client, so I hear. This isn't even your real face, is it?' The Gravedigger pulled out a chair and sat, looking back at The Broker. 'I understand you're pursuing Thomas Marlowe. A fascinating coincidence, as I've recently developed a professional interest in him myself.'

From the phone, forgotten on the table, Steele's voice cut through the tension.

'What is this? A convention?'

The Broker glanced between the two assassins, his carefully orchestrated morning suddenly spinning beyond his control.

'It seems,' he said carefully, 'that our hunt has attracted some very specialised attention.'

9

THE OTHER BROKER

THE *IMPETUS COURIER* DEPOT LOOKED LIKE ANY OTHER warehouse in North London. A row of white vans lined the front, and all anyone would see as they passed by were drivers in high-vis jackets loading parcels. Nothing special, and definitely nothing that screamed "secret front for professional killers".

But Marlowe knew better. He'd been here before, after all.

His tooth still hurt like hell despite the painkillers, the rough temporary crown constantly whispering at his tongue to prod at it, a constant reminder of Steele's elaborate game.

Time to play my own bloody game.

This time, Marlowe wasn't breaking in. No cutting through fences, no sneaking around in the shadows, like he had when hunting a killer sent by Taylor Coleman. He'd simply walk through the front door and ask for Pauline Faulkner.

What could go wrong?

THE RECEPTION AREA WAS SMALL AND PLAIN, EXACTLY WHAT you'd expect, and a woman with her hair pulled back tight looked up from her computer as he entered.

'I need to see Pauline Faulkner,' Marlowe said.

'Do you have an appointment?' She didn't sound like she cared either way.

'No. Tell her Thomas Marlowe is here.'

The receptionist's eyes widened just enough to tell Marlowe his name meant something. She picked up her phone, turning away slightly as she spoke.

'End of the corridor, last door on the left,' she said after hanging up. 'She's expecting you.'

Marlowe had been down the corridor before, and just like last time, it was lined with shipping papers and manifests. *All part of the act.* Pauline ran a tight ship, and everything looked legitimate on the surface. But under, well ...

There be dragons.

Pauline was waiting behind her desk when Marlowe reached her office. Her black bob was exactly as he remembered, and even the clothing was the same. Marlowe had to push away a thought that she never left the desk, and that she was some kind of avatar of death.

'Marlowe,' she said as he closed the door behind him. 'No gun this time?'

'Thought we'd try talking first,' he replied. 'Seems more grown-up.'

He looked through the window, out into the warehouse, aware he was being watched.

'Sit down before my staff starts wondering why we're staring at each other,' Pauline smiled coldly, and with a nod, Marlowe took the chair opposite her desk. Pauline Faulkner had once sent an assassin after him, then later offered him a job. She was practical that way. Nothing personal, just business.

'Six million dollars,' Pauline said straight away. 'That's what you're going for now. Down from twelve after you killed one of them. Not bad work before breakfast.'

'You've heard about the Marlowe Coin, then.'

'Hard to miss,' Pauline leaned back. 'It's causing quite a stir. Cryptocurrency coin tied to a hit contract. Very "now". Very public. Not how most of us like to work.'

'That's why I'm here,' Marlowe said. 'I need information about The Broker; the one running this show.'

Pauline took a moment, weighing something in her mind. Then she reached for a bottle of water, took a sip and continued.

'You've met him?'

'At an auction in Punta Cana. Nothing major.'

'Well, he works for people who've met you,' Pauline replied. 'Been around for years. Fifteen, maybe more. Before that, he was somebody else. Raymond Kinley.'

'Kinley?'

'Money man. Worked with spooks, crime outfits, anyone who needed cash moved without questions.'

'What happened?'

'Vienna happened,' Pauline said, lowering her voice. 'Fifteen years ago. A hit that went to shit. Foreign diplomat, civilians killed, big international mess. The kind that gets agents cut loose and handlers forced into early retirement.'

'And Kinley was involved?'

'He sorted the money, supposedly. When it all went wrong, he vanished. Six months later, The Broker showed up—no face, no name, just a reputation for being careful and getting results.'

'You're sure they're the same person?'

Pauline gave him a look that suggested he was being idiotic with his question.

'The Broker might be behind the scenes, but he does make appearances. As you said, Punta Cana–although I heard that was a special case. Some kind of AI drone I understand?'

Marlowe nodded but didn't elaborate–Pauline may have known more, but it felt like she was fishing.

'Anyway, people who knew Kinley recognised him over the years,' she continued. 'In our line of work, you learn to spot patterns. The Broker is Kinley. And whatever happened in Vienna made him bloody paranoid.'

'How so?'

'Never meets clients face-to-face any more, unless it's an important hit, only appears at the big-money events, or when owing favours.'

'The Broad Sword auction? Punta Cana?'

'That was a favour. He usually works through middlemen nowadays. Guy called Hargrove. And he keeps paper records of every job.'

This caught Marlowe's attention.

'Actual paper? These days?'

'Can't hack paper,' Pauline said with a shrug. 'The Broker doesn't trust computers. Bit odd, given this cryptocurrency thing he's running now.'

'Which is why I think he's working for someone else on this,' Marlowe said. 'Someone who pushed for the digital approach. Someone like Steele.'

Pauline's eyebrows rose slightly as she gave a small smile.

'Heard some things about St John Steele lately.'

'What things?'

'That he's tearing apart some shadow outfit from the inside. Called Orchid.'

Marlowe kept his face blank, but inside he was surprised. Orchid wasn't common knowledge, even among criminals. If Pauline had heard the name, Steele's moves were making bigger waves than he'd thought.

'If The Broker once worked with intelligence agencies,' Marlowe said carefully, 'he might have crossed paths with Orchid.'

'Makes sense,' Pauline nodded. 'There were always whispers about a group above the agencies, pulling strings. Most thought it was just paranoia.'

'If Steele is taking down the old guard of Orchid, and if there's any chance The Broker was connected to them ...'

'Might explain why he's suddenly so active after years of keeping quiet,' Pauline finished.

Marlowe nodded, pieces clicking together.

'What about the killers involved? I've already run into a few.'

'Some of the best in the business,' Pauline confirmed. 'The Swede is in–efficient but has a breathing problem. Can't handle smoke or gas.'

'Useful.'

'Rostov's team is there too. They're good but won't work with others, which you can use against them. There's a woman from Jakarta who's deadly but won't take jobs on certain dates–thinks they're unlucky. Then there's the Ukrainian, Volkov–that means "wolf", apparently. Claims you blew him up once and met him already in Vegas.'

Marlowe nodded. *The blond that had worked for Stepan Chechik.*

'Anyone else I should watch for?'

'Posh prick called *Passive*, but he's more a try-hard voyeur than anything else. I also heard The Gravedigger is joining in, though.'

Marlowe kept his face expressionless at this.

'I've also heard talk about Mister Bones,' Pauline added.

'What is it about hitmen and stupid names that start with "The"?' Marlowe almost laughed.

'Whatever you think of the name, don't cast him aside. He's a top-tier operator. Been around for years but doesn't take many jobs. Him being involved means this is something special,' Pauline paused. 'Though it's odd that nobody seems to know what he looks like.'

'Maybe he's a ghost,' Marlowe suggested. 'Or, like The Broker, people have seen him but don't talk about it.'

The suggestion hung between them. Marlowe changed the subject.

'I appreciate this,' he said. 'I'm aware you're giving me this for free—'

'While you live, Kinley looks stupid, and that's good for my branding,' Pauline smiled. 'But I will expect something for the love I give you.'

'In that case, I have something for you,' Marlowe smiled, pulling the small USB card from his jacket and placing it on the desk. 'Payment for your help.'

Pauline didn't touch it.

'What is it?'

'Access to one million Marlowe coins. Worth a lot now, and probably more soon.'

'You're paying me with cryptocurrency named after you, from a hit on your own life?' Her eyebrows went up, but this time there was no humour to it.

'Bit strange, isn't it?' Marlowe gave a thin smile. 'Steele

gave them to me as a "gift". I don't want to profit from this game, but you might.'

Pauline picked up the card.

'And if you die? Do these become worthless?'

'Just the opposite. If I die, the price will jump before the crash. Sell at the right moment and you'll make a fortune.'

'So, you're giving me a reason to keep you alive until the best-selling time,' Pauline said, almost smiling as she pocketed the drive. 'Smart. What else do you want to know?'

'Any idea where The Broker works from?'

'Multiple places, but there's a private club in Mayfair he sometimes uses for business. Very exclusive. Very secure.'

'Name?'

'The *Monarch*. Members only, with fees that would buy you a house outside London. If you're hunting Steele, he uses the same place. If you can't find him there, try the *Labyrinth Club*. Swanky Knightsbridge location that's so exclusive it won't allow working-class folk like me to join–but I know Steele has worked out of there before. And I hear there's a lot of renovation work happening there right now. Almost as if they want to hold some kind of event.'

She thought for a moment.

'Tower Bridge, too.'

'Tower Bridge?' Marlowe frowned at this. 'I thought that's just, well, a bridge?'

'Well, obviously the bit above the water is,' Pauline smiled now. 'But there's a whole ton of underground rooms and shit on either side. Temperature controlled and all that. There was talk it was going to be an information hub for your old employers, with a secret route from the Tower of London itself, but it's not finished yet. The tender went out a while back, but I hear that while it's still in "building red tape", someone's making use of the space.'

Marlowe filed that away.

'One last thing. Vienna. Any details on what actually happened?'

Pauline's face turned serious at the question.

'Diplomatic summit. Target was a Saudi prince. The hit went wrong–bombs instead of a sniper. Seventeen civilians killed, including kids. Two spy agencies publicly denied everything, which meant they were likely definitely behind it.'

'And The Broker –Kinley–was directly connected?'

'Nothing was ever proven, but in our world, word gets around,' she leant forward. 'Whatever happened, it changed him. There was talk he had an asset, maybe even a mentor who got screwed over during it. Made him obsessive about controlling everything. That's why this cryptocurrency business is so out of character. It's public, it's flashy, it's unpredictable. Either he's desperate, or someone has something on him.'

'Or both,' Marlowe suggested.

'Or both,' Pauline agreed.

Marlowe stood up, done with their business.

'Thanks for your time, Pauline. It's appreciated.'

'We're not friends, Marlowe,' Pauline said as he reached the door. 'But maybe we're not enemies any more. Some advice? This game's set up so you can't win. The only way to survive is to change the rules completely.'

'That's the plan,' Marlowe assured her.

'In that case, good luck,' she replied, already turning back to her paperwork. 'You'll need it.'

Outside, the morning had turned to afternoon, the sky

the usual London grey. Marlowe walked back to a road, intending to call a taxi, still finding himself watching every face he passed, in case they were an enemy. The pieces were fitting together now. Not the whole picture yet, but enough to start planning his counter-attack. The assassins thought they had Marlowe cornered, but he was hunting them right back.

THE SERVER FARM WASN'T MUCH TO LOOK AT FROM THE outside. A converted warehouse in East London, just off Cable Street, its windows blacked out and security cameras mounted at every corner. The only hint of what lay inside was the massive cooling units on the roof and the thick power cables running into the building from the rooftops.

Trix had been watching the place for three hours, positioned in a trucker cafe across the street with a clear view of the main entrance. In that time, two security guards had changed shifts and three IT technicians had arrived separately.

No one had left.

'Another coffee, love?' The server hovered with a pot of what barely qualified as coffee.

'No thanks,' Trix said without looking up from her laptop. 'Just the bill.'

The cafe was emptying out as afternoon headed slowly towards evening. Soon she'd lose her cover among the other customers.

Time to move.

Trix packed her equipment into her backpack: laptop, signal booster, and the small electronic device she'd built last night. It looked like a standard external hard drive, but inside was custom hardware designed to create a backdoor into closed networks. The guys in *Mission Impossible* would have been proud–if they weren't, like, fictional.

Ciaran's security would be good. He was always obsessed with it, even back when they were together. But Trix knew his methods, his thinking patterns. More importantly, she knew his weaknesses.

The side entrance was used mainly for deliveries. A keycard scanner-controlled access, with a camera positioned directly above. Trix approached confidently, wearing the outfit she'd purchased that morning–blue overalls with *"Swift IT Solutions"* embroidered on the breast pocket, and a baseball cap pulled low over her face. In her hand, she carried a tablet displaying what appeared to be a work order.

The trick wasn't to avoid the cameras. It was to give them exactly what they expected to see.

She reached the door and swiped the blank card she'd programmed twenty minutes earlier. The scanner would record an attempt, but the signal interceptor in her pocket would block the failed authorisation message from reaching the security system. Meanwhile, her device transmitted the code she'd extracted while watching the technicians arrive earlier, as she did some mid-distance cloning of the data, keeping what was needed. Distance degraded the coding, but this was simple "open door" data, so easy to reverse engineer with AI to fill the gaps in.

The door clicked open. Inside, the temperature dropped immediately–this wasn't a surprise, though, as server farms always ran hot, and cooling was essential. The hum of hundreds of servers filled the air; a white noise that would mask her movements.

Good.

Trix moved purposefully through the aisles of server racks, appearing to check her tablet periodically as if verifying locations. Two technicians were visible at the far end of the room, but neither looked up. IT people generally avoided interaction when possible.

She needed to find Ciaran's personal setup; he'd always kept his most important work separate from standard infrastructure, especially since recent events had shown him how catastrophic holding the information on your person could be.

Trix wondered if he was even here, and if so, what he'd say if they bumped into each other; after all, the last time they spoke was on the roof of a Berlin Opera House, when he was unceremoniously dumped in a dog cage for the police to find.

The police never did, though–someone else got to him first.

Steele, perhaps?

Near the back of the facility, she found what she was looking for; a cluster of high-performance servers separated from the others by a glass partition. Inside, the hardware was newer, the cables more neatly organised. This was *special project* territory.

The security here was tighter–a biometric scanner requiring both fingerprint and retinal verification ... but Trix had expected this. From her backpack, she removed a small device and attached it to the scanner's data port. *Old-school hardware hack to bypass new-school security.*

She held her breath as the device cycled through programmed responses. Three seconds. Five. Ten.

ENTER OPTICAL DATA

Trix rummaged in her bag–usually this was where people would falter, unable to break the retinal scanner, but Trix had an Ace in her pocket. Over the last year or two, she'd started a habit of 3D scanning people's eyes for fun, before recreating them in acrylic duplicates. It'd helped both her and Marlowe over the years, and of *course* she'd scanned Ciaran. In fact, the multiple times she'd surreptitiously done it, all brought together, gave probably a more accurate retinal representation than his actual eyeball.

She held the acrylic eyeball up, watching the scanner line pass across.

The lock clicked. The door opened.

Once inside, Trix worked quickly. She located an open USB port on the main control terminal and plugged in her backdoor device. It would take thirty seconds to install itself and establish a secure connection to her external systems; after that, she was good to go. While waiting, she scanned the room. Multiple screens displayed data flows, network maps, and what appeared to be facial recognition algorithms running against CCTV feeds. One screen showed a scrolling list of wallet addresses and transaction records.

Marlowe Coin.

This was it, Ciaran's command centre for tracking Marlowe through London's surveillance network. The chances were he was looping in remotely, but this, if it wasn't the brain at least, was definitely the nervous system.

The device beeped softly, indicating successful installation. Trix was about to remove it when a door at the far end of the server room opened.

She froze, crouching lower behind the servers.

A man entered, speaking loudly into his phone.

Ciaran.

He looked exactly as she remembered–tall, slim, with short, wild ginger hair and a wispy attempt at a beard–with the perpetually distracted expression of someone whose mind was always half in the digital world.

'—tracking system is working perfectly,' he was saying. 'We lost the dental implant signal, but the facial recognition is compensating. We've got nearly eighty per cent coverage of Central London.'

Trix held perfectly still, barely breathing.

'No, Steele, I don't need more resources,' Ciaran continued, irritation creeping into his voice. 'What I need is for your people to stop interfering with my systems. The Broker's team keeps trying to access my network.'

He paused, listening to the response.

'Fine. But remind them I designed this system. Nobody knows it better than me. If Marlowe reappears on the grid, you'll be the first to know.'

Irritated, Ciaran ended the call and moved to the terminal where Trix's device was still plugged in. Her heart hammered in her chest. *If he noticed it ...*

But Ciaran was distracted, muttering to himself as he typed on the keyboard, seemingly oblivious to the small device attached to the adjacent USB port. After what felt like hours, but was probably less than a minute, Ciaran straightened and walked out, still muttering to himself about algorithm modifications.

Trix waited thirty seconds, then disconnected her device. The backdoor was established; from now on, she could access Ciaran's systems remotely, see what he saw, and more importantly, feed false information when needed.

She was about to leave when a notification flashed across one screen. An auction listing for Marlowe Coin.

Exclusive livestream access to next assassination attempt.
Current bid: 50,000 coins.

People were actually bidding to watch Marlowe die.

Trix took a quick screenshot with her phone, then reattached the USB into the system, although this time in a far more hidden junction. This done, she made her way out, following the same confident walk she'd used to enter. Ten minutes later, she was three streets away, heart still racing.

She found a quiet corner in a coffee shop and opened her laptop. The connection to Ciaran's system was live now, and data streamed across her screen–facial recognition hits, CCTV access points, transaction records for $MARLOWE.

Trix smiled grimly as she began downloading everything. Ciaran thought nobody knew his system better than him.

He was *wrong.*

10

MEMBERS' CLUBS

The Monarch Club occupied a Georgian townhouse in Mayfair, its entrance marked only by a discreet brass plaque beside a glossy black door. No signs, or advertisements, just the kind of place that relied on whispered recommendations, rather than social media presence.

Mister Bones adjusted his tie as he approached. The steel-grey suit he wore was bespoke, Italian cut, tailored to disguise the lean muscle beneath. His face once more bore subtle alterations to his actual structure; he wore cheekbone prosthetics, a slightly wider nose bridge, and different tinted contacts shifting his eyes from the previous blue to a flat grey. Even his walk had changed, the measured stride of a predator who never needed to hurry.

Nobody in this business had seen Mister Bones' true face, in all the years he'd existed.

The doorman, ex-military by his posture nodded in recognition—although he'd never seen the man before—as Mister Bones held up a phone, the screen showing a code sent to his dark web message inbox earlier that day.

'Good evening, sir,' he said, noting the number and knowing it was accurate. No names were exchanged. This was, after all, the kind of place where identity was both crucial and never spoken aloud. He opened the door and Mister Bones entered.

Inside, The Monarch Club revealed itself as a study in understated luxury. Dark wooden walls, surrounding leather chairs that'd seen better days. Crystal decanters caught the light from low-hanging fixtures, the lighting precisely calibrated–bright enough for faces to be seen but dim enough for conversations to feel private.

A dozen or so patrons occupied the main lounge; business executives, politicians, the occasional celebrity, and others less easily categorised, but carrying the same dangerous competence as Mister Bones himself.

Contractors, specialists, even people who solved problems discreetly. All were here tonight, it seemed.

A hostess in a tailored black dress approached.

'Mister Stone. How lovely to see you again. I'm Elizabeth.'

Mister Bones had never been here before, but knew the name had been given so The Broker's enemies didn't work out who The Broker was inviting. It had been explained as he left the breakfast earlier that day; it was always element-connected, so *stone, water, fire, air,* and was a name used many times in the past for different people. Mister Bones–or, rather, "Mister Stone" followed Elizabeth through the lounge to a secluded alcove; a single table, positioned to allow clear sight lines to both exits while keeping his back to a solid wall. The table had been chosen with professional paranoia in mind.

'Will you be dining with us this evening?'

'Just drinks for now.'

'Very good, sir.'

As Elizabeth departed, Mister Bones scanned the room properly. There were three exits including the main entrance; security cameras disguised as light fixtures. Two men sat at the bar who didn't belong among the wealthy clientele– internal security, and almost certainly armed. In the far corner, a table occupied by a large man nursing what appeared to be sparkling water.

The Swede.

Easily two hundred and twenty pounds, with the flat, expressionless face of a career killer, his size belied his reputation for swift, efficient work; the man could move when necessary.

Mister Bones settled in, accepting a glass of eighteen-year-old Macallan from a passing server without having to order. The Monarch prided itself on learning and remembering preferences, and this impressed Mister Bones–as he'd only ever publicly ordered this the once, in a Swiss restaurant just under three years earlier.

The Broker was showing he knew everything about everyone, it seemed.

Ten minutes passed in careful observation. The Swede didn't look Mister Bones' way once–too professional to show interest. Across the room, a silver-haired man in a navy suit entered from a side door, his gaze sweeping the room before settling on Mister Bones.

Hargrove. The Broker's right-hand man. He approached with the confidence of someone accustomed to power.

'Mister ... Stone. A pleasure, as always.'

'Mister Hargrove. You're looking well.'

Mister Bones moved in; hand outstretched for a handshake. It was a move that surprised Hargrove, although there was every chance this was for show, to lessen the importance of the meeting to the others. *A friendly chat rather than a business opportunity.* They shook hands warmly; Hargrove now close enough to see the tinted contacts.

'May I?' The handshake over, and with Mister Bones stepping back and sitting back down, Hargrove gestured to the empty chair. Mister Bones nodded. Hargrove settled in, placing a slim leather portfolio on the table between them.

'I understand you've expressed interest in our current ... opportunity.'

'I have.'

'Rather high-profile for your usual tastes.'

Mister Bones took a measured sip of whisky.

'The compensation is proportionally attractive.'

'It was, although it's now six million, after our Swedish friend's colleague made his unfortunate attempt,' Hargrove's smile didn't reach his eyes. 'The Broker values your interest, but I should mention there's significant competition.'

'I don't compete. I *complete*.'

The rehearsed line came out with just the right amount of practised arrogance. Ignoring the comment, Hargrove opened the portfolio, revealing photographs, maps, and what appeared to be surveillance reports, all focused on Thomas Marlowe.

'Our target has proven ... resilient. He's currently operating with limited resources, having lost his primary base of operations. We believe he'll attempt to establish contact with previous associates.'

Hargrove tapped a photograph, showing Marlowe entering an internet cafe in Shoreditch.

'This was taken yesterday, caught from CCTV attached to the next building. By the time we sent our assets, he was long gone.'

Mister Bones studied the image with clinical detachment. 'Recent intelligence suggests he's in Mayfair tonight.'

Hargrove's eyebrows rose slightly.

'That's not information we've circulated. I'm curious how you've heard?'

'I maintain my own sources. Ones I won't be sharing.'

'May I ask why?'

'Why give my rivals the same advantage I currently have?' Mister Bones shrugged. 'They can find their own assets.'

'Interesting.' Hargrove studied him with new consideration. 'Well, you may be right. We've received similar reports within the last hour. If accurate, this presents an opportunity.'

'Indeed.'

'The Broker has authorised me to provide additional resources should you require them.'

'I work alone.'

'Of course.' Hargrove slid the portfolio closer. 'Nevertheless, these materials may prove useful. Target history, known associates, behavioural patterns. The usual dossier. For a small percentage of the fee, of course. A "helpers" fee, as such.'

'Appreciated, although being paid to kill someone, and then finding the client taking money from that payment because they told me information I already knew ... it doesn't sit well with me.' Mister Bones closed the portfolio without examining it further. The message was clear; he didn't need their intelligence.

Hargrove stood, straightening his already immaculate suit.

'The Broker has particular interest in this contract. Success would be ... remembered.'

'As would failure, I imagine.'

Hargrove's smile tightened.

'Precisely.'

'And The Swede?'

'Enjoying our food, nothing more.'

'And The Gravedigger?'

Hargrove went to reply, but then simply smiled.

'Good hunting, Mister Stone.'

As Hargrove departed, Mister Bones allowed himself a moment of satisfaction.

The meeting had gone exactly as planned.

Now for phase two.

He finished his whisky and rose, moving towards the men's room located off the main lounge. As he passed The Swede's table, he made brief, deliberate eye contact; a professional courtesy tinged with challenge.

The men's room at The Monarch Club continued the old-world luxury theme; marble sinks, private stalls with actual doors and a dedicated attendant who discreetly stepped out as Mister Bones entered. He washed his hands slowly, watching the door in the mirror.

Three.

Two.

One.

The door opened. The Swede stepped in, his massive frame filling the doorway.

'Mister Bones, I believe?' His accent was barely detectable, his voice surprisingly soft for a man his size. 'I heard you were playing. Surprised you would be so visible.'

'Lindström.' Mister Bones turned, drying his hands with a thick towel. 'I thought we might have a word.'

'About Marlowe?' The Swede moved further into the room, positioning himself between Mister Bones and the door. Not overtly threatening, but a professional claiming territory.

'I understand you've taken an interest in the contract.'

'As have you, apparently.' The Swede smiled thinly. 'Unusual for you to join such a ... public competition.'

'The terms are unique.'

'Six million now.' The Swede nodded. 'Down from twelve. Someone got close.'

'Close isn't completed.'

'No.' The Swede studied him with cold blue eyes. 'I've wondered about you, Bones. So few have seen your face. Even fewer have seen the real face under all that latex crap.'

'I value my privacy.'

'As do I. Yet here we are, discussing business in a bathroom.' The Swede reached into his jacket, slowly enough to telegraph the movement wasn't threatening, and withdrew a silver case. From it, he removed an inhaler, taking a quick puff.

'Marlowe's in the building,' Mister Bones said abruptly.

The Swede froze, inhaler halfway back to his pocket.

'Here? Now?'

'Information suggests he's meeting someone. Third floor. Private gaming room. No cameras.'

'And you're sharing this why?'

Mister Bones shrugged.

'Professional courtesy. The contract doesn't specify a solo capture.'

'You're proposing cooperation?' The Swede sounded sceptical.

'I'm proposing efficiency.'

The Swede considered this, eyes narrowing.

'And the split?'

'Even. Three million each.'

'Generous.'

'Practical. Half the fee for effectively half the work.'

The moment stretched between them, two predators assessing each other's intentions. Finally, The Swede nodded.

'Show me.'

Mister Bones led the way out of the bathroom, through the main lounge, and towards a discreet elevator at the back. The third floor housed private gaming rooms and meeting spaces, restricted to the club's most exclusive members. The elevator required a key card, which Mister Bones produced from his pocket.

'How?' The Swede was surprised at this.

'Do you not have one?' Mister Bones was dismissive, aware the conversation distracted The Swede from the key card, naming "Hargrove, Lewis" as the card owner.

As the elevator doors closed, The Swede's professional demeanour shifted subtly. His stance widened slightly; hands loose at his sides–a fighter preparing for potential action.

'After you,' The Swede said as the doors opened, revealing a plushily carpeted corridor.

Mister Bones stepped out, walking with confidence towards the last door on the right. This section of the club was quieter, the sounds from downstairs muffled by expensive insulation.

Perfect for what came next.

He reached the door, turned the handle, and pushed it open to reveal a small gaming room, complete with green baize table, leather chairs and crystal decanters on a side table.

Empty.

'Where is he?' The Swede's voice had hardened.

'He'll be here.' Mister Bones stepped into the room, moving towards the centre. The Swede followed, letting the door close behind them. The soft click of the latch engaging sounded unnaturally loud in the quiet room.

'I don't appreciate games, Bones.'

'Then you've chosen the wrong profession.' Mister Bones turned slowly to face The Swede. 'And the wrong opponent.'

The subtle shift in his voice–from Mister Bones' controlled precision to something more familiar, caught The Swede's attention. The big man's eyes narrowed as he studied Mister Bones' face more carefully.

'You said Marlowe would be here.' The Swede's hand was moving towards his jacket, where a weapon was undoubtedly holstered.

Mister Bones moved with explosive speed. The distance between them vanished in an instant, and his first strike targeted The Swede's throat–a vicious, precise blow that sent the larger man staggering back, gasping.

The Swede recovered quickly though, professional training overriding surprise. He countered with a vicious hook that Mister Bones barely avoided, the fist brushing past his cheek with enough force to displace air.

'I am,' he said, and his voice wasn't Mister Bones any more; instead it was the voice of Thomas Marlowe.

As The Swede paused in surprise, Marlowe pressed his advantage, knowing he couldn't match the larger man for raw strength. Speed and precision were his only edges. He delivered three rapid strikes to the solar plexus, each impact driving breath from The Swede's lungs. The larger man retreated, fumbling for his inhaler, but Marlowe kicked it from his hand, sending it skittering across the carpet.

'You ...' The Swede wheezed, recognition dawning in his eyes. 'Impossible.'

'Yet here we are.'

The Swede lunged, desperation adding power to his movement. He caught Marlowe in a bear hug, massive arms constricting like steel bands. Marlowe felt his ribs protesting, breathing becoming difficult, and in desperation he drove his forehead into The Swede's nose.

Once.

Twice.

Blood fountained between them. The grip loosened just enough.

Marlowe twisted free, immediately targeting The Swede's already compromised breathing. A knife-hand strike to the throat; an elbow to the diaphragm, anything to attack his breaths. The big man was struggling now, face reddening as his damaged respiratory system failed him.

The Swede made a final, desperate move–drawing a compact pistol from a shoulder holster. Marlowe caught his wrist, forced it upwards. The weapon discharged, the sound deafening in the confined space, the spent round embedded itself in the ceiling.

They grappled for control, Marlowe using The Swede's declining strength against him. He forced the larger man's arm down, back, but The Swede pressed back, aiming it towards Marlowe, who squirmed to get out of the way. However, The Swede's strength was fading, and the gun now moved back, and eventually pressed against The Swede's own chest. There was a moment of perfect stillness, held in stasis by eye contact between two professionals.

'Professional courtesy,' Marlowe said softly, and squeezed The Swede's finger against the trigger.

The report was muffled by the press of bodies. The Swede's eyes widened in surprise, then dimmed as he slumped forward. Marlowe stepped aside, letting the body fall heavily to the carpet.

He stood for a moment, breathing hard, adrenaline still coursing through his system. Then, methodically, he began returning into character, becoming Mister Bones once more.

The door opened behind him.

'Impressive work.'

Marlowe turned, the Mister Bones persona firmly back in place. In the doorway stood The Gravedigger.

For a long moment, neither spoke. Then The Gravedigger stepped fully into the room, closing the door behind him.

'I always wondered when we might meet again,' The Gravedigger said, his accent cultured, precise. 'I was over-joyed when I saw you with The Broker earlier today. Your reputation precedes you, Mister Bones. Or should I say ... Thomas?'

'You seem to have me in a positional disadvantage,' Marlowe's hand tightened around The Swede's pistol, still warm in his grip.

'In more ways than one.' The Gravedigger's gaze flicked to the dead man, then back to Marlowe. 'Though I must say, the dual identity is a clever approach. Hunting yourself while others hunt you?'

'How long have you known?'

'When I met "Mister Bones" today,' The Gravedigger moved further into the room, seemingly unconcerned by the weapon in Marlowe's hand. 'You tend to remember the smallest details of a man after they shoot you.'

'I let you live,' Marlowe offered. 'I'd hope you'd see that as a form of—'

'Do you see me trying to kill you?' The Gravedigger smiled. 'Believe it or not, I'm not here to kill you. I have bigger prey.'

'The Broker?'

'His paymaster,' The Gravedigger muttered.

'Steele?'

The Gravedigger said nothing for a moment, then a thought came to mind.

'You set me up for the death of Razor Gibson,' he said calmly. 'I wasn't happy about that.'

'You killed my friend. I wasn't happy about that either.'

'You should have killed me in Cupertino.'

Before Marlowe could respond, muffled shouting came from the corridor outside. The gunshot had been heard, despite the room's insulation.

'Security will be here momentarily,' The Gravedigger said calmly. 'You have approximately thirty seconds to decide whether to attempt to add me to today's body count or accept my assistance.'

'Why would you help me?'

'As you said, you let me live. I repay my debts.' The Gravedigger glanced at the door. 'Twenty seconds.'

Marlowe lowered the weapon slightly. 'What exactly are you offering?'

'Verification of The Swede's death. Confirmation to The Broker that Marlowe was here and escaped during the confrontation. Your Mister Bones identity remains intact, the bounty drops to three million, and you gain an ally with access to information you need.'

'And your price?'

'Steele.' The Gravedigger's expression hardened. 'When the time comes, he's my kill.'

The footsteps outside were louder now. Any moment, the door would open.

'Deal,' Marlowe said, just as the handle turned.

Two security guards burst in; weapons drawn. They froze at the tableau before them; The Swede's body on the carpet, Mister Bones standing over him with a gun, The Gravedigger calmly observing from the side.

'Gentlemen,' The Gravedigger said smoothly. 'A regrettable incident. Mr. Lindström encountered our mutual target and was, unfortunately, outmatched.'

'Marlowe was here?' the lead guard asked, weapon still trained on Mister Bones.

'Indeed. My colleague here confronted him as he was escaping, and gained the gun back,' The Gravedigger gestured to Marlowe, now back to being "Mister Bones". 'Unfortunately, Marlowe slipped away during their altercation. I suggest you lock down the building immediately. He can't have gone far.'

The guards exchanged glances, then the leader spoke into his radio, ordering a complete lockdown of The Monarch Club. Within seconds, alarms began sounding throughout the building.

'We need to secure the scene,' the guard said. 'Both of you will need to remain for questioning.'

'Of course,' The Gravedigger replied. 'Though Mister Stone here has sensitive information for The Broker regarding the target's movements. Perhaps he could deliver that report to Mister Hargrove while I assist with your investigation?'

The guard hesitated, then nodded curtly.

'Fine. Mister Stone, Mister Hargrove is in the main office.

Second floor, end of the hall. He'll want to hear about this immediately.'

'Thank you,' Marlowe handed the weapon to the guard, careful to maintain his persona's cold detachment. 'I won't be long. Check this for fingerprints.'

As Marlowe left the room, he caught The Gravedigger's slight nod. A promise kept. A debt repaid ... and a new alliance formed in the process.

Although, for how long, he had no idea.

———

THE CHAOS OF THE LOCKDOWN PROVIDED PERFECT COVER. Staff and patrons were being directed to secure areas, security personnel rushing to cover exits. No one questioned Mister Bones as he took the stairs to the second floor, projecting the confidence of someone with authorisation to move during a crisis.

Mister Hargrove's–and by default The Broker's–office when he was here was marked by a simple plaque reading 'Private'.

No name. No title. Just a statement of exclusivity–likely because it wasn't just The Broker who used this. If Pauline Faulkner was to be believed, St John Steele also utilised it.

Marlowe tried the handle. *Locked.* He removed a thin pick from his jacket lining, working quickly while keeping an eye on both ends of the corridor.

The lock surrendered after fifteen seconds of careful manipulation, and inside, the office spoke of old-world wealth and careful curation. Leather-bound books lined mahogany shelves, and an antique desk dominated the centre, its surface organised with what felt like military precision. Oil paintings–originals, not reproductions–hung on the walls.

Marlowe moved immediately to the desk, searching methodically. The drawers revealed nothing of immediate value: standard office supplies, a few files with client information but nothing directly related to the Marlowe situation.

Time was ticking. Security would eventually verify his identity, or The Gravedigger's diversion would reach its limits.

A painting behind the desk–a moody London cityscape–caught his attention. It hung slightly off-centre. Marlowe moved it aside, revealing a wall safe. In a way, it'd been expected. Neither Hargrove nor The Broker struck Marlowe as the type of person to allow a painting to hang at an angle.

It was a matter of seconds to open the safe; Trix had expected this and his phone also doubled as a digital cracking device. Inside the safe, Marlowe found what he was looking for; a leather-bound ledger, exactly as Pauline had described ... The Broker's physical insurance policy. He flipped it open, scanning pages of handwritten notes documenting contracts, clients, payments, dates going back years.

And there, marked with last week's date, details of the Marlowe hit.

Client: St. John Steele.

Terms: Twelve million, reducing by half with each confirmed kill by target.

Special conditions: Digital tracking and audience participation.

But it was the note in the margin that captured Marlowe's full attention.

Final meeting–Tower Bridge facility–Friday 8pm. Answers given.
Debt paid.

Today was Wednesday. Just over forty-eight hours until Steele and The Broker would meet at whatever facility was being established at Tower Bridge, according, once more, to Pauline Faulkner. Interestingly, this was four hours after the game was believed to end, if the details he had gained while at the crypt were to be believed.

Marlowe pulled out his phone, quickly photographed the relevant pages, then returned the ledger exactly as he'd found it, leaving the safe and painting as he'd discovered them. A quick sweep of the remaining office revealed nothing else of immediate value, and he was about to leave when a framed photograph on a side table caught his eye. It was an old image, at least fifteen years old judging by the style and quality; a group of men in suits, standing before what appeared to be a Viennese landmark. Among them was a younger version of The Broker–Raymond Kinley–and beside him, unmistakably, St John Steele, back in what was likely his MI5 or MI6 days.

Marlowe photographed this as well, before replacing it exactly as he'd found it.

Voices in the hallway outside indicated his time was up. Marlowe slipped out of the office, locking the door behind him, and moved confidently towards the stairs. He nodded to a pair of security guards rushing past, the Mister Bones persona firmly back in place.

'Any sign of him?' one guard called over his shoulder.

'Nothing on the second floor,' Marlowe replied in Mister Bones' clipped tone. 'I'm checking the roof access.'

The guard nodded and continued on, not questioning his authority.

TWENTY MINUTES LATER, AMID THE CONTINUING CHAOS OF THE lockdown, Mister Bones walked calmly out of The Monarch Club's service entrance. No one stopped him, no one questioned him. The hunt for Marlowe continued inside, while the man himself disappeared into the London night, the identity of Mister Bones protecting him like a shield.

Only when he was six streets away, in the anonymous safety of a late-night cafe, did Marlowe finally check the photographs he'd taken.

The evidence connecting Steele and The Broker.

The details of their upcoming meeting at Tower Bridge on Friday night.

And Marlowe would be there, too.

11

PLANNING SESSION

MARLOWE ARRIVED BACK AT HIS KENTISH TOWN SAFE HOUSE apartment shortly after midnight, still running through the events at The Monarch Club in his mind. The Swede's death was unfortunate but neccessary, and there had never been any love lost between them, and Marlowe was very aware that if he'd entered as himself, The Swede would have taken no time whatsoever in pulling out his pistol and shooting Marlowe in the face before claiming his bounty.

Killing The Swede first was nothing more than pre-emptive self-defence, if such a thing actually existed.

Then, there was The Gravedigger's unexpected alliance; when Marlowe, as "Mister Bones" had seen the man enter, he thought there was a strong chance his ticket was punched– the strange alliance that then unfolded was still fresh in his mind, and confusing.

Could he trust Peter Jericho, the man known as The Gravedigger? Or was this another set-up?

He'd taken three separate transport modes to reach the safe house, even doubling back twice to ensure he wasn't followed, keeping in character all the time, in case someone had decided to follow him, and had managed to keep up. There was a note on his laptop screen as he arrived; the message board he frequented with Trix had a full page of random characters, which, when placed through his decrypting software, Marlowe found was a secure server link to a video chat.

He connected, and a moment later, Trix Preston appeared on the screen. She went to speak, paused, and then started laughing.

'Jesus, you prick,' she muttered. 'You scared the shit out of me wearing that!'

Marlowe grinned. Trix was one of the few people in the world who knew he was Mister Bones, a character created while at Section D in MI5, under the watchful gaze of Emilia Wintergreen. He'd been created to "take out" assets who were under threat, providing them with new identities and lives, in return for their undying loyalty to MI5, of course. In fact, the first time he met The Broker, Marlowe had agreed to kill French diplomat Jean-Pierre Moreau, who, instead of dying in the Swiss alps, now ran a guest house in York, having decided to lead a quiet life after realising someone hated him enough to place a million-dollar bounty on his head. He wasn't the first, either. In total, "Mister Bones" had "killed" a dozen assets, three of which weren't even Marlowe, simply credited to him when actual accidents did the job while he was on the case.

Trix had been there for the last few of these and had even helped him with "reassessing" his legend's history.

'Nice place,' he said as he started pulling off the pros-thetics.

Trix glanced behind her–she was currently in a hotel

room, likely a more "budget-travel-friendly one" than the "luxury boutique" level suites Marlowe usually supplied.

'Yeah, well, it's got free breakfast,' she replied in response. Marlowe could see she'd transformed the hotel room into a makeshift command centre, with three laptops running simultaneously, a tangle of cables connecting various devices, and a whiteboard covered in her unreadable handwriting. 'Still alive, then?'

'For now,' Marlowe replied, dropping into a chair opposite the laptop, and by default, her.

'How's the tooth?'

'Had some issues, needed more surgery,' he touched his jaw automatically; the pain had receded to a dull throb. 'Chopra was paid to place a tracker in.'

'You should kill him.'

'Someone beat me to it,' 'Marlowe shrugged. 'You find anything useful on your own travels?'

Trix's expression shifted to one of grim satisfaction.

'Ciaran's the one who created your coin,' she said. 'Had a look at his server farm; he's built an impressive tracking system. The moment your tracker turned off, he sorted backup facial recognition software, setting it running through London's CCTV network–thousands of cameras scanning for you constantly.'

'Perfect,' Marlowe paused from removing the makeup. 'Maybe I should stay as Bones a little longer.'

'It gets better. I've created a backdoor into his system. We can feed false positives–make it think you're anywhere we want,' Trix suggested. 'Although currently chatter on the dark web thinks you're at some Mayfair club. Did you kill The Swede?'

Marlowe nodded, placing the latex nose bridge onto the table.

'Him or me,' he replied. 'This code of Ciaran's. How accurate is it?'

'About seventy-eight per cent, according to his own documentation. Good enough to narrow down search areas, not enough for precision targeting.'

'And the Marlowe Coin stuff?'

Trix turned one of her laptops towards the screen's camera, displaying complex financial data.

'I can't read that,' he replied. 'Can you share the screen?'

'Not on this secure server,' Trix replied. 'I'm having enough issues as it is, just keeping video. Basically? It's bigger than we thought. Over three hundred investors holding significant amounts of your bloody coin right now. Most are anonymous, but I've identified several high-profile names through transaction patterns–politicians, tech billionaires, even a few celebrities.'

'People paying to watch me die,' Marlowe said flatly. 'Orchid?'

'A few old guard, but more like people who like Steele and don't like you. Entertainment for the elite.' Trix's disgust was evident. 'The coin's value has jumped fifteen per cent since The Swede's death. Scarcity driving demand. Good job we have a million coins. You might make something out of this.'

'About that ...' Marlowe winced. 'I might have given them away.'

'Well, I hope whoever got them gave you worthwhile intel for it,' Trix mocked. 'What about The Broker's connection to Steele?'

Marlowe pulled out his phone, bringing up the photos he'd taken of younger versions of both men.

'The Broker used to be Raymond Kinley, financial specialist for intelligence operations. According to Pauline Faulkner, something went catastrophically wrong in Vienna several years ago. Seventeen civilians killed, including children.'

Trix was already typing, pulling up information.

'Vienna, fifteen years ago ... diplomatic summit ... bombing that killed a Saudi prince and seventeen bystanders. No one claimed responsibility, blame was placed on the Russian delegation there.'

'The perfect black operation gone wrong,' Marlowe said. 'Also, the kind that ends careers.'

'Or creates new ones,' Trix finished. 'I'm deep diving some GCHQ files I really shouldn't have access to, and it says here that after Vienna, Kinley disappears, and shortly after that The Broker emerges, while Steele rises through intelligence ranks. Now, Steele's got some leverage over The Broker. Maybe that's why he's running this cryptocurrency game despite his usual caution. So what's our next move?'

Before Marlowe could answer, one of Trix's laptops emitted a sharp alert sound. She turned to it immediately, her expression shifting from confusion to alarm.

'What is it?' Marlowe asked, moving to look closer at the screen, even though he couldn't see what was on it.

'New auction just announced on the Marlowe Coin network,' Trix replied, bringing up details. 'This is different from the usual bounty. They're calling it "Justice for Rule-Breakers.".'

The screen displayed an elaborate graphic–a gavel striking a block, with text announcing a special event for

Marlowe Coin holders. From what Marlowe could see, participants could bid on "appropriate punishments" for those who had aided Thomas Marlowe.

'Who?' Marlowe's voice was suddenly tight.

Trix scrolled down, her face paling.

'Marshall Kirk—'

'He gave me the prosthetics and the suit. Dammit, I knew I shouldn't have called him. Who else?'

'DI James Morris.'

Marlowe felt a cold weight settle in his stomach.

'How the hell did they know he was involved?'

'Some Ukranian grassed him up, it looks like.' Trix frowned.

Marlowe winced. *His bloody tooth.*

'They've been taken? Or they have hits on them?'

'According to this, they've been taken.' Trix continued reading. 'The auction starts midnight. Investors can bid on execution methods using Marlowe Coins.'

'Location?'

'Not specified yet. "To be announced to qualified bidders.".'

Marlowe stood abruptly, pacing the small room.

'This is on me. I involved them both.'

'Look Tom, I might not have been there, but I can pretty much guarantee you didn't force them to help you,' Trix countered, though her voice lacked conviction. 'Marshall's usually champing at the bit to get involved with shit like this.'

'Doesn't matter,' Marlowe checked his watch. 'I need to confirm this is real.'

'How? We can't exactly go visit Marshall's house–they'll be watching for that. And calling Morris won't help, as it's one in the bloody morning.'

'I'll try his partner. She can look into it,' Marlowe carried on pacing now. 'I also need to know where Tessa is—'

Trix looked up sharply, facing the camera, as if looking through the laptop screen.

'Tessa? I thought you knew. She's back in London. Finished her MI5 counter-op training last month according to Marshall.'

Marlowe was already dialling a number from memory. Unsurprisingly, at one in the morning, the call went to voice-mail. He left a brief message.

'It's me. Um, hi. Need a meet set up. Usual place, urgent matter regarding your dad. Text the number I'm using with a time.'

'What now?' Trix asked as he disconnected.

'We wait, and plan,' Marlowe returned to the chair, grabbing a wet wipe to continue removing his makeup. 'If this is real, we need to get into that auction.'

'You mean Mister Bones needs to get into the auction,' Trix corrected.

'Exactly,' Marlowe nodded. 'The Gravedigger will be there too. Between us, we should be able to locate and extract them.'

'Wait ... *What*?' Trix's eyes opened wide.

'Oh, yeah, I forgot to mention. The Gravedigger seems to be on our side right now. Claims he owes me a life debt or something.'

'Great. The Gravedigger is actually on our side ... until he decides he isn't and shoots you in the back of the skull.'

'He had the chance to expose me at The Monarch Club and didn't,' Marlowe shrugged. 'That's as close to trust as we get in this game.'

Trix didn't look convinced.

'And if it's a trap?'

'Then we'll need a better plan.' Marlowe's phone buzzed with a text–it seemed Tessa Kirk had checked the voicemail.

Embankment. One hour.

'If that's Tessa, go speak with her,' Trix replied, already typing. 'But take the rest of that creepy bloody disguise off before you do.'

THE VICTORIA EMBANKMENT WAS EERILY QUIET AT TWO IN THE morning. A few taxis passed along the road, but the pedestrian path along the Thames was nearly deserted.

Perfect for a discreet meeting.

Marlowe stood by the river railing, watching the dark water flow beneath Blackfriars Bridge, the city lights reflecting in rippling patterns. Somewhere to the left and down by the Thames was an outlet that led to the Fleet river, running under London. Layers upon layers of London history, right where he stood.

He sensed rather than heard Tessa's approach. He'd expected this, though; she'd been trained as a child by the *spetsial'noe naznacheniya,* known by their more public name "Spetsnaz", or the "Grey Men" who were the bogeymen of the Russian army, planned to be a sleeper agent for Russia. She'd even spent her holidays in Averkyevo training camp.

'You've got a lot of nerve.' Tessa's voice came from behind him, cold and precise.

Marlowe turned. Tessa Kirk stood ten feet away, hands in the pockets of her Barbour jacket. Her short blonde hair was partially hidden under a grey baseball cap pulled low over her eyes. Despite the casual outfit, her posture was rigid, radiating tension.

'It's good to see you too, Tessa.'

'Is it?' She stepped closer, her face now visible in the dim light of the embankment lamps, fury barely contained beneath a professional mask. 'My dad's been missing since lunchtime, you've been off grid, your church apartment looks like a war zone, and suddenly you want to meet?'

'I just found out,' Marlowe said quietly. 'That's why I called.'

'Bullshit,' Tessa's voice remained controlled, but her eyes flashed. 'You got him involved in whatever mess you're in. Again.'

'That wasn't my intention, I swear.'

'It never is, Tom.' She moved to stand beside him at the railing, both looking out over the Thames. 'But people around you tend to get hurt anyway, don't they?'

Marlowe couldn't argue with that. And even if he did, he wasn't going to argue with Tessa. She'd proven herself too many times to be someone who could go toe to toe with him.

'What do you know about his disappearance?'

Tessa was silent for a moment, professional training visibly wrestling with personal anger. Finally, practicality won out.

'Dad called me this morning. Said he'd helped you with something and needed to check some intelligence through back channels. Nothing unusual for him.' She gripped the railing tightly. 'When he didn't check in by noon, I went to his flat. Front door splintered. Signs of a struggle.'

'Any surveillance footage?'

'Wiped. Cameras in a two-block radius all conveniently

malfunctioning.' Tessa turned to face him. 'Wintergreen's looking, but it's early days. Officially, he's just a missing retired agent who's wandered off grid for a few hours.'

She watched Marlowe for an uncomfortable moment, biting her lip, frowning.

'What don't I know?' she asked.

Marlowe, sighing, told her. About the coin, the hitmen, the rich men paying for their sport. This done, he then explained about the auction, watching Tessa's expression shift from anger to horror.

'An auction for execution methods? Using cryptocurrency named after you? Jesus, Tom.' Tessa pulled the cap off and ran a hand through her hair. 'What the hell have you gotten into? You know I should report this.'

'But you won't,' Marlowe said. 'Curtis has already said there could be moles in MI5 and MI6 who are helping Steele. We can't let anyone know until we get your father back.'

'We?' Tessa's eyebrow arched.

'I'm going to fix this, Tessa. I promise you that.'

'How, exactly? You can't exactly walk into their auction.'

'No,' Marlowe agreed. 'But Mister Bones can.'

Understanding dawned on Tessa's face.

'Of course you were Bones,' she said in realisation. 'You're going to infiltrate using the same bullshit assassin identity that my dad must have been holding for you. I knew it was something like that.'

'It's the only way in.'

'It's suicide,' Tessa countered. 'If anyone recognises you—'

'They won't. And your dad won't have given anything up. They think I'm legit and one of the hunters in the game. Also … I'll have help.'

'Trix?'

'Her, and The Gravedigger.'

'You trust him?' Tessa's eyes widened slightly. 'I thought you shot him?'

'As much as I trust anyone in this game–and everyone shoots everyone in this game. You know that.'

Tessa turned back to the river; her profile sharp against the city lights.

'What do you need from me?'

'Official channels won't help, but you've got access to MI5 resources. We need everything on Tower Bridge: security systems, maintenance schedules, structural blueprints.'

'Tower Bridge?'

'That's where this ends in a couple of days. I need to know how and why.'

Tessa was silent, calculating, and for a split-second Marlowe recognised Marshall Kirk in her methodical thinking.

'I can get what you need,' she finally said. 'But I'm coming with you to the auction.'

'Absolutely not,' Marlowe replied immediately.

'It's not negotiable.' Her voice was steel as she glared at him. 'That's my dad they're planning to execute for entertainment. I'm trained. I can handle myself. Ask MI5. Ask the Russians.'

'This isn't a training exercise, Tessa.'

'And it's not your call.' She stepped closer, eyes level with his. 'You owe me, Tom. You got my dad into this. You don't get to shut me out of getting him back.'

'Fine. But you follow my lead. No heroics.' Marlowe recognised the futility of arguing.

'Understood,' her posture relaxed fractionally and he

could still tell she was pissed at this. 'I'll get the Tower Bridge information by morning. Where do I send it?'

Marlowe gave her the address for his safe house.

'Come in person. Bring whatever you can about the auction too.'

Tessa nodded, already turning to leave.

'Tom,' she paused. 'If anything happens to my dad ...'

The threat remained unspoken, but perfectly clear.

'We'll get him back, Tessa. I promise.'

She studied his face for a moment, then melted into the darkness of the embankment path, leaving Marlowe alone with the flowing Thames ... and the weight of another promise he wasn't certain he could keep.

12

DA INFORMANT

Tessa Kirk's grey Ford Focus pulled up outside the Kentish Town estate at precisely eight-thirty. Marlowe watched her arrival through a gap in the curtains of his apartment, noting her baseball cap pulled low, the almost instinctive tactical awareness in how she scanned the street before exiting the vehicle.

Marshall's daughter had learned well.

After buzzing her through the main entrance, he met her at the door, coffee already poured.

'I have a lead,' she said, accepting the cup but not sitting as she entered the apartment.

'Someone from MI5?' Marlowe raised an eyebrow, sipping at his own drink.

'No. Viktor Orlovsky.'

'The Spetsnaz trainer?' Marlowe leaned against the kitchen counter. '*Your* trainer? I thought he ran a Paris delicatessen now?'

'He'd like you to think that,' Tessa shrugged. 'I know he said he'd left the business when we last needed his help, but you never truly get out. We've kept in contact.'

'Rubicon reunions and all that?' Marlowe smiled.

'Surprisingly similar,' Tessa replied icily. 'Anyway, no matter what the international spy community thinks of him, the fact is he has connections to underground auctions. If anyone knows where they're holding my dad, it's him.'

'And he'll help us?'

Tessa's expression remained neutral, professional.

'He owes me. And he respects me, in that way a trainer respects their favourite student–even if he doesn't like you personally.'

'Me? What the hell did I do?'

'Exposed Rubicon, repeatedly placed me in harm's way ...'

'Okay, point taken,' Marlowe nodded, draining his coffee. 'When?'

'Now. He's expecting us,' Tessa placed the coffee down. 'So, come on then. Chop chop.'

TESSA TOOK A CIRCUITOUS ROUTE THROUGH LONDON'S morning traffic, doubling around the one-way system twice, making sure they weren't followed–even if Marlowe didn't think they were. However, the extra precautions were well needed as far as he was concerned, and so he left her to it. He'd also had a text from Wilcott while driving; Morris hadn't come to work that day and according to his wife, he'd not arrived home the night before. Wilcott had claimed a work situation to her and promised to get him to call later that day.

The message had basically been her telling Marlowe not to make her a liar.

He'd stared out of the window after that, silently berating

himself for getting people involved, remembering St John Steele's last words.

'*You should contact your friend, and then you should start running. But that'll be the last time you can. Once we start playing, anyone who helps you? Well, they become fodder for the gaming mechanics.*'

'Trix is working on accessing the club's security system remotely,' Marlowe muttered, half to himself, breaking the silence. 'But we need a location first.'

'That's why we're seeing Viktor.' Tessa took a sharp left, avoiding a delivery truck. 'He's been in London since Christmas. Runs a deli in Farringdon as cover. Apparently, he still has connections to Orchid's High Council.'

'Depends which one,' Marlowe muttered. 'If he's sided with Steele, that's a whole new High Council he could be working with.'

'Old or new, he still hates you, so don't worry,' Tessa smiled as they looked for a parking place.

MIROSLAV'S DELICATESSEN OCCUPIED A SMALL CORNER storefront in a row of what looked to be struggling businesses, in what felt to be a section of Farringdon that hadn't gained the memo that this was a time for progress and gentrification. Its windows displayed Eastern European speciality foods, the paint on its sign faded from years of London weather.

A bell jingled as they entered, and Marlowe wasn't surprised to see the shop was empty of customers. Behind the counter stood a short, squat man with a bald head, wild, salt-and-pepper eyebrows above a bushy dyed-brown beard and a vicious scar split his left eyebrow in two. At five feet six inches, Viktor Orlovsky shouldn't have been intimidating, but decades of Spetsnaz operations had left their mark in his posture, his calculating eyes, and the economical precision of his movements.

'Little Weber ... or is it Kirk?' he said, his Russian accent still thick. 'You bring trouble to my door.'

'We need information, Viktor,' Tessa replied, approaching the counter without hesitation.

Viktor's gaze shifted to Marlowe, assessing him coldly.

'Thomas Marlowe. The three-million-dollar man. Your price drops quickly.'

'I've been working hard,' Marlowe replied.

Without another word, Viktor moved to the door, locking it and flipping the sign to "Closed". He gestured towards a curtained doorway behind the counter.

'Come. Not safe to talk here.'

The back room contrasted sharply with the shabby storefront–modern, clean, with multiple screens showing security feeds of the surrounding streets. Viktor gestured for them to sit at a small metal table, then moved to a samovar in the corner, preparing tea with practised movements.

'Why this visit?' he asked, placing steaming glasses before them. 'You know price of meeting when there is bounty.'

'My dad's been taken,' Tessa said, her voice flat. 'Along with a Metropolitan police detective. They're being held for auction. We need to know where.'

Viktor went still, only his eyes moving as he regarded Tessa.

'Authorities being taken off the street ... this is not how things should be done.'

'And you're the expert on that?' Marlowe replied defensively.

Viktor said nothing, simply glaring at him, before waving around.

'You see this? It is all because of you,' he explained coldly. 'I got out of the "spy business", as you say–but my favour to Tessa in Paris, it reminded people I still lived. That I still had debt. So now I monitor once more, stuck in this shithole of a city. You did this, Marlowe. You.'

Marlowe swallowed.

'I'm sorry,' he said. 'I really didn't know this. I'll see if I can fix this.'

Viktor snorted at this.

'We believe it's connected to The Broker,' Tessa added, trying to defuse the situation. 'And the Marlowe Coin.'

Viktor's eyebrows rose fractionally, as he returned his attention to Marlowe now.

'You know the digital money with your name?'

'We know it's funding a hit on me, and now they're using it to auction off execution methods for Kirk and Morris.'

Viktor sipped his tea, considering.

'I knew there were captives, I did not know it was your father, as the identity was only given with clients with more coins than I have. If it helps, they are at The Labyrinth Club. Knightsbridge. Very exclusive. Very secure.'

'When?' Tessa leant forward.

'Today. Second round of auction begins at midday.' Viktor checked his watch. 'Less than three hours.'

'You're certain?' Marlowe asked.

Viktor's expression hardened.

'I do not speak unless certain, Marlowe. This is not year of training in cold lake, yes?'

At Marlowe's confused expression, Viktor sighed and looked at Tessa.

'Your father would understand this,' he muttered, as if annoyed that his well-thought-out barb had failed to hit the mark.

'Security?' Marlowe moved on quickly.

'Extensive. Biometric scanners. Armed guards. Members only, with guest privileges for special events.' Viktor set his glass down. 'This auction is special event. Very exclusive entertainment for wealthy clients.'

'Is there another way in?' Tessa asked.

'Service entrance, east side.' Viktor rose, moving to a drawer from which he extracted a folded piece of paper. 'Building plans. Old, but structure unchanged.'

He spread the paper on the table, and Marlowe rose to examine them, seeing that they were detailed schematics of a Victorian townhouse, now converted to a private club. He guessed the Labyrinth Club was a place of interest for a while now; Viktor wouldn't have just had these to hand like this.

'Main floor, reception, bar,' Viktor pointed. 'Upstairs is public face. First basement, gaming rooms. Second basement, private entertainment venues. Auction will be here.'

His thick finger tapped a room on the upper floor marked *Theatre.*

'How do you know all this?' Marlowe studied the plans, memorising the visible exit routes.

'I was invited.' Viktor produced a black card from his pocket. 'As investor in Marlowe Coin.'

Tessa's expression flickered with surprise.

'You're involved in this?'

'Investment opportunity only,' Viktor shrugged, before looking at Marlowe with a dark smile. 'In my position, good to know what games are being played. Even better to make money on the problems of someone you do not like. So far I am up seven hundred grand. Good profit. Stay alive. Make me more money.'

His face fell as he looked back at Tessa.

'I swear though, I did not know your father would be involved.'

'Will you help us get in?' Marlowe asked directly.

Viktor considered for a long moment.

'I cannot be seen to help. But this ...' He slid the black card across the table. 'Club membership. Good for guest access.'

'Won't this come back to you?'

'I shall tell them you demanded it from me. I am old man now, and I cannot "kick your arse" any more.'

He punctuated this with another dark smile.

'Although this is a lie to help you. I could and would very much like to, "kick your arse".'

'A single guest won't be enough,' Tessa pointed out, once more diverting the conversation back on target.

'This is for you, as my emissary,' Viktor replied. 'He can enter on his own as Mister Bones.'

Marlowe stilled.

'You know about that?'

A thin smile cracked Viktor's weathered face.

'Old spies know many things, Marlowe. Your Mister Bones identity is professional work. Nobody outside Thames House knows; it's almost Russian quality. But several of the defectors Mister Bones "killed" now buy food from me under new, MI5-given identities. I work things out.'

Marlowe exchanged a glance with Tessa. Viktor knowing

about Mister Bones was concerning, but time was running out for Kirk and Morris.

'Why help us, Viktor?' he asked. 'What's your angle? You could make more if I die.'

'Angle?' Viktor seemed almost amused. 'Always suspicious, Marlowe. Good trait for survival. Two reasons. First, I train little Tessa. Her father was good man, even as enemy. Never fought his wife for custody of Tessa. Which allowed training to complete.'

'And second?'

Viktor's expression hardened.

'The Broker. Raymond Kinley. We have ... history.'

'Vienna,' Marlowe said, watching Viktor's reaction closely.

The Russian's eyes narrowed, his body tensing subtly.

'You know this name?'

'Kinley was involved in a Vienna operation gone wrong. He disappeared, emerged later as The Broker.'

Viktor was silent for a long moment.

'Vienna was ... miscalculation. Kinley promised clean operation. No civilians. No children,' his voice had dropped, heavy with old anger. 'He lied.'

The smile came back.

'Besides, longer you live, higher coins go up. The Broker does not know you are Mister Bones?'

'Not yet.'

'He will, at club. This is very likely a trap.'

'Probably,' Marlowe agreed. 'But we're out of options.'

Viktor nodded, understanding the calculation, and tapping back at the map now.

'Second basement has entire area off map. Reinforced steel. Where they will take prisoners if something goes wrong.'

'Access?'

'Biometric lock. The Broker's thumbprint only.'

Tessa leant forward, examining the schematics. 'Can that be bypassed?'

'Not easily.' Viktor's gaze shifted to Marlowe. 'Unless you have specialist equipment.'

'We do,' Tessa answered before Marlowe could respond. 'Trix can help remotely.'

Viktor seemed satisfied.

'One more thing. Broker's office, main floor, back corridor. Currently been given to your friend St John Steele as his own office. Perhaps personal files kept there.'

'Noted,' Marlowe said, folding the plans and pocketing them.

Viktor moved to a small safe concealed behind a false electrical panel, extracting a thin manila folder which he placed on the table.

'Labyrinth Club members. Names, faces. Know your enemies, Marlowe.' He tapped the folder. 'Russian among them. Alexei Voronin. Former FSB liaised with us when we trained Tessa here. Now private contractor. Dangerous.'

'If he watched you train, he'll recognise you,' Marlowe said to Tessa.

'Not a worry as she will be there on my behalf. We keep her in the open. Kinley will assume she's there to politic for father's life and will be distracted from you.' Viktor studied Tessa. 'But be careful. Voronin is suspicious man.'

Tessa nodded, her expression betraying nothing of what she might be feeling right now about infiltrating a club containing someone from her training days.

'Time is limited,' Viktor said, checking his watch again. 'You must prepare.'

As they moved to leave, Viktor caught Marlowe's arm, his grip surprisingly strong for a man his age.

'Marlowe,' Viktor said quietly. 'When you confront Broker, remember–Kinley's entire operation was built by Mikhail Gregorovich.'

'Gregorovich?' Marlowe frowned. 'The name's familiar.'

'Should be. KGB colonel who turned double agent for MI5 in eighties. Kinley's mentor and financial backer, but was one of the Russians blamed for the ... how you say? Saudi Prince Fiasco.' Viktor's expression darkened. 'After Vienna, Gregorovich was the only one who stayed allied with Kinley, and provided new identity, new resources. Without him, no Broker.'

'What happened to him?'

'St John Steele happened,' Viktor's voice lowered further. 'Three years ago, Gregorovich disappeared. Rumour says there was an investigation started by the son of the Saudi Prince, and Steele, through allies at MI6 captured and placed Gregorovich in black site–one that doesn't exist on any record. Insurance policy against Broker stepping out of line but also keeping one of the only people who can prove Steele caused Vienna disaster out of the light.'

'And you think The Broker might turn on Steele if he learned Gregorovich's location?'

'Not might. Would.' Viktor's certainty was absolute. 'The Broker owes Gregorovich everything. Loyalty deeper than any contract. The Broker probably doesn't even know Steele took his mentor, so if you find Gregorovich's location in Steele's files—'

'We'd have leverage to force The Broker against Steele,' Marlowe finished.

'Da. And more important—you would have ally in Broker himself.'

As Tessa drove, Marlowe studied the club members in Viktor's folder. Most were wealthy entrepreneurs, politicians, a few celebrities with darker tastes than their public images suggested. Then he spotted him—Alexei Voronin. Cold eyes and a definite military bearing even in his tailored suit. Former FSB, now in private security.

'You know him well?' Marlowe asked, showing Tessa the photo.

Her expression tightened almost imperceptibly.

'We've met. Training exercises in Russia. He was FSB liaison to Spetsnaz when I was there.'

'Problem?'

'Shouldn't be. It was years ago and as Viktor said, I'll be there as Viktor's emissary.' Her tone was professional, but Marlowe detected the slight tension beneath it. 'And we know how that worked *so well* for me in Paris.'

'If he recognises you—'

'He won't,' Tessa cut him off. 'And if he does, I'll handle it.'

Back at the safe house, Marlowe found Trix had ignored his rules on keeping away from the location for her own safety and was now sitting at the kitchen table, having accessed the building through some tech voodoo that Marlowe really didn't want to know.

It was good to see her, though.

Trix had already made significant progress as well; her laptop showed building schematics, security protocols, and staff rotations.

'The Russian was right; the Labyrinth Club uses a tiered access system,' she explained as Marlowe began applying the Mister Bones prosthetics. 'Biometric verification at the entrance, key cards for internal areas, separate system for the lower levels.'

'Can you bypass them?' Tessa asked, changing into a black cocktail dress she'd picked up on the way back from Camden.

'Already have. I've checked, and "Marcus Stone"– Marlowe's Mister Bones identity–is already on their guest list for today's event, although it's unlikely he'd have been stopped. As for you, I didn't need to do anything. Your old friend has already informed them you'll be going in his place.'

Marlowe carefully applied the facial alterations that would eventually transform him into Mister Bones–subtle changes to his cheekbones and bearded jawline, tinted contacts shifting his eyes to a flat grey, silver threaded through his hair at the temples, and through his beard. The voice would be different too–slightly lower, with a faint accent that was hard to place.

'This is too risky,' Tessa shook her head, watching him. 'If it's a trap, they'll be waiting for you.'

'Which is why I'll need to access The Broker's office–I mean *Steele's* office, according to Viktor–before anything else,' Marlowe said. 'According to Viktor, that's where he'll likely keep physical records, possibly leverage we can use. They'll think I'll go for the hostages, so they'll place more guards there.'

Trix nodded, typing rapidly.

'I've got the office location. Main floor, rear corridor. Separate security system, but I should be able to loop the cameras when you're ready.'

'Once I have what we need from the office, I'll move to the auction.' Marlowe continued applying his disguise, the transformation nearly complete. 'Tessa will be positioned for backup and extraction.'

'What about The Gravedigger?' Trix asked.

'Uncertain ally,' Marlowe replied. 'We play it cautious.'

'And me?'

'Same as always,' Marlowe smiled. 'Stay here, work the systems and keep me alive.'

AN HOUR LATER, THE TRANSFORMATION WAS COMPLETE. Marlowe checked his appearance in the mirror–Marcus Stone, better known as "Mister Bones", professional problem-solver, looked back at him. The ceramic knife concealed in his suit cuff wouldn't trigger metal detectors; neither would the lock picks disguised as cufflinks, while the earpiece connecting him to Trix was virtually invisible.

'Communications check,' Trix said through the earpiece. 'Receiving?'

'Clear,' Marlowe confirmed.

Tessa had finished her own transformation–gone was the worried daughter of Marshall Kirk; now she looked every inch a woman who deserved to dine with the elite, dripping with jewellery and looking a million dollars. Of course, half the jewellery was filled with items like Marlowe had, but with luck she wouldn't need to use them.

'Separate approaches,' Marlowe said. 'I'll go in through

the main entrance as a guest. You come in a few minutes after.'

'I'll monitor all communications and security systems from here,' Trix added. 'If anything changes, I'll let you both know immediately.'

As they prepared to leave, Marlowe caught Tessa's eye.

'We'll get him out.'

Her expression remained professionally neutral, but something flickered behind her eyes: fear, determination, maybe something else, too complex to name.

'I know,' she said simply.

Marlowe checked his watch. Almost eleven. Just over an hour until the auction ended, and the real money was spent.

Time to walk into a trap and hope they could turn it to their advantage.

13

TRAPS CLOSING

THE LABYRINTH CLUB OCCUPIED A VICTORIAN TOWNHOUSE IN one of Knightsbridge's most exclusive squares, surrounded by wine bars and posh bread shops. Nothing about its discreet frontage suggested what lay within–a playground for the wealthy elite, where anything could be purchased for the right price.

Marlowe approached the unmarked entrance at precisely eleven-thirty, giving himself enough time to locate and access The Broker's office before the auction ended.

Two men in impeccable suits flanked the door, their military postures betraying security backgrounds.

'Good morning sir,' one said, his gaze assessing Marlowe critically. 'May I ask your name?'

'Stone,' Marlowe replied, his voice pitched slightly lower than usual, with the faint accent he'd crafted for Mister Bones.

The doorman checked a tablet discreetly, then nodded.

'Welcome to The Labyrinth, Mister Stone. We've been expecting you for today's special event.'

He gestured to a biometric scanner beside the door.

'If you'll verify your identity, please.'

This was the first true test of Trix's digital infiltration. Marlowe had spent years building Mister Bones as a real person, but not once had he gone near anything like this, mainly as he knew that on a normal day it'd flag him as *Thomas Marlowe, MI5*. Sighing, he placed his hand on the scanner, maintaining a bored expression that suggested he'd done this countless times before.

The scanner hummed softly, creating a moment that stretched uncomfortably long, before giving a soft chime.

Success.

'Thank you, Mister Stone,' the doorman said. 'Please proceed to reception.'

Inside, The Labyrinth's interior revealed itself as what looked to be a study in calculated luxury. Dark-wood panelling ran along the walls, under art that suggested wealth without ostentation, and in front of him, the reception desk was staffed by a woman whose elegant appearance was matched only by her studied indifference.

'Mister Stone,' she greeted him. 'We're pleased to welcome you to today's event. The auction ends in the Hades Lounge at noon, and then the games will start. In the meantime, may I direct you to the Dionysus Bar?'

'That would be perfect,' Marlowe replied. 'May I ask, what games are these? I've yet to speak to Mister Hargrove. I was simply told to be here.'

It was a lie, but vague enough to not pique the receptionist's attention.

'There's an extra round of bidding,' the receptionist replied. 'I don't know what for.'

Marlowe paused, forcing himself to not react. The

auction was for "appropriate punishments", interesting and twisted ways of execution. Another auction meant either some extra twist in the tale, or a bid on who got to do it.

Would they make Marshall and Morris fight to the death?

Marlowe didn't want to know. And, as he followed the receptionist's directions through a series of corridors most likely designed to disorient, Trix's voice came through his nearly invisible earpiece.

'Security scans show movement in the lower levels. Eight guards. Two prisoners confirmed.'

Marlowe gave no indication he'd heard, moving smoothly towards the bar, where several guests had already gathered. Most were men in expensive suits, though a few women in designer attire mingled among them. All of them projected the particular confidence that came with extreme wealth, and Marlowe had to wonder if he was the only "hired gun" here; that would make him stand out a little more than he wanted.

He ordered a sparkling water and positioned himself with clear sight lines to both entrances. As he surveyed the room, he spotted a familiar face, one he'd seen earlier that day. Alexei Voronin, the former FSB agent Viktor had warned about, was engaged in quiet conversation with two men near the bar, a shot of vodka in his hand.

'Tessa,' Marlowe murmured, barely moving his lips, 'Voronin is in the main bar.'

No response, which was expected. Tessa would be maintaining strict communications silence until necessary–there was even a chance she wasn't even in the building yet.

Through his earpiece, Trix updated him.

'The Broker's office is on your level, east corridor. Security cameras show it's currently unoccupied. Looks like Steele isn't here.'

Marlowe waited, sipping his sparkling water, observing as more guests arrived, including Tessa, now walking with a determined stride to the bar. She stopped beside Voronin and Marlowe paused, watching, wondering whether this was something he needed to get involved in, but instead she took the vodka shot from Voronin's own hands, downed it, and then slapped him in the face. It was softer than a full-on slap, but it echoed around the bar.

'That's for not informing me you were in town,' she said loudly. 'And from Viktor, as you didn't visit him.'

Voronin went to reply, paused, and then laughed.

'Little Weber,' he said, and his eyes narrowed. 'Here to watch your father die?'

'You think he can't handle himself against a close-to-retirement copper?' Tessa shook her head sadly. 'Your tactical evaluations used to be legendary. So sad you've fallen so far.'

More laughter.

'I'm here to pay for my father's release,' she replied. 'And watch for Thomas Marlowe's appearance.'

At the name, more people stopped their conversations, looking over at her. The Dionysus Bar was filling with the kind of people who could afford to bid millions on the death of a man they'd never met, and all wanted an inside scoop.

'To help?' Hargrove, the man from the Monarch Club had approached now.

'To negotiate a freedom, Mister Hargrove,' Tessa replied. 'I reckon if I can bring you Thomas, you'll allow my father his freedom.'

'It might cause our bidders some concern.'

'Really?' Tessa frowned. 'I got the impression they'd be over the moon about the "entertainment" value of today's auction. Apparently each coin's worth over a dollar now.'

Hearing that, Marlowe actually regretted giving Pauline Faulkner the USB card.

Hargrove gave a smile, a slight nod.

'Let's see what happens first,' he said, leaving the conversation as he turned his attention to Marlowe, across the room.

'Mister Stone,' he said as he approached, Tessa now forgotten as she ingratiated herself with the Russian contingent at the bar. 'First time at one of these events?'

Marlowe shook the offered hand.

'Depends what the event actually is,' he said.

Hargrove nodded, understanding the vagueness.

'Today's entertainment should be interesting. Two men who chose the wrong side of a very expensive game.'

'I heard they helped Marlowe.'

'Indeed. A cautionary tale about the consequences of interfering in matters beyond one's station.'

'And yet you may release one?' Marlowe nodded over at Tessa.

'We'll see if her game makes it worth our while, and her target actually appears,' Hargrove sipped his drink, studying Marlowe over the rim of his glass. 'You've already had a run-in with Marlowe. I do hope you won't fail us again.'

The statement carried a subtle probe. Marlowe maintained his neutral expression.

'As far as I can see, prolonging the hunt makes your master's *master* money.'

It was deliberate, and Marlowe saw Hargrove twitch.

'My boss has no master,' he smiled, the humour missing.

'My apologies,' Marlowe raised a glass. 'I was under the assumption he worked for St John Steele, who was effectively his boss, and who's taken his office here. The video call I witnessed gave a very strong "master and servant" vibe. I'd like to be sure of whom I provide services for.'

'There is a working arrangement and The Broker does his part for a percentage of the winnings. As do we all. And besides, The Broker very much prefers his other office at The Monarch Club.' Hargrove checked his watch. 'The second auction will begin shortly. The truly interesting bidding happens early, before the anticipation builds.'

'I'll keep that in mind. What is the second bidding, by the way?' Marlowe leant back in the chair. 'I was under the assumption the execution weapon was the bidding.'

'Yes, but there are other things.' Hargrove's eyes sparkled, and Marlowe had to fight back the urge to strangle him there and then. *The bastard was enjoying this.* 'Who dies first, how slow, who does it ... all the good stuff is yet to come.'

'Marlowe?'

'We're still waiting for sources to find him,' Hargrove replied. 'And, after all, you did say you had your own.'

'My sources were right last night,' Marlowe replied calmly.

'Well maybe your sources will help you kill him.'

'As I said, the longer it takes, the more his crypto coin money goes up. And I don't care about the fee dropping. It's never about the money for me.'

'Didn't you ever read those warnings about playing with crypto, Mister Stone?' Hargrove had obviously tired of this conversation. 'Your stocks can go down as well as up. Pray we don't reach a point where the coin's candle flickers out.'

This stated, Hargrove moved away–though Marlowe noted he remained within observational distance. The encounter had been a test–of what, exactly, remained to be determined.

'Cameras in the east corridor looping now,' Trix informed him through the earpiece. 'You have three minutes.'

Marlowe finished his water and set the glass on the bar–ignoring Voronin and Tessa, who were arguing about favoured fighting knives–then moving casually towards a corridor marked "Private" with the confidence of someone who belonged, nodding to a staff member as he passed.

The corridor was deserted, lined with doors marked only by small brass plaques. At the end, he found what he was looking for.

Club Administration

The lock yielded quickly to the specialised cufflinks, but Marlowe found himself struggling, mainly as this was an exposed area, and anyone seeing him would instantly know he wasn't "looking for the men's room". Once inside, he relaxed for a moment, before looking around at a well-appointed office with leather-bound ledgers on shelves, and a polished desk with a computer.

'Two minutes,' Trix warned in his ear.

Marlowe moved directly to the desk, checking drawers methodically. Steele would likely avoid leaving items in the safe, as others would know the code. However, a locked drawer needed a key, and that could be held on his person–

This is stupid. You should be rescuing Marshall and Morris. Steele wouldn't leave anything here.

Marlow straightened, considering this.

Or would he?

Steele had a weakness, something Marlowe had seen in Berlin, Rushmore, even in Vegas. When working with others, he utilised their infrastructure. Why build your own secret base when you could use someone else's? As such, a locked box in a secret club, with all details aimed at someone else meant he was effectively out of the loop.

That said, there was also a feeling of control here–Steele loved control. He loved to show he had the authority, the gameplay ... maybe this came from his upbringing, or maybe this came from his time in Orchid or the Security Service ... he probably gained some kind of sick relief from keeping his secrets in plain sight.

Or, Marlowe's first thought was correct, and this was a wasted effort.

However, this opinion seemed to change quickly, as the third drawer he pulled at, keeping them opened only by a sliver, in case of any traps, wouldn't budge, and contained what he was seeking–a lock, easily picked, and within a folder with no name. He carefully noted the exact position of the folder in the half-opened drawer before removing it, observing how it sat in relation to the drawer's other contents. A fine hair was positioned across the fold–one of the oldest tricks in espionage, but effective. Steele was thorough.

And no-named folders were always interesting.

It was a Whitehall file, the date on the printout only a day or two old. Steele obviously had someone in Whitehall on his side still–and from the coding text on the bottom this was high level, maybe government, possibly Russell Robertson, the current Minister for Defence. He was ex-Orchid, and Marlowe remembered he was an ally of both Charles Garner–owner of the Scottish golf club that helped steal *Broad Sword*–and Steele, too. Steele probably gained the file while in this office, and hadn't had a chance to move it yet, so locked it away for later.

All the better, then.

Marlowe quickly went through the printouts, photographing them with his phone–although one document in the pile particularly caught his attention. It was a security report on a black site facility in northern Scotland. The file detailed the transfer there of a prisoner codenamed "Patriarch" three years earlier.

Handwritten in the margin was a single word.

Gregorovich

'Thirty seconds. Wrap it up.'

As Marlowe replaced the folders exactly as he'd found them, he quickly snapped some last photos before returning everything to its precise position, including the hair, re-locking the drawer and moving to the door.

But then he paused.

Steele wasn't that stupid.

Marlowe walked back to the desk, scanning it with fresh eyes. Something felt off about how easily he'd found those documents. Steele was methodical, paranoid even–he wouldn't rely solely on a simple locked drawer.

Had this been a test? Was Steele leaving this for Marlowe to find, or was he testing The Broker's loyalty?

Suddenly, Marlowe didn't know whether the information he'd just found was real or not. He'd have to check–although that might flag up a search, and Steele would then know.

He crouched down, examining the underside of the desk. Steele was old school, but he knew how to run a good surveillance. He'd have had time to set something up here, but it would have been portable, something he could do on the fly.

There.

Barely visible in the dim light, was a hair-thin wire running along the drawer's track. It was a rudimentary but effective alarm trigger–if the drawer was opened too quickly or carelessly, the wire would break the circuit.

The wire wasn't broken yet; Marlowe had been lucky in his opening, keeping the drawer half opened as he searched. Half an inch more, and it would have been. Quickly, he re-checked the wire.

That was too easy.

'Time,' Trix whispered.

'Give me a moment.'

'I can't,' Trix snapped irritably. 'The guard is coming now.'

Marlowe looked up at the door, debating whether to run, but instead carefully ran his fingers along the edge of the desk, feeling for any other triggers. Near the right corner, his fingertips detected the slightest indentation–a pressure plate. Leaning closer, he examined the plate more closely. It held a small screw with a marked orientation, currently aligned with a nearly invisible pencil line on the wood.

Clever bastard.

If someone searching the desk leaned too heavily on that corner, the screw would move out of alignment, signalling an intrusion. With delicate precision, Marlowe confirmed the screw's exact position, glad he hadn't leant on the desk.

Satisfied that he'd left no trace of his intrusion, Marlowe moved to the door–

As the door handle turned, and it opened.

It seemed that his time was over, and the guard was now checking the room.

14

BIDDING TIME

Slipping to the side, Marlowe pulled the ceramic blade from his cuff, allowing the door to open, blocking the guard's view of him.

'Nothing,' Marlowe heard the guard speak, likely into an earpiece. 'Moving on to the next room now.'

Only once the door was closed and relocked did Marlowe let out his breath.

That was too close.

Giving the guard a moment to leave, Marlowe used his lock-pick cufflinks to open the door once more, before leaving, again locking the door behind him. He was curious why the guard had checked the office–was it routine, or had they been alerted?

'Now you're finally done, the route is clear,' Trix confirmed as he re-entered the corridor. 'Security guard's finished his rounds, though, and is approaching back from the north. Take the service stairwell to your right and head down to the basement.'

Marlowe slipped through a door marked "Staff Only",

finding himself in a utilitarian stairwell, heading down quickly, but also noting the lack of any security cameras here. Either they were lax, which didn't really fit the brief, or they didn't want any evidence of what happened on the stairs.

When people were dragged down them, perhaps.

Marlowe forced the thought from his mind and stopped, quickly sending the images to Trix and, once done, completely deleting all evidence of them from his phone–the last thing he wanted, if caught was to show he'd been in the office after all. Then Marlowe took a moment to check his makeup with the phone camera as he headed through the lower-level door.

The first basement level housed private gaming rooms–poker, baccarat, roulette–each behind discreet doors, each with a brass plaque describing the games played within. There was another staircase at the far end, and continuing down to the second basement, Marlowe found himself in a corridor leading to what the floor plan had identified as the "Hades Lounge".

Two security guards flanked the entrance, checking invitations on tablets. Now back into his "Mister Bones" persona, Marlowe approached confidently, providing his name and after a brief verification, they allowed him to enter.

The Hades Lounge proved to be a theatre-like space with tiered seating facing a stage area. Unlike a conventional theatre, however, each tier featured comfortable chairs arranged around small tables, creating an atmosphere more akin to an exclusive cabaret. About forty people were already seated, drinks in hand, quiet conversation filling the space with a low murmur.

Marlowe selected a seat in the second tier, positioned with good views of both the stage and the exits, while also trying to commit any faces he recognised to memory, in case he ever needed a blackmail victim. From his vantage point, he could see a door to the left of the stage that likely led backstage–where Kirk and Morris would be held.

As if reading his thoughts, Trix's voice came through the earpiece again.

'Backstage security includes four guards and biometric locks. Prisoners are in a holding room twenty metres beyond the stage-left door.'

'I could go now,' he muttered, accepting a passing glass of champagne and speaking into it.

'That's Tessa's job,' Trix chided. 'Yours is to screw up whatever else is going on.'

The lights dimmed slightly and The Broker appeared on stage. He carried himself with the easy confidence of someone accustomed to addressing wealthy audiences and Marlowe knew this was true; he'd seen the same patter and attitude in a Punta Cana auction for military grade weapons.

'Distinguished members and honoured guests, welcome to today's special presentation.'

A screen descended behind him, displaying the Marlowe Coin logo–a silhouette of a man's head with a target superimposed over it.

Nice. Tactful. Not oppressive at all, you elitist prick.

'As you know, our primary entertainment–the hunt for Thomas Marlowe–continues to provide exceptional returns,' The Broker explained. 'Following recent developments, the bounty now stands at three million dollars, with corresponding increases in coin value. Right now, we're selling at just under two dollars a coin.'

Murmurs of approval rippled through the audience and Marlowe tried to work out the internal maths. Excluding the burnt coins, Steele would now have hundreds of millions of dollars. And the coins in the auction all went to him, too. Millionaires who bought the coins for pennies didn't care, as they had hundreds of thousands of them.

They cared that they could use it to reveal their baser instincts.

The Broker, however, was continuing.

'Today, however, we address a different matter. Rules must be enforced for any game to maintain integrity. Those who assist our target must face consequences.'

The screen changed to show images of Marshall Kirk and James Morris. Next to them, Marshall's now-expired MI5 credentials displayed alongside Morris's police background.

'These men chose to aid Marlowe, directly contravening the terms of our entertainment package. As investors, you have the privilege of determining their fate.'

The auctioneer gestured, and the backstage door opened. Four guards appeared, escorting Marshall and Morris onto the stage. Both men walked under their own power but showed signs of rough treatment. Marshall's expression remained impassive, his long-time MI5 training clear in his controlled demeanour, while Morris looked more openly defiant, his bloodied jaw set in anger despite the split lip and bruising.

Marlowe glanced around; Tessa wasn't in the room. There was every chance she had been barred from attending, or maybe she was planning her own extraction. Marlowe couldn't let it distract him, though.

'We've just ended the online auction, and the method of execution for one of these men is death by skinning,' The Broker said, to a small amount of cheers. 'Now, we get to decide the second method, and which of these dies first. Bidding begins at ten thousand Marlowe Coins for choice of execution method, and five thousand for which one gains the honour of dying right now. Minimum increments will be of five thousand coins. Successful bidders may select from our menu of options or propose their own, subject to technical feasibility. Please note, we do have a substantial offer for keeping one of them alive, so bidding higher is the only way to ensure full *performance*.'

Marlowe maintained his neutral, almost bored expression with effort, anger building beneath the carefully constructed image. Through the earpiece, he heard Trix's voice, tight with controlled fury. She'd heard everything, too.

'Tessa states security diversion in place. Ready to trigger on your mark.'

On the stage, The Broker continued his grotesque pitch, detailing the "menu" of execution methods available–from the quick and clinical to the prolonged and performative. On stage, Marshall suddenly caught Marlowe's eye. Though Marshall had never seen this particular "Mister Bones" disguise, something in Marlowe's posture or attention must have registered–or maybe Marshall Kirk had been playing with the prosthetics while they were in his possession and now recognised them. Marshall gave no obvious reaction, but his gaze lingered a fraction longer than normal before moving on.

He knows.

The bidding began, with the numbers climbing rapidly as wealthy patrons competed for the privilege of determining how the second of these two men would die for their entertainment. The display screen tracked the top bids, updating in real-time.

'Mark,' Marlowe whispered, barely audible.

'We have fifty thousand coins for "Hung, Drawn and

Quartered",' The Broker crowed. 'That could ruin the carpet. Who else wants to push it higher? Also, currently DI Morris is first, with twenty thousand coins–who knew you hated the police so much—'

He didn't finish the jibe because as he spoke, commotion erupted from the direction of the kitchens. Alarms sounded–not the shrill evacuation bells, but a more subdued alert that had security personnel touching their earpieces.

'Fire in the eastern kitchen quadrant,' Trix reported. 'Small, contained, but security protocols require response.'

Tessa had been busy, it seemed.

As expected, two of the four guards on stage received instructions through their earpieces. After a brief conference, they departed, leaving just two guarding Marshall and Morris. The Broker, watching them leave, paused for a moment, as if gathering his thoughts before he continued smoothly.

'Ladies and gentlemen, please remain seated. Our security team is addressing a minor situation. The auction will continue without interruption.'

'Is it him?' One of the bidders asked loudly, as the guards dragged Marshall and Morris off the stage and back through the door–and Marlowe couldn't tell if he was scared, or excited. Deciding he'd had enough, Marlowe rose casually, as if heading to the bar at the back of the room. As he passed through the rear section, he noted that several security personnel had been drawn away by the kitchen incident.

Perfect.

'Service corridor clear,' Trix informed him. 'You have access to the backstage area through the maintenance door to your left.'

As The Broker kept up with his pantomime auction of

horrors, Marlowe slipped through the indicated door, finding himself in a narrow utility corridor that curved around behind the stage. He moved quickly, encountering no resistance until he reached a door marked "Stage Access". Here, an electronic lock required key card access.

'I can override, but it'll trigger a system notification,' Trix warned.

'Do it,' Marlowe replied softly. 'We're out of time.'

A moment later, the lock clicked open with a green light and a small *beep*, and Marlowe slid through, entering a dimly lit backstage area. For the small size of the stage, Marlowe was surprised at the amount of equipment cases, lighting rigs, and various props that lined the walls. Ahead, he could hear The Broker's voice continuing the bidding process.

'Current high bid stands at eighty thousand coins for the acid immersion option ...'

Moving silently, Marlowe navigated through the backstage clutter towards the holding area. As he approached, he spotted the two remaining guards stationed outside another, this time, unmarked door.

'Kitchen diversion escalating now,' Trix said in his ear.

On cue, a more urgent alarm sounded, and one of the guards tapped at his ear, obviously receiving new instructions through his earpiece. After a brief exchange, he departed, leaving just one guard at the door.

Marlowe drew the ceramic knife from his sleeve, approaching from the guard's blind spot. Before the man could react, Marlowe had him in a chokehold, the knife pressed against his throat.

'Key card for the door,' Marlowe whispered. 'Now.'

The guard reached slowly for his belt, producing a plastic card, which Marlowe took with his free hand. A moment later, the guard slumped unconscious from Marlowe's blood choke hold. Sitting him up, Marlowe swiped the card against the reader, and the door unlocked with a soft click.

Inside, he found a small room with medical equipment arranged as if for a procedure, while nearby, an array of implements were laid out on a table that made Marlowe's stomach turn–clearly the "menu" options the audience was bidding on.

'Tessa,' he murmured into his communications device. 'Southeast corridor, behind stage. Need extraction route.'

'Moving to position,' came the terse reply. 'Two minutes. Need to get away from some Russians.'

Marlowe continued through to an adjoining room where Marshall Kirk and DI Morris were sitting, secured to metal chairs. Both men looked up as he entered, expressions guarded.

'Mister Bones, I presume,' Marshall said, his voice steady despite his situation. 'Or should I say you *over-theatrical prick*?'

Morris looked horrified at Marshall, who nodded his head back at the new arrival.

'It's Tom, in another of his bloody identities,' he muttered to Morris's surprised expression.

'Explanations later,' Marlowe interrupted, moving to release their restraints with the ceramic blade. 'We have about sixty seconds before they realise something's wrong.'

Morris looked between them; confusion evident.

'What the hell is going on?'

'The short version?' Marlowe freed Marshall's bonds. 'I'm rescuing you and we're leaving. Now.'

As Marshall Kirk stood, rubbing his wrists, the door

behind them opened. Marlowe spun, knife ready, but froze at the sight of the figure in the doorway.

The Gravedigger stood there; his distinctive scarred face partially visible in the dim lighting. For a tense moment, no one moved.

'Three guards approaching from the main corridor,' The Gravedigger said calmly. 'You'll want to use the service exit.'

He gestured to a door on the opposite wall.

'It leads to a back room with a laundry chute. Drop down to the sub-level, head east. Your extraction team is waiting.'

'Why help us?' Marshall eyed The Gravedigger warily.

'Professional courtesy,' The Gravedigger replied. 'And common enemies. Go. I'll delay them.'

Decision made, Marlowe nodded to The Gravedigger before urging Marshall and Morris towards the door.

'Move. Now.'

As they reached the door, Marlowe heard footsteps approaching rapidly from the corridor.

'Go,' The Gravedigger urged. 'I'll handle this.'

Instead, however, it was Tessa who appeared.

'What the hell—' Marshall muttered but stopped as she hugged him tight.

'More coming,' she nodded back at the door, kneeling by the unconscious guard and pulling his weapon, checking it before looking back. 'Go now. We'll speak later.'

Knowing there was no point arguing, Marshall pushed through the door first, followed by Morris, and through the door, Marlowe could hear them opening the laundry chute and jumping. As Marlowe moved to follow, however, The Gravedigger suddenly seized his arm in an iron grip.

'One thing before you go,' he said, his voice dropping. 'Raymond Kinley isn't who you think he is.'

Before Marlowe could respond, The Gravedigger shoved him backward–not towards the escape route, but into the centre of the room–and, as Marlowe struggled to regain his balance, The Gravedigger raised his voice.

'In here! I've got him!'

Marlowe turned to Tessa, who'd raised the guard's gun at The Gravedigger, but now, seemingly torn, she turned the gun on Marlowe.

'Sorry,' she said. 'But I made a deal. My dad for you. Don't think badly of me—'

As if by magic, the door burst open as she finished and security personnel flooded in, weapons drawn.

Behind them entered The Broker.

'Mister Bones,' he said, his voice cultured, precise. 'Or should I call you Mister Marlowe?'

He nodded to The Gravedigger.

'Well done. The payment will be transferred as agreed.'

Marlowe looked at The Gravedigger, betrayal settling like ice in his stomach.

'You sold me out.'

'It's nothing personal,' The Gravedigger replied, though something in his eyes suggested otherwise. 'It's simply that three million dollars is three million dollars.'

'And my friends?' Marlowe asked.

'Made it to the laundry chute,' Tessa confirmed, looking at The Broker. 'As promised. Our deal was for you, not them.'

Marlowe went to reply, to say something back, but paused, as if he realised he had no words.

'Judas,' he muttered, simply.

'I'm my father's daughter, Tom,' Tessa said sadly. 'But I'm also my mother's daughter. You should have thought of that when you called for my help. Did you seriously think I hadn't already started making plans with the Russians to free my dad before you contacted me?'

Marlowe said nothing, his posture slumping slightly.

'The bidders won't be happy I let their tasty treats go, and I'll have to refund the winners bids,' The Broker stepped forward, studying Marlowe with clinical interest. 'Remarkable. Even knowing what to look for, I might have been fooled under different circumstances. You should have shaved the beard, though. Even with the makeup, with hindsight it's a dead giveaway.'

'What now?' Marlowe asked, acutely aware of the guards surrounding him.

'Now?' The Broker smiled thinly. 'Now we modify our entertainment package. The hunt for Thomas Marlowe has become ... predictable. Our investors demand innovation. And we need to find new ways to make them spend their coin.'

'What does that mean?'

'It means, Mister Marlowe, that you'll be providing our clients with a more immediate form of entertainment. Gladiatorial combat. You, against a series of professional assassins. The ultimate test of skill. Our investors are already expressing considerable interest.'

The Broker gestured to the guards.

'Secure him. And wipe that stage-show crap off his face.'

As the guards moved in, Marlowe attempted to fight back–a brief, furious struggle that ended with him pinned to the floor, a knee in his back, arms wrenched behind him. As handcuffs clicked into place, Trix's voice came through his earpiece, frantic now.

'Marlowe! Security systems are showing multiple alerts—'

'And I think we've had enough of her, too,' The Broker

approached, bending to remove the nearly invisible earpiece from Marlowe's ear. He examined it briefly before crushing it under his heel.

'Ingenious,' he said. 'But ultimately futile.'

The Gravedigger stood to one side, face impassive, Tessa beside him as Marlowe was hauled to his feet.

'You won't get away with this,' Marlowe said, the words sounding hollow even to his own ears.

'I already have,' The Broker replied. 'But take comfort in this, your friends are free, by the selfless acts of your acquaintances here. And by this time tomorrow, your value to our investors will have increased tenfold.'

As the guards dragged him from the room, Marlowe caught Tessa's eye one last time. She couldn't meet it back, and Marlowe knew the trap had closed, but not as anyone had expected. Marshall and Morris were free, but he was now in the hands of the very people he'd been hunting–and who'd been hunting him. And ahead, lay something more dangerous than a simple assassination ...

Instead, he was to be part of a spectacle, designed to entertain the wealthy elite who had turned his death into a commodity.

Wonderful.

15

GLADIATOR

THE HOLDING CELL WAS SMALL, CLEAN, AND UTTERLY inescapable. Marlowe had spent the first hour examining every square centimetre–the reinforced door with its electronic lock, the smooth walls offering no purchase, the ceiling too high to reach; it had all been designed to make sure anyone inside had no option but to sit still and shut the hell up. Which also concerned Marlowe–*why would a club have such a room in the first place?*

Eventually, he'd settled onto the narrow cot, conserving energy and considering his options, which were currently limited to virtually none.

They'd been thorough, stripping him of every possession, every potential tool, even the ceramic blade he'd kept hidden in the lining of his cuff. His captors had been professional and were definitely experienced in handling dangerous individuals. Not a word was spoken during the search, and there was no unnecessary force, just cold, brutal, unnerving efficiency. In fact, the only time anyone had spoken was when one of the guards had muttered, 'Clean him up,' before he was escorted to a small shower room, given fresh clothes and brought to this cell.

The Broker clearly wanted him presentable for whatever came next.

Footsteps approached from the corridor outside. Marlowe remained seated, apparently relaxed, though his muscles tensed in preparation. The electronic lock disengaged with a soft click and the door swung open to reveal The Broker, flanked by two security personnel.

'Mister Marlowe,' The Broker spoke, worryingly relaxed as he faced his prisoner. 'It seems this is the first time I see you as you truly are.'

Marlowe said nothing, wondering where this conversation was going.

'Punta Cana was too short a time for us to truly get to know each other.' The Broker shut the door behind him as he entered the room–or was it still classed as a cell? Marlowe wasn't sure. 'The only times we've really spoken, you've been behind prosthetics.'

Marlowe made a point of stretching back in the chair, lacing his fingers behind his head.

'We all wear masks, Broker,' he said. 'Or should I say *Raymond*.'

If The Broker was surprised that Marlowe knew his name, he didn't show it. He simply nodded as he pulled a chair from beside the wall, placing it in front of Marlowe and sitting down. He was strangely relaxed for such an intense conversation; Marlowe wondered if The Broker simply knew how many people were on the other side of the door with guns.

'So, is this me apologising for leading you on?' Marlowe

asked. 'Is this you annoyed at being conned? Because you weren't the only one, believe me.'

'No,' The Broker shook his head. 'I admire what you did to keep an identity in such a community secret for so long. No wonder The Gravedigger respects you.'

'Peter Jericho respects me because I shot him, beat him and still let him live,' Marlowe replied. 'And I will point out, he didn't know I was turning up here. I don't want him connected to whatever I did.'

'It almost sounds like you're concerned about him, when he was one of the people who captured you.'

Marlowe chuckled.

'No,' he replied. 'It's just when it comes out that I went against you and won—as I will, Broker, believe that—I don't want him gaining any subsidiary credit for helping me when he didn't.'

The Broker said nothing, watching Marlowe for a long quiet—and, if Marlowe was being honest—slightly uncomfortable moment.

'And Miss Kirk?'

'Did what she had to do. She had no loyalty to me; I get why she betrayed me.'

The Broker mouth shrugged, understanding.

'What happened to the diplomat?' he eventually asked.

Marlowe hadn't expected this question, and it took a moment for him to understand who The Broker was asking about.

'The one in Rome?' The Broker encouraged.

Marlowe, realising what The Broker was asking, finally grinned.

'We faked his death,' he said, as if it was the simplest thing in the world. 'We had a couple of assets on the slopes. We bundled him into a van where no one could see him. And we left a body for the authorities to find.'

'Do you have many bodies around?'

'You'd be surprised,' Marlowe shrugged. 'You find them here and there.'

'And the money?'

'The money went into giving him a new life,' Marlowe replied, 'and funding some off-books operations. The hits that Mister Bones did over the years took a lot of people off the table and placed them in little doggie bags for MI5 and MI6 to play with. Sometimes they were removed and placed in black bag sites. Sometimes it was new identities. Sometimes ...' he shrugged. 'Sometimes they simply didn't make it.'

'But all the time you took the payments.'

Marlowe nodded.

'There was a warlord who we were trying to extract,' he explained. 'There was a half a million hit on him so I was there as Mister Bones to take what I could. I broke into his mansion late one night, found him in bed and prepared to extract him.'

'What happened?' The Broker leant forward, intrigued.

Marlowe shook his head with a smile.

'Stupid bastard woke up, saw a man at the end of his bed and had a heart attack,' he replied. 'Died there and then.'

'Which of course meant that you fulfilled your task and killed the man,' The Broker nodded. 'And your clients wouldn't know how you did it. As far as they were concerned, you'd managed to make it look as if he had a heart attack in his bed. Even better for you.'

'That's the thing with assassins,' Marlowe nodded. 'How many of them have claimed credit for God's work? An accident that happened while a target was being hunted? A death that occurred while in the crosshairs, yet not with the gun fired?'

The Broker shook his head.

'You're wrong, Mister Marlowe,' he replied.

'Am I?' Marlowe raised an eyebrow. 'Can you be sure about that?'

'Very much so,' The Broker leant back on his chair now. 'But not about the deaths. You're right about that. You're wrong about assassins. You see, you just said "how many of them", when actually, you should be saying "how many of *us*"? Because let's face it, Mister Marlowe, whether you like it or not, you are an assassin.'

'I don't get paid to kill.'

'No, you're convinced by a sense of patriotism or national duty to kill.' The Broker shook his head sadly. 'Or is this a lie you tell yourself that you don't do this? A lie that keeps you able to sleep at night?'

He gave Marlowe a moment before he continued.

'Because, let's face it, Mister Marlowe, I think Gabriel Rizzo or Lucian Delacroix, maybe even Stefan Chepik, all of these people might want a word with you. You could give every victim of yours a playing card, and by the end you wouldn't have enough cards left for a game of poker, maybe not even a *hand* of poker.'

'Every person I've killed has deserved it,' Marlowe said coldly, his eyes narrowing as he stared at the man in front of him. 'Or it's been in self-defence.'

'And what of the people who have died because of their connection to you? What of the people that died when you tried to save them, even misguidedly? Kate Maybury, perhaps?'

At the name, Marlowe rose.

'Are we done?' he asked, 'because if not, I would like to add a Marlowe coin rule.'

'Oh yes?' The Broker was still relaxed as he watched Marlowe.

'Yes. If you want to talk to me about my life, pay me some bloody coins,' Marlowe snapped.

'I think you'll find you've already received enough coins.' The Broker rose to face Marlowe. 'Last I understood, St John Steele had sent you a million. At the time, they were worth percentages of pennies. But now, those coins have made you richer than you could ever perceive.'

'Pretty pointless when you think I'm going to die before I get a chance to spend them,' Marlowe replied. 'Although perhaps I could get somebody to buy out one of your plans. Maybe get it that my assassins have to kill me with a baguette or something. That'd be great.'

'Fun but surprisingly not exciting to our watchers,' The Broker said almost apologetically. 'Perhaps we can find another way down the line.'

Marlowe gave it a moment, turning away, making sure The Broker couldn't see his face.

Never let them see what you're planning.

'Why are you working with Steele?' he asked.

'Steele is a valued client and, over the years—'

Marlowe spun back.

'Don't give me that,' he snapped. 'You didn't give him what he wanted in Punta Cana. You were working for someone else then. You didn't give him what he wanted in Cupertino, because again, you worked for someone else. Now you work for Steele, and it's almost as if he owns you, body and soul.'

'Steele has an answer that I've been looking for, for a very long time,' The Broker explained. 'When this is done, I will gain my answer.'

Marlowe nodded, sitting back on his chair, kicking his feet up and resting them on the cot beside him, staring up at the ceiling, almost as if ignoring the fact that The Broker was even in the room still.

'If you're looking for Gregorovich,' he whispered, 'there are other people who can provide you answers.'

'What do you know about Gregorovich?'

Marlowe turned his head to the side, now looking at The Broker at an askew angle.

'I know everything about Vienna,' he said. 'I know what happened, what you believe yourself to be blamed for, what you blame yourself for even.'

He shook his head.

'I also know who took Gregorovich–your mentor–and I believe I know who has Gregorovich.'

The Broker went to reply, paused and then smiled, and it was as if the man had hard rebooted, his entire attitude and expression now different.

As if he was on show again.

'I trust you've found your accommodations adequate?'

'A bit spartan for my taste,' Marlowe replied. 'But I've had worse.'

The Broker smiled thinly.

'Indeed. I imagine your experiences in ... where was it? A dog crate in Berlin? It gives you a certain perspective.'

So, Steele had updated The Broker, it seemed.

'What happens now?' Marlowe asked, cutting to the chase. 'I assume we're not here for tea and reminiscing.'

The Broker gestured for him to rise.

'Walk with me. There are some things you should under-stand before we proceed.'

Marlowe stood, noting that the guards remained close enough to intervene if needed, but also far enough to give the appearance of a civilised conversation.

As they exited the cell, he caught a glimpse of the broader facility; the club must have owned all the upper floors of the entire block, as the corridor stretched in both directions, other doors similar to his own, and spaced at regular intervals. There was a piped smell, though. Air conditioning perhaps? That and the lack of windows made him wonder if instead of being on the upper floors, he was in fact on one of the lower basement levels–the place had the clinical sterility of a private medical facility, combined with the security features of a military installation.

Not the kind of thing you find in Knightsbridge.

'This way,' The Broker directed, leading him to the right. 'The situation has evolved somewhat since our plan was formulated. Your ... unexpected intrusion as Mister Bones created certain complications.'

'Sorry to inconvenience you,' Marlowe replied dryly.

'On the contrary,' The Broker said, 'it's added a fascinating dimension to our entertainment package. The hunter becoming the hunted–it's a narrative our investors find quite compelling.'

They passed through a security checkpoint, where both Marlowe and The Broker were subjected to biometric scans before being allowed to continue.

'Thorough,' Marlowe observed.

'Necessarily so. The value of assets under our protection requires it.'

So, this wasn't just a club, Marlowe thought to himself.

Other people are here. Prisoners? Voluntarily? Is this the effective black site for the new Orchid of St John Steele? Is that why he took the office?

The corridor opened into a large control centre. Multiple workstations lined the walls, each staffed by technicians monitoring various displays. In the centre, a holographic projection against a glass screen showed what appeared to be transaction data–blocks of code flowing in real time, numbers shifting, changing.

'The Marlowe Coin network,' The Broker explained, gesturing to the display. 'Currently trading at just over five dollars per coin. It dipped when you were caught, but since we pivoted, it's had a remarkable increase in a brief period. Your continued survival–and especially your eliminating The Swede–has created quite the market excitement.'

Marlowe studied the display.

'So, this is what a gamified assassination looks like from the inside.'

'Such a crude characterisation,' The Broker frowned. 'This is finance, Mister Marlowe. The marketplace of risk and reward, skilfully designed by specialists.'

'By specialist, you mean Ciaran Winston?' Marlowe chuckled. 'At least tell me he's moved out of his mum's house in Ireland.'

The Broker's expression flickered–surprise, quickly masked.

'You're well-informed,' he said, recovering fast. 'Yes, Mister Winston provided the technical framework. His understanding of cryptocurrency structures is ... exceptional.'

'His understanding of loyalty, less so,' Marlowe observed.

'Loyalty is a variable commodity in our world,' The

Broker replied smoothly. 'As I believe you've discovered first-hand.'

He gestured towards another door, leading Marlowe through into what appeared to be a preparation area. Racks of clothing, equipment, and various stations for what looked like medical examinations or physical assessments lined the walls.

'The rules have changed, Mister Marlowe,' The Broker continued. 'The hunt, while entertaining, was proving somewhat ... inefficient. Our investors desire more immediate gratification.'

'So, instead of waiting for assassins to find me, you're staging a show.'

'Precisely. Controlled environment, guaranteed entertainment, measurable outcomes.' The Broker's professional demeanour slipped slightly, revealing an undertone of genuine enthusiasm. 'The original bounty remains in play, but the mechanics have been changed, now it's dropped considerably. You'll face a series of challengers–professional operators, each with their own specialties. Survive, and the bounty decreases as before. Fail ...'

He didn't need to finish the sentence.

'And the audience watches, in HD full surround sound,' Marlowe replied.

'For a premium, yes. The highest-tier investors receive livestream access, betting privileges, even limited input on conditions or weapons.' The Broker paused at a table displaying various combat implements. 'The greater their holdings in Marlowe Coin, the more ... interactive their experience becomes.'

Marlowe examined the weapons–knives, batons, even

metal crowbars, all items that could inflict damage without immediately ending the spectacle.

Nothing with range. Nothing that could kill too quickly.

'You've thought of everything,' he murmured.

'It's my job to anticipate variables, Mister Marlowe. Just as it was when I operated in more ... official capacities.'

There it was–the first direct reference to his previous life.

Marlowe filed it away.

'When does this circus begin?'

'Tonight. Eight o'clock. We've already sold almost all available viewing packages.' The Broker adjusted his cuff-links–Marlowe had seen it before and wondered if it was an almost habitual gesture of a man accustomed to control. 'Your first opponent will be relatively straightforward. We need to establish the format, build audience engagement.'

'Before bringing in the actual killers,' Marlowe hadn't missed the usage of "first".

The Broker expected him to win.

For a moment Marlowe was brought back to his father, hiring a second-rate killer, just to gain his son's attention.

The Broker smiled thinly.

'As I said, entertainment, especially a story like yours, requires pacing.'

'And if I refuse to participate?'

'There are two outcomes to this scenario, Mister Marlowe,' The Broker replied. 'Either you die in the arena, providing our investors with the resolution they've paid for, or ...'

He paused for effect.

'Or you survive long enough to make yourself more valuable alive than dead.'

'You're suggesting there's a way out.' Marlowe raised an eyebrow.

'There's always a way out. The question is whether you're capable of identifying it before it's too late.' The Broker checked his watch. 'You have five hours to prepare. Food, medical attention if needed, physical conditioning–all of this is available to you. We want a good show, after all.'

He gestured, and the guards moved forward to escort Marlowe back to his cell.

'One more thing,' The Broker added as Marlowe was led away. 'Mister Steele sends his regards. He's looking forward to the finale. Make us proud. Make us money.'

16

DEADLINES

MARLOWE WAS RETURNED TO HIS CELL, THE DOOR LOCKING behind him with a decisive click. Alone again, he processed what he'd learned.

The Broker, Steele, the arena concept, even the transaction data he'd glimpsed; all were pieces of a larger puzzle, which currently he still didn't have the full picture to work from.

Place the straight edges and work in from the outside.

He lay back on the cot, closing his eyes. The Broker had revealed more than he'd intended–which was always typical of men who believed themselves to be in complete control. All leverage, if used correctly.

The escape offer was the most interesting. There was every chance this was part of the new narrative; Marlowe escapes, the hunt continues, people pay more coins. Or, Marlowe keeps killing, the coins get burnt up still, and the holders make more and more.

Or The Broker hated Steele as much as Marlowe did and was starting to see him as a potential ally against a common enemy.

Marlowe allowed himself a small smile. They thought they'd written the script, defined the rules of engagement. But they'd made a critical error.

They'd put Thomas Marlowe exactly where he wanted to be.

———

TRIX WORKED FRANTICALLY, HER FINGERS FLYING ACROSS TWO laptop keyboards simultaneously. The temporary setup in the safe house apartment wasn't ideal–nothing compared to her lost equipment in the crypt–but she'd managed to establish a workable system within hours of arriving.

Morris paced behind her, watching the screens with a mixture of confusion and concern.

'Anything?' he asked, not for the first time.

'Not yet,' Trix muttered, not looking up from her work. 'Problem I have is Marlowe's tracker went dead after Canary Wharf. He did such a job on it I can't pick up anything.'

Marshall, seated across the room cleaning a disassembled Glock 17, caught her eye.

'He's alive,' he spoke with quiet confidence. 'Tom's harder to kill than cockroaches after a nuclear winter.'

'I know,' Trix replied, turning back to her screens. 'But being alive doesn't mean he's not in serious trouble. I've got multiple processes running concurrently–one tracking Marlowe Coin transactions, another attempting to penetrate Ciaran's security systems, a third monitoring emergency services and police communications across London. Something has to give us a lead.'

'I still don't understand why someone would create an

entire cryptocurrency just to kill one man,' Morris muttered, finally sitting down across from her.

'It's not just about killing him,' Trix explained, eyes still on her screens. 'It's about making it a spectacle. Entertainment for the elite. And more importantly, making obscene amounts of money in the process.'

'Also, Tom knows how to piss people off so much they want him dead in style,' Marshall grinned, seemingly unconcerned.

'But how does that work? I thought cryptocurrencies were just digital money?'

Trix paused her typing for a moment.

'Crypto is primarily driven by scarcity and demand,' she said. 'They created a billion Marlowe Coins and sold them cheap to their wealthy friends. Every time Marlowe kills an assassin, a chunk of the unsold coins get "burnt" according to the protocol.'

'Reducing supply,' Marshall nodded, following.

'Exactly. With each reduction, the remaining coins become more valuable. If Marlowe started with a billion coins at a fraction of a penny each, and now they're worth over five dollars each with a reduced supply ...'

'Someone's making millions,' Morris concluded.

'Billions,' Trix corrected. 'And the people holding the coins get special perks–like tracking data on Marlowe, exclusive viewing rights to assassination attempts, even the ability to influence how he's targeted. I've seen operations like this before, though never this sophisticated or public.'

One of Trix's screens flashed an alert. She leaned forward, typing rapidly.

'What is it?' Morris asked.

'Large transaction block just processed,' Trix replied, her

voice tightening. 'Multiple premium packages being purchased for something happening tonight. Eight in the evening.'

She pulled up the transaction data, analysing it quickly.

'They're calling it "The Arena". Looks like ... some kind of staged combat event.'

Marshall set down the pistol components and moved to look over her shoulder.

'Can you see where?'

'Not yet, but I'm tracking the data flow. If I can isolate the network architecture—'

Her phone buzzed–a secure messaging app she'd set up after losing her equipment. She checked it quickly.

'Marlowe's being held in a facility beneath the Labyrinth Club,' she said. 'They're preparing him for some kind of gladiatorial combat tonight.'

'Who sent that?' Marshall frowned.

'I have my sources.'

Marshall checked his watch.

'That gives us just over five hours, if his combat is the event at eight.'

'To do what, exactly?' Morris asked. 'Storm a high-security club filled with assassins and criminals?'

'No,' Marshall shook his head. 'To get someone inside.'

All eyes turned to him.

'I don't like where this is going,' Trix murmured.

'You don't need to like it,' Marshall replied. 'You just need to help make it happen. You said these cryptocurrency investors get special access depending on how much they hold?'

'Yes, but—'

'Then I need to become a major investor,' Marshall said firmly. 'Quickly.'

'With what money?' Morris asked.

'I've got resources,' Marshall said, the set of his jaw indicating this wasn't up for discussion.

Trix studied him for a moment, then nodded slowly.

'I'd need to create a secure wallet, route the purchase through multiple shells to avoid detection, establish a plausible identity ...'

'How long?'

'Two hours, maybe three.'

'Make it two,' Marshall said, returning to the pistol he'd been cleaning. 'I'm going to need appropriate attire for tonight's entertainment.'

'They only just released you,' Trix shook her head. 'Why would they let you back in?'

'Because I won't be bait, I'll be a game player,' Marshall smiled. 'And as we've seen, they seem to have rules.'

'I'm coming with you,' Morris stated.

'No,' Marshall replied without looking up. 'Too many faces increase the risk of detection. I'll go alone. Besides, Tessa's still in the system. I can use her help if it all goes to shit.'

Trix turned back to her screens.

'Tessa's been dark since you escaped,' she said. 'There's a chance she's compromised, or I'd have suggested giving her the coins and letting her play.'

There was a moment of silence at this. All they knew from that afternoon's excitement was that Tessa hadn't managed to get Marlowe out in time, and was probably radio silent for a reason. It'd been one quick message and then static.

'I'll work on getting you that investor access,' Trix relented. 'But there's something else we need to consider.'

'What?' Marshall asked.

'Ciaran Winston,' Trix said, her expression hardening. 'He's the architect of this whole system. If we're going to disrupt it–really disrupt it–we need to target him directly.'

'You want to go after him while we're extracting Marlowe?' Morris asked incredulously.

'No,' Trix replied. 'I want to break his system from the inside while you and Wilcott start investigating him, creating a diversion. The coin, the tracking, all of it–it's just code. Complex, brilliant code, but still just code. And I know how Ciaran thinks.'

'What do you need?' Marshall asked.

'Remote access to their primary systems.' Trix gestured to one of her screens, where a complex network diagram was displayed. 'I've been mapping their infrastructure since this began. There's a central node–if I can get a direct connection, even briefly ...'

'You could crash the whole thing,' Morris concluded.

'Not crash,' Trix corrected. 'Control. Take over the coin's protocol, corrupt the smart contracts, maybe even redirect funds. Make it look like everything's normal until exactly the right moment.'

'When the coin hits peak value,' Marshall nodded. 'Maximum damage.'

'Exactly.' Trix's eyes gleamed with determination. 'We don't just want to save Marlowe. We want to destroy their entire operation and leave them with nothing.'

'You can still walk away,' Marshall offered to Morris. 'No one would blame you.'

Morris shook his head.

'Too late for that. I'm already accessory to whatever the hell this is,' he smiled grimly. 'Might as well see it through.'

'Good,' Marshall said, reassembling the Glock, inserting a full magazine and racking the slide. 'Because if we're doing this, we're doing it right. No half measures.'

'I'll need equipment,' Trix said, already making a mental list. 'Customised hardware, signal boosters, proximity readers.'

'I can get those,' Marshall assured her. 'Just tell me what you need.'

'And we'll need a way to communicate securely during the operation,' Trix continued. 'Something they won't detect or jam, and I can't ask MI5, as I'm unsure how deep they've been compromised.'

'I might have a solution for that,' Morris offered. 'A friend in counterterrorism has access to some interesting tech.'

Trix nodded, turning back to her computers, a grim smile playing at the corners of her mouth, but there was a beep on one of her laptops, and she held her hand up to pause the conversation, flicking through some images.

'I've had AI checking those file photos Marlowe provided,' she said, reading. 'They're definitely genuine.'

'So, this isn't some kind of weird setup?'

'No,' Trix replied, leaning back in her chair. 'They're also coded with cabinet access.'

'What's that mean?' Morris inquired. 'Are we talking government?'

'More than that,' Trix looked over at the Detective Inspector. 'These were provided at a request from cabinet level. But this isn't the Education Minister asking, or whoever does Food, Farming and Fisheries. This has to be either the Home Secretary, the Prime Minister or the Minister for Defence.'

'So, Charles Baker, Joanna Karolides or Russell Robertson,' Marshall stroked at his chin as he considered the names. 'Baker's a gutless piece of shit, but at the same time, he's one of the people who kept Section D going and has a personal connection to Marlowe and yourself. Wasn't he the guy who brought you in?'

'Yes,' Trix replied. 'I don't think it'd be him. Also, Karolides owes us for when we saved her arse on the A40 during the whole *Fractal Destiny* thing. We've dealt with her a few times since. She mightn't be a solid ally, but she's definitely not an enemy.'

She pursed her lips.

'That said, she did want *Broad Sword*, and we managed to screw that one up for her, so perhaps she's decided it's time for us to go. I can't see her working with Steele, though. In fact, the only one I can see working with Steele is Robertson.'

'Well, that's a given, isn't it?' Marshall replied. 'Considering the fact we know he's old school Orchid.'

'That doesn't necessarily mean he's an enemy,' Trix raised an eyebrow. 'Remember, there's a lot of old school Orchid who are siding with Marlowe *against* Steele and his radical reimagining of the society.'

She rubbed at the back of her neck.

'If Robertson is providing Steele with real-time intelligence, then there's something else going on here.'

'What do you mean?'

'If Steele's the one who put Gregorovich in a black site three years ago, why's he gaining files telling him about it?' Trix shook her head, rising from her chair, walking over to the small kitchenette area and pouring herself a glass of water from the sink. 'Steele would know exactly what's going on. So what are these papers, and who are they for? There's something more here that I'm missing—'

She slapped her forehead as realisation came to her.

'He wanted this to be found,' she said. 'It's bait.'

'But how would that affect Marlowe?'

'Not Marlowe,' Trix replied, looking back to Marshall. 'He wanted The Broker to see this–he wanted The Broker to realise that Steele definitely had an idea of where Gregorovich was, giving a location and providing details of where the man is.'

'But surely if Gregorovich *is* in a black site in Scotland, the last thing Steele wants to do is provide anybody with information of how to get to him?' Marshall walked over, staring at the image on the screen.

'Yeah, but black bag sites are impenetrable, right?' Morris frowned at the comment.

'And thus speaks the voice of the law,' Marshall chuckled. 'You're not the first to think that. Tom and Trix have learned first-hand how black sites can be stopped.'

Trix stared back at the documents on the screen; Marshall was correct. One reason why Marlowe had eventually left the service was because a black site holding a serial killer had been compromised. Marlowe had been part of a team moving him, but the information had been leaked and they were ambushed, Marlowe was shot several times and left for dead. The serial killer in question was now long dead history, as was everything that had happened back then. But one thing it showed was that being in a black site wasn't exactly the cast iron dungeon it once was. There were no *Count of Monte Cristo in Chateau D'If* moments to be had here.

'It's a test,' she said. 'Steele's placed this information here to see what The Broker does, if he finds it.'

'But what could he do?' Morris asked and then held a hand up to stop them from replying as he realised the answer instantly. 'The Broker has the contact list of every major mercenary and assassin in the world, doesn't he? That man would have no trouble putting a team together, especially one that was made purely to rescue someone, but if it's a trap ...'

'Exactly,' Trix said. 'We need to confirm, off books, that the Ayrshire black bag site is real and whether Gregorovich is actually there, because if it *isn't* real, and Steele's aiming everyone in that direction, it means that he wants to see who's against him and knows where Gregorovich is already. Knowing him as we do, I reckon the chances that it's somewhere very close are–'

She cursed.

'What now?' Marshall asked.

'I can't tell Marlowe we believe it's fake,' she said. 'Which means if anybody asks him about Gregorovich, he's going to tell them exactly what Steele wants him to say. He's become one of Steele's own informants, and there's nothing we can do about it.'

'All the more reason to get to him as soon as possible,' Marshall mused. 'Now, about my invite to the gladiator arena ...?'

IN A PRIVATE OFFICE WITHIN A SERIES OF ROOMS UNDER TOWER Bridge itself, Ciaran Winston watched multiple screens displaying code, transaction data, and security feeds. His wild ginger hair was even more dishevelled than usual, his eyes bloodshot from too many hours staring at monitors.

The intercom on his desk buzzed.

'Mister Winston,' a cultured voice announced. 'Mister Steele for you on line one.'

Ciaran sighed, reaching for the phone.

'Steele,' he answered, not bothering with pleasantries.

'How are our numbers looking?' St John Steele's voice was calm, measured.

'Coin value hit almost six-dollars-ten an hour ago. We've sold out of premium packages for tonight's event. Total current market cap just crossed five hundred million.'

'Excellent,' Steele replied down the line. 'And the system integrity?'

Ciaran glanced at a monitoring screen that showed attempted intrusions into his network–a constant stream of probes and attacks. One particular signature, however, kept appearing, methods he recognised all too well.

'Someone's been poking at our infrastructure,' he said carefully. 'Nothing concerning yet.'

'You mean Miss Preston,' Steele said, and it wasn't a question.

'Most likely,' Ciaran agreed. 'She's good, but not good enough to break my encryption. Not without direct access.'

'Ensure she doesn't get it,' Steele's tone hardened slightly. 'And the asset?'

'Marlowe's been processed and prepped. The Broker is handling that personally.'

'As expected. And our special guest?'

Ciaran checked another screen, showing a holding area where a tall, lean figure with distinctive scarring sat calmly reading a newspaper.

'He's chilling out until he gets to fight. The Gravedigger is also ready. Still maintains he has a personal stake in this.'

'He does,' Steele replied cryptically. 'Keep him in reserve until I give the word.'

'Understood.' Ciaran hesitated, then added, 'There's been significant buy-in from an anonymous wallet in the past hour. Large enough to qualify for top-tier access.'

'Expected,' Steele said dismissively. 'As word spreads of tonight's entertainment, we'll see more wealthy players entering the market. Monitor, but don't intervene.'

'And the Tower Bridge preparations?'

'On schedule,' Steele answered. 'The vault access has been arranged, and you can start connecting into the infrastructure right now.'

Ciaran nodded, though Steele couldn't see it.

'Will you be attending tonight's event?'

'Remotely only,' Ciaran replied. 'I have other matters requiring my attention. But I'll be watching with great interest.'

'You should be there.'

'I think I'd be better off–'

There was a chuckle down the phone.

'It's Miss Kirk, isn't it? You're scared of seeing her?'

Ciaran shifted in his chair uncomfortably.

'Why is she even there?' he muttered. 'You know she's planning to screw us over.'

'The Russian contingent vouches for her, and she did, after all, deliver Marlowe to us.'

'Screwing us over,' Ciaran muttered again. 'Remember I said this when it all goes to shite.'

'You're just pissed she locked you in a doggie cage.'

'You're damn right I'm pissed!' Ciaran exclaimed. 'I think we–'

'I pay you to think in code, Ciaran. Not to think about the

real world,' Steele chided. 'Our investors expect a spectacle. Make sure they get one.'

The line went dead.

Ciaran turned back to his monitors, scanning the security feeds that showed various areas of the Labyrinth Club. Staff were making final preparations for the evening's event; the arena being set up in what had once been the club's main entertainment space. Medical personnel stood by, ready to intervene should the combat go too far too quickly. Technical teams adjusted lighting, sound, camera positions. One camera feed lingered on Tessa Kirk, who'd spent the last couple of hours sitting in the bar talking to some Russians who looked terrifying.

His gaze lingered however on the feed showing Marlowe's cell. The man sat perfectly still, eyes closed, appearing to rest. But Ciaran knew better. He knew Marlowe well now; the man wasn't resting. He was planning.

Ciaran zoomed in slightly, studying Marlowe's composed features. For a moment, he felt a twinge of something–not quite sympathy, but perhaps professional respect. After all, how many men could turn being hunted into a leverageable position?

The thought of Trix unwittingly helping his operation brought a smile to Ciaran's face. She'd be furious when she realised how thoroughly she'd been manipulated, how each attempted intrusion only strengthened his systems by revealing potential vulnerabilities.

His attention was drawn to an alert on one of his secondary monitors. Another probe attempt, but this one coming from inside the Labyrinth's own network. *Interesting*. Someone had planted a device on their internal systems.

Goddamned Tessa Kirk. It had to be. But she'd been in the bar. He'd been watching there. How?

Ciaran's fingers flew now, tracing the signal, isolating its source. There–a small transmitter hidden within the staff area, disguised as part of the electrical system.

Clever, but not clever enough. So, Marlowe has friends still.

He considered alerting security, then decided against it. Better to let this play out, see where it led. He would have said it was The Gravedigger, but he'd proven himself an enemy to Marlowe when he captured him. Perhaps Trix would make an appearance after all? That'd add a delicious element of personal satisfaction to the evening's entertainment.

Ciaran leaned back in his chair, a confident smile playing across his features. By midnight, the Marlowe Coin would be worth at least seven dollars. By the time everything was done and dusted, it might hit ten.

And by the time anyone realised what was *really* happening, it would be far too late.

For everyone except those who knew the *truth*, that was.

17

PICK A WEAPON

MARLOWE STOOD IN THE PREPARATION AREA, ROLLING HIS shoulders as a man in a white coat circled him, performing what appeared to be a final medical assessment. The room was stark–white walls, bright lights, and a selection of various pieces of medical equipment arranged ominously along a side table.

Two guards observed from the doorway; their posture relaxed but alert.

'Heart rate normal. Blood pressure slightly elevated but within acceptable parameters,' the doctor noted, speaking into a small recording device. 'Subject shows minor lacerations to right forearm, partially healed. Recent dental trauma, upper right molar.'

Marlowe smiled thinly.

'Sorry about the tooth. Self-dentistry isn't my speciality.'

The doctor didn't respond, continuing his clinical assessment as if Marlowe hadn't spoken.

'Physical conditioning excellent. Reflexes above average. Combat-ready.'

He stepped back, nodding to someone Marlowe couldn't see beyond a one-way glass observation window, then turned to a steel table where several more worryingly painful items were laid out.

'You may select two,' the doctor said, his tone entirely professional. 'No firearms, and no ranged weapons.'

Marlowe approached the table, examining the offerings. These included combat knives of various designs, a telescoping steel baton, brass knuckles in three different styles, fighting sticks, and an extendable self-defence chain not unlike his own, usually clasped around his right wrist, but which he hadn't worn as Mister Bones. Each item was designed to extend combat, to provide a show without ending it too quickly.

'Should I be flattered by the variety?' he asked, lifting a knife to test its balance.

'Standard procedure,' the doctor replied, making another note. 'Your opponent will have the same options.'

Marlowe set the knife down, selecting instead the chain and brass knuckles. It didn't really matter which he picked, the fight would still be bloody and brutal and, at least with these, he had nothing with an edge that could be turned against him too easily, instead using tools that required skill and offered versatility.

If punching someone with brass knuckles needed skill, that was.

The choices made, the doctor nodded, removing the remaining weapons.

'Five minutes until you're escorted to the arena. Water?'

'Please.'

A paper cup was handed to him, and Marlowe drank slowly, using the moment to catalogue his surroundings once more. The preparation area was connected to the main arena through a short corridor, currently blocked by a heavy steel door. It felt way sturdier than something on an upper level should be, so Marlowe guessed this was definitely more a basement level area than upper floors. Security cameras in each corner tracked his movements, and the guards were armed but carried non-lethal options prominently–tasers, batons, restraints. They weren't taking chances on him escaping, but they also didn't want him dead before the main event.

'Who am I fighting?' Marlowe asked, crumpling the cup when finished.

The doctor glanced at his tablet.

'Subject designation: Volkov.'

Marlowe felt a jolt of recognition as Pauline Faulkner's words came back.

'Then there's the Ukrainian, Volkov–that means "wolf", apparently. Claims you blew him up once and met him already in Vegas.'

The Ukrainian from Vegas. One of Stepan Chechik's men. Blond, muscular, and an incredibly efficient killer.

'We have history,' he muttered. Which was an understatement–the last time they met, Marlowe had gained Volkov into a chokehold using his chain and slammed his head into a Formula One barrier. He even remembered the last words he'd spoken.

'That's twice you've hunted me and twice I've beaten you. If there's a third, you won't be around afterwards.'

Marlowe grimaced.

Looks like there's going to be a third time after all.

'So I understand,' the doctor replied, showing the first hint of actual engagement. 'Makes for better entertainment.'

A buzzer sounded, and the guards straightened.

'Time,' one of them announced.

The doctor nodded to Marlowe.

'Good luck, Mister Marlowe. Medical team standing by.'

'Comforting,' Marlowe muttered, moving towards the guards who now flanked him, leading him through the corridor.

The noise hit him first–a low, expectant murmur of voices, growing louder as they approached the arena entrance. The space opened up before him, and Marlowe took in the setup with a quick, professional assessment.

The Labyrinth's main entertainment venue had been transformed. Tiered seating surrounded a central area approximately ten metres in diameter, enclosed by transparent barriers that reached three metres high. The floor was matted but firm–offering some protection against falls, but nothing that would significantly impede movement. Lighting focused inward, making the audience difficult to see clearly but perfectly illuminating the arena itself, and cameras were positioned at various points, capturing multiple angles. It reminded him of the gaming area Gabriel Rizzo had built in Vegas, the one he'd fought in–perhaps Rizzo had been involved with this before he died.

Waiting in the centre, Volkov stood with the relaxed posture of a predator. Blond hair cropped military-short, and a face set in an expression of cold determination, he'd selected a knife and what appeared to be a set of reinforced fighting gloves, it seemed.

'Marlowe,' Volkov acknowledged as he approached, his accent thick but his English precise. 'I hoped perhaps Rizzo had killed you, before the contract went out and I realised you still lived.'

'Disappointed?'

'The opposite,' Volkov replied. 'Now I get to finish properly.'

A voice boomed over the sound system–The Broker, addressing the assembled audience.

'Distinguished guests, welcome to tonight's exclusive presentation. The rules are simple. Combat continues until submission, incapacitation, or ...' there was a dramatic pause, 'more permanent resolution. Intervention will occur only if both participants are rendered unable to continue, or if our investors signal for a conclusion through the auction interface.'

Marlowe glanced up, noting a large display screen showing real-time bidding metrics. Apparently, the audience could pay to influence the outcome or conditions–medical supplies, adrenaline, bandages–all could be bought with Marlowe Coins, it seemed.

Democracy for the wealthy.

'As a reminder,' The Broker continued, 'all premium package holders have access to exclusive camera angles and biometric data. Bidding closes in thirty seconds.'

Volkov flexed his hands, testing the fighting gloves.

'Nothing personal, Marlowe. Just business.'

'It's always just business,' Marlowe replied, unwinding the chain, feeling its weight. 'Until it becomes personal. This is the second time you've accepted a hit on me. I thought you'd have learnt your lesson by now.'

Before a response could be given, a loud tone sounded, and Volkov moved immediately, closing distance swiftly. No hesitation, no posturing–just the direct approach of a professional who knew his craft.

Marlowe sidestepped, whipping the chain to create space

between them. The Ukrainian adjusted instantly, feinting left before striking right, his knife flashing under the arena lights. Marlowe felt the blade catch his shirt, missing flesh by millimetres.

They circled each other, the audience's murmur growing with anticipation. Marlowe kept moving, analysing Volkov's style, recognising the *Systema* training in his fluid movements.

Former Spetsnaz, most likely. Dangerous at close quarters.

'This isn't your usual work,' Marlowe said, testing a strike with the chain that Volkov easily evaded. 'Staging fights for rich voyeurs.'

'Times change,' Volkov replied, advancing again, knife and fist working in coordination. 'After Vegas, work become scarce. Reputations damaged after you made us look like fools.'

He launched a series of strikes, forcing Marlowe to give ground. One caught Marlowe's side, not deep but enough to draw blood.

The audience responded with appreciative sounds.

Marlowe countered, the brass knuckles connecting with Volkov's shoulder, throwing him slightly off balance. He followed with the chain, catching the Ukrainian's wrist, momentarily immobilising the knife hand.

'The Broker recruited you specifically?' Marlowe asked, maintaining pressure on the chain.

Volkov twisted free with impressive strength, resuming his fighting stance.

'For you, specifically.'

He attacked again, this time with a different rhythm, mixing Systema with what looked like Krav Maga techniques. Marlowe absorbed a blow to his ribs, countering with a strike that snapped Volkov's head back and opened a cut above his eye.

'They're watching us,' Volkov said quietly as they grappled briefly before separating. 'Listening.'

Marlowe caught the slight emphasis, the meaningful glance upwards towards the observation booth where The Broker likely sat.

Interesting. Volkov was telling him something.

'Does it bother you?' Marlowe asked, circling again. 'Being part of this ... spectacle?'

'Work is work,' Volkov shrugged, but there was something in his expression–a flash of something beyond professional detachment. 'I'm not the one with the bounty. Or the crypto coin.'

They moved in again, exchanging strikes with what Marlowe felt was an increasing intensity, but Volkov was holding back slightly. Not enough to be obvious to observers, but enough that a trained fighter would notice. Their eyes met briefly during a clinch, and Marlowe saw confirmation there.

The Ukrainian wasn't trying to kill him–at least not quickly.

Had he been paid to slow the fight, to gain more money for the gamemasters?

On the display screen, bidding numbers shifted rapidly. The audience was engaged, digital assets flowing as they bet on outcomes, purchased influence options. The Broker's voice occasionally interjected with updates or special announcements. Marlowe took a calculated risk, allowing Volkov to manoeuvre him towards the arena barrier closest to the main entrance and, as they neared it, the Ukrainian pressed his advantage, his knife seeking vital targets with a clear determination that seemed to delight the audience.

'Vienna,' Marlowe said quietly during a close engagement, testing a theory.

Volkov's rhythm faltered momentarily—almost imperceptible, but it was definitely there.

Recognition.

'Gregorovich,' Volkov murmured, the word barely audible as they separated again, resuming their combat dance for the audience.

So, he knew about that connection.

Marlowe filed the information away, reassessing the Ukrainian's position in this game. Not just a hired killer, then, but someone with deeper knowledge of The Broker's past—and possibly his vulnerabilities.

The display screen flashed with a new announcement.

SPECIAL CONDITION ACTIVATED: WEAPONS EXCHANGE.

The Broker's voice returned, echoing through the arena's speakers.

'Our platinum-tier investors have approved a modification. Combatants will exchange weapons immediately.'

Volkov raised an eyebrow slightly, then held out the knife, handle first. Marlowe reciprocated with the chain, as they exchanged weapons under the watchful eyes of the audience and cameras.

'Better for you,' Volkov commented as they resumed fighting. 'Knife suits your style.'

'Thoughtful of our benefactors,' Marlowe replied dryly. 'The gloves are too small, though. You have tiny hands.'

They continued, the pace quickening as both fighters

adjusted to their new implements. Blood glistened on the arena floor–some Marlowe's, some Volkov's–but neither showed signs of significant fatigue or impairment, and Marlowe knew this was in effect nothing more than a slightly painful sparring match. The audience was growing restless, sensing the measured pace of professionals conserving energy rather than seeking a decisive conclusion.

Marlowe saw the shift in Volkov's eyes a moment before it happened. The Ukrainian suddenly escalated, launching a blistering series of attacks that forced Marlowe to defend more urgently. This wasn't for show–Volkov was deliberately pushing towards what would appear to be a genuine climax.

'Time to end this,' Volkov said, loud enough for nearby microphones to catch. 'Nothing personal.'

He drove Marlowe towards the centre of the arena, creating the impression of dominance. Marlowe allowed it, unsure if this was reality or yet another feint on Volkov's behalf, taking a calculated hit to create the impression of increasing vulnerability. The chain lashed out, catching his injured arm, and genuine pain flared through him.

On the screen, betting odds shifted dramatically, Marlowe Coins flowing as investors sensed a conclusion approaching. The Broker's voice added commentary, highlighting Volkov's apparent advantage, and Marlowe's increasing difficulty.

Volkov closed for what appeared to be a finishing sequence. As they grappled at close quarters, he spoke again, voice barely a whisper.

'Tower Bridge. Friday. The server core. This is his endgame, if you live.'

Then louder, for the benefit of their audience:

'For Chechik.'

Marlowe understood the game now. Volkov was performing–creating a convincing show while passing information. But why? What stake did he have in this beyond the contract?

There was no time to consider it further, though. The Ukrainian was committed to his performance, and Marlowe needed to play his part. They exchanged another rapid series of blows, Marlowe deliberately leaving an opening that Volkov exploited with more than a little amount of theatre, driving him to the ground.

The crowd's excitement peaked as Volkov stood over him, chain raised for what appeared to be a finishing strike. Marlowe lay seemingly dazed, calculating angles, timing, the perfect moment to reverse the situation.

The display screen flashed again.

OUTCOME VOTE INITIATED: CONTINUE OR CONCLUDE?

Digital numbers raced across the screen as investors registered their preferences, spending Marlowe Coins to influence the outcome. The majority seemed to favour continuation–they weren't ready for the entertainment to end so quickly.

The Broker's voice announced:

'Our investors have spoken. The combat continues!'

Volkov nodded slightly, acknowledging the command, and adjusted his grip on the chain. As he moved to strike again, Marlowe executed his reversal–a swift sweep that caught the Ukrainian's legs, bringing him down. The knife flashed, coming to rest against Volkov's throat in a position that looked decisive ... but actually applied minimal pressure.

For a second, Marlowe remembered a UK wrestler he'd trained with a couple of years earlier, explaining to him the psychology of the sport. And it was a sport; the moves they made and the risks they took were real, even if the "story" was created in advance, and the implied pain and potential casualties were more visible than actual.

That was what Volkov wanted, and Marlowe was happy to follow his lead.

A collective gasp rippled through the audience, followed by appreciative applause at the sudden turn. The betting display erupted with activity as odds recalculated and new wagers poured in.

'Well played,' Volkov murmured, genuine professional appreciation in his eyes.

'Not over yet,' Marlowe replied quietly, pulling back.

They continued for what felt like hours but was actually no more than another ten minutes–a carefully choreographed dance of near-misses, convincing blows, and dramatic reversals. Both men were bleeding from multiple cuts, breathing heavily, showing the genuine fatigue of extended combat. The audience was fully engaged, digital assets flowing freely as they purchased influence, placed bets, and rewarded particularly impressive sequences. Finally, when both men appeared completely spent, the display flashed once more.

FINAL OUTCOME VOTE: DECISIVE VICTOR REQUIRED.

The Broker's voice carried a note of satisfaction:

'Distinguished investors, the time has come for resolution. Voting closes in thirty seconds.'

Volkov met Marlowe's eyes, a silent communication passing between them. Whatever happened next, the Ukrainian had played his role perfectly–creating a convincing spectacle while subtly assisting Marlowe. The question of "why" remained, but that'd have to wait. The digital tally appeared on screen; votes tallied in real-time as Marlowe Coins flowed into the system. Investors clearly preferred drama over a quick resolution–Marlowe's come-back and the extended combat had pleased them.

They moved in again, but Volkov's grip was now slick with his own blood and his chain slipped from his grip, lowering his guard, and creating an opening that Marlowe exploited with apparent ruthlessness. Or, rather, that was what Volkov had meant it to look like. The Ukrainian fell to a knee, Marlowe's knife coming to rest at his throat once more– this time with genuine pressure, though still carefully controlled.

'Finish it,' Volkov said, loud enough to be heard. 'You've earned it.'

Marlowe hesitated, making a show of considering it, even if that wasn't his plan. *What was Volkov playing at? Surely he knew Marlowe had to kill him to stay alive? Why wasn't he trying to survive?*

The audience's excitement built, sensing the possibility of a definitive conclusion. The screen showed new options appearing, and Marlowe could see that investors could now pay premium amounts to influence the exact nature of the finish.

The Broker's voice returned through the speakers.

'Mister Marlowe, our platinum tier has expressed a pref-erence. They would like to see you complete your victory with the blade.'

Marlowe maintained the knife's position, seemingly contemplating his decision. He could see the calculation in Volkov's eyes–the Ukrainian understood what was at stake. A real death would reduce the bounty to one and a half million dollars, further disrupting Steele's plans while adding credibility to the spectacle.

But then Marlowe stood.

'Screw you,' he replied to the audience. 'I'm not helping your snuff fantasies.'

There was a definite murmur of discontent here–the audience weren't expecting Marlowe to go full "Gladiator" and not do what they asked.

'They'll kill us both,' Volkov whispered. 'You need to stay alive and avenge Gregorovich.'

'What's your connection?'

'He was my grandfather. Steele killed him.'

Marlowe adjusted his grip on the knife, looking up as the audience started to boo.

'Mister Marlowe, by refusing to kill your vanquished opponent, all you do is hasten his death regardless.' The Broker's voice was angry now.

'At least let me speak to him,' Marlowe shouted up. 'He deserves a warrior's last confession.'

There was no answer and, taking that as confirmation, Marlowe looked down.

'You're wrong with "was",' he said softly. 'He *Is*. He was in an MI6 black bag facility three years ago in Ayrshire. His codename was Patriarch. Is that enough for you to find him?'

Volkov's eyes had widened, and he nodded. Then, in a swift, precise movement, Marlowe flicked the blade up once more and drew it across Volkov's throat–with just enough pressure to create a convincing spray of blood without severing anything vital. The Ukrainian's performance was flawless, body convulsing in apparent death throes, eyes going vacant.

Marlowe crouched down to check the body.

'When you find him, tell me,' Marlowe whispered, head down. 'It's the only thing keeping The Broker under Steele's control. But you knew that already, didn't you?'

Volkov couldn't reply, of course, as he was playing dead. But, as Marlowe rose back to his feet, the audience erupted in a mixture of gasps, applause and excited chatter. On the display, however, the bounty figure immediately updated.

$$\$3,000,000 \rightarrow \$1,500,000.$$

'Ladies and gentlemen,' The Broker announced, voice perfectly controlled despite the unexpected development, 'Thomas Marlowe advances to the next level. The bounty is reduced accordingly. Market adjustments will process automatically and another percentage of unspent coins will be burnt.'

Medical personnel rushed in, surrounding Volkov's apparently lifeless form. They made a show of checking vital signs, then covered him with a sheet, strapping him to a stretcher for removal. As they lifted him, Marlowe caught the barest movement from beneath the sheet–acknowledgement of their successful deception.

Guards approached Marlowe; weapons raised but not threatening.

'Quite a performance,' one commented quietly. 'The Broker wants to see you.'

Dropping his weapons, Marlowe allowed himself to be escorted from the arena, the audience's excited discussions fading behind him. Blood–both his own and Volkov's–stained his clothes, hands and the knife, now left on the floor of the arena.

He'd survived the first test. The bounty was halved again.

Somewhere, Steele would be recalculating, adjusting his plans.

And Marlowe had gained a potential ally–though Volkov's true motivations remained unclear.

All he needed to do now was survive long enough to work out what was really going on.

———

18

THE OLD GUARD

TRIX WATCHED THE LIVESTREAM WITH A MIXTURE OF professional assessment and personal concern. The safe house had fallen silent as they observed Marlowe's performance in the arena, the combat's shifting dynamics, and the eventual "death" of his opponent.

'He's playing them,' Marshall Kirk had commented at one point, his experienced eye recognising Marlowe's moves.

'You could be right,' Trix agreed. 'I've seen Marlowe fight for his life before and that felt a little more staged. That Ukrainian wasn't fighting to kill.'

Morris leaned forward, studying the screen where the feed continued to show aftermath footage–medical personnel removing the body, while cleaning crews swooped in behind them, preparing the arena for the next event, audience members mingling in exclusive lounges.

'So, what does that mean?' he asked.

Trix didn't reply; she was too busy focused on a different aspect of the feed–the digital infrastructure visible in the background. Camera positions, control interfaces, networking equipment, cataloguing each element, building a mental map of the system architecture.

'There,' she said suddenly, pointing to a brief glimpse of what looked to be a server rack visible through a doorway as they wheeled the body on a gurney through it, leaving the empty arena. 'That's a distribution node, not the main core. Wires all the feeds out of the arena together and sends them off to God knows where. But it confirms what The Gravedigger said–the primary systems must be elsewhere.'

There was the faint sound of scuffling outside the door and Trix paused, looking over, her eyes wide. Morris rose, about to open the door, but Marshall grabbed his arm, picking up his weapon and sliding over to the side. Morris, realising once again that this was a little more outside of his wheelhouse than he preferred, stepped back, allowing the expert to move in.

There was a knock on the door. Three short raps, two short raps, and then one. Three, two, one.

Marshall relaxed.

'It's Tessa,' he murmured. He opened the door, but Trix noted that he still had his gun prepared, just in case. Tessa slipped through, still wearing the cocktail frock she'd worn earlier that day.

She saw Morris and Marshall and her shoulders relaxed.

'Thank God,' she breathed. 'I was worried you didn't make it.'

'We're not the ones who needed to worry,' Trix snapped. 'What happened with Marlowe?'

'We were intercepted before we could leave,' Tessa replied calmly.

'Bullshit,' Trix shouted, looking at her directly. 'At what

point did the plan turn into "betray Marlowe and leave him for The Broker"? And don't give me any shit that you didn't.'

Tessa nodded, waiting for Trix to calm.

'When we first met, Trix, you thought I was a double agent, and in a way I was. But not one that would've hurt you or Marlowe,' she said. 'The last time we met, I helped you place your abusive ex-boyfriend in a dog cage. Do you really have so little faith in me that you'd think I'd betray Marlowe at the first opportunity?'

She looked over at her father.

'We discussed it on the way back from Viktor's delicatessen,' she went on. 'Marlowe knew that if he told his plan to Trix, she'd have arguments about it. Or that if you and Morris learnt it as you left, you might try to go back and stop things.'

'And what exactly would we have been stopping?' Morris asked coldly.

'I was supposed to go in and be the one to betray Marlowe,' Tessa replied. 'As far as The Broker was concerned, I was there to get my father out, nothing more. Once he was, I did what I said I would and gave The Broker Marlowe.'

'And Marlowe was happy with this?'

'I wouldn't say "happy" was the term I'd use,' Tessa shrugged, 'but he knew he had to do something. Running around London being chased by nameless hitmen was tearing him down. This way he had a chance to get things moving *his* way.'

'His way? He was almost bloody killed!' Trix snapped. 'You might not have seen the fight, being on your way here—'

'I watched it,' Tessa said. 'I was given a feed for my phone. I saw what happened.'

'Which was?' Marshall asked.

'That Volkov pulled his blows, and that Marlowe didn't kill him at the end.'

'And why would that be?'

Tessa leant back against the wall.

'Because Volkov's the grandson of Gregorovich,' she explained. 'When I saw Alexei Voronin at the bar, I gave the impression I was there purely for my dad, but that I was still the Russian Spetsnaz wannabe he knew. When Hargrove spoke to me, I offered him a deal. Free my dad–or at least allow him to escape if he managed to get out–and I'd give him Marlowe. The Broker spoke to me later and confirmed he was happy for me to do that, as long as my father escaped and wasn't freed–that way he didn't void the betting.'

'So, let me get this right,' Marshall murmured. 'If I hadn't escaped, Marlowe would still be safe.'

'No. They knew he was Mister Bones from the moment we arrived.' Tessa shook her head. 'Voronin told me–even nodded across at him and said, "that's your friend Marlowe". I had to argue, say I didn't believe him. But when I realised Marlowe was about to be outed, I used it to my advantage. The Gravedigger too.'

There was no response to this. The revelation that The Gravedigger had also betrayed Marlowe was fresh in everyone's minds.

Tessa smiled.

'Stepan Chechik also trained under Alexei Voronin,' she said. 'Back when Ukraine and Russia were friends. Volkov worked for Stepan. Voronin mentioned Volkov was Gregorovich's grandson. Once we'd captured Marlowe, I asked if I could speak to Volkov. Made out I was feeling guilty for screwing over Marlowe, and I wanted Volkov to give my last words of apology to him during the fight. As it was, I pointed out that Marlowe may have known where Gregorovich was, and it was in his interests to see if he could help him.'

'Yeah, well, that might not be the case any more,' Trix replied. 'We think it was a test–and definitely a lie. We need to find somebody at MI5 or MI6 who can give us an honest answer.'

She looked back at the screen.

'But if Marlowe did pass the message to Volkov, he'll be looking to get out, go to Ayrshire, find his grandfather–and alert Steele that he's gained information left by him. We probably need to find a way of stopping him before he does that. Did Marlowe say why he wanted to do this?'

'He wanted to bring the money down, and he wanted to piss off Steele,' Tessa shrugged. 'With each reduction in the bounty, the remaining coins become more valuable. People are rushing to buy in before the next value jump, creating a feedback loop.'

'If the bounty drops once more ...' Marshall began.

'We could see ten dollars per coin,' Trix finished. 'Billions in virtual value created from nothing.'

'Until it collapses,' Tessa noted. 'It's paper money until Steele cashes in. Marlowe wanted it to rocket and then crash before he could do anything. Best way to hurt him was cut off his cash and air supply.'

'And it will,' Trix confirmed, 'when I trigger the cascade once it's set up. But until then, it'll keep rising.'

'Unless Marlowe dies first.'

'Well, obviously, unless Marlowe bloody dies before we can sort this,' Trix said as she turned her attention to Marshall.

'I'm not happy about this, but your wallet's loaded,' she

told him. 'A hundred thousand Marlowe Coins, acquired through six separate proxy purchases to avoid triggering security flags. Should be enough to get you top-tier access.'

'They're going to recognise you,' Morris muttered, annoyed he wasn't going. 'You were literally on stage, strapped to a chair a few hours back.'

'What's this?' Tessa looked around the room.

'Your dad wants to be a hero and suicide mission his way back in to save Marlowe.'

'No,' Tessa shook her head. 'They'll taser you the moment you arrive. Christ, they'll probably taser me too, now. Especially when they learn what I did to Volkov.'

'What did you do?'

'Paid off the medics, told them The Broker needed a show, so if they were to find Volkov wasn't dead, to pretend he was, get him out and let The Gravedigger finish Marlowe off.'

'Jesus! How do you know The Gravedigger won't—'

'Because The Gravedigger has this weird debt thing going with Marlowe,' Tessa replied. 'I suggested that saving Volkov would partially repay it.'

'So, if I can't go, and you can't go, then what do you suggest?' Marshall replied irritably.

'Someone else?' Morris deadpanned.

'We don't have anyone else,' Marshall replied irritably. 'You think we haven't considered it? Anyone who's helped Marlowe in the past is off limits. Anyone we can call is known by Steele.'

'That could work to our advantage,' Trix looked back. 'Look Marshall, he's right. If you go back, you'll be distrusted. Probably executed or used as a pawn. We need someone they won't suspect ...'

She paused, typing on her keyboard. A moment later, she grabbed her phone, dialling a number shown on the screen.

'No names,' she said when whoever answered. 'It's me, the one who shot you in the foot.'

There was a moment, as Trix listened to the voice of Sir Walter McKellan, likely telling her, without naming her, exactly what he thought.

'Yeah, whatever, love you too,' she said. 'Can we meet? Like right now? I have a favour to ask.'

IN HIS PRIVATE VIEWING SUITE ABOVE THE ARENA, THE BROKER watched the cleaning crew prepare for the next event. The first round had definitely exceeded expectations–Marlowe's performance, the audience engagement, even the digital assets flowing through the system. The Broker was however surprised and disappointed by the unexpected death of Volkov–he'd hoped the crowd would let him live to fight another day, perhaps–but he knew it served a purpose, driving coin value higher while adding authenticity to the spectacle.

Gregorovich's grandson deserved better.

The door opened behind him and Hargrove entered, a tablet in his hand, currently displaying updated metrics.

'Coin value holding at six fifty-three,' he reported. 'Volume up three hundred per cent since yesterday. New investors continuing to enter the market at an accelerated rate.'

The Broker nodded, accepting the tablet.

'And our special guests?'

'Arriving as scheduled. VIP sections at capacity.'

'Excellent.' The Broker scrolled through the data, noting particularly the distribution of high-value wallet holders. 'Any unusual patterns?'

Hargrove hesitated briefly.

'Just the wallet that acquired significant holdings. Anonymous routing, multiple shell purchases aggregating to hundreds of thousands of coins.'

'Could be real, could be Steele testing us.' The Broker returned the tablet. 'Monitor, but don't interfere. Let's see what move they make.'

He looked out at the arena.

'And Marlowe?'

'Currently being treated by our medical staff. Minor injuries only–he paced himself well.'

The Broker moved to the window, overlooking the arena.

'Has Steele been informed about Volkov?'

'His death? Yes. He expressed ... displeasure.'

'I'm sure he did.' A thin smile crossed The Broker's face. 'The bounty reduction accelerates his timeline, forces adjustments. He dislikes improvisation.'

Hargrove waited, but when nothing else was forthcoming, he shook his head.

'Going against Steele won't end well.'

'Steele has yet to provide me what I asked for,' The Broker shrugged. 'And his pet hacker is pissing people off at Tower Bridge.'

He sighed.

'I mean, Tower Bridge? How more "Bond villain" can you get?'

There was another long moment of silence in the room.

'And the incoming investor?' Hargrove continued, changing the subject.

'Standard procedure. Full access commensurate with their spending level. Excellent service. Complete cooperation.' The Broker straightened his already impeccable tie. 'After all, customer satisfaction is our primary concern.'

His tone made it clear the matter was concluded. Hargrove exited silently, leaving The Broker alone once more, gazing down at the arena where, in a few hours, the next spectacle would unfold.

Everything was proceeding according to plan.

Different than Steele's plan, certainly, but then Steele had never fully appreciated the human elements of the game. The psychological nuances. The importance of perception over reality.

The Broker checked his watch.

Soon, the show would continue. And what a show it would be ... if not *exactly* the show St John Steele expected.

———

BENEATH THE MAIN LEVELS OF THE LABYRINTH IN A SECURE medical facility, Volkov lay perfectly still on an examination table as a doctor checked his vital signs. The blood had been cleaned away, revealing the precision of Marlowe's performance—a convincing but superficial wound across the throat, designed to appear fatal while actually causing minimal damage.

'Remarkable control,' the doctor commented, applying a specialised skin adhesive to close the laceration. 'Another millimetre and we'd be having a very different conversation.'

Volkov remained silent, eyes fixed on the ceiling. His role required complete commitment—as far as most of The Labyrinth's staff and security were concerned, he was being prepared for discreet disposal, and the cameras in the corner could still pick up movement. He wasn't sure, but he believed only The Gravedigger, and this particular doctor knew otherwise. Perhaps The Broker? Maybe not.

When the doctor finished, he moved Volkov into the corner, placing a shield around the "body", as if to stop anyone gaining a shock on entering the room. However, what it did was allow Volkov to finally relax, as he closed his eyes, his mind returning to Marlowe's comment.

His grandfather could still be alive.

He knew there was a shift change in half an hour. There'd be a moment where he'd be able to leave without being watched. Once done, he could look for this "Patriarch", and ruin St John Steele's day completely.

All he had to do was take him from the fools at MI6, of course. And how hard could that be?

LONDON'S FINANCIAL DISTRICT STOOD NEARLY DESERTED AT this hour, the towering glass monuments to capitalism emptied of their daytime occupants, as Trix guided the "borrowed" Audi through streets slick with recent rain, her eyes constantly checking the mirrors for any sign of surveillance.

The car–taken from a long-term car park with the help of a device she'd built specifically for bypassing modern security systems a couple of years earlier–was anonymous enough to avoid immediate attention, but at the same time, paranoia wasn't a bad thing to have in these challenging times.

St. Dunstan-in-the-East had provided the perfect meeting place; an old church destroyed during the Blitz and preserved as a garden, its stone walls open to the sky, and with trees and vines growing through what had once been sacred space. At night it was officially closed to visitors, but the wrought-iron gates yielded easily to Trix's lock picks, nothing more than a woman leaning against the church, if anyone passing bothered to examine closer.

Once inside–although for a series of ruins with no roof, the term "inside" didn't exactly sit right–she positioned herself in the shadowed remains of what had once been a side chapel, her back to a solid wall, checking the burner phone's signal strength.

Twenty minutes early. Good.

The gardens remained silent, save for the occasional rustle of leaves in the night breeze and distant sounds of late-night traffic. Trix used the time to mentally run through calculations, projecting how the Marlowe Coin's value would respond to the latest reduction in bounty. At current growth rates, they could easily hit ten dollars within twenty-four hours, possibly twelve by tomorrow night. Ciaran's system was working exactly as designed–creating artificial scarcity, driving up value, generating billions in phantom wealth, that would evaporate the moment she triggered her cascade.

The burnt billions, however, were of interest. Ciaran was a hoarder. He wouldn't have agreed to this unless there was something in it for him, and not just from Steele, and the "New Kid" Orchid he was creating. *But what was it?* It was annoying, for sure. Trix had been closer to Ciaran than most people when they were in their relationship–but at the same time he had a long-term girlfriend she didn't even suspect about; so off-the-records that even Trix didn't see her. Which meant that something like this would be ten times more important–and ten times more secured.

At precisely midnight, a black Jaguar pulled up outside the garden gates, its engine cutting to silence. Trix watched as a tall figure emerged, moving with the measured caution of a man who'd spent decades in intelligence work. Sir Walter McKellan–silver-haired, immaculately dressed despite the hour, carrying the weight of his seventy-plus years with dignity, if not with a slight limp, and assisted by a cane. He entered the garden alone, moving directly to her position with unerring accuracy. Of *course* he'd know where to find her–the man had forgotten more about fieldcraft than most agents ever learned.

'I hope your foot's recovered,' Trix said by way of greeting, not moving from her shadowed position.

'It hasn't,' McKellan replied dryly. 'The doctors tell me I'll have a permanent reminder.'

'Consider yourself lucky. I was aiming for the knee.'

McKellan's lips twitched in what might have been amusement.

'Why this meeting, Miss Preston? I assume it has something to do with Marlowe's current ... predicament.'

He held a hand up to pause her inevitable question.

'The Marlowe Coin has created quite a stir in particular circles. I understand half of Thames House have wagers on him or are pooling together coins to bid for more amusing ways for him to fight.'

Trix stepped forward, close enough now to see the lined face clearly in the dim light filtering through the ruined church windows.

'We need someone who can pass as a wealthy investor. Someone with enough legitimacy to gain top-tier access to a private club event.'

'The gladiatorial entertainment at The Labyrinth,' McKellan nodded. 'I've heard whispers.'

'Marshall Kirk was going to do it, but he's too recognisable now–they've seen him. We have a copper who wants to do it, but ...'

'They'll be on record. And I'm guessing Miss Kirk, or your pet gangster Maguire aren't options. Your CIA friend? The sexy one with the identity issue?'

'Hates Steele, and visibly so, which means I can't see that working,' Trix shrugged. 'We need someone whose presence wouldn't raise suspicion, who could lie away how they gained enough money, and is maybe there for a secret benefactor.'

'And you thought of me?' McKellan raised an eyebrow. 'I'm flattered, but I'd hardly call myself inconspicuous in those circles.'

'Not you,' Trix shook her head. 'Someone you might provide. Someone with the right credentials, the right bearing–someone Steele and The Broker wouldn't immediately connect to us.'

McKellan studied her for a long moment, his expression unreadable.

'I might have someone suitable,' he admitted eventually. 'But you won't like it.'

'I don't need to like it. I just need it to work.'

'Even if the person has a ... complicated history with Marlowe?'

Trix's expression hardened.

'Sir Walter, Marlowe is currently being held in a facility where wealthy elites are paying to watch him fight to the death with hand tools and garden implements. We're well past being picky about our allies.'

McKellan nodded, apparently satisfied with her answer.

He turned slightly towards the Jaguar and made a small gesture with his hand.

The rear door opened immediately.

'I guessed this was what you wanted after Marlowe freed Kirk,' he said. 'Yes, we watch the same feeds you do. And I realised after your call that this had to be your Hail Mary.'

Trix felt her body go rigid, hand instinctively moving towards the concealed weapon at her waist as a man emerged from the back seat, his movements fluid and controlled. He was average height, compact build, and wearing an immaculately tailored suit that couldn't quite disguise the athletic frame beneath. He was a man of Indian ancestry, thick black eyebrows over watchful brown eyes that missed nothing as they scanned the garden perimeter before settling on Trix.

The faint scar on his shoulder and neck–visible just above his collar–seemed to catch the moonlight. Somewhere beneath that expensive shirt lay another scar, once a black-light Orchid tattoo marking him as a member.

'Hey Trix,' Vic Saeed smiled. 'Long time, no see. So, who do I have to kill?'

19

DOUBLE JEOPARDY

THE LABYRINTH CLUB MAINTAINED AN AESTHETIC OF OLD wealth rather than new money, Vic Saeed noted as he adjusted his Brioni suit cuffs, stepping from the taxi, the doorman already moving to greet him. The rain from earlier had stopped, but the pavement still glistened under the streetlights, and Saeed's handmade shoes left momentary imprints as he approached the entrance.

Marshall Kirk had needed to play dress up to look this good, he thought to himself. *I do it naturally.*

'Good evening, sir.' The doorman's assessment was swift but thorough–the suit, the watch, the bearing. All acceptable. 'Do you have membership?'

'I'm a guest,' Saeed produced the encrypted access code Hargrove had supplied, displayed on a phone that itself cost more than most people's monthly salary. 'For tonight's special event.'

He paused.

'It's two in the morning,' he continued. 'At what point does "tonight" become "this morning"?'

The doorman ignored the question as he examined the phone, nodded, and opened the door with a small amount of deference.

'Welcome to The Labyrinth, sir. Reception will assist you further.'

Saeed paused, opening his jacket and removing, with two fingers, a Kershaw Shallot folding knife.

'This is not a weapon,' he explained as he passed the knife across. 'This is something I'd like passed into the game. I expect to pay for the privilege, of course.'

The doorman checked it over, then passed it back.

'I'll let them know,' he said, and Saeed noticed the utter lack of care in the weapon. *Obviously a blade meant nothing in here. Good to know.*

Inside, the understated opulence continued: oak panelling, discreet lighting, staff that appeared when needed and vanished when not. The receptionist, an elegant woman in her thirties, scanned Saeed's credentials.

'Ah, Mister Reynolds. We've been expecting you,' she said as she handed him a small black card embossed with gold lettering. 'This will grant you access to the premium viewing area for tonight's entertainment.'

'Reynolds is an alias,' Saeed replied, taking the card. 'I prefer my own name. Vikram Saeed.'

The receptionist's expression remained professional, but something flickered in her eyes–recognition, perhaps, or maybe confirmation.

'Of course, Mister Saeed. We were informed you might use various identities. Would you care for refreshments before the event begins?'

'The most expensive malt whisky you have. Neat.' Saeed pocketed the card, his eyes already scanning the surroundings, noting camera positions, staff movement patterns, exit routes.

'Right away.'

'I understand the previous bout was quite ... spectacular.' Saeed maintained the confident bearing of someone accustomed to exclusive environments. 'I hope tonight's entertainment proves equally engaging, and worth staying up for.'

'I believe you'll find it most satisfying, sir.' The receptionist gestured towards a side corridor. 'The premium viewing area is through there. Your drink will be brought to you immediately.'

Saeed followed the indicated route, entering a lounge area where perhaps two dozen people mingled. The quiet hum of conversation, the occasional clink of glasses–wealthy speculators discussing their investments with the detached interest of those who wouldn't miss the money if it disappeared.

A server approached with his whisky–a Macallan 25, served in crystal without him having to specify; the attention to detail was impressive. Saeed took the glass and moved towards a quieter corner, sipping his drink, definitely worth the two grand a bottle price tag, before activating his communications device, hidden deep in the ear and undetectable to standard security scans.

'In position,' he murmured, the sound barely audible even to himself. 'Premium access secured.'

Trix's voice came through, equally soft.

'Any sign of Marlowe?'

'Not yet. Preparations for the next event appear to be underway. Coin value displays showing just shy of seven dollars and climbing.'

'The extraction window opens in thirty-five minutes.

Morris and Wilcott are in position outside if needed, disguised as maintenance staff near the east service corridor.'

Saeed took a careful sip of his drink, maintaining the appearance of a wealthy investor sampling the club's offerings.

'Security is comprehensive, but standard. Four-man teams, rotational patterns, communications on closed circuit.'

'The Broker?'

'Private viewing booth overlooking the arena. Limited access, dedicated security.'

'I'm working through their network architecture now,' Trix replied. 'Multiple nodes, all routing back to the external source, probably a server at Tower Bridge, judging from the traffic. Not accessible from current position.'

'Plan B then,' Saeed murmured behind his glass. 'I'll need to get a message to Marlowe directly.'

'Too risky,' Trix replied. 'Not including the fact that he'll probably kill you the moment he sees you.'

'He wishes,' Saeed smiled as he raised a glass to someone across the room, who'd raised their own to him. They looked familiar and Saeed wondered if he'd worked with them in the past. After all, over the years many of his "employers" had always been in the shadows.

'You screw us, Vic, and I'll make sure you're left with nothing,' Trix said, her voice cold. 'I don't trust you, no matter what McKellan says.'

'McKellan understands talent.' Saeed leant back on a chair now, cricking his neck as he did so. 'And while he has my balls in a box, I'm forced to work for him–while Robertson believes I work for *him*.'

'And Steele.'

Vic Saeed took a mouthful of drink to stop a curse word escaping.

'Steele believes he owns me, but I was never one of his gang. No matter what happened in California.'

'I'll believe that when you prove yourself.'

'I don't need to prove myself to anyone, Preston. I'm doing this because I was ordered to. And, being honest, Marlowe's not as much of a prick as people make him out to be.'

'You might think that about him, but I'll promise you he doesn't feel the same warm fuzzies,' Trix replied.

'No choice. He needs to know about Volkov's discovery,' Saeed finished his drink, setting the glass aside. 'I'll improvise, and if things kick off, it'll make my cover look even better.'

'Proceed with caution,' Trix replied. 'Initial breach in twenty-eight minutes.'

Saeed deactivated his comms as a tall man in his fifties approached–Hargrove, The Broker's right hand.

'Mister Saeed,' Hargrove greeted him. 'Welcome to The Labyrinth. I understand you've acquired a significant position in our venture recently.'

'I recognise opportunity when I see it.' Saeed met the man's assessing gaze without hesitation. 'The scarcity mechanism is particularly elegant.'

'You have experience with cryptocurrency?'

'Among other things.' Saeed allowed his expression to suggest connections better left unmentioned. 'I've found that diversification is essential in uncertain times. Especially since the ... disruptions in certain circles.'

It was a calculated reference to Orchid's fragmentation, something Saeed knew was on The Broker's, and by default

Hargrove's radar. Hargrove's slight narrowing of the eyes confirmed he'd caught it.

'Indeed. Many established networks have experienced ... restructuring.' Hargrove gestured towards a door at the far end of the lounge. 'The premium viewing area is through there. Tonight's format should be particularly engaging. If you wish for a closer perspective, front row access can be arranged for investors of your calibre.'

'I'm not a high spender like some of the others here.'

'True, but you have connections that are far more valuable.'

'You mean Robertson?' Saeed nodded. 'He sends his apologies. He can't really be seen attending something like this. I hope you understand.'

'We do. And the invite is still there for you.'

'I'd appreciate that. I've always believed in being within a close proximity to my investments.'

'I understand you have a gift?'

Saeed pulled out the Kershaw folding knife.

'Last time I saw Marlowe I was cut with this, a Kershaw Ken Onion 1840 shallot,' he said carefully. 'I offer a hundred thousand Marlowe Coins as a Joker to call, in a potentially new rule.'

'That's over half a million dollars currently,' Hargrove replied. 'It'd have to be an impressive rule.'

Saeed turned the knife over in his hands.

'When I call my Joker, I want whatever Marlowe's using taken, and I want to give this to him personally,' he said. 'It's a three-and-a-half-inch blade, so pretty useless against a bigger weapon, and the locking mechanism can cause issues.'

Hargrove took the blade, opening it up, examining it, before closing it and passing the blade back.

'We'll take that bid,' he said. 'After all, by the time you call the rule, we could be closer to a million.'

'If it is, I might change my own mind,' Saeed smiled as he returned the folding blade into his pocket. As Hargrove moved away, he reactivated his comms.

'Front row access secured. Direct contact may be possible.'

'Understood,' Trix replied. 'But priority remains system infiltration. I'm detecting unusual activity in their network– Ciaran's implementing additional security protocols. He may suspect something.'

'Time frame?'

'Accelerating breach to coincide with bout commencement. Be prepared for earlier extraction if necessary.'

Saeed made a subtle sound of acknowledgment, then moved towards the premium viewing area. Once through the door, he was shown to a front-row seat directly against the transparent barrier, providing an unobstructed view of the arena below.

He withdrew a leather notebook from his inner pocket– the kind of accessory a wealthy investor might use to track his holdings. Inside, and without anyone noticing he carefully tore a small page and folded it precisely, tucking it into the folding part of the blade. The message on it was concise but critical:

Gregorovich not in Ayrshire. Steele using info as test. McKellan checking real location. Trix says you're an idiot.

The last part was so Marlowe knew he was working with the angels. Now he just needed the right moment to pass it to Marlowe without alerting security, or the cameras constantly scanning the arena–or ending with Marlowe ramming a knife into the side of his throat.

As the house lights dimmed, signalling the imminent start of the event, Saeed calculated angles, timing, the precise opportunity that would present itself during the chaos of combat.

One chance–that's all he'd have.

But then he'd done far more over the years with one chance.

MARLOWE EXAMINED THE ARRAY OF WEAPONS LAID OUT BEFORE him. No chain this time, no brass knuckles; just an assortment of bladed implements that spoke to The Broker's refined understanding of audience preferences. The bounty had been halved, now sitting at one and a half million, while the coin value had surged to seven dollars and climbing.

'Choose one,' the white-coated attendant instructed.

'Just one?' Marlowe raised an eyebrow. 'Generous.'

'New format,' the man replied without emotion. 'This round has ... different parameters.'

Marlowe selected a Cold Steel SRK combat knife, testing its balance. Not his first choice, but it would serve its purpose–assuming he had the opportunity to use it before being overwhelmed.

'Different parameters,' Marlowe repeated. 'You mean two opponents.'

The attendant's expression flickered–surprise quickly masked.

'You've been briefed?'

'No. Just observant.' He'd motioned over to the double preparation stations and the additional medical equipment.

'Let me guess. The Broker wants to avoid another reduction in the bounty.'

'I'm not authorised to discuss the format.'

'Of course not,' Marlowe replied, slipping the knife into the sheath he'd attached to his belt. 'Lead on, then.'

The corridor leading to the arena felt longer than before, the murmur of the crowd already audible through the thick walls. After the unexpected outcome of his bout with Volkov, the audience would be expectant, hungry for escalation, even at this time of night. The Broker would need to deliver.

Marlowe intended to stop that.

As he approached the entrance, Marlowe took stock of his physical condition. The medical team had patched him up effectively after the Volkov fight, and currently he had nothing that would significantly impair his movement, but his real problem would be stamina. Fighting two opponents simultaneously would drain his reserves quickly, and he'd only had a few hours break since Volkov, and no food or drink during that time.

The arena had been subtly reconfigured since his last appearance. The transparent barriers remained, but the floor had been modified–sections now at slightly different elevations, creating uneven terrain that would favour the agile over the strong. The audience was larger too, the premium viewing section packed with investors eager to protect their stakes in the Marlowe Coin. Or maybe the more public evening events in London had ended now, allowing them to sneak out "after hours" for a little dogfight or two.

Marlowe scanned the VIP area briefly, noting the presence of several new faces–including one that shouldn't have been there at all. Vic Saeed sat in the front row, immaculate in a tailored suit, looking for all the world like a wealthy investor enjoying an exclusive entertainment.

Prick.

Marlowe instinctively thought back to the last time he'd seen Saeed, bleeding from the wrist, the shoulder and a vicious blow to the temple.

He liked him better that way.

Their eyes met briefly–no recognition displayed, nothing to suggest they were anything but strangers, yet Marlowe felt the calculated intent behind Saeed's presence.

Something was coming. But what? He'd heard rumours McKellan had turned Saeed while he was in holding, and his Whitehall job for Robertson was nothing more than a smokescreen. *Was he here for McKellan? Or had Robertson sent him to report back?*

The Broker's voice came over the sound system.

'Distinguished guests, welcome to our second presentation. Following the unprecedented conclusion of our first event, we've enhanced tonight's experience to ensure maximum entertainment value.'

Marlowe's opponents entered from the opposite side of the arena–a matched pair that moved with the synchronised precision of partners who had trained together for years. Both were tall, strikingly similar in appearance–dark skin gleaming under the arena lights, shaved heads and lean, powerful physiques that reminded Marlowe of Olympic sprinters. The woman wore fitted combat gear that emphasised her statuesque frame, while the man displayed ritual scarification across his shoulders and chest. Both carried identical traditional Liberian fighting knives–long, dagger-pointed blades that looked a lot like a Fairbairn-Sykes, designed for maximum damage at close quarters.

'Tonight,' The Broker continued, 'we present a unique challenge. Thomas Marlowe versus The Shadows–Nyala and Abasi Konate, specialists in coordinated elimination from our partners in Liberia.'

A murmur of approval rippled through the audience. Marlowe retained his neutral expression while assessing his opponents. West African special forces training, most likely, combined with traditional combat disciplines. The woman–Nyala–maintained eye contact as they approached, while her brother scanned constantly, seeking tactical advantages in the modified arena. She looked like Grace Jones, and he wondered if this was the woman who'd originally spoken to Doctor Chopra, pretending to be MI5, who'd planted the tracker in his tooth.

Maybe this was their reward for good work–or their punishment for not keeping the tooth in play, perhaps.

Either way, it was two on one with two fresh players, with knives they'd probably grown up with, while Marlowe was battered, tired, and being watched by one of his most hated rivals.

Marlowe hated to admit it; he was *screwed*.

20

FIGHT NIGHT

'The parameters for tonight's event are straightforward,' The Broker explained as Marlowe stretched his shoulders, trying to warm up before the fight started. 'Combat continues until one side can no longer continue. Investment options remain available through your personal interfaces.'

The display screens showed the real-time Marlowe Coin value: almost eight dollars and rising steadily. The mechanism was working perfectly—billions in virtual wealth created from scarcity.

'Begin,' The Broker announced without ceremony.

The Shadows moved immediately, splitting to approach from different angles. No wasted motion, no posturing—pure calculated efficiency. Marlowe stepped back, seeking higher ground on one of the elevated platforms to limit their ability to flank him.

Nyala reached him first, her blade flashing in a tight arc aimed at his midsection. Marlowe countered, his unfamiliar blade meeting hers with a metallic ring that echoed through the arena. Abasi attacked from the left, forcing Marlowe to disengage and move laterally.

Their coordination was impressive–one always pressing, the other recovering, constant pressure applied from multiple angles. Marlowe found himself perpetually responding rather than initiating, using precious energy to maintain a defensive position.

'You chose wrong,' Nyala said during a brief engagement, her accent carrying the rhythms of West Africa but her English eerily precise. 'You should have taken a dagger, like us.'

'I'll keep mine, thanks. Gives me a bit of reach against yours,' Marlowe replied, deflecting another strike.

'Not against two of us,' Abasi added, closing again.

Marlowe pivoted, using one of the level changes to create separation, then launched a counterattack aimed at Abasi's lead shoulder. The blade connected, drawing first blood, but the victory was momentary; Nyala exploited the opening to score a shallow cut across Marlowe's back.

On the displays, betting odds shifted as investors responded to the exchange. Money flowed through the digital interfaces as they purchased influence options, placed wagers on outcomes, timing, methods.

Marlowe retreated again, using the arena's geography to force his opponents to adjust their approach. The Shadows adapted quickly, modifying their formation to maintain pressure from opposing directions.

Professional. Dangerous. Potentially fatal.

As he manoeuvred for position, Marlowe caught sight of Vic Saeed in the VIP section; the man had risen from his seat, approaching the barrier as if seeking a better view of the action. Not unusual–other spectators were doing the same during particularly intense exchanges.

'You're bleeding already,' Abasi observed, circling left while his sister moved right. 'More than from Volkov.'

'Volkov was making it personal, playing with his food,' Marlowe replied, scanning for options. The elevated sections created both opportunities and hazards, better visibility at the cost of restricted movement. What he needed was a way to separate the Shadows, break their coordinated attack pattern.

The display screens flashed with a new announcement.

PREMIUM ACCESS ACTIVATED: ENVIRONMENT MODIFICATION.

The Broker's voice returned.

'Our Platinum tier has triggered a special condition. Arena lighting reduced to thirty per cent for two minutes.'

The illumination dimmed significantly, plunging the combat area into partial darkness. The audience murmured with anticipation; this introduced a new variable, advantage shifting unpredictably. The Shadows hesitated momentarily, recalibrating for the changed conditions.

Marlowe didn't wait. He moved immediately towards Abasi, the more physically imposing of the pair, recognising that reduced visibility would impact their coordinated tactics. The man reacted quickly despite the darkness, bringing his machete up in a defensive position, but Marlowe had anticipated this, feinting high before striking low, catching Abasi's thigh with a slash that elicited a grunt of pain.

Nyala responded instantly, moving to support her brother, but the darkness complicated their usual synchronisation. Marlowe used the momentum of his attack to carry him past Abasi, then changed direction suddenly, doubling back towards the arena wall where the transparent barrier met one of the elevated platforms.

A message tone sounded, and one of the display screens updated with new betting metrics.

UNEXPECTED DEVELOPMENT: ODDS RECALCULATING.

The audience was responding to his change in tactics, recognising that he was attempting to use the environment rather than directly confront the superior numbers. Money shifted as new wagers were placed, predictions adjusted.

Marlowe reached the barrier wall, directly in front of where Saeed now stood, apparently caught up in the spectacle like the other investors. As Marlowe pressed his back against the wall, he glanced up briefly, meeting Saeed's eyes for a fraction of a second. Then he launched himself towards the approaching Shadows, an aggressive move that caught the audience by surprise. But, as he passed near the barrier, he stumbled slightly. It was an accidental move, distracted by Saeed, but it seemed to be a catalyst for Saeed now raised his hand and shouted.

'I call my Joker!' he cried out.

At this, the lights lit back up, and the screens all changed to the face of a playing card Joker.

JOKER PLAYED: COST: 100,000 MARLOWE COINS

The VIP guests seemed confused, probably annoyed they hadn't thought of such a rule, especially as the amount of coins was now worth just shy of nine hundred thousand dollars. Guards entered from the side, motioning for the Shadows to step back, approaching Marlowe.

'Blade,' one ordered, holding out his hand. Marlowe went to argue but noticed the tasers in the other hand. He looked back to Saeed to see him moving to the entrance of the arena, reaching into his jacket.

What the hell was going on?

Marlowe handed off the combat blade as Vic Saeed now entered the arena arrogantly, walking over to the guards and holding up what looked to be a folding knife.

'Marlowe once used this very blade to fight me in America,' he cried out, holding it up. 'It's a Kershaw Ken Onion 1840 shallot, with a three-and-a-half-inch blade. Which is shorter than his current weapon.'

He stared at Marlowe.

'I return it to him, with the command that he uses it for the remainder of this fight.'

The crowd liked this new rule; the blade was a definite drop from the one he'd used, and Marlowe reluctantly took it, his mind whirling.

He knew of the blade–but he'd never used it. The Kershaw Ken Onion shallot had been the blade Vic Saeed had passed *Brad Haynes,* not Marlowe, on a flight from Seville to California, one that, once Brad had realised Vic Saeed was playing them, had been stabbed back into his shoulder during a vicious fight in the offices of Spencer Neville the Third.

So why the lie?

Saeed moved close to Marlowe now.

'I hope it fails you and you die,' he said loudly, winking at the cameras as he continued. 'You might want to check the locking mechanism. It's temperamental.'

'I need a moment to check the blade,' Marlowe shouted out. 'This guy wants me dead. If the knife's doctored, then I'm at a disadvantage.'

'Should we allow Marlowe a moment to examine his new weapon?' The Broker's voice asked as Saeed and the guards left. 'Bid now!'

The screens above flashed and Marlowe saw he'd been given thirty seconds to examine the blade by a factor of fifty-two to forty-eight per cent. It was good for him, but also good for The Broker–and by default Steele, as more coins were now in his pocket.

The lights began to gradually return to half illumination as across the arena The Shadows regrouped, adapting their formation to account for Abasi's injury. Marlowe retreated to a higher platform, using the brief respite to examine the blade's locking mechanism while catching his breath. He saw the hidden paper and quickly fell to a knee, as if winded, taking a couple of seconds to read the note, absorbing the information in an instant, before he crushed the paper in his fist, faking a cough to place the small ball in his mouth and swallowing it down as he stared back at his weapon.

So, Saeed was an ally, then. Shame he had to screw Marlowe over to pass the message across.

Sighing, he returned his full attention to the fight. But the dynamics had changed–not just of the combat, but of his entire understanding of the situation.

The Shadows were advancing again, Nyala now taking the lead, her movements economical, while her brother provided support from a more defensive position. Marlowe met them halfway, engaging Nyala directly while maintaining awareness of Abasi's position.

Marlowe now had to be absolutely precise to stay alive,

relying on careful parrying; the Kershaw was eight inches locked open and had excellent balance, but he'd lost two inches of fighting range. They clashed repeatedly, neither gaining decisive advantage. Marlowe felt a sting as Nyala's dagger caught his forearm, adding another shallow wound to his collection. He countered with a strike from his Kershaw, the folding blade's serrated edge barely missing her throat before grazing her shoulder.

The crowd responded to each exchange, digital assets flowing as they bet on outcomes, purchased influence options, speculated on resolution timeframes. The Marlowe Coin value continued its steady climb.

On the other side of the barrier, Saeed had returned to his seat, appearing to study the betting interface embedded in his chair arm. His hand moved almost casually to his ear, and Marlowe guessed he was activating a communication device.

Trix.

Saeed's intervention had altered the equation. But first, Marlowe needed to survive long enough to escape.

The Shadows pressed their advantage, executing a pincer movement designed to limit his options for evasion. Marlowe countered with a risky manoeuvre, dropping to one knee before launching himself forward in a rolling dive that carried him between them, coming up behind their position, the Kershaw folding knife clutched in reverse grip for greater slashing power and better defensive capability.

The audience responded with appreciative sounds–the dramatic movement was providing excellent entertainment value. The displays showed more rapidly shifting betting patterns as investors responded to the unexpected tactic.

But something had changed in the arena's atmosphere;

subtle, but definite. The steady hum of the ventilation system had altered pitch, and there was a faint odour that hadn't been present before–something metallic, chemical.

The Shadows noticed it too, exchanging a brief glance before returning their attention to Marlowe. They adjusted their approach, movements becoming more urgent, as if sensing a change in parameters they hadn't been briefed on.

In the premium section, Saeed had risen once more, moving with casual purpose towards a staff member stationed near the service corridor. He appeared to be requesting something–another drink perhaps, or information about the betting system. Nothing to draw undue attention, but Marlowe recognised the calculated positioning.

A message tone sounded through the arena speakers.

SYSTEM DISRUPTION DETECTED: STANDBY FOR RECALIBRATION.

The displays flickered momentarily, digital metrics disappearing before reappearing with altered values. The Marlowe Coin price feed showed sudden volatility–nine dollars to eleven dollars, and then back down to eight dollars in rapid succession.

Trix was making her move.

The Shadows pressed their attack with renewed intensity, perhaps recognising that something unexpected was developing. Marlowe found himself forced into a purely defensive posture, the compact Kershaw proving more manoeuvrable in close quarters than he'd expected as he parried Nyala, conserving energy while watching for whatever was about to happen.

It came in the form of a momentary power fluctuation–

the arena lights dimming for precisely three seconds before returning to full illumination. To the audience, it would appear to be part of the same system disruption affecting the displays.

To Marlowe, it was the countdown.

Saeed, meanwhile, had continued to engage the staff member in conversation, angrily gesticulating, gradually manoeuvring them both towards the service door. As security personnel responded to alerts in their earpieces, and audience members now reacted to the strangely metallic smell–likely nothing more than filings heating up, but enough to cause concern as to some kind of bioweapon attack–Saeed appeared to become agitated, gesturing towards the digital display where the Marlowe Coin value continued to fluctuate wildly, before pointing over at Marlowe.

The distraction was perfectly timed; security's attention was now divided between the arena, the system disruptions, and an apparently irate high-value investor demanding explanations.

A second power fluctuation occurred, longer this time, accompanied by a low-pitched tone from the sound system. Additional security personnel moved towards the premium section, responding to the developing situation.

On the screen, a new message appeared, as something burnt out in the back of it, adding a second, vicious odour to the room.

$£*K YOU CIARAN *** $£*K YOU CIARAN

As the three words scrolled continually across the screen, The Broker's voice came over the speakers, the usual calm professionalism now edged with something else.

'Ladies and gentlemen, we're experiencing technical difficulties. Please remain in your seats while our staff resolves the issue. The fight is momentarily paused, while our tech department work out what's happening.'

Marlowe smiled. By "tech department", The Broker meant Ciaran, who by now had realised that somehow Trix had entered the arena's security. But how? Anything brought in would have been examined and taken away–

The Kershaw.

Oh, you clever, devious bloody woman. You stuck your cloner into the weapon I'm using. A weapon that sat in Saeed's pocket until the moment you told him you were done.

The Shadows hesitated momentarily, uncertain whether to continue their attack or await further instructions. Marlowe didn't hesitate–he launched himself towards the nearest elevated platform, flicking the Kershaw closed with practised ease before biting it, freeing his hands for climbing as he used the height to gain visibility.

From this vantage point, he could see Saeed in heated argument with three security personnel, his back strategically positioned to block their view of the service door behind him. As Marlowe watched, the door opened slightly, revealing maintenance uniforms in position–the extraction team, there to return him to his cell.

The arena lights flickered again, this time accompanied by a series of sharp pops from the sound system; feedback loops created by deliberate signal interference, and the audience's attention was now divided between the continuing combat and the technical disruptions affecting their viewing experience.

The Shadows recovered from their momentary uncertainty, resuming their attack, with Abasi taking a more aggressive role despite his injury. They reached the base of Marlowe's platform, splitting to approach from both sides.

Marlowe waited until the last possible moment, then launched himself from the platform; not towards either of the Shadows, but towards the transparent barrier near where Saeed was creating his distraction. He hit the barrier with controlled force, using the impact to direct his momentum along the wall rather than rebounding back into the arena.

The audience members nearest the barrier drew back in surprise as Marlowe moved rapidly along the perimeter, heading towards the service door that was now standing partially open. The Shadows pursued, but the arena's configuration slowed their approach, giving Marlowe precious seconds.

Saeed's voice rose above the growing confusion, demanding compensation for investment losses, physically placing himself between security and Marlowe's approach path. The perfect cover, wealthy entitlement creating chaos at the critical moment—

Abasi moved in front, his dagger raised.

'No—' he started, but as he spoke, a final power fluctuation plunged the arena into complete darkness for five critical seconds. In that moment of blindness, Marlowe flicked open and then slammed his Kershaw knife into Abasi's chest, one quick strike perfectly aimed between the ribs to sever the aorta, letting the assassin fall lifeless to the side as Marlowe reached the service door, slipping through the opening and into the corridor beyond. When emergency lighting activated, he had vanished from the combat area entirely. Behind him, he could hear The Broker's voice attempting to restore order, Nyala's screams of anger, security alerts sounding throughout the facility, and the confused reactions of the audience.

An extraction window had opened, and Thomas Marlowe had stepped through it.

Behind him, in the arena, Vic Saeed was being forcibly removed by security, protesting loudly about his treatment and threatening legal action. No one noticed the slight smile that crossed his face as he was escorted from the premises–his mission accomplished, his cover maintained.

The game had changed.

21

INTERVIEW WITH A BROKER

MARLOWE WAS TIRED, BEATEN AND BLOODY, BUT HE WAS FREE for the moment. Although he was still trapped within the basement area of the Labyrinth club, he'd been far more injured and in far worse predicaments and had survived; besides, he had an ace up his sleeve that, if it came to it, he could play first.

However, he needed to get out.

The obvious answer was to find one of the security or service exits, but security would immediately look there. He knew that this would be nothing more than a blip as far as The Broker and Steele were concerned; the hunt would return, and the coins would be back on Marlowe's head, wherever he was.

However, now the cost was less than a million with Abasi dead in the arena, so people might not be so sure to come after him.

Again, Marlowe felt no sadness at his death–it had been self-defence. But he also knew that he now had a new enemy in Nyala, who would stop at nothing to kill him.

That, however, was a problem for another day.

Marlowe knew he could have tried the laundry chute escape that Marshall and Morris had done earlier, but that would have been blocked. Instead, he went an alternate route. The first door he reached, however, was already blocked by a security guard–broad, solid, and with his weapon–a suppressed Glock–already drawn and levelled at Marlowe's chest.

His eyes narrowed, finger tightening on the trigger.

'Don't mo—'

Marlowe ignored the command and lunged. His shoulder crashed into the man's sternum, driving him back into the corridor. The guard staggered but stayed upright, however, twisting his body to slam Marlowe against the wall, the suppressed Glock jamming into his ribs.

Marlowe grabbed the guard's wrist, forcing the muzzle away as it fired with a muted *phut* noise, and they grappled, the guard's forearm grinding into Marlowe's throat, cutting off air.

Pain flared through his already bruised ribs as Marlowe's hand found the Kershaw in his pocket. He flicked the blade open and with a swift movement he slashed it across the guard's arm. Flesh parted; the man grunted and jerked back. Marlowe ripped the Glock free from his now blood-slicked grip, and as the guard came at him again–fast, reckless–Marlowe pulled the trigger; one suppressed shot to the chest.

The guard jerked, breath catching, eyes wide with shock. He staggered back, collapsed heavily against the wall, then slid to the floor, dead.

Marlowe crouched, wiping blood from the Kershaw and his hands on the man's shirt. He ejected the Glock 17's magazine and counted fourteen rounds before he slipped it back home. Checking the dead guard, he pocketed a loaded spare magazine, a key card, and a collapsible baton before pulling on the black security jacket. It was long in the shoulders, but it would have to do–at least it hid the bloodstained shirt he'd been wearing in the arena.

He stepped over the body without hesitation, rolling his shoulders as he moved deeper into the basement area. He was annoyed at the lack of a radio; it would have been good to know what was going on, but he needn't have worried. The moment he opened the door to head through to the upper level, he found himself facing The Gravedigger.

'What's your plan, Marlowe?' The Gravedigger asked, gun in hand.

'They'll look for me outside,' Marlowe replied. 'I'm heading to the office.'

'Do you want company?'

Marlowe considered the question briefly and then shook his head.

'I'm hunting a chat with The Broker.'

The Gravedigger smiled.

'In that case, I'll lead the guards away and suggest to The Broker that he visits his office—'

Marlowe grabbed his arm as he turned.

'Did Tessa get out okay?'

'Tessa did everything you asked,' The Gravedigger nodded. 'She probably won't be allowed back in.'

'Gregorovich?'

'Not in Scotland, but he's alive,' The Gravedigger continued. 'My own sources have pointed out that St John Steele has recently brought somebody under great security to a holding cell he's had made near Tower Bridge, in what used to be the Shad Thames Sub-Basements, near Butler's Wharf.'

Marlowe knew the location.

'South side of the Thames? You think that's where he is?'

'If I'm wrong, we'd find out quicker than if he were in Scotland,' The Gravedigger replied, while above them, sirens wailed. 'Go. I've got this.'

'At what point does our debt end?' Marlowe asked.

The Gravedigger smiled.

'When you allow me to kill Steele,' he said. 'Then all bets are off.'

He looked down the corridor.

'I think by now I've already paid off my life debt to you.'

Marlowe said nothing, continuing up the corridor quickly as behind him he could hear The Gravedigger shouting out that he'd seen Marlowe going to the left–the other direction. As he ran, Marlowe examined the Kershaw knife. He'd been correct–this wasn't the one originally used by Brad Haynes, and the handle had been carbon printed, but it was a quick job, the grip itself rough and unfinished.

Why carbon print a new handle?

Pulling at it with his nails, he found that it popped off, revealing a selection of small electrical wiring; this was likely what Trix had used to hack into the system. There were a couple of long, thin pins that had held it together, and Marlowe quickly took them out, bending them into a crude lock pick as he arrived at the door to The Broker's office. Quickly, he attacked the lock with them, opening and shutting it behind him as he entered and checked the drawers and side cupboards, looking for something he could use as a weapon.

In a mid-level drawer under a shelf, one he hadn't looked in earlier, he found a Glock 17 with a full round. *Excellent.* Marlowe placed it into his waistband, then sat behind the desk and waited. And, as he did so, he considered The Gravedigger's words.

The file in the drawer had been a setup. But for who? Words spoken earlier by Viktor Orlovsky echoed in his mind.

'The Broker probably doesn't even know Steele took his mentor, so if you find Gregorovich's location in Steele's files ...'

That was where Marlowe had been led to the office, literally aimed at the trap Steele had set.

'I was invited. As investor in Marlowe Coin.'

Now Marlowe wondered whether Viktor had been on his side at all.

There'd be a reckoning after this was over.

If he even survived, of course.

It was only a matter of minutes before the door opened and The Broker walked in, curious, shutting it behind him.

'I could make one call right now and you'd be ended,' he said.

'Yes, but then you'd lose all your nice fake money, because it looks like it's tanking,' Marlowe smiled. 'I do hope you're getting out while the money's high enough.'

'It'll recover,' The Broker replied, 'We'll adjust again. It seems we have some new rules you'd like to discuss?'

'Actually, I was thinking of a hostile takeover,' Marlowe replied.

'You want to take this over?'

'No,' Marlowe shook his head. 'I want *you* to take this over. I know that you're being forced to do this–that Steele has information on Gregorovich, keeping you in line ... but he'll never give it to you.'

The Broker waited.

'And how do you know about—'

'Come on, Raymond, I know everything,' Marlowe interrupted. 'I also know that in this desk drawer here, Steele's left you a little gift–something that, if you act upon it, will immediately show that you've gone against his wishes. He's wired it to let him know when it's been read, and he's testing you.'

'Gregorovich is dead.'

'Is he?' Marlowe asked, 'or is he off underneath Butler's Wharf, held by Steele while you become a good boy and do what he says?'

The Broker said nothing for a moment, staring at Marlowe, and then eventually ... he nodded.

'Interesting. What's your suggestion?'

'You find me a way to get out and I'll take down Steele,' Marlowe suggested. 'I'll lead a team to extract Gregorovich, and once he's in your possession, you can do whatever you want. Burn Steele, dump him, anything that leaves him open for me–or, rather Peter Jericho.'

'The Gravedigger? Curiouser and curiouser. And you want me to believe that after all this, you're happy to let me walk?'

'I don't want you,' Marlowe shifted in the seat, aches and pains starting to make their presence known from the vicious fighting he'd just escaped. 'As much as you're a sadist–and I really should have a chat with a therapist at some point if I was you–you're just a middleman and you're being forced to do the same dance as everybody else. Although I will say... skinning alive?'

'Not my choice,' The Broker replied. 'Steele wanted it. Said the visuals would increase bids.'

'And that's the only reason you still breathe,' Marlowe growled. 'Steele's running the game here, and I want him more than I want you.'

The Broker considered this.

'You let Volkov live.'

'To hunt Gregorovich, but he's going the wrong way,' Marlowe replied. 'Set up by Steele and Orlovsky.'

'Viktor too? That's interesting.' The Broker looked towards the door, and Marlowe wondered briefly whether all of this had been in vain, and that The Broker was too institutionalised into Steele's service now to even consider moving away.

'If you escape,' The Broker said, 'the hunt will still continue.'

'I understand,' Marlowe nodded. 'But the alternative is to stay here and keep fighting to the death until someone eventually wins. I don't really see how that's going to work.'

The Broker considered this.

'We have to announce that your escape was created by Volkov,' he said, rubbing at his chin, working through the angles already. 'That you didn't kill him and that he helped you.'

Marlowe watched carefully. Everything The Broker said was truthful. Volkov *had* faked his death, although he hadn't been an active part of Marlowe's rescue.

'This means the hit would now go back to one and a half million,' The Broker carried on. 'If you stayed here, if we were to capture you and place you back in the game, I don't know how useful you would be to me.'

'Tell people Orlovsky was working with Volkov. It might not be true, but there's enough plausible deniability there to screw around.'

'True. And he did train Tessa Kirk, after all.' The Broker bit at his lip and Marlowe could see genuine concern on his face, likely wondering whether this was a good idea or not.

'I can take the hits,' Marlowe said. 'And one and a half million is still better than twelve. It'll thin the market out—'

'You don't understand,' The Broker snapped. 'They'll go for everyone connected to you now. Morris and Marshall, that was nothing; whoever helps you in any way now becomes part of the game. It's the only way I could make this work.'

'They were anyway.'

'Not to the level they are now. Before, it was only worth chasing when there was something juicy. Now? It's scorched earth tactics.'

Marlowe understood exactly what The Broker was saying; if he was to carry on the way he was going, then Marshall, Tessa, Trix–none of them could be used. And, as for Morris, well, the detective hadn't even been a friend, just some poor sod Marlowe had used and almost killed in the process.

'Done,' Marlowe nodded, rising. 'You get me out of here, I'll get you Gregorovich and I'll kill Steele. Once that's done—'

'Once that's done, Mister Marlowe, the hit will be removed from your head, and the coin will be stopped.'

Marlowe gave a small smile.

'No offence, Raymond ... but I think by the time we kill Steele, the coin will be the least of your worries.'

He walked to the door.

'So, how do I get out?'

'Easy,' The Broker smiled. 'I kill you.'

———

THE GUARDS HAD WHEELED THE BODY BAG OUT THROUGH THE same entrance that Volkov had been wheeled out several hours earlier. As far as they were concerned, they were removing the body of Abasi, unaware that his body was still in the morgue.

The van waiting outside had been instructed by The Broker to take Marlowe half a mile away and drop him off on a random street; it was the best The Broker could do–no money, no credit, no phone. Marlowe would have to continue alone, but in a way it was the best option all round. This way, Marlowe's friends wouldn't be in the firing line and, for once, Marlowe was happy about that.

His friends, however, had a different opinion.

No sooner had Marlowe walked a street away from the drop-off point, now finding himself heading towards Green Park, he saw a black BMW X5 series pull up with Trix, Marshall, Tessa and Saeed climbing out.

'Wow. You gave us a bloody scare,' Trix said, running a hand through her blonde hair. 'Walking around in London this time of night, you're an idiot.'

'I think I'm pretty safe at four in the morning,' Marlowe grinned. 'Even the gangsters have gone to bed by now.'

'You look like shit,' Marshall said, noticing the blood-stained shirt. 'We need to get you to a doctor.'

He moved forward but stopped as Marlowe held a hand up.

'The hunt is back on,' he said. 'I made a deal with The Broker.'

'Of course you did. That was the plan,' Tessa said. 'Why do you seem so weird about it?'

'Because part of the *revised* plan was making sure that you weren't involved,' Marlowe continued.

Ignoring the comment, Trix moved back towards the car.

'I've got my own plan. What we can—'

'No plans,' Marlowe interrupted, placing a hand on her shoulder to pause her. 'If you've found a way to screw over the Marlowe Coin, great. Go do it. But I can't come with you.'

'You *what*?' It was Marshall Kirk who spoke now, his eyes widened in shock. 'We've just come all this way—'

'I get that you've come all this way,' Marlowe cut in, turning to face his mentor. 'But this is a fight that is purely on me. If you hadn't got involved, you wouldn't have been captured. Morris wouldn't have been captured. Trix wouldn't have been on the run. St John Steele is pretty serious with what he wants to do, and if I call on any of you, he'll kill you. No bullshit auctions or games. We've gone way past that now.'

He looked over at Saeed.

'The only reason Vic got out of there is because they didn't for one second think he could be allied with me. I know you're considering some bloody foolish idea of putting Marshall in prosthetics or something stupid like that, maybe one of your acrylic eyeballs to give him a different identity– actually, I don't know what you're thinking, but it won't work. Not this time.'

'So, what do you suggest?'

Marlowe looked back at the park.

'I'm going to continue playing,' he murmured. 'But not in the way they think I should. They want me as a running man, fine. Every person who fails to kill me drops my money down and takes a potential threat off the table.'

He gave a small, wry smile at this.

'How many coins do you have?'

'I don't know,' Trix replied. 'There's a chance I could have quite a few if I managed to hack Ciaran's systems.'

Marlowe nodded.

'Whatever you've given Vic for helping out, class them as gone,' he muttered. 'He's earned what he got today.'

He turned back to Saeed.

'I know you're in a strange position, having to work for the people you hate, and spy for people who class you as an enemy. But whatever our problems were, you stepped up for me today, and for that, it's only fair you get something from it.'

'I could use them to have you killed in some other way,' Saeed replied with the slightest of smiles.

Marlowe smiled back, but there was no humour in it.

'You've just watched me close my entire group,' he said. 'You've no idea what I intend to plan.'

Saeed considered this.

'How can I help?'

Marlowe hadn't expected the question, and his eyebrows shot up in surprise.

'Come on, Marlowe, you're not an idiot,' Saeed smiled. 'Sure, you've given me some money and that's lovely. But when I got screwed over with the whole Broad Sword drone fiasco, Steele didn't help. He left me to rot just like all the other tech billionaires he'd screwed over. It was MI6 and McKellan that gave me a lifeline, pretty much because they knew I had nowhere else to go. Even Robertson had to be pressured to bring me in.'

He rubbed at the back of his neck as he considered his next words carefully.

'They're hunting your allies and, as you just said, nobody thinks I'm one of them. They still don't. As far as they're concerned, I've got some money and I wanted to see you die. Steele, as far as he's concerned, thinks I'm still a friend. But I want that bastard taken down for what he did to me.'

When Marlowe didn't respond, Saeed tapped his shoulder where the scar was, under the expensive suit.

'It was Steele who inducted me into Orchid,' he said. 'And whether you believe I was playing both sides, or his loyal man or whatever, I was Orchid through and through. The same as Kate Maybury was, the same as Oliver Casey was. We weren't Steele's people; we were Orchid people. Steele seems to think we're loyal to him, when actually we're pretty pissed at what's happened.'

Marlowe decided not to mention that *Kate Maybury and Oliver Casey wouldn't be as pissed as Vic Saeed was because they were both dead,* but then he smiled as a sudden realisation crossed his mind.

'You think they'll take you back!' he blurted. 'You think if you help me, Orchid–not Steele's splinter but the *other* Orchid, the old guard–they'll bring you back into their bosom? Maybe even find a way for you to get out of whatever agreement you've had to take with McKellan?'

'Is it wrong to hope?' Saeed asked.

'No.' Marlowe shook his head. 'And actually, you help me out, I'll put in a good word to Falkenberg, Shida, Gonzalez– whoever it is I need to speak to. If you want to side with us instead of Steele, I'm overjoyed.'

Saeed nodded, and Marlowe wondered whether he'd picked up on Marlowe saying "us" instead of "them", something even Marlowe hadn't intended to say. Deciding to change the subject, Marlowe looked back at Trix.

'I want this coin destroyed, Trix.' he said. 'I want it ruined. I want–what's the term–the "rug pulled" so badly that everybody who spent millions of their money to fund St John Steele's power-hungry takeovers is left in the dark with nothing.'

'That can be arranged, although it could take a little time to get a way back in, as Ciaran will have found and killed my entryway after I outed him on the Marlowe Coin display,' Trix gave a smile. 'But I'll have it done within twenty-four hours, I reckon. And you're not going to begrudge me making some money out of the process?'

'If it hurts him, I don't care,' Marlowe muttered, looking back to Saeed. 'You have a way to be contacted?'

Saeed looked at Trix, who, realising what he wanted, passed over a pen and piece of paper. Saeed jotted a number down.

'This is my burner,' he said. 'If you send me a message, say you're my Uncle Akbal. If I see that, we can meet. Prearranged location.'

'London?'

'Makes sense. Preferably somewhere near Trafalgar Square. Means I can get out of Whitehall quite easily.'

Marlowe considered this and then, taking the pen, wrote an address on the piece of paper, tearing it off as he passed it over to Saeed. Trix tried to see the address, but Marlowe held it from her.

'No,' he said. 'I've told you, you can't be involved in this.'

'The hell I can't be involved,' Trix snapped back angrily. 'You know damn well this is everything I do.'

'And for once it's something *I'm* going to have to do.' Marlowe looked back at Marshall and Tessa. 'I appreciate what you've done, but I'm going to dance with the devil for a while. And the steps are too fast and way too hot for you to join in.'

'You'd better bloody know what you're doing,' Tessa said, stepping forward and kissing Marlowe on the cheek. 'Because if you die, I am going to be very pissed off.'

'I will raise a glass in your honour, but I won't be pissed off,' Marshall smiled. 'Because you're suicidal and it's a bloody shame.'

'I don't intend to die anytime soon,' Marlowe replied, 'but I appreciate the sentiment. Do you have my go bag?'

This last part had been to Trix, who shook her head.

'I've got some funds,' she replied, 'and I always keep a couple of Helen Bonneville blanks you can use. Also, I have a CZ 75 and a few spare magazines in the glove box in case you needed it.'

'It'll be enough.' Marlowe held out his hand. 'I don't need IDs, I just need a working credit card and some cash.'

'How much?'

'Whatever you've got. And a jumper if you have one; this shirt's a bit of a giveaway something bad's been going on.'

'I'd also like some cash,' Marshall offered, but when there was no response, gave a shrug. 'Worth a try.'

Trix passed across a small bag, but held it tight, stopping Marlowe from taking it.

'At least give me a clue as to what you're about to do,' she said. 'Show me you're not winging it.'

Marlowe smiled darkly.

'How many is a few spare magazines?' he asked in a stage whisper. 'I'm going to go play spies, and I'm going to need to kill a *lot* of people.'

22

BROKER VS BROKER

THE EMBANKMENT WAS ALWAYS QUIET AT SIX IN THE MORNING. The theatre-goers and nightclubbers had long gone home, while the office workers, shopkeepers and shop staff were only just waking in their homes. Only the homeless, the locals and the night-time clean-up crew bothered to spend their time on both the Embankment and the South Bank of the Thames.

This was the time when Alexander Curtis went for his runs.

He'd started running again after he'd been injured; he was told he needed to regain his strength, but cardio and VO2max were important. Curtis was of an age where he didn't understand what VO2max even meant, but he knew that if he wanted to stay in his job, he had to stay fit and healthy, as heart attacks while in your office were a common way to go for people involved with the security service.

And so, at around six a.m. every morning, before everything landed on his desk and the world woke up screaming, Alexander Curtis would change into some running gear, strap on his running shoes, and force himself around his route.

It was a simple one; he would start at Thames House, making his way clockwise –if you were looking at a map – heading past Westminster, turning towards Westminster Bridge, and then left onto the Embankment itself. He'd then carry on down to the Golden Jubilee Pedestrian Bridge, run across it, carry on eastwards along the South Bank, and then cross back northwards on Blackfriars Bridge, returning along the Victoria Embankment past Cleopatra's Needle. He would then head past the Houses of Parliament one more time and arrive back at Thames House. The entire journey took him just under forty minutes at a distance of six and a half kilometres, or, as he preferred to think of it, four miles.

He didn't run with music or even listen to podcasts; he was too paranoid to have anything distracting him from things around him. He was, after all, London section chief of MI5; there was every opportunity for someone to take him off the street. He wasn't a fool, of course, and twenty yards further back, he often had a younger operative pacing, watching, armed in case something went wrong, and likely annoyed at the slow pace.

This morning, however, he was alone.

It hadn't been a conscious choice. He simply needed the run and had arrived earlier than usual, having been up most of the night gaining real-time intel on this bloody gladiator issue Thomas Marlowe had been thrown into.

Marlowe was out and on the run again–he'd been informed of this a few hours back–and now, filled with nervous energy, he needed to clear his mind.

He'd been doing well, keeping to time, and was approaching his last kilometre, marked by the statue of

Boudicca beside Westminster Bridge, when he saw the figure watching him.

He paused, taking a moment to gather his breath.

'I thought you'd be dead by now,' he muttered.

Marlowe gave a small, almost apologetic shrug.

'People are trying,' he replied. 'I'm surprised you haven't bought some coins and tried it yourself.'

'You know, there are easier ways to talk to me,' Curtis straightened, hands on hips as he gulped in air.

'No offence, Curtis, but the last time we chatted, not only did you drag me to Rochester and a strange cathedral, I then had hitmen try to kill me,' Marlowe responded. 'So forgive me if I'm a little suspicious about what happens when you tell your people about meetings.'

Reluctantly, Curtis accepted the comment.

'I suppose I did tell you we were a leaky sieve,' he admitted. 'That doesn't necessarily mean you get to stop me in my private moments.'

'Curtis, it means the only time I *can* talk to you is during your private moments,' Marlowe explained. 'Anyway, you're going to want to hear this.'

'Fine,' Curtis agreed. 'Is there anywhere, though, that we can talk that isn't so public? We're right by Westminster, and there's an operative following who's about to turn up any second from now, and once he sees me talking to you, he's going to probably pull his service revolver out and put two in the back of your head.'

Marlowe grinned.

'If he did I'd be impressed, considering the fact that I think he's still in the office wondering where you've gone.'

He nodded to the base of the statue.

'We could go back the underground route if you wanted.'

Curtis shook his head in disbelief but couldn't stop the smile on his face. The first time he'd ever met Marlowe, they'd had him in an interrogation room in the basement of Thames House, believing him to be a Cold War Russian asset. Marlowe had managed to escape, though, and had used the subterranean passages created during the Second World War to escape, the exit being the same spot they were now at.

'I'm guessing this wasn't by chance,' he remarked.

Marlowe shook his head.

'It gets us out of the cold,' he replied, 'and won't it surprise your crew when you appear out of nowhere?'

The doors to the tunnel underneath Boudicca's statue opened easily, and Curtis was momentarily surprised at the speed that Marlowe had opened it–until he realised that Marlowe had probably already picked the lock before Curtis even arrived. In fact, there was every chance Marlowe had been waiting for Curtis since he had run past the other way, hoping to catch him in a more exhausted state.

Once they were down the stairs into the tunnel system itself, however, Marlowe stopped.

'You know I can't go with you,' he said, 'I'm sorry. The moment I turn up in Thames House, I'm expecting a dozen agents to take me out.'

Curtis smiled darkly.

'While it's true you've got enemies there,' he said, 'I don't think they'd want to pop you.'

'They might not want to kill me,' Marlowe continued. 'But I'd definitely find myself in some kind of underground cell, wrapped up in bubble wrap and held tight, while MI5 decide to try to save the day.'

He stretched, looking around.

'I mean, let's be honest, Curtis. I used to be one of them. It's what I did. It's what I was good at.'

'So, if you weren't that fussed about walking down these corridors with me, why all the cloak and dagger?' Curtis frowned.

'I can't be seen publicly with you,' Marlowe replied, 'I don't know how close I'm being monitored, but the hunt is still on for me, and I was pretty much informed that anybody I went to for assistance couldn't be a friend or an ally.'

'I don't know how to take that,' Curtis gave a tight smile. 'I thought we had a good relationship.'

'We do,' Marlowe said, holding a hand up to pause Curtis. 'But *MI5* and I have a bit of an issue, so anybody looking will see you as the voice of authority, rather than the man you are. This means that if you're checking into things, people won't think it's on my behalf. They'll believe you're doing it because you're like the others.'

Curtis nodded.

'I get that. So, what do you actually want from me?'

'Gregorovich,' Marlowe said. 'You know the name?'

'I know an Alexei Gregorovich,' Curtis replied. 'Used to be an arms dealer. Russian linked, KGB, then FSB when it tried to rebrand. Disappeared a few years ago. There was talk it was an MI6 op.'

He paused.

'What don't I know?'

'Raymond Kinley, better known as The Broker,' Marlowe continued. 'Gregorovich was his mentor. Fifteen years ago there was an event that happened in Vienna, something to do with a diplomat. Gregorovich was involved. Volkov, the assassin that tried to kill me in Vegas—'

'The one you killed in the arena last night,' Curtis said

with a surprising knowledge of what had been happening recently in Marlowe's life.

'I didn't kill him,' Marlowe replied. 'We faked it. Volkov's Gregorovich's grandson. The Broker, meanwhile, is under the assumption that St John Steele knows where Gregorovich is, and that he was taken three years ago as part of an MI6 sting and placed in a black bag site in Ayrshire.'

Curtis shook his head.

'Steel wasn't MI6 three years ago. Or MI5, for that matter.'

'No. But there was every chance he could have been assisting someone,' Marlowe replied. 'Three years ago he still had an excellent cover, he was Arbitrator of Orchid and he had a solid mole network. Kate Maybury, Oliver Casey, Vic Saeed–they were all deep, and that's just the ones we know about.'

Curtis considered this, nodding.

'So, you want to know whether Gregorovich is in this black site?'

'I get the impression he's not. Or if he is, he's been moved–I need confirmation.'

'Do you have any idea where?'

'Somewhere near Butler's Wharf,' Marlowe said. 'Underground basement, perhaps? Somewhere near Shad Thames.'

Curtis ran his hands through his damp hair as he thought about this.

'There used to be a small pop-up black site, shall we say, that worked from there about ten years ago.'

'What the hell is a pop-up black site?' Marlowe asked.

'Well, you know how pop-up shops appear out of nowhere and last for a little while and go? This was like that. It was a spot where we could interrogate people,' Curtis replied. 'Your mum might even have been one of the people who helped get it sorted. It was created a year or two before the seven-seven attacks. After your mum died during them, it was used quite liberally, shall we say?'

Marlowe understood what Curtis was saying. His mother, Olivia Marlowe, had been a high-level Military Intelligence operative in the security services. She had been involved in a lot of counter-terrorism based in London, and it was intel she had on insurgents that cost his mother her life in a train explosion during the seventh of July attacks.

'Steele would have been involved in those "interviews",' Curtis continued, musing. 'But anyway, around ten years ago, the place was boarded up, left to rot. Everything was being gentrified around the area, which made black SUVs dumping bound and gagged prisoners down there a bit too public, but rather than sell on the space, we kind of just let it stay there. Chances are it's probably not on any books any more, which makes it the perfect spot for Steele to use.'

He nodded to himself.

'I can send a team—'

'No,' Marlowe interrupted. 'No teams. No MI5, no MI6. As I said, The Broker and Steele have been one step ahead of us at all opportunities, which to me says you've still got people working for them in there. I'm hoping Vic Saeed might be able to help with that respect.'

'Saeed?' Curtis shook his head now. 'I saw he was at the event. You're playing a dangerous game there. Are you sure he's on your side?'

'As I said,' Marlowe grinned, 'I can't use friends to assist me. I'm having to rely on enemies.'

'Shaky ground,' Curtis stretched at his sides and Marlowe knew his muscles were starting to tighten and cramp.

'Look,' he said, 'I'm going to check out Shad Thames. But if you can provide me any information of where it was ...'

'It would be in your mum's files,' Curtis said. 'Although I'm guessing at the moment they're not easy to find.'

Marlowe considered his burned-out church base.

'Let's just say I need an alternative way of getting hold of them.'

'Trix?'

'Can't use her.'

Curtis thought for a second.

'Wintergreen would know, but ...' he tailed off. 'McKellen, perhaps. Let me see what I can do off books. How can I contact you?'

'Get whatever you can to Saeed,' Marlowe replied. 'He might be late into work today, but he'll be there. I have an arrangement with him.'

Curtis nodded as, from down the corridor there was a noise.

'Sounds like movement sensors have been tripped,' he said. 'We stuck them in here after you pissed off with Tessa Kirk that time.'

'Will you be okay?' Marlowe asked, already returning to the door.

'Marlowe, I run this place. I'll just claim that I was getting cold, or wanted a distraction from my run,' Curtis gave a smile, this time with humour behind it. 'Just try not to die until we sort this out, yeah? If MI6 and MI5 are as mole-ridden as we seem to think, I might be on the lookout for some ex-operatives to come home.'

'We'll see,' Marlowe smiled. 'We'll see.'

ONCE MARLOWE LEFT CURTIS, HE'D SPENT A GOOD HOUR travelling randomly through London, just in case somebody had decided to follow him or he was being caught in some random game that he wasn't aware of. Once he was one hundred per cent sure that he was free, he found a cafe, grabbed himself some early breakfast–or was it dinner, as even though it was now eight in the morning, he couldn't remember the last time he ate–regained some energy and then stole a car from a small side road, making his way to the North London courier company named *Impetus Couriers*, and Pauline Faulkner.

He knew he could have used a cab, or called a rideshare, even rented a car–but he only needed something short-term and fast. The car would be found, it wouldn't be connected to him, and by the time the police arrived, he'd have been long gone.

He didn't intend to leave more than the smallest of shadows today.

Pauline Faulkner, meanwhile, didn't seem to be surprised to face Marlowe sitting at her desk when she walked into her office at nine in the morning.

'You know, I thought I had superb security,' she shouted out to a portly, miserable-looking man sitting in the other room, who looked up with resignation in his eyes.

'What did you expect?' he said. 'Bloody guy's like a ghost.'

'If you're here for your money back,' Pauline smiled, 'I'm afraid I've already cashed it in. Four million dollars–too good to risk waiting.'

She looked a little embarrassed and Marlowe knew exactly why.

'You didn't think I'd last, did you?' he said. 'You cashed out because you thought it was about to plummet.'

'Do you blame me?' Pauline asked. 'You were going up against people with far greater armouries than you. And the money was definitely placed against your favour.'

'No, I completely get it,' Marlowe replied. 'And, if I'd been in your situation, I'd probably have done the same.'

He gave the slightest of smiles.

'I'm glad you made money from me. It means that the favour I ask for will be easier to give.'

'Oh, so we're giving favours now, are we?'

'Class it as a return on the four million dollars that you made from me.'

'What do you need?' Pauline Faulkner sighed.

'I want to put a hit on St John Steele,' Marlowe said.

For once, Marlowe saw genuine emotion on her face; this surprised Pauline, but she quickly shook her head.

'You don't want to do that,' she replied. 'That way lies madness.'

'How so?' Marlowe asked. 'Let's be honest. I'm only doing what he did to me. How much would it cost to consider killing Steele?'

'He's an important man,' Pauline continued to shake her head slowly, as if non-verbally warning him off. 'You won't find many people that would take on the hit, let alone manage to do it.'

'I didn't ask how much to kill him,' Marlowe said. 'I asked what was the figure that people would take to consider it.'

'You're talking millions,' Pauline replied. 'More than you own.'

'I wouldn't be sure about that,' Marlowe gave a tight smile. 'After all, as you said, the Marlowe Coin is doing incredibly well right now.'

Pauline considered the question and then nodded to herself.

'Realistically, if you're looking at money, I'd say ten million, maybe fifteen. Dollars.'

'Good,' Marlowe said. 'I want you to put a hit out on St John Steele in my name. Speak to all intermediaries.'

'Okay, and what am I saying when I speak to everyone?'

'Tell them that the price I'm offering is one dollar.'

'I can't do that!' Pauline's eyes widened.

'I know, your ten per cent would be fractional, but take it out of the four million—'

'It's not that! Something like this? It's suicide. They would hunt *me* down.'

'You'll be safe,' Marlowe replied. 'Tell them this is on me, my personal request. Tell them it was at gunpoint if it helps. One dollar. And a favour from Orchid, once we're back in control. That's all I offer.'

'No one will take it.'

'I don't want anybody to take it.' Marlowe smiled. 'I want St John Steele to *hear* that I've done it.'

'Oh, he'll hear, all right,' Pauline laughed. 'He'll definitely hear.'

23

OLD ENEMIES, NEW ALLIES

THE MOMENT HE LEFT THE BUSINESS BRUNCH, MAXIMILIAN Schen knew he was being followed. You didn't get to where you were in the community of dark, shadowy dealings without knowing when someone was deliberately making a pass. He didn't know who the man was, but he was Indian in looks and very competent at what he did.

Schen had seen him during the brunch; a black-tie event in Pall Mall. It had been part of the Institute of Directors' current networking outreach plans and if he was being brutally honest, although it wasn't that important in the grand scheme of things, Maximilian Schen, or Max to his friends, was finding himself a little friendless right now. For the last few months he'd found that his rivals, in particular one annoying thread that wouldn't be pulled, were continually attacking his stocks and his shares, and he'd lost millions because of this.

Not to mention the gold, bearer bonds and blackmail material he'd lost in a Berlin safe deposit box.

If, however, he had to swear on a stack of Bibles, Max

Schen would admit he'd brought it upon himself. In Berlin, he had decided that caution was the best form of valour after learning of what was about to happen from Orchid High Council member Ingrid Falkenberg, and had left his partner– if only in name rather than responsibilities–St John Steele to the wolves, deciding that rather than try to continue a lost cause in Berlin, it would be far better to attempt something from the safety of his own home.

By the time Thomas Marlowe had destroyed every plan they had made, Max Schen was already landing at Biggin Hill Airport, sipping champagne and waiting for his driver to appear in his Rolls Royce.

Surprisingly, Steele had survived; this was something that Max hadn't really expected. More importantly, he'd heard rumours of Steele after Berlin, having taken Max's money and blackmail material for himself. First, there'd been some kind of issue in Vegas, involving old members of Orchid, and his currently cursed takeover of such aforementioned group, and then there was some kind of spat on the top of Mount Rushmore that ended with a body count higher than most Schwarzenegger movies, and Steele returning, once more, into hiding, unable to raise his head above the parapet.

Max had considered reaching out at that point, offering an olive branch; he probably could have got Steele back on his side for a fraction of what he'd originally been offered. Steele would have understood why Max disappeared. He'd seen more than anybody else that Thomas Marlowe was not somebody to go to war with.

But he hadn't. Because he knew that St John Steele was a *petty little bitch* when he really wanted to be, and a traitorous piece of shit by default. He knew that if he'd brought Steele in too close, the viper would have struck at some point, maybe even fulfilling what he had attempted to do back in Berlin, and take over Max Schen's entire empire.

This didn't mean, however, that Max was an idiot. He knew that if St John Steele was making serious money, and once more becoming a player in the game, at some point there would be an opportunity for recompense and retaliation—if only to ask politely for his safe deposit box back.

Today, Max hadn't been the keynote speaker for the event. That honour, as much as it was, had been given to some junior entrepreneur, who had made several million on some world-saving device. Max hadn't really been paying attention, if he was being honest—the man was only a year or two older than he was, which in his mind meant he wasn't "junior", as Max didn't class himself as such. But that wasn't the reason he'd been distracted, oh no—he'd been paying attention more to the Asian woman across the table from him. She was the wife of Josh Van Camp, a high-roller hedge-fund manager in his forties who thought he was the big dog in the room. But all Max could think of was how he could convince her that one night with him was worth the rest of her life lying to her husband. He was half the age and twice the man, it seemed.

Eventually, however, he tired of considering how he could achieve such a task, primarily because she had noticed him watching her and flipped him the finger, her expression showing it wasn't some kind of flirtatious act.

She genuinely didn't like him. Max accepted that. He was an acquired taste, after all. But he also decided that because of this rather rude rebuke, he would now destroy her husband's empire, forcing him to be left with nothing. Then, maybe, when he was begging anyone for scraps to pay off his immense debts, Max might swoop in like a hero, offer to "rent" his wife for a night of rough shagging, paying pennies on the dollar for the opportunity, with maybe a cash bonus added if she seemed *encouraging* during the session.

Yes. That would be a far better revenge.

It was while he was considering this, he'd noticed the man. He looked familiar; Max was sure he had seen him in one of his earlier meetings with Steele. The man was MI5 or perhaps MI6, possibly even Orchid–definitely a team player rather than a lone wolf. If he was here, and as he seemed to be staring directly at Max so hard that he could burn holes in his expensive shirt, then this was a time for prudence.

He had made sure that his men were ready for action–he paid them enough after all–and while they kept an eye on the stranger with the piercing eyes, taking the more public route down to the car park, Max and one of his guards doubled back, heading towards the side exit. Anybody watching would still think that the crowd of men surrounding somebody in the middle was a very loyal security force. What they didn't realise was that the man in the middle, his hair almost exact to Max's trendy blond hairstyle, was nothing more than a diversion. An expensive one, as he still had to pay them for their time, but if it kept him alive, he was quite happy to pay the price.

Ever since Berlin, Max had been incredibly paranoid about an attack.

Although, was it really paranoia when you expected it to happen? Surely that was foresightedness or being prepared.

Either way, every event he went to, he always made sure now that he had at least one, maybe two backup plans, maybe even a body double for the bigger ones, kept in a car around the back. This brunch event was no exception. He had his car out the front, a second in the car park for emergencies, where his men were now going, and a third, a motorcycle locked up to the side, out of sight in the car park but close enough to the main exit that he could clamber onto it, his lone security behind him, and ride.

When he'd first suggested this, his close protection security originally suggested that they should ride the bike if there was a problem, and that he would be the one behind– but Max had pointed out that not only did he understand how to ride a motorcycle and had done so for many years, if they'd got to the point where he was having to use Plan C to get out of a location, he wanted his security guard to not only be behind him, effectively a human shield for anybody firing at him, but also he wanted him to be able to use his own weapon and *fire back*, something Max was unsure he could do to his full effect.

Besides, he was paying some of the best soldiers in the world to secure him. Why would he train up to be as good as them, when he could just pay them to do it for him?

As he walked down towards the car park, a safe distance behind his primary group, now wearing a baseball cap and a brown leather jacket instead of his tuxedo, he heard the squawk in his companion's earpiece. The guard paused, tapped his ear to listen and then turned to face Max.

'We go now,' he muttered. 'They've had fire.'

'Flames or gunshots?'

'Someone's opened up on them.'

'Are they okay?' Max asked and then shook his head. 'Scratch that, I don't care, just get me out of here.'

They hurried down a side staircase, exiting only feet from where the motorbike was. It was a Kawasaki Bandit, fast and agile, matte black and dangerous. There were two helmets attached by a security lock and the guard removed this, throwing one helmet to Max. As Max pulled his helmet on, the guard had already prepared himself, pulling a small Beretta from a shoulder holster and racking the slide to chamber a round. The bandit also had a back rail, which meant that the security guard could sit behind Max and hold on to that, which made it easier for him to turn and fire backwards if need be. But, more importantly, it meant that the guard didn't have to put his arms around Max.

That was a little bit of intimacy he didn't want to know about, no matter how hard he'd tried with whatever her bloody name was–the woman he'd screw one day for pennies.

This was the same car park that his other men had gone to, albeit a further location across the entire building away, but Max couldn't hear anything; no bullets, no gunfire, no screams, and he wondered whether his other team had managed to chase off the assailant. He turned to his guard who seemed to have wondered the same thing, now connected to his helmet's headphone and microphone.

The guard, however, shook his head.

'No response, no signal,' he mumbled. 'It's probably because we're underground. Once we get out, we'll find out what's happening.'

He looked back towards the car park.

'There's no way they would have been taken out this fast. The chances are he took off and they'd gone after him.'

'Good.' Max climbed onto the bike, starting the engine and revving the throttle. 'We go now.'

The guard went to reply and then jerked back in a spasm, as if suddenly electrocuted. A positioning that was actually pretty correct, as Max now noted the taser tines sticking into his back, fired from somewhere in the corner of the car park.

Shit, they found me.

Max didn't wait. The guard was on the car park floor, twitching uncontrollably as he slammed the bike into gear with his foot and pulled hard on the throttle, sending the bike forward at speed. But then, as it stopped abruptly, he went flying over the handlebars, clattering to the floor.

The bike, now on its side, revealed a chain that had been wrapped through the wheel and secured to a concrete bollard.

Max cursed as he struggled to get back up. *He'd been so careful about the other issues; he hadn't considered that someone might doctor his bike.*

A figure emerged from the shadows and Max Schen felt a shiver of fear as Thomas Marlowe emerged.

'Your man's okay,' he said, 'and so are the others. They're currently having a merry old time chasing a friend of mine.'

Max stood up, pulling off the helmet, tossing it to the side, hoping that the sound of the clattering helmet might pull in some help.

'I wouldn't call out,' Marlowe said and Max noted that the Taser Marlowe had taken out the guard with, had now been replaced with what looked to be an automatic pistol.

'So, this is how you want to end it?' Max asked. 'You want to kill me? Don't you have more problems on your mind right now? Last I heard you had millions on your head.'

'Not so much any more,' Marlowe replied calmly, motioning for Max to follow him. 'Don't worry, Max. I'm not here to kill you or even hurt you. In fact, I'm here to make you a deal.'

Max frowned at the comment.

'What kind of deal would I make with you?' he questioned. 'You destroyed everything we were planning in Berlin. You cost me millions.'

'No,' Marlowe said. 'We both know St John Steele cost you the millions. I was just the tool he used to do it.'

Max paused as Marlowe holstered the pistol. Now unarmed, Marlowe held his hands up to make the point.

'You can run if you want,' he said. 'I won't stop you, but you'll eventually have someone connected to Steele catch you, paid for by your own bearer bonds, or blackmailed by your own gathered information, ruining your day and losing out on an offer.'

'And what kind of offer do you have for me?' Max pouted. He was annoyed, mainly because he knew Marlowe was right.

'The enemy of your enemy is your ally,' Marlowe said. 'The last I heard, you're still on the run from St John Steele, who blames you for leaving him in the lurch in Berlin, and who currently wants to kill you.'

Marlowe gave a wide smile, in what was known as a shit-eating grin.

'How would you like to kill him first?'

24

CASH OUT

ST JOHN STEELE WASN'T HAVING A VERY GOOD DAY. FOR A start, his plans, well laid out and ready to go were falling apart around him. Marlowe had always been nothing more than a distraction, a way of making money–The Marlowe Coin, created by Ciaran, would make them millions. Maybe not the billions he was once promised in Germany, but enough to keep him moving as he gained more allies. "You spend money to make money," was something he'd been told by his "betters" in boarding school when he was a young, wet-behind-the-ears student, and this was what Steele planned to do.

The money that *Operation Quicksilver* had supposedly had within its slush funds had been nothing but a pipe dream, a PR exercise by both America and the UK, convincing each other that they hadn't removed the money so the others shouldn't either, while both had secretly removed every single penny. Before that, the money he intended to make in Berlin had turned to nothing.

Even the box he'd been given by Marlowe, Max Schen's own personal lockbox, had provided him with nothing more than pennies, a few euros and heartache.

But Steele wasn't a loser. He understood how to gain back what he had lost and for two months had been rebuilding his empire. Orchid–the *old* Orchid that was, the one he'd once been a member of before they unceremoniously kicked him out–was struggling. All he had to do was keep pushing at it, prodding at it, allowing more people to consider joining his revised organisation. As soon as they arrived and the funding returned, then he could use this new Orchid's finances to do what he needed ... but currently, he was quite happy with the money he was making off the Marlowe Coin.

The only problem he had, was every time Marlowe survived and killed an assassin, the hit fee would go down– but so would the number of coins in supply, as Ciaran Winston had created a way of creating scarcity by burning more and more of the stock they had. By now, over twenty per cent of the original billion coins had been destroyed; two hundred million coins in total. And with the coins now holding at around seven dollars after a worrying dip the previous night, that so many spare coins had been lost was nothing more than tragedy as far as Steele was concerned.

He was aware this wasn't the way it worked. Ciaran had tried to explain to him like a parent talking to a five-year-old child about how if they *hadn't* burnt the coins, the price wouldn't have gone up as much, and that even with the coins burnt, they were still making the same amount of money they would have beforehand, just convincing the buyers it was a race to gain them before there were no more.

But the fact of the matter was, Steele liked the idea of

making a lot of money, and he was worried that at some point everything would go wrong.

Marlowe not dying was also a major issue here.

Steele had taken a quarter of a billion coins as his original investment, while Ciaran was given a hundred million coins. Currently, Steele was wealthier than half the people he used to work for, as each coin, now worth just over seven dollars meant that after some smaller sales, he had a crypto worth of over a billion dollars.

The problem with that, however, was this was a *crypto worth*, only on paper–or rather, in his cold-crypto wallet. To make a billion or more from these coins, he had to find people willing to *pay* a billion or more to *buy* those coins.

He'd expected Marlowe to be hard to kill. This, in fact, had helped him build up what he needed. Originally, when the coin had hit three dollars per unit, he'd wanted to sell up. But Ciaran had pointed out that the moment he started dumping large amounts of coins, millions of coins appearing out of nowhere would bring it right back down to cents upon the dollar. It was far better to build up and then sell them slowly as they burnt more.

But Steele was now realising that although it had sounded great on paper and that Ciaran Winston had sold him a great idea, it wasn't actually as feasible as he had thought it would be. For a start, once Marlowe was dead, there was no reason to have the coins, which meant they needed to find a way to find buyers quickly before that happened. Sure, the coin was worth seven dollars now, but once Marlowe died and they started selling, he'd be stunned if they managed to make half of that. The entire thing so far had cost no more than six or seven million dollars to set up and put together, and at least he'd be saving on the hit placed on Marlowe, now it was down to six figures, but if he played his cards right and if Ciaran kept his nerve, he could still find himself with a fortune in the hundreds of millions. And more importantly, when he sold he'd make sure that everybody he wanted on his side in the new Orchid sold as well; warlords, industrialists, billionaires, the ones he wanted to succeed would make money even if it was only a little more than they'd spent.

Whereas the people who were in it for the money and the ones he didn't care for would be the ones who funded this.

The problem was that Marlowe shouldn't have escaped. Now he was out there again, and this time, the facial recognition software didn't seem to be working. Either that or Marlowe was once more dressing like Mister Bones, his stupid bloody assassin character, causing the software to glitch.

This had been a massive oversight for Steele. He'd always claimed that he was a spymaster second to none in MI6, that he knew everything that was going on at any time–and yet at the same time he had never known that Mister Bones, one of the most feared assassins out there, was actually an MI5 agent gathering assets in witness relocation. Sure, most of the hits had been "completed" after he had left and it'd been bloody Wintergreen playing silly bastards, but it still grated at his professional side that such a simple thing had been missed.

All he could use in his defence was that he simply didn't have the right staff. Oliver Casey and Kate Maybury had been working on their own plans. Lucien Delacroix had been trying to take over without bothering to check what else was going on. And St John Steele had taken his eye off the ball, something he wouldn't do again.

There was a buzz on his intercom. Steele leant back in what was technically Kinley's chair and pressed the button, allowing it to go to speaker.

'What?' he asked.

'There's been a disruption in Pall Mall.'

'What about it?'

'Gunfire. We believe Max Schen was targeted.'

Steele smiled. *Perhaps today wasn't going to be a washout after all.*

'Tell me he's dead,' he muttered.

'No, sir,' the voice replied. 'However, we believe he has been taken.'

Steele hadn't stayed alive for decades because of dumb luck. He had a sixth sense, a gut feeling when something was off and this felt as off as anything else.

'Do they have any information of who it could have been?'

'No, sir, but we've seen some of the security footage and we believe that one of the people trying to take him had been in this club earlier today. I believe you know him as Vikram Saeed.'

Steele chuckled.

'Well, well, well,' he said. 'Looks like little Vickie's picked a side.'

He disconnected the call, reached into one of the drawers, pulled out a Glock 19, checked the magazine, racked a round... and fired the entire magazine into the wall. As security guards came bursting through, he stared at them, tossing the gun to the side.

'Get me The Broker,' he instructed. 'It's time to cash up and move out.'

In a London bar, Marlowe sat in the corner nursing his Guinness as Max Schen, sipping happily at a Bloody Mary, carried on talking. Once Max had realised there was an opportunity here to take down a mutual enemy, the bloody man hadn't stopped talking, and Marlowe was already regretting taking him in the first place.

Amusingly, while everyone looked for Max Schen, believing he'd been kidnapped, Marlowe and Max had actually simply wandered twenty yards down the street, entering a bar on King Street. Both huddled conspiratorially, the two discussed plans.

'What can you tell me about Gregorovich?' Marlowe asked.

Max shrugged.

'Only what I heard from Berlin,' he said. 'Lazarev used to talk about him. He was some big shot in Russia, and Lazarev, being from Azerbaijan had a hard on for Russian spies and oligarchs. Until Gregorovich was taken out.'

'Taken out as in ...' Marlowe mimed a gunshot to the head.

'Christ, no,' Max shuddered, as if the idea made him feel queasy. 'Look, all I know is Gregorovich was somebody that Steele had beef with when he was in MI6. He'd done some sting of some kind in Vienna that ended with a bombing that killed a Saudi prince and a dozen or so randoms. Gregorovich was there with the Russian ambassador, and he was blamed for it, though nobody could prove it.'

'What happened to him?'

'No idea. Lazarev reckoned Steele set him up when he

was high in Orchid a few years back, dumped him in a black site.'

'In Scotland?'

'Maybe. I was never given the name. All I heard was second-hand information. When I hired him to buy Broad Sword, I found out he'd already offered his services to the Russians, but they apparently really hate him,' Max shrugged, taking another sip of his Bloody Mary, wincing. 'I hate it when they put too much Worcester sauce in.'

'That's the problem with the Bloody Mary? The Worcester sauce?' Marlowe shook his head. 'Okay. So, Gregorovich is held because Steele knows he's the only bargaining chip he has. That's why The Broker's working with him so closely.'

Max nodded.

'He's kept as an ace in the pocket for when Steele needs it.'

Marlowe considered this.

'I think he's going to be needing that ace pretty soon.'

'That's the thing about Steele,' Max shook his head, leaning back on the cushion of his chair. 'People always think when he's got his back to the wall, he's screwed, but that's when he does his best work. If you've got Steele against the ropes, there's every chance you've lost.'

It made no logic, but Marlowe understood what he was saying.

'If the Russian powers that be want him dead, and Gregorovich is keeping them from doing that, then him not having Gregorovich means he's vulnerable. If he doesn't have Gregorovich, The Broker is also free and can do what he wants and Steele loses a chunk of his power.'

Max swirled the ice in his glass, looking thoughtful.

'I could help you, you know. Get to Gregorovich.'

'How?' Marlowe narrowed his eyes.

'I've still got connections. When someone's worth billions, even when they've fallen from grace, people pick up the phone,' Max leaned forward. 'And I've got something better than that. I've got the Tower Bridge plans.'

'Tower Bridge? What do you know about that?'

'I know that's where Steele's running his operation from,' Max replied with a sly smile. 'Not the bridge itself, though God knows that would be appropriately dramatic for the pompous prick. The facility beneath it. There's a whole underground complex there—old storage vaults, maintenance tunnels, some newer additions. All very hush-hush. I was approached to invest in it six months ago.'

'By Steele?'

'Through intermediaries. I didn't know it was him at the time and it was before ... well, our unpleasantries.' Max's expression darkened. 'I've still got the proposal documents, hired some people to get a basic security layout, all of it. Was going to toss it, but something told me to hang on to it.'

Marlowe sat up straighter, suddenly much more interested.

'Where are these documents?'

'Secure storage, not far from here. But that's not all I can offer,' Max said, lowering his voice. 'You want to really cut Steele off at the knees? I can get you to Robertson.'

'Russell Robertson? The Defence Minister?'

'The very same. He's one of Steele's most powerful backers in government. Without him, Steele loses his official cover.'

'We have someone there already.'

'Saeed? Robertson treats him like an errand boy,' Max

sniffed. 'He knows MI6 are playing him along. At best you're getting old intel and at worst? Second-rate shit.'

Max checked his watch.

'Robertson's having a private lunch at the Baker Club in an hour. Members and their guests only. I'm a member.'

'And you'd take me in? Just like that?'

Max's smile didn't reach his eyes.

'Steele screwed me out of millions. Made me look like a fool. I want to watch him burn and I don't much care who lights the match.'

He finished his drink.

'Besides, Robertson's been avoiding my calls since Berlin. I'd love to see the look on his face when I walk in.'

'There's more you're not telling me,' Marlowe said, reading the man's expression.

Max hesitated, then sighed.

'Fine. There's something else. Orchid's still fragmenting– the old High Council is in disarray. Falkenberg reached out to me last week, looking for allies against Steele's faction. She doesn't trust anyone who might be compromised by intelligence services, and no offence, but she's not expecting you to come up with much.'

'And she trusts you?' Marlowe ignored the jibe.

'She trusts my hatred for Steele,' Max replied. 'And my money. What's left of it, anyway.'

Marlowe considered his options. Two valuable opportunities were now laid out before him; Tower Bridge plans, and access to Robertson–he'd hold the Falkenberg news until a time when it helped him more. All from a man he'd wanted dead just months ago. But desperation made for strange bedfellows, and Max Schen's thirst for revenge seemed genuine enough.

'Why didn't you tell me this from the start?'

'Needed to be sure you weren't just going to put a bullet in my head the moment I wasn't useful,' Max shrugged. 'I've got a healthy sense of self-preservation. Plus, I wanted to know what you were planning first.'

Marlowe nodded once.

'Get the Tower Bridge documents. Then we pay Robertson a visit.'

'And my part in all this? After I've helped you?' Max asked.

'You get to watch Steele fall,' Marlowe replied. 'Isn't that what you want?'

'I want more than that,' Max leaned forward. 'I want my place back. My standing. I want those high-society bastards who've been laughing behind their hands to choke on it. And I want my bloody money back.'

'One step at a time,' Marlowe stood up. 'Let's start with Robertson.'

Max drained his glass and rose, straightening his expensive suit.

'One more thing,' he said. 'Your man Volkov's in London. I saw him at my hotel this morning.'

'He's not my man,' Marlowe frowned. 'And how would you know him?'

'I make it my business to know the faces of professional killers,' Max replied. 'Especially ones connected to Steele. Besides, I have a friend who owns Marlowe Coins, so I was quite surprised when I saw him, considering he's supposed to be dead.'

Marlowe decided not to answer this, and sensing the conversation was over Max motioned for Marlowe to follow. They left the bar together, stepping into the grey London afternoon, as Max pulled out his phone, making a quick call to arrange retrieval of the Tower Bridge documents while Marlowe scanned the street for threats. No sign of surveillance, but that didn't mean they weren't being watched–especially with the facial recognition back on. There was only so many times you could hide from a camera before it caught you. As far as Marlowe knew, he could already have been picked up on a camera, his location broadcast out.

The Marlowe Coin hunters could be anywhere.

'Car's waiting around the corner,' Max said, pocketing his phone. 'It's not the guard you tasered, but be wary when you see him next, as he'll probably want your balls for what you did. We'll grab the documents on the way to the club. And Marlowe?'

'What?'

'Try not to get us killed between now and then, would you? I've got plans for after we destroy Steele.'

Marlowe said nothing, but his expression made it clear–Max Schen's plans were very low on his list of priorities. Staying alive, finding Gregorovich, and dismantling Steele's operation piece by piece–those plans were what mattered. But for now the billionaire was useful towards those ends.

Maybe then he'd kill Max. If only to shut him up.

MAX'S DRIVER TOOK THEM TO A PRIVATE VAULT FACILITY IN Knightsbridge, where Max retrieved a slim portfolio containing the Tower Bridge plans. Back in the car, he spread them out on his lap, pointing out key features as they drove towards Whitehall.

'Main server room is here.' He indicated a large space near the north tower foundation. 'Security checkpoint here, here and here. This section was being retrofitted as some kind of vault system when I was approached; I believe the plan was to build a server farm there or something. Perfect place to hold a high-value asset like Gregorovich.'

Marlowe studied the layouts, committing them to memory.

'Security?'

'Cutting edge when this was drawn up,' Max replied. 'Biometric access, armed guards, the works. Supposedly part of a government initiative to secure key infrastructure, but that was obviously a cover for whatever MI6 wanted it for. Whole thing's caught up in bureaucratic bullshit which'll take years to clear, which is great for whatever Steele's really doing down there.'

'And Robertson? How does he fit into this?'

'He pushed the funding through the Defence Ministry,' Max said. 'Classified project, minimal oversight. Typical black ops or security service setup, but with the kind of money that requires ministerial sign-off.'

'So, he knows exactly what's happening there.'

'Down to the last detail. He's Steele's buddy, after all.' Max's smile was unpleasant. 'And because of that, he's about to have a very uncomfortable afternoon.'

He paused, wrinkling his nose.

'But first, may I suggest another trip to my tailor?' he asked, waving a hand at Marlowe's dishevelled appearance. 'You look like you've come from a fight to the death in a gutter.'

Marlowe raised an eyebrow at this. It was true he'd been in the wars recently, but he'd used the money and cards Trix had passed him to freshen up at a hotel and gain a change of clothes.

'What's wrong with what I'm wearing?' he asked.

'Nothing, if you want to pretend you're a spy,' Max sniffed. 'But, where we're going, you'll be rubbing shoulders with billionaires. Unfortunately jeans and a t-shirt simply don't suffice.'

25

SECOND LUNCHES

THE BAKER CLUB OCCUPIED A DISCREET GEORGIAN TOWNHOUSE just off Whitehall's wide and well-known route to the Houses of Parliament.

No sign announced its presence; only a polished brass plate beside the door displayed its name in incredibly understated lettering. As they arrived at the entrance, a doorman in formal attire nodded to Max with the practised deference of old money institutions.

'Mister Schen. Good to see you again, sir. The news said you'd had some trouble today.'

'Likewise, Phillips, and the rumours of my "kidnapping" are just that. I simply wanted out of a dreadfully boring party,' Max smiled broadly. 'I've brought a guest with me. This is Mister John Smith, a business associate from overseas.'

The doorman didn't blink at the obviously false name, simply looking Marlowe up and down, noting the expensive pinstripe suit, pale-blue shirt and burgundy tie before checking the polished Oxfords on Marlowe's feet–all provided by Max so that Marlowe "didn't make him look a fool"–eventually checking a leather-bound register before opening the door.

'Very good, sir. Minister Robertson is in the Oak Room, as you've requested.'

Marlowe raised an eyebrow at this, but Max simply smiled.

'I called ahead,' he said as they entered. 'I'm not stupid enough to walk in blind.'

Inside, the club was a shrine to a long-forgotten world of British Empire autonomy–Marlowe could see leather armchairs worn to a buttery softness, walls of oak panelling darkened by decades of cigar smoke, and an atmosphere of hushed importance. Men in expensive suits moved through the rooms with the quiet confidence of power, while white-gloved staff appeared and disappeared as needed, never lingering and certainly never seen.

Marlowe followed Max Schen through the main hall and up a flight of stairs, constantly hyperaware of how exposed they were. If any of Steele's Marlowe Coin game hunters had connections to this world, this would be the perfect killing ground and the security here meant CCTV that went straight to the source; that source being MI5 or MI6 and the moles Steele paid for.

But something told him The Broker's assassins–or rather the ones left in the game now the fee was so low–wouldn't have access to establishments like this.

Christ, Marlowe was the golden boy of Orchid and even *he* didn't.

Max paused outside a door at the end of a corridor, straightening his tie.

'Let me do the initial talking,' he murmured. 'Robertson will try to leave the moment he sees me. We need him cornered before you start. And for God's sake, straighten your tie.'

Marlowe nodded once, resisting the urge to strangle Max with his own tie, and Max pushed open the door.

The Oak Room was a private dining space, intimate enough for confidential conversation but large enough to not feel cramped. At a table by the window sat a man in his sixties–distinguished, silver-haired, with the polished appearance of a career politician. His eyes widened in genuine shock as he spotted Max.

'Schen? What the devil are you—'

His words died as Marlowe entered behind Max, closing the door firmly.

Russell Robertson, Minister for Defence and believed member of both the old Orchid, and St John Steele's "New Kid" variant went very still, his fork suspended halfway to his mouth.

'Afternoon, Minister,' Max said cheerfully, pulling out a chair and sitting without invitation. 'Hope we're not interrupting anything important. Just a friendly catch-up between old associates.'

Robertson carefully set down his fork, his face a mask of serene neutrality, though Marlowe noted the slight tremble in his hand.

'I'm afraid I'm in the middle of a private lunch, gentlemen. Perhaps we could speak another time.'

'Oh, I think now works best for all of us,' Max replied, gesturing for Marlowe to sit. 'After all, we have so much to discuss. Tower Bridge. Gregorovich. The Marlowe Coin. All those fascinating projects you've been helping provide for our mutual friend.'

Robertson's eyes flickered to Marlowe, then back to Max.

'I have no idea what you're talking about. Now if you'll excuse me—' He began to rise.

'Sit down, Minister,' Marlowe said quietly. It wasn't a request.

Robertson hesitated, then slowly sank back into his chair, his political instincts clearly calculating the optics of a scene in the club versus whatever dangerous conversation was about to unfold.

'I have a meeting,' he muttered petulantly, as if this would save him from whatever was about to occur. 'What do you want?'

'The truth would be a good start,' Marlowe replied. 'About Steele. About why a senior cabinet minister is backing a rogue intelligence operative with a vendetta and a cryptocurrency built around my assassination.'

Robertson's expression flickered through a variety of responses, including surprise, calculation, and then ended on something like resignation.

'You have no idea what you're meddling with, Marlowe,' he said finally. 'This goes far beyond your personal grudge with Steele.'

'Then enlighten me.'

Robertson glanced around the room, then leant forward.

'Steele represented stability,' he said, voice barely above a whisper. 'Control. A unified Orchid could maintain the balance between competing powers, keep the worst excesses in check. When you shattered that, you created a vacuum. Do you have any idea what's rushing in to fill it?'

'Spare me the lecture on geopolitical balance,' Marlowe replied coldly. 'You're funding a man who's put a bounty on my head and is holding a Russian intelligence asset–actually, from what I can work out, a Russian and MI6 intelligence asset–in an unauthorised black site beside one of London's most recognisable landmarks.'

'It's more complicated than that.'

'It always is with your type,' Max interjected. 'Right up until someone puts a bullet in your head. Then it gets remarkably simple, remarkably quickly.'

Robertson paled slightly.

'Is that a threat?'

'Just an observation,' Max replied. 'Though I'm sure Thomas here has considered it.'

The door opened and a server entered with a bottle of wine. Robertson waved him away with a terse, 'Not now,' and the man retreated, closing the door behind him.

'You need to understand,' Robertson continued once the server was gone, 'Steele was containable. Predictable. He wanted power, yes, but within established parameters. What's emerging now is far worse–fragmented power centres, no accountability, old vendettas being settled violently. At least Steele has a vision.'

'A vision that includes putting me in a gladiatorial arena for the entertainment of the wealthy?' Marlowe asked.

'That was ... unfortunate.' Robertson at least had the grace to look uncomfortable. 'An unorthodox fundraising mechanism. But necessary, after the Berlin and Rushmore setbacks.'

So, Robertson knew about these. Interesting.

'Unorthodox,' Marlowe repeated flatly. 'Is that what they teach you to call murder in Westminster these days?'

'It was never supposed to go this far,' Robertson insisted. 'The coin was meant to be a controlled exercise; create some excitement, attract investment, establish a new financial foundation for the reorganisation. Nobody expected you to actually start killing the assassins.'

'Nobody expected me to survive, you mean.'

Robertson didn't deny it but then sighed.

'We thought you'd defeat them, but that you'd leave them alive. Maybe one or two would die, there'd be a small drop, but we didn't expect what you did with The Swede, for example. Or Volkov.'

He leant back, licking his lips nervously.

'You want to be careful,' he breathed. 'I could be an excellent ally for you. Baker's on the way out and I'm a front runner for the job. If I get in, and you play nice ...'

The offer was unspoken; it didn't need to be given voice. Everyone at the table knew what Russell Robertson was suggesting.

Max leaned forward; his expression suddenly serious.

'Here's what's going to happen, Russell. You're going to withdraw your support from Steele. Completely. Financial, political, all of it. Today.'

'That's impossible.'

'Is it?' Max slid his phone across the table. On the screen Marlowe could see a document–bank transfers from an account in The Cayman Islands to various shell companies. 'These look familiar. I kept copies of everything while we were prepping Berlin. Just in case.'

The colour drained from Robertson's face.

'Where did you get this?'

'I may have been cut out of the operation, but I'm not an idiot,' Max smiled thinly. 'I always keep insurance. These transfers–authorised by you, personally–funded some very interesting activities in Eastern Europe. Activities that would raise some extremely uncomfortable questions in Parliament.'

Marlowe read the data on the phone, even though it was upside down. *Had Vic Saeed provided this? Was he working for more than just McKellan? The man had expensive tastes, so it made sense he'd sell copies to the highest bidder. Or was this Max Schen using other assets?*

'This is blackmail,' the response from Robertson was almost a whine.

'This is consequence management,' Max corrected. 'You backed the wrong horse. Now you're going to make it right—'

The door opened and closed suddenly, causing all three men to start. A tall man in an impeccable suit now stood in front of the door, his eyes scanning the room before settling on Marlowe.

Marlowe recognised him instantly. It seemed like the assassin known as "Passive" had decided *not* to be his namesake any more.

For a fraction of a second, nobody moved.

Then Passive's hand moved to his jacket, but Marlowe was already diving sideways as the muffled cough of a suppressed pistol filled the room.

The CCTV must have flagged him. Or the doorman.

Or bloody Max Schen was playing games.

The round shattered the wineglass on the table where Marlowe had been sitting moments before. Robertson scrambled backwards with a startled cry as Max upended the heavy oak table, creating a momentary barricade.

'Friend of yours?' Max hissed at Marlowe.

'Unlikely,' Marlowe replied, drawing his own weapon. 'More like another bounty hunter.'

Passive advanced methodically, taking measured steps into the room. Expensive shoes, bespoke suit, professional bearing–this wasn't some amateur thug. This was a high-end professional, the kind who would carry the most current version of Marlowe's location data from the cryptocurrency network.

'Come, Mister Marlowe, don't make this hard on us both,' he said through the chaos. 'Stand up, give a smile, and let me finish this.'

As a response to this, Marlowe fired twice from behind the table, forcing the assassin to take cover behind a fake divider bookcase.

The gunshots were thunderous in the confined space and somewhere in the distance, alarmed voices could be heard responding to the commotion.

'We need to move,' Marlowe said to Max. 'Stay low, head for the door when I give the signal.'

'What about Robertson?'

'He's on his own–but his close protection officers will be in at any second and they won't be taking prisoners.'

Max nodded, wide-eyed, but understanding the calculus of survival.

Robertson, meanwhile, had crawled behind a sideboard, making himself as small a target as possible and was screaming for his bodyguards.

Passive fired again, wood splintering from the table inches from Marlowe's head. Then there was the distinctive metallic click of a magazine being changed–the opening Marlowe had been waiting for.

'Now!' he shouted to Max, rising to return fire as Max dashed for the door. But before either of them could make it halfway across the room, the door burst open again–and a familiar blond figure charged in, weapon raised.

Volkov.

For a disorienting moment, Marlowe thought he was facing a second attacker. But Volkov fired precisely at Passive, three rapid shots that drove the man back against the bookcase. Passive returned fire wildly, missing his targets as Volkov advanced relentlessly, putting another round into the man's chest. The assassin known as Passive collapsed, blood blossoming across his white shirt.

Silence fell abruptly, broken only by the distant sound of alarmed voices and the approaching wail of police sirens.

Volkov turned to Marlowe, his expression unreadable.

'You lied about Ayrshire,' he said flatly.

'I told you what I believed was true at the time,' Marlowe replied, keeping his weapon raised. 'Why are you here?'

'Following him,' Volkov nodded towards the fallen body of Passive. 'I knew he was coming for you once you'd escaped. When I saw what he planned, I decided to intervene.'

'Out of the goodness of your heart?' Max asked sceptically, emerging from behind an overturned chair.

'Out of self-interest,' Volkov replied coldly. 'Marlowe knows where my grandfather is. Marlowe dead and in God's hands–or the Devil's, perhaps–means I never find out.'

He looked at the body.

'I killed him,' he said. 'Does that lower your price?'

'I really don't know and I really don't care right now.' Marlowe started to calm a little as the adrenaline left his system. 'But thanks.'

Robertson chose that moment to rise shakily from his hiding place, straightening his tie with trembling hands.

'This is outrageous,' he began, his politician's instincts asserting themselves. 'I'll have all of you—'

'Shut up,' Volkov and Marlowe said in unison.

The sirens were getting closer.

'We need to leave,' Volkov said. 'Immediately.'

Marlowe moved to the downed assassin, quickly searching his pockets. He found what he was looking for–a smartphone with the Marlowe Coin tracking application open on its screen. He pocketed it, then turned to Robertson.

'Remember this moment,' he whispered. 'When the police ask, you'll tell them it was a lone gunman, a crazy. You defended yourself.'

'With what?'

Marlowe took the gun from Volkov, giving it to Robertson. Then, with Robertson's finger in the trigger guard, Marlowe aimed the gun at the body of Mister Passive and fired it once.

'That way, you'll have resin on your fingers. Makes the story believable. You'll be an action hero. Remember this when you take Baker's job–that it was *this* that did it for you.'

The sound of running steps was closer now; Marlowe guessed Robertson had told his unit to stay away during his lunch, and although the fight was over, only seconds had truly passed.

'What do you want of me?'

'You'll protect Max. You'll cut all ties with Steele. Because if you don't, Max's insurance policy will be the least of your worries.'

He turned to Volkov.

'You want to find your grandfather? Come with us.'

Volkov nodded once and the three men slipped out of the Oak Room's rear entrance, leaving Robertson alone with a corpse, a gun in his hand and a lot of explaining to do.

'The lack of response there, was that you?' Marlowe asked as, once in the corridor, Max led them to a service staircase that descended to the kitchen level and out through a delivery entrance. 'We were left alone for way too long.'

'That's my fault and I'm sorry,' Max sheepishly admitted. 'I had my guard pay off people, say we needed some personal time with Russell and not to bother us, no matter what. They probably didn't realise what was happening until it was too late.'

'I hope you paid them well, because I think there's a lot of guards about to lose their jobs over that,' Marlowe muttered.

They emerged into an alley just as police cars screeched to a halt in front of the club's main entrance.

'My car's three streets east,' Max said, already walking briskly in that direction. 'I told him to go there after ...'

'After you sent anyone who could stop Mister Passive away,' Marlowe gave a thin smile. 'Almost as if you wanted him to kill me?'

'Oh, believe me, I want nothing more than to attend your funeral after Berlin,' Max replied coldly. 'But perhaps after we screw over Steele, yeah?'

'We shouldn't stay together,' Volkov objected. 'Too obvious a target.'

'We need what Max has,' Marlowe replied. 'And you need what I know. For now, we stick together.'

Volkov's expression suggested he wasn't entirely convinced, but he fell in step beside them, his eyes constantly scanning for threats.

'The Shad Thames warehouse plans,' Marlowe said to Max as they walked. 'Time to put them to use.'

Max nodded, pulling out his phone.

'We'll need more people, maybe one or two more, who can help us with the next part, too,' he said. 'Someone Steele would never expect you to work with.'

Marlowe's thin smile held no warmth.

'I know just the man.'

26

PLANNING SESSION

'YOU WANT TO WORK WITH VIKRAM SAEED?' MAX SCHEN stared at Marlowe like he'd suggested partnering with St John Steele himself. 'The man's a snake. Worse, he works for Robertson.'

They were back in Max's hotel suite, a surprisingly understated location in Marylebone. Volkov leaned against the wall, arms crossed, watching the exchange with the calculated indifference of a professional who'd seen too many planning sessions dissolve into ego battles.

The plans for the Butler's Wharf facility lay spread across a dining table, weighted down with coffee mugs and a half-empty bottle of Glenfiddich.

'That's precisely why we need him,' Marlowe replied, as Max, shaking his head helped himself to another measure of the scotch. 'Think about it. Robertson's rattled after our little chat. He'll be calling Steele, trying to distance himself from whatever's coming. Saeed will know exactly what buttons to push to get what we need.'

'Assuming he doesn't immediately sell us out,' Max countered.

'You don't understand Saeed,' Marlowe leant against the table, stretching out his back. 'He's not loyal to Robertson or Steele–he's loyal to whoever offers the best angle. Right now, that's us.'

'How do you figure?'

'Because we're winning,' Marlowe said simply. 'The Marlowe Coin is already creating chaos. Saeed knows me, and he helped me escape. I paid him handsomely for it, true, but he's also caught between Robertson and McKellan at MI6. He wants to get out, he wants back into Orchid, preferably in a position of power, and he's calculating enough to see which way the wind is blowing.'

Volkov spoke up for the first time since they'd arrived at the suite.

'In Russia, we have saying; when the bear is wounded, even its cubs will bite it. Steele is wounded. Saeed will sense this.'

'Fine. Contact him,' Max conceded. 'But if he betrays us, he's your responsibility.'

'Fair enough.' Marlowe nodded, already pulling out his phone.

AFTER HE SENT HIS TEXT AS "UNCLE AKBAL", MARLOWE returned to studying the Shad Thames plans. The facility to the south side of the bridge was more extensive than he'd initially realised–a labyrinth of interconnected chambers, storage vaults and security checkpoints.

According to the documents, the main detention area was

two levels down from the primary entrance, accessible only through a series of biometrical secured doors.

'If Gregorovich is there, he'll be in this section,' Marlowe traced a finger along a high-security zone marked as "Special Containment". 'Heavy security, limited access points, emergency protocols in place.'

'They'll have modified the layout since these plans were drawn,' Volkov observed, moving closer to examine the documents. 'Steele is not stupid, and these were public.'

'They were for investors,' Max argued.

'Exactly. People not in the business. So, public.'

'He's right, but bureaucracy is predictable,' Marlowe interjected. 'Changes require permits, contractors, inspections. Even black sites have to follow building codes to some extent, especially in central London. The core structure will be the same.'

'We still need a way past the security checkpoints,' Volkov pointed out. 'And the guards. There will be many guards.'

'That's where Morris comes in,' Marlowe said. 'A Metropolitan Police Detective Inspector with a warrant makes for an excellent distraction.'

Volkov raised an eyebrow.

'You trust this police officer?'

'As much as I trust anyone,' Marlowe said with a shrug. 'He was almost killed because of me. And he doesn't know the full plan, just his part in it.'

'Which is?'

'Lead a raid on what he believes is a human trafficking operation. With enough evidence planted beforehand to make the warrant stick.'

Max chuckled.

'What?' Marlowe turned to face him.

'You just said "he was almost killed because of me". What in God's name makes you think he'll help?'

'Morris is a straight edge, but he's also ambitious. A high-profile raid leading to the rescue of a supposed kidnapping victim? That's career advancement material.'

Marlowe's phone beeped. He checked the message and smiled.

'Saeed's in.'

'Let's hope it's worth the risk,' Max muttered.

'I'll bring in someone else, too,' Marlowe added, texting a reply. 'But I'll hold on anything more until I know if he can make it.'

'What about The Broker?' Volkov asked suddenly. 'When he discovers the one thing holding him in line is missing, he will move against Steele.'

'That's the idea,' Marlowe nodded. 'Steele's been holding Gregorovich over The Broker's head to keep him in line. Once Gregorovich is free, that leverage disappears, but only if we get Gregorovich out alive and into The Broker's hands. Which means we need to be clean. No casualties if we can help it.'

Volkov's expression suggested he wasn't entirely on board with the "no casualties" approach, but he nodded regardless.

'I want Gregorovich safe and alive. That is all that matters to me.'

THE SUITE DOOR WAS KNOCKED UPON PRECISELY AN HOUR later. The guard at the door, apparently one of Max's most loyal "soldiers" looked over and, at a nod from his boss, opened the door. Moments later, Vic Saeed strode into the apartment with his usual confident swagger, impeccably dressed in a charcoal suit.

Behind him came a face Marlowe had expected to see, but the others hadn't.

'Hello, Tom,' said The Gravedigger, his scarred face impassive as ever, as he moved into the room, casting a professional eye over the plans on the table. 'Didn't expect to see you so soon. These current?'

'As current as we could get,' Max replied. 'We were hoping Saeed might have updates. And you are?'

'Oh, sorry,' Marlowe smiled. 'Max Schen, meet The Gravedigger.'

Max had obviously heard the name before and Marlowe had a moment of satisfaction as the billionaire paled. He wasn't sure, but Marlowe believed that if he'd had a little less whisky in him, he might even have wet himself.

Saeed, ignoring this, smiled thinly, setting his briefcase on the table and removing a sleek tablet.

'Robertson was kind enough to leave his office unlocked when he departed Whitehall in a hurry after your little meeting,' he said, powering up the device. 'Amazing what you can find when people panic.'

He pulled up a series of schematics, more detailed than the ones they already had, with security notations and what appeared to be recent modifications.

'Tower Bridge facility, latest update from three weeks ago,' Saeed explained. 'Complete with guard rotations, security protocols, and–most importantly–the location of one Alexei Mikhail Gregorovich, formerly of the KGB's First Chief Directorate, and then MI6 asset.'

'Tower Bridge Facility?' Marlowe frowned. 'We're looking at Butler's Wharf.'

'It's all the same thing,' Saeed shrugged. 'Connected by underground tunnels. Think Whitehall and Westminster? Same thing.'

Volkov leaned forward, his cold and calm persona cracking slightly at the sight of his grandfather's name on an official document.

'He's alive, then,' he said quietly, looking at Marlowe. 'You were right, it seems.'

'You don't have to sound so surprised,' Marlowe muttered.

'Not only alive,' Saeed confirmed, 'but valued enough to be kept comfortable, if not free. Private quarters, medical attention, decent food. They want him functional.'

'As leverage against The Broker,' Marlowe nodded. 'Steele always had the talent of knowing where all the bodies are buried. Knowing everybody's pressure points.'

'So, we have updated plans,' The Gravedigger said, returning focus to the operation. 'What about access? These security protocols look formidable.'

'That's the other thing I brought,' Saeed reached into his briefcase again, producing what looked like four security badges. 'Tower Bridge maintenance credentials. Level three access, which gets us through the first two checkpoints.'

'And after that?' Max asked.

'After that, we improvise,' Saeed replied with a thin smile. 'Or rather, I improvise. McKellan's had me spending the past six weeks building a backdoor into their security system as part of Robertson's "infrastructure review". One terminal access is all I need to create a little chaos.'

'McKellan knew of this?'

'Just that Steele had been allowed to use the space by

Robertson as one of the "reviewers",' Saeed admitted. 'He was suspicious. I mean, apart from it being Steele, McKellan would have been suspicious anyway. The man's constantly paranoid.'

'What about the police raid?' Volkov asked. 'How does that fit with this plan?'

'That's our extraction,' Marlowe explained. 'Morris leads a legitimate raid on what he believes is a human trafficking operation. In the confusion, we get Gregorovich out, supposedly "arresting" him as one of the perpetrators. Once he's in police custody, we have friends in MI5 and MI6 who can take over. By the time anyone realises what's happened, Gregorovich'll be with The Broker, and Steele will have lost his leverage.'

'Neatly played,' The Gravedigger commented, sounding almost impressed. 'If it works. But it doesn't give me Steele to kill, so as a plan it fails.'

'I've got one more card to play on that point,' Marlowe said, pulling out his phone. 'I've put a contract on Steele. It's set to be announced before six, which is any time now.'

There was a moment of stunned silence as everyone in the room took in the words that had just been spoken.

'You *what*?' Max finally asked.

Marlowe smiled, relaxing his shoulders a little as he leant back against the table.

'I contacted Pauline Faulkner. Put a hit on Steele for one dollar and a favour from my branch of Orchid.'

'One dollar and a favour?' Saeed looked incredulous. 'Nobody will take that.'

'That's not the point,' Marlowe replied. 'The point is to make it public. To make him a joke. To show everyone that the great St John Steele, who put a twelve-million-dollar bounty on my head, is worth exactly one dollar and a moment of my time to me. It's about humiliation, not elimination.'

'That'll certainly get his attention,' The Gravedigger said with a grim smile. 'And distract him right when he needs to be focused.'

'Exactly,' Marlowe nodded. 'While he's dealing with the public embarrassment and the sudden flood of amateurs hoping to claim Orchid's favour by taking potshots at him, we'll be freeing his most valuable asset from right under his nose.'

'I hate to be the voice of reason here,' Max interjected, 'but what about the Marlowe Coin? Even if we pull this off, there's still millions of dollars in cryptocurrency incentivising your death. That doesn't disappear overnight.'

'Trix is working on that,' Marlowe replied. 'If anyone can crash a cryptocurrency, it's her.'

'And if she can't?'

'Then I'll keep dealing with assassins one by one until the price drops to pennies and nobody bothers any more,' Marlowe said with a shrug. 'But let's focus on tomorrow's problem tomorrow. Right now, we need to finalise this plan. Get some rest, we start this tomorrow. I'll contact you all by six p.m. with what needs to happen.'

As the others walked over to the door, discussing Steele's reaction to the upcoming hit, Volkov lingered, his expression unusually uncertain.

'My grandfather,' he whispered. 'What condition will he be in?'

'I don't know,' Marlowe admitted. 'But Saeed says he's being kept comfortable. That's a good sign.'

Volkov nodded, his face returning to its usual impassive mask.

'Thank you,' he said stiffly, clearly uncomfortable with gratitude. 'For doing this.'

'Don't take this the wrong way, Volkov, I'm not doing it for you,' Marlowe replied. 'Or even for Gregorovich. I'm doing it because it hurts Steele.'

'I know,' Volkov said. 'That doesn't change what it means to me.'

With that, he turned and left, following The Gravedigger out of the suite door. Saeed was next, pausing at the door with a faint smile.

'For what it's worth, Marlowe, I always thought you'd win this game. That's why I'm betting on you.'

'This isn't a game, Saeed.'

'Everything's a game for men like us,' Saeed replied. 'The difference is some of us admit it.'

Then he, too, was gone, leaving only Max and Marlowe in the apartment.

'You really think this will work?' Max asked, pouring himself a last measure of scotch.

'No plan survives contact with the enemy,' Marlowe said, gathering up the remaining documents. 'But it doesn't need to be perfect. It just needs to create enough chaos for us to get Gregorovich out and to The Broker.'

'And after that?'

'After that, Steele loses his leverage over The Broker. The Marlowe Coin crashes. And then it's just him and me, with nowhere left to hide, probably fighting to the death somewhere in Tower Bridge, as that's where he's decided to make his stand.'

Max raised his glass in a mock toast.

'To chaos, then.'

'To chaos,' Marlowe agreed.

'You know,' DI Morris said as he opened his front door, staring at Marlowe, 'when you said you were going to leave me alone so I could spend time with my children, I didn't expect you to keep turning up.'

Marlowe gave a small smile.

'How would you like to be a hero?'

'My kids have known I've been a hero for years,' Morris looked around. 'Do I have to invite you in, or can we talk on the doorstep?'

'We can talk,' Marlowe. 'It'll be quick. I don't want to get you into trouble.'

He passed across a scrap of paper.

'Gregorovich, the one The Broker's got the hard-on for? He's here, being held by Steele, or someone on behalf of Steele. I intend to free him.'

'And why are you telling me?'

Marlowe tapped the address.

'Because I believe that this is within your jurisdiction, DCI Morris.'

Morris looked at the map and then frowned.

'I'm not DCI,' he said. 'You should know that by now.'

'Oh, I do,' Marlowe gave a wide smile. 'But you see, after you bring in the bust of the century, I'm sure that you'll be promoted. Don't you?'

Morris sighed, and it looked for all intents and purposes

like the air had simply fallen out of his body, with the resignation of what was about to happen.

'Fine,' he said, waving Marlowe into his house. 'Just stay quiet, yeah? My wife and kids are asleep. Come in, we'll have a cup of tea, and you can tell me what the bloody hell you want me to do.'

————

27

BUTLER'S WHARF

THE SHAD THAMES AREA NEAR BUTLER'S WHARF HAD changed dramatically since its days as a Victorian warehouse district. Once the largest tea warehouse complex in London, its cobbled streets and iron footbridges now housed luxury apartments, boutique shops and restaurants with views of Tower Bridge. But beneath the gentrified surface, remnants of its industrial past remained–forgotten spaces, maintenance tunnels, and subterranean rooms that had never made it into the modern blueprints.

Perfect places to hide someone you didn't want found.

Marlowe checked his watch–it was eleven forty-seven in the morning. Thirteen minutes until noon, when DI Morris would arrive with his warrant, DS Wilcott and likely armed police backup.

The narrow alley behind a row of converted warehouses was deserted, the steady drizzle discouraging casual passersby. Marlowe pulled his collar higher against the rain and studied the unassuming metal door set into the brick wall. According to Saeed's intelligence, this maintenance entrance led directly to the sub-level where Gregorovich was being held.

As if by magic, Volkov appeared at his side from the shadows with a silence that marked him as a serious threat ... if they ever found themselves on opposite sides. The Ukrainian's face betrayed no emotion, but Marlowe noticed his hand checking his concealed weapon for the third time in as many minutes.

'Nervous?' Marlowe asked quietly.

'Cautious,' Volkov replied. 'I haven't seen my grandfather in years. Remember, Marlowe, I was told he was dead.'

'Family reunions can be complicated,' Marlowe conceded. 'Especially when they involve breaking into black sites.'

A soft footfall announced The Gravedigger's arrival, followed by Saeed's more purposeful stride. Both men were dressed inconspicuously in maintenance coveralls, blending perfectly with the working environment of the area.

'Security scan shows minimal activity,' Saeed reported, checking a device that looked like a modified smartphone. 'Two guards on rotation, plus whatever automated systems they've got running. The trick will be the biometric locks– we'll need to bypass at least three. Is your woman able to do that?'

'I'm not using her for this. That's why we have you,' Marlowe said. 'To prove to me why MI5 thought you were such hot stuff and all that.'

'Always nice to be appreciated,' Saeed smirked.

The Gravedigger, likely not trusting Saeed's tech, produced a small electronic device, attaching it to the door's security panel, watching the screen fill with details. Marlowe was about to ask how he had his own devices, but then remembered that when he was Peter Jericho, The

Gravedigger trained under a pre-knighted Walter McKellan and was one of MI6's brightest and best–before going it alone.

He tutted as he read the display.

'Standard Governmental maintenance encryption. Would have expected better upgrades from Steele.'

'He relies on obscurity more than security,' Saeed replied. 'Nobody's supposed to know this place exists–or if they do, that it's operational. New security just makes it interesting.'

The device beeped softly, and the door's lock disengaged with a subtle click. The Gravedigger pulled it open just enough to check inside, then nodded to the others.

Time to do this.

Marlowe led the way, his senses heightened as they entered the dimly lit passageway. The air carried the familiar mustiness of long-disused spaces, overlaid with the industrial scent of machinery and concrete. Emergency lighting cast everything in a sickly green glow, creating pockets of shadow between fixtures.

'Primary security checkpoint should be thirty metres ahead,' Saeed whispered, consulting the building plans on his own phone screen. 'Then down one level to the containment area.'

They moved silently, alert for any sign of guards or surveillance. The first checkpoint was unmanned–a simple camera above a reinforced door with a biometric scanner.

'They're confident,' The Gravedigger observed. 'Too confident.'

'Or understaffed,' Marlowe countered. 'Steele's been bleeding resources since Rushmore. The camera?'

'For show only, the feeds have been fluctuating badly since they brought the servers into the main vaults,' Saeed approached the scanner, removing a thin film from his pocket. 'They're rotating their operational assets, so if we're in and out fast, they'll miss us on the screens. And if they don't miss us? They're not staffed enough to check every maintenance worker with level one access.'

'And how do we get through?'

'This,' Saeed waved the film. 'Lifted from one of Robertson's glasses during a cabinet meeting. His prints have level five access to all government locations, and this, even though it's "borrowed" by Steele, is still on the books.'

He pressed the film against the scanner, which pulsed blue, then green. The door unlocked with a heavy clunk.

'Parliamentary privilege has its uses,' Saeed remarked dryly.

Beyond the door, a narrow stairwell descended into darkness. They proceeded single file; The Gravedigger taking point, Marlowe close behind, with Volkov and Saeed following. At the bottom, another corridor stretched before them— although this one seemed better maintained, with proper lighting and recently painted walls.

'We're entering the active part of the facility,' Saeed whispered. 'Stay alert–the CCTV here won't be rotated.'

They had progressed perhaps twenty feet, when a door ahead opened suddenly. A guard emerged, back turned to them as he spoke to someone inside the room.

'Making another coffee run. Want anything?'

The reply was inaudible, but the guard laughed and began turning towards them.

Volkov moved with startling speed. Before Marlowe could react, the Ukrainian had closed the distance and knocked the guard unconscious with a vicious blow to the base of the skull. He caught the man's body before it hit the floor, dragging him silently back towards their position.

'No killing,' Marlowe reminded him sharply.

'He's breathing,' Volkov replied, sounding almost offended. 'Help me drag him into that storage closet.'

The Gravedigger helped secure the unconscious guard, using zip ties from his pocket to bind the man's wrists and ankles. They gagged him with his own tie and closed the closet door, continuing down the corridor with heightened caution.

'That was one of two,' Saeed murmured. 'Where's the other?'

They received their answer moments later as they approached the final security door. Through its reinforced glass panel, they could see a small control room with multiple monitors. A single guard sat at the desk; his attention focused on a tablet in his hands.

'Biometric lock again,' Saeed observed. 'But we need him distracted or neutralised before we can use the print film.'

Marlowe considered their options. Direct confrontation risked noise and potential alarms. Stealth approach would be difficult with the guard behind the door.

The Gravedigger solved the problem by removing what looked like a pen from his pocket.

'Smoke pellet,' he explained. 'Small enough to fit through the air vent beside the door. It'll create enough confusion for us to enter.'

Volkov's eyes narrowed.

'He'll trigger the alarm.'

'Not if we're fast enough,' The Gravedigger replied. 'And we need to be fast anyway. Marlowe's man Morris will be here in minutes. Besides, curiosity killed the cat.'

Marlowe nodded his approval and The Gravedigger carefully inserted the device through the small ventilation grille. A moment later, wispy tendrils of smoke began filling the control room. The guard looked up in surprise, walking to the door to examine this potential fire hazard–

Marlowe was through the door before the guard could complete the call, Saeed's print film having disengaged the lock. The guard turned back to the desk, reaching for his weapon, but Volkov was already there, delivering another blow with the butt of his gun to the head that rendered the man unconscious without causing permanent damage.

Well, apart from a likely concussion, anyway.

Marlowe moved immediately to the security monitors.

'Saeed, find Gregorovich's exact location.'

Saeed slid into the chair the guard had vacated, fingers tapping on the keyboard as he navigated the security system, at a speed that for a second made Marlowe regret not bringing Trix into this.

Saeed noticed Marlowe's sour expression.

'Look, I'm a two finger typer, yeah? Get over it,' he snapped. 'Three detention cells in the east wing. Only one is occupied according to the system logs.'

The monitors displayed various angles of the facility–corridors, storage rooms, and a section marked "Detention". In one cell, a figure sat on a narrow bed, reading what appeared to be a book.

'That's him,' Volkov said quietly, staring at the grainy image. Despite the poor quality, the family resemblance was evident–the same sharp cheekbones, the same watchful stillness.

'Can you disable the remaining security?' Marlowe asked Saeed.

'Working on it.' Saeed's fingers continued their annoyingly slow dance across the keyboard. 'They've got a redundant system. If I disable everything, it triggers an automatic alert to their offsite monitoring. I need to create a loop in the camera feeds first, then selectively disable the cell locks.'

He grinned.

'See? If you bother to attend the briefings, you can learn a lot in the Security Service.'

'How long?'

'A minute or two.'

Marlowe checked his watch again. 'Morris will be here around the same time. Perfect.'

After a long, awkward minute of silence, broken only by the methodical, slow tap tap tapping of the keyboard, Saeed hit the return button with purpose.

'Cameras are looped, cell locks are on manual override,' he announced triumphantly. 'We can proceed to the detention area.'

Marlowe nodded to Volkov.

'You lead. It's your grandfather we're here for.'

Something like gratitude flickered across the Ukrainian's face. He moved to the door connecting the control room to the detention wing, Saeed's electronic bypass making quick work of the lock.

The detention area consisted of a central hub with three cells branching off it. Only one door showed the red indicator light of an occupied cell and Volkov approached it cautiously, peering through the small observation window.

Inside, an old man sat completely still, his posture erect despite his age, eyes fixed on the door as if he'd been expecting visitors. He wore simple clothing–navy trousers and a white shirt–but carried himself with unmistakable dignity.

Saeed activated the override and the indicator light changed from red to green. Volkov hesitated, his hand on the door handle, a rare moment of uncertainty from the usually implacable assassin.

'He might not recognise you,' Marlowe said quietly.

'He'll recognise me,' Volkov replied and pushed the door open.

Mikhail Gregorovich rose from his seat with the deliberate movements of a man conserving energy. He was tall, still powerfully built despite his age, with thick white hair and penetrating blue eyes that assessed each person entering his cell with cold efficiency.

His gaze settled on Volkov and for a moment, time seemed suspended between them.

'Grandson,' he said finally, his voice a deep, gravelly rumble. 'You took your time.'

Volkov's usual impassivity cracked, a fleeting smile touching his lips.

'I was told you were dead, Grandfather.'

'And yet here I am.' Gregorovich's attention shifted to the others. 'You've brought friends. Unusual for you.'

'Circumstances required it,' Volkov replied. 'We're extracting you. Now.'

Gregorovich nodded once, without surprise, and moved towards the door with the gait of someone managing chronic pain. Marlowe noticed he favoured his left leg slightly–an old injury, perhaps, or simply the wear of advanced age.

'You have transport prepared?' Gregorovich asked, addressing Marlowe directly.

'Of a sort,' Marlowe replied. 'Metropolitan Police will be

arriving momentarily with a warrant. You'll be "arrested" as part of a human trafficking operation. Once in custody, arrangements have been made for your release.'

Gregorovich raised an eyebrow.

'Creative. And who orchestrated this particular ballet?'

'I did,' Marlowe said. 'With some assistance from your grandson.'

'And you are?'

'Marlowe.'

Recognition flashed in the old man's eyes.

'Ah. You're the one with the price on his head. The guards have a sweepstake on you.'

'Well, I hope they're not expecting to win.'

Before anyone else could respond, Saeed checked his now flashing phone.

'Police are at the entrance. Right on schedule.'

'Time to move,' Marlowe said. 'Gregorovich, can you walk unassisted?'

'I've been walking unassisted since before you were born, young man,' Gregorovich replied dryly. 'Lead the way.'

They exited the cell, Volkov staying close to his grandfather as they returned to the control room. On the monitors, they could see Morris and Wilcott leading a team of armed response officers through the entrance corridor, warrant in hand.

'Perfect timing,' The Gravedigger observed. 'Though your Detective Inspector brought more backup than expected.'

'Let's give them something to find,' Marlowe decided. 'Saeed, can you trigger a limited alert? Something that suggests activity in this area without specifying exactly what's happening?'

Saeed grinned.

'With pleasure.'

Moments later, a muted alarm began sounding through the facility.

Marlowe turned to Gregorovich.

'When they arrive, let me do the talking. You're just another suspect as far as they're concerned.'

Gregorovich nodded, though his expression suggested he found the entire situation faintly amusing.

'What about the guards?' The Gravedigger asked.

'Leave them,' Marlowe replied. 'They're part of the evidence now. Adds credibility to Morris's raid.'

They didn't have to wait long. Within minutes, they heard the rapid approach of multiple footsteps in the corridor outside. The door burst open and Morris entered, followed by two armed officers.

'Metropolitan Police!' he announced. 'Nobody move!'

Marlowe raised his hands slowly, a gesture copied by the others. Only Gregorovich remained perfectly still, his posture relaxed despite the weapons pointed in his direction.

Morris's eyes paused momentarily on Marlowe but, to his credit, he didn't break character.

'All of you, on your knees, hands behind your heads!' he ordered.

They complied, though Gregorovich moved more deliberately, his age clear in the stiffness of his joints.

'Detective Inspector,' Marlowe said calmly. 'I'm glad you're here. We were just conducting our own investigation into this illegal detention facility.'

'Save it,' Morris replied curtly, though Marlowe caught the faint hint of a nod–acknowledgment that he was playing along. 'Henderson, Williams, search them for weapons.'

As Wilcott stood beside the door, Marlowe wondering

whether she'd been informed on what was happening here, the officers moved forward, conducting professional pat-downs. They recovered weapons from Volkov and The Gravedigger, but Marlowe and Saeed had wisely left theirs behind, knowing this moment would come.

'Sir,' one officer called to Morris, 'we've found a security guard locked in a closet. Alive but restrained.'

'And the control room shows this is some kind of detention facility,' Marlowe added, nodding at the monitors.

Morris made a show of looking around, his expression hardening into convincing outrage. 'Illegal detention. Just as our informant suggested.'

He turned to Gregorovich.

'Sir, were you being held here against your will?'

Gregorovich considered the question with theatrical gravity.

'I have been a prisoner for three years and was brought here a month ago,' he said, his Russian accent thickening slightly. 'Kept in that cell. Not allowed to leave.'

He gestured towards Marlowe and the others.

'These people were trying to free me when you arrived.'

'Vigilante justice is still illegal,' Morris replied firmly. 'All of you are under arrest. You have the right to remain silent ...'

As Morris continued the formal arrest process, Marlowe caught his eye briefly. A silent message passed between them.

Everything was proceeding according to plan.

The officers handcuffed all five of them, leading them back towards the entrance in a single file, and Marlowe noticed Morris was careful to maintain the appearance of a legitimate arrest, keeping his distance, treating them as suspects rather than allies.

They had almost reached the main entrance when a new,

unexpected figure appeared stepping through the doorway with casual confidence.

The Broker.

He was dressed impeccably in a pinstripe suit that probably cost more than most of the officers made in a month, his silver hair perfectly coiffed, his expression one of mild interest as he surveyed the scene. Behind him stood Hargrove, his ever-present assistant, holding an umbrella to shield his employer from the drizzle outside.

'Detective Inspector Morris,' The Broker said, his voice carrying the polished tones of expensive education. 'Excellent work. I see you've apprehended the suspects.'

Morris paused–and Marlowe held his breath.

The last time Morris met The Broker, he was secured on stage, while the man auctioned off his death. This could ruin everything if Morris reacted the wrong way.

To his credit though, Morris took a moment, straightened and regained his composure.

'And you are ...?' he asked coldly.

'Raymond Kinley,' The Broker replied smoothly, offering a business card. 'Home Office consultant on special operations. We've been monitoring this facility for some time.'

It was, Marlowe had to admit, a masterful performance. The Broker precisely projected the right mixture of authority and bureaucratic confidence to make his presence seem legitimate. The business card, no doubt, contained a phone number that would connect to someone who would verify his credentials–all part of the elaborate machinery that kept men like The Broker operating in the shadows of official power.

Morris examined the card sceptically–rightly so, given his unofficial knowledge of the man–but didn't challenge the claim directly.

'This is an active crime scene, Mister Kinley. I'll need to ask you to wait outside.'

'Of course, Detective Inspector. I merely wished to confirm that you had secured the primary asset.' The Broker's gaze moved to Gregorovich and something unspoken passed between the two old men. 'I see that you have.'

Gregorovich's expression revealed nothing, but Marlowe noted the slight straightening of his posture, the fractional narrowing of his eyes. Recognition, certainly. Perhaps even relief.

'All suspects will be processed at the station,' Morris stated firmly.

'Naturally,' The Broker agreed. 'Though I should inform you that certain ... diplomatic considerations may come into play regarding that particular gentleman.'

He nodded towards Gregorovich.

'My office will be in touch with your superintendent within the hour to arrange the appropriate protocols.'

Morris nodded curtly.

'We'll follow procedure, sir.'

'I would expect nothing less,' The Broker replied with a thin smile. 'As I said, excellent work, Detective Inspector. You've done your country a service today.'

He stepped aside, allowing the procession of officers and handcuffed suspects to continue past him. As Gregorovich passed, The Broker spoke quietly in Russian, too low for anyone but the old man to hear. Gregorovich gave no visible reaction, but Marlowe, watching closely, caught the faintest nod of acknowledgment.

Welcome back, master.

Outside, police vehicles waited to transport them to the station. The rain had intensified, turning the cobblestones

slick and casting everything in a grey haze that reduced visibility–perfect conditions for what came next.

As they were led towards separate vehicles, The Broker
approached Morris once more.

'Detective Inspector, a moment of your time?'

While Morris was distracted, Hargrove moved subtly
closer to Marlowe, speaking without looking directly at him.

'The Broker wishes to express his gratitude for your
assistance in this matter,' he murmured. 'He will ensure all of
you are released within hours, with no charges filed.'

'That's not why we did this,' Marlowe replied quietly.

'Nevertheless, the debt is acknowledged,' Hargrove
continued. 'He also wishes you to know that tonight's event at
Tower Bridge has been ... modified. Steele has taken the news
that you've placed a hit on him quite personally. He's called
off all hits and demanded the network find and inform you of
his plan.'

'Which is?'

'A final fight. You versus Steele, Tower Bridge, eight p.m.
tonight. Winner takes all.'

Marlowe absorbed this information, the implications
sending a chill through him despite the handcuffs digging
into his wrists.

One way or another, this ended in eight hours.

'Why tell me this?'

'Because The Broker believes you are the only one with
both the motivation and the capability to finish this with no
messy strings,' Hargrove replied simply. 'And because he no
longer wishes to be associated with an operation of this
nature.'

Before Marlowe could press for more details, an officer
approached to escort him to a waiting police car. Hargrove

stepped back, his expression returning to professional blankness.

As Marlowe was led away, he caught a last glimpse of The Broker standing beside his sleek black car, watching the proceedings with the calculated interest of a chess master observing the board. Their eyes met briefly and The Broker gave an almost imperceptible nod–acknowledgment, perhaps even a kind of gratitude.

Marlowe would even have bought it–if it wasn't for the fact that days earlier The Broker had been happy to skin his friends alive for coin raises.

Then the car door closed, and Marlowe was being driven away, ostensibly into custody but in reality towards the next phase of his confrontation with Steele.

The extraction had succeeded. Gregorovich was free, or would be soon enough. The Broker's debt to him was acknowledged, his loyalty to Steele broken.

But the news about Tower Bridge changed everything. This wasn't about money or power any more.

This was anger and hatred, primal and fierce.

Steele had always intended to end that evening at eight– from the start, Marlowe had known that whatever Steele planned, it would be then, and after Marlowe had been milked for every dollar his death could provide. Now, with a last fight in plan, Steele obviously believed it was time to end Marlowe *before* moving on.

And, now in the back of the police car, hands cuffed behind him as it navigated the rain-slicked streets towards the station, Marlowe decided he was absolutely fine with that.

28

FINAL BOSS

THE TEMPORARY WORKSTATION TRIX HAD SET UP IN THE service van was cramped but functional, parked in the shadow of Tower Bridge's north tower, as she worked on the small military-grade laptop on the bench table in front of her. Rain drummed on the roof, providing a rhythmic backdrop to her work as she executed the final phase of her plan.

On one screen, lines of code scrolled past as her virus worked its way through the Marlowe Coin blockchain. On another, security camera feeds cycled through various angles of the building's interior. In minutes, Marlowe would arrive, taking St John Steele's offer for one-on-one combat to end this whole damned show, while on either side of the bridge, official looking teams of workmen had closed off the bridge, making sure that nobody could enter Tower Bridge.

Except for Ciaran Winston, that was. He was already in there, deep in his little web, spinning his crypto lies.

But it was the third screen that held her attention now–a direct connection to the Marlowe Coin's primary server, where she could see active attempts to block her intrusion.

Someone was fighting back, recognising the attack and deploying a variety of impressive countermeasures with impressive speed.

Ciaran.

She recognised his coding style immediately–as ever, it was efficient but slightly over-engineered, with characteristic flourishes that were as identifiable to her as a hand-written signature. *For all his genius, he'd never been able to resist showing off in his work.*

'Found you,' she whispered, tracing his counter-program to its source. As she'd believed, the signal was coming from within the Tower Bridge complex itself–a server room two levels below where Marlowe was headed. It looked like Ciaran had finally ported everything across.

Trix grabbed her backpack, checking the equipment inside one last time. Inside it, she had additional hardware, emergency tools, and the thin USB-C drive containing the last phase of her attack. According to the building schematics, there was a maintenance entrance on the east side that would give her access to the lower levels without crossing the path of the fake roadmen–who, being on Steele's payroll would as likely shoot her in the face than tell her to move on.

Pulling on a rain jacket with the *Thames Water* logo–courtesy of Marshall Kirk, but why he had it, Trix had no idea–she stepped out into the downpour. The service entrance was thirty metres away, guarded by a single security camera that she'd already looped with footage from an hour earlier.

The electronic lock yielded easily to her cloned access card from earlier that week, taken from Ciaran's other facility. Inside, the utilitarian corridor was silent except for the distant hum of machinery. Trix consulted her phone, which displayed the building schematic with a blinking dot representing Ciaran's location.

Two levels down, three corridors over. It wasn't the important area, so security should be light.

She moved quietly, avoiding the main pathways where any of Steele's remaining security might be patrolling, but she wasn't expecting any, and her footsteps echoed slightly on the concrete floors despite her efforts to move silently.

Better safe than sorry.

The deeper she went, the more the building's infrastructure became apparent: massive power conduits, server racks, climate control systems. Steele hadn't just chosen this location for its symbolic value; the bridge's infrastructure provided access to London's traffic systems, power grid and communications networks. The perfect hub for whatever demonstration he'd planned before Marlowe's one-dollar bounty had forced him to change tactics.

Maybe the demonstration had just been delayed an hour.

Approaching the server room, Trix slowed. Light spilled from beneath the door and she could hear the rapid click of keyboard strokes from within. She checked her phone one last time, confirming her virus was still executing its initial phase, camouflaged as routine system maintenance.

Taking a deep breath, she pushed the door open.

Ciaran Winston sat hunched over a command console, his wild ginger hair even more dishevelled than usual, his attention fixed on a wall of screens displaying code sequences and transaction data. He wore the same rumpled Oxford shirt he'd favoured during their relationship, sleeves rolled up to reveal forearms covered in lines of hastily scrawled notes in black marker.

He didn't immediately look up as she entered, too engrossed in his work.

'I told you I don't want to be disturbed,' he snapped, fingers still flying across the keyboard. 'Whatever Steele wants can wait until I've contained this breach.'

'Hello, Ciaran,' Trix said quietly.

His hands froze mid-keystroke. For a moment, he remained perfectly still, as if processing a particularly complex line of code. Then he turned slowly, his expression shifting from disbelief to wariness.

'Trix,' he said finally. 'I'd say this is a pleasant surprise, but we'd both know that's a lie.'

'Not enjoying my little software update?' She nodded towards the screens, where alert messages were multiplying rapidly.

Ciaran's eyes narrowed as understanding dawned.

'Of course it's you. I thought you were one of the attacks, but I thought Whitehall was the other. Makes sense you're all of them.'

'Oh, I'm not all of them,' Trix smiled darkly. 'You and your master have pissed off a lot of dangerous countries. They're all having a pop. Let's see how good you really are.'

Nodding at this, Ciaran turned back to the screens, scrolling through lines of code.

'Clever cow. Using my own obfuscation techniques against me. But you always were a quick study.'

'Quick enough to see what you were doing with the Marlowe Coin from the beginning,' Trix replied, moving further into the room, positioning herself between Ciaran and the door. 'A cryptocurrency built around assassination. Classy.'

'It's more than that,' Ciaran said, his fingers resuming

their dance across the keyboard. 'It's a completely new financial architecture. Self-regulating scarcity, usage-based value correlation, predictive market integration ...'

'Spare me the white paper,' Trix cut him off. 'I've seen the code. You created a digital bloodsport and got rich off it.'

'*We* could have gotten rich off it,' Ciaran countered, still typing. 'If you hadn't been so bloody righteous about Marlowe.'

Trix set her backpack on an adjacent desk, removing her laptop.

'Is that why you never told me about your *other girlfriend* while we were together? My righteousness?'

That got his attention. Ciaran's hands paused again, and something that might have been shame flickered across his face before vanishing.

'Ancient history,' he said dismissively. 'Just like whatever you're trying to do here. Your attack's impressive, but ultimately, you're a school kid trying to win against her teacher. I designed this system with multiple fail-safes.'

Trix pulled her tablet from her bag and opened it.

'Should I be worried that you saw us like that?' she asked. 'You're like a year older than me.'

'And yet years more advanced.'

Trix shook her head sadly, entering a series of commands into the tablet.

'I think you'll find your "advances" aren't as advanced as you thought,' she said. 'Did you design it to handle *this?*'

On the main screens, new alerts began flashing. The Marlowe Coin value suddenly dropped by thirty per cent, then by another forty as previously burnt coins flooded *back* into the system.

Ciaran's eyes widened, his face pale in the glow of the monitors.

'That's not possible. Those coins were permanently removed from circulation.'

'Nothing's permanent in crypto,' Trix replied, her lips curving into a satisfied smile. 'Just hidden until someone finds the right key. You never actually burnt those coins, did you, Ciaran? Just moved them to cold wallets only you could access. Guess what? You used wallets I still had codes to, and you never found the flash drive I stuck in your other server system. Whoops.'

'How did you—' Ciaran stopped, his jaw clenching as he saw the transfer logs scrolling across her screen.

'Your code was elegant, I'll give you that, even if you couldn't help shouting from the rooftops you'd written it. Stole some of my own code, too, I saw,' Trix continued, enjoying the moment more than she probably should have. 'That fancy burn function that supposedly removed coins from circulation? It actually just shuffled them sideways into segregated wallets that nobody else could see. Very clever. When the price peaked, you'd have cashed out with hundreds of millions, while Steele wondered what happened to his golden goose.'

Ciaran's face flushed crimson, his fingers jabbing frantically at his keyboard.

'The burn mechanism was necessary for the price stability algorithm, I couldn't just—'

'Oh, save it for your trial,' Trix rolled her eyes. 'You were planning to screw Steele all along, weren't you?'

'Steele was using me,' Ciaran snapped, his composure finally cracking. 'Just like he uses everyone. Did you really think I'd build something this bloody brilliant just to let him walk away with all the profit? After what happened in Berlin?'

'If I recall, we left you in a dog cage in Berlin,' Trix said with a smile that didn't reach her eyes. 'Too bad I'm triple-crossing both of you.'

She hit *Enter* on her tablet with probably a little too much dramatic flair and on the screens, transaction logs showed the Marlowe Coin collapsing as people, previously unable to afford coins now found the falling cost profitable, while people who'd bought at the top were now trying to dump their own wallets at a substantial loss, realising the selling market was way higher than the buying one.

In less than a minute, the price had fallen from seven dollars to two and was still plummeting.

'The cold storage wallets were air-gapped,' Ciaran protested, real panic in his voice now. 'Those keys were stored offline in a bloody vault!'

He launched into a frenzy of countermeasures as he tried to stem the bleeding. Trix watched calmly, however, executing her own commands at a measured pace, systematically dismantling his defences.

'You'll crash the entire market,' Ciaran said, a note of desperation entering his voice. 'Not just the Marlowe Coin, but every associated blockchain. The investors will lose millions.'

'The investors knew what they were funding,' Trix replied coldly. 'They put money on Marlowe's death. They deserve to lose it. Sorry ... that made it sound like *future* tense. Let's be honest here. They've *already* lost it. The coin's now under a dollar. Soon it'll be lower than the original price and you'll have investors after your head.'

'Some of those investors are very dangerous people,' Ciaran warned. 'They won't take this lightly.'

'I know,' Trix smiled. 'They'll come hunting for who did this. You.'

A shadow crossed Ciaran's face.

'Bullshit. You did this—'

'How?' Trix gave her most innocent face. 'Using coins you stole, that you told people were burnt and launching it from your own servers right here? Come on, mate. You know you'll be the one blamed. Even Steele can't be accused of this.'

'It wasn't personal, Trix. It was just business.'

'Funny,' she replied. 'It felt pretty personal when you gave Steele access to Marlowe's house so you could blow it up.'

Ciaran abandoned his keyboard, turning to face her fully.

'It was the opportunity of a lifetime!' he exploded, running his hands through his wild hair. 'Do you have any idea what it's like creating something this revolutionary? This elegant? The Marlowe Coin isn't just a cryptocurrency, it's a new economic paradigm!'

'It's blood money,' Trix countered. 'And I'm taking it all down.'

On the screens, the Marlowe Coin's value continued its precipitous fall, now down over eighty per cent from its peak. Investor wallets were emptying at unprecedented speeds as panic selling accelerated.

Ciaran watched in horror.

'Do you realise what you've done? Months of work, destroyed in minutes.'

'Not destroyed,' Trix corrected, executing her final command sequence. 'Transformed. Just like our relationship. Game over, Ciaran. Go back to playing in *Crime City* servers. You're not ready for the real game yet.'

Ciaran had hit his limit though, and lunged suddenly, reaching for the emergency shutdown button on the console. Trix intercepted him, grabbing his wrist with surprising strength, twisting until he gasped in pain.

'Don't,' she warned. 'It's too late, anyway. The transactions are already confirmed on multiple blockchains. Even if you shut down this entire facility, you can't stop it now.'

Ciaran sagged against the console, defeat clear in every line of his body.

'Steele will kill me for this.'

'Steele has bigger problems right now,' Trix said, releasing his wrist. 'And I've sent enough evidence of your activities to Interpol, Scotland Yard, the FBI—hell, you name them, I sent it over to them—to keep you occupied for years to come.'

She turned off the tablet, packing it into her backpack.

'I'm curious, though—did you ever actually care about me?' she asked. 'Or was I just another system to be manipulated?'

For a moment, genuine emotion flickered across Ciaran's face—regret, perhaps, or something close to it.

'It wasn't all a lie,' he mumbled. 'But when it came down to it, I chose the work. I always do.'

Trix nodded, unsurprised.

'That's something I figured out long before Berlin. Some things matter more than code.'

She moved to the door, pausing with her hand on the handle.

'You should tell him,' Ciaran muttered.

'Tell who and what?'

'Marlowe. How you feel about him.'

'You don't get to give advice,' Trix shook her head. 'Get whatever funds you can and run. I don't ever want to see you again. And I sure as hell don't want to be forced to finish you permanently.'

Ciaran's head snapped up.

'What do you—'

'I'm very good at what I do,' Trix interrupted. 'Better than you. Remember that.'

As she stepped into the corridor, closing the door behind her, Trix felt a weight lift from her shoulders. The Marlowe Coin was crashing, Ciaran was defeated and now it was Marlowe's turn to finish what they'd started.

Trix checked her phone one last time, confirming that her final message had been sent to Curtis at MI5–the complete evidence package on Steele, Ciaran and everyone else involved in the operation.

Whatever happened next on Tower Bridge, the digital battlefield had been won. The Marlowe Coin and everyone connected to it was now destitute.

Trix gave a little grin.

Well, Maybe not everyone.

She kept that smile until the moment she turned the corner and found the armed men with assault rifles waiting for her.

29

TOWER BRIDGE

It was eight o'clock when Marlowe arrived at the north side of Tower Bridge. As expected, there was a selection of roadwork vans and men in high-vis jackets blocking the way, waving traffic on, signs saying the bridge was closed for essential building works ... and Marlowe knew that if he asked, they would be able to provide the exact paperwork needed for such an event.

Motorists were complaining–after all, Tower Bridge was one of the main routes across the Thames following the recent Mayor of London's decision to start charging on the Blackwall Tunnel later that year. But the road workers simply shrugged, claimed it wasn't their problem and kept their guns hidden in case things escalated.

Marlowe, however, had no problems. He hadn't driven; his Jaguar was still undercover in a car park in West London. Which had been lucky, really, because he was sure that if he had parked outside his church, it would probably have been destroyed in the same explosion and fire that had taken out the building. Instead, he had caught a cab, been dropped off at St Katherine's Docks and had walked along the wharf front, up the stairs and onto the bridge.

The guards seemed very well informed. The moment they saw him, they stepped back, allowing him to enter.

Of course they did, he thought to himself. *St John Steele wanted him there. The fact that Marlowe had turned up alone was probably exactly what he wanted.*

Tower Bridge stood before him, an iconic landmark spanning the Thames. Built in the late eighteen hundreds, the bridge was designed with two massive towers and a unique bascule mechanism that allowed it to open for passing ships. Its distinctive Victorian Gothic style made it instantly recognisable–a symbol of London that tourists flocked to photograph. But Marlowe knew it was more than just a pretty structure. The bridge contained hidden walkways, mechanical rooms and spaces most visitors never saw. Its towers housed exhibition spaces now but had once contained various offices and control rooms. The bridge had survived the Blitz and witnessed decades of London's history, standing as a silent observer to the city's evolving story.

And now, under its south side, was Steele's glorious new empire.

As Marlowe walked towards the North Tower, a guard, not bothering to wear the same road worker uniform as the others, was waiting for him.

'St John Steele is waiting for you on the visitors' gantry,' he said, nodding upwards. Tower Bridge did still open up for boats at times, and at the top of the towers were two equidistant walkways which over the last few years had become tourist attractions, where people could watch this from above. Marlowe had even been here on quieter days; the gantries provided amazing views over London, glass-walled and even glass-floored in sections–reinforced glass where one could look down at the cars passing underneath.

There were no cars passing tonight, but the fall would probably still hurt, if not kill.

'Is he alone?' Marlowe asked.

'As much as a man like him can be,' the guard nodded.

'What's that supposed to mean?'

The guard waved at himself.

'Well, I'm not exactly a nobody.'

'Right, so what you're saying is he's got muscle?' Marlowe smiled. 'You won't mind if I make sure that I have my own muscle here, then?'

'As long as they stay on the road level, we've got no problems,' the guard replied. 'They can take your body away when he's finished.'

Marlowe gave a dark smile in response.

'You know, you could always go up there for me if you wanted,' he said. 'Pop him in the head, come back down and show me a photo. You'd get the hit.'

'What, a dollar and a bullshit promise from you for something? I think I'd rather take cash.'

The guard shifted uneasily, though. Marlowe knew that this was bravado and bluster. The guard was concerned.

Good.

The guard motioned for Marlowe to raise his arms and patted him down, taking the CZ 75 from his holster.

'You don't need that,' he said. Reaching down to his legs, he found the Fairbairn-Sykes dagger that Marlowe often had on him.

'You can keep that.'

So, close combat weapons only, it seems.

Marlowe raised his wrist, showing the self-defence chain upon it.

'And this?'

'Maximum length?'

'Three foot? A metre?'

'Yeah, you can keep that too.'

Marlowe frowned. The lack of interest the guard had for these items made him wonder exactly what was about to happen. He guessed he'd be fighting, but this felt less like a duel and more like he was walking into a lion's den–an arena with people who knew a game that he didn't. It could simply be that Steele thought he had an advantage because Marlowe was injured, tired and hadn't really slept in almost a week.

Of course, he could be right.

With a wave from the guard, Marlowe slowly walked up the steps that led to the upper gantry.

It was dark outside and the lights of London lit up the sky as Marlowe arrived at the top. A sign had suggested he go into the right-hand side gantry rather than the left, and Marlowe chuckled. He could just imagine the situation if he had gone into the wrong gantry to face his final battle–only to wave across an open space at an annoyed St John Steele. But he had made the right choice, because at the other end of the gantry, wielding a combat knife of his own–what looked to be an American Marines Forces one–and with what looked to be an extendable baton in the other, St John Steele stood waiting.

The last few times Marlowe had seen Steele, he was always impeccably dressed. Suited, Kent-collar shirt, sometimes jeans, often trousers, and it was a coin toss whether he wore a tie or not, but he always looked every inch the gentleman spy he claimed to be. He was a figure of authority and he dressed to show this.

But today, he hadn't. He wore black combats with a webbing belt, looking as though he was about to go on some kind of black ops mission. And Marlowe wondered if this was his actual black ops uniform, worn to make him feel a little better in the upcoming fight. Marlowe, meanwhile, had simply turned up in his usual jacket, T-shirt and jeans–all of which had been picked up in the last couple of hours, replacing the expensive suit that Max Schen had provided him the previous day.

St John Steele cricked his neck as he watched Marlowe enter the gantry and Marlowe paused as the door behind slammed and locked shut.

'Looks like we're stuck together now,' he said, pulling off his jacket and placing it in the gantry's corner. The floor was strangely lit, glowing with the thousands of energy-efficient LED lights that lit up the road beneath. 'So, what's the plan? I'm guessing it wasn't to fight to the death from the very beginning.'

'No,' Steele replied. 'You were supposed to die a long time ago, but like a cockroach, you just won't do it.'

'You should be happy about that,' Marlowe raised an eyebrow. 'Your coin went up because of that.'

'My coin has collapsed because of that as well,' Steele said. 'Do you know how much money I had this morning? Over a hundred and fifty million dollars. Do you know how much I have now? Nothing. Nobody wants to buy my coins.'

'Should've sold when it was high, then. That's the problem with investing. You always wait a little bit too long.'

'Oh, don't get me wrong.' Steele replied, shaking his head. 'I sold some, but not all. The plan was to sell up this afternoon. But then you had to rescue Gregorovich at lunchtime. That bollocks hit on me became public knowledge, made me a laughing stock. Then The Broker began closing down his system and his assassins told me they weren't going for you any more. People who would still try for the money. They weren't on your level. It would have just been more and more killing until there was no hit money left to spend. Witnesses tell me Volkov killed Passive, so that doesn't count. And then your woman—'

Marlowe chuckled.

'I can tell you without any doubt, Trix Preston is not anybody's woman.'

Steele shrugged.

'Miss Preston screwed over Ciaran. Or so he claimed.'

'So he claimed?'

'Let's just say he gave her full blame for what happened. Yet, the mechanics of her actions seem to have involved burnt coins that weren't as burnt as he claimed.'

'Oh no,' Marlowe gave mock innocence. 'You're not telling me that Ciaran Winston tried to cheat you, are you? Because if you genuinely thought he was on your side, I've got a bridge I can sell you.'

He looked around.

'Oh wait, we're already on it.'

St John Steele considered the words and then laughed– but it was a short, bitter bark of one.

'You were going to make me millions, if not billions,' he said. 'The money would have funded my new Orchid, gained me enough funding to bring in new money. That money, in turn would have changed the balance of the organisation.

Three or four other smaller secret societies would have joined. By the end of today, I would have been God.'

He looked around the bridge, staring out of the window towards the other side where, too far to be seen, would be the lights of Westminster.

'You know, I was intending to screw with the infrastructure of the UK,' he said. 'Robertson was going to help me. We were going to provide tariffs to take out our enemies and cash incentives to bring others in. By the end of the year, I would have controlled most of the country's infrastructure. Trains, buses, airports–all while building up my network. Who knows, maybe I would have become Prime Minister. Although that's a little small for what I wanted to do.'

'Well sure,' Marlowe replied mockingly. 'As you just said, you wanted to become God.'

'Yes, well that's not going to bloody happen now, is it?' Steele seemed to tire of the reminiscing, glaring back at Marlowe. "You know, you've got some nerve, bringing in Max Schen. Dick move.'

'It wasn't just Schen who wanted to see you fall,' Marlowe replied. 'How do you think I got out?'

He waited for realisation to cross Steele's face.

'I promised Raymond Kinley I'd provide Gregorovich for him. And what a surprise, I did. Sorry to spoil your plans, St John.'

He had deliberately emphasised the *Sin-jen* of "St John", waiting to see what happened next. Steele, however, simply watched Marlowe, as though judging or estimating him.

'So, what are we doing here?' Marlowe asked eventually. 'I'm guessing you've got nothing left. You've spent millions on a coin and an elaborate fighting pit and a series of assassins who have all failed in their tasks. Your investors are probably preparing to hunt *you* for sport, and your target is now facing you across a gantry.'

'Nobody wants my money any more,' Steele shrugged, 'apart from, of course, the investors who believe I've screwed them over. *They* want my money–the money they believe I've stolen from them.'

'But you haven't, have you?' Marlowe replied. 'You're just as much a victim as everybody else. It's amazing how fast a coin can crash.'

He relaxed his stance, actually going so far as to lean against the wall behind him as he watched Steele across the gantry.

'You've spent so many years believing you were the greatest spy around; you didn't even consider the fact that you could be taken down by someone who wasn't an even greater spy.'

'Are you saying that you're better than me?'

'No, that's the point,' Marlowe replied. 'You've proven time and time again that you're playing chess when I'm playing Cluedo or Tiddlywinks. You entered my apartment without breaking a stride. You've put together plans that would destabilise the world, while at the same time working out your shopping list. And yet here I am, once more, screwing your shit up. That must really piss you off–almost as much as the hit I placed on you.'

'Your hit did nothing but make me laugh,' Steele replied, but from the lack of humour in his voice, Marlowe could tell this wasn't exactly true. 'A dollar and a favour from a defunct organisation. Oh, please, line me up. I'd love to get involved in that.'

Marlowe said nothing, allowing the moment to stretch

out. Tired, Steele straightened–Marlowe mimicking him, preparing for whatever was going to happen.

'I'm tired of you, Marlowe, and it's time for you to die,' Steele said, slowly walking towards him.

Marlowe decided to mirror this and, as he did, noted that all along the gantry's ceiling were cameras. He stopped, looking at them.

'Oh, you see what's actually happening now,' Steele smiled. 'You've taken my money, but I *will* gain something from you. Your death will be broadcast to everyone who purchased Marlowe Coins. They'll see that, as a man of my word, I provided the death they paid for. With luck, this will stop some of them demanding outrageous fees. For others, it will prove I should be trusted, especially with more of their money. So we're going to fight and it's going to be live-streamed.'

'How unoriginal.' Marlowe paused as his foot stepped on the first of the slices of glass embedded into the walkway. As he looked down, he saw that the glass led to the road beneath, but there was a small black square in the middle, obscuring the view.

'Ah,' Steele smiled, 'you've seen the first part of the game.'

He pointed back at all the pieces of glass embedded into the floor.

'Do you know why these are called the sacrificial sheets? It's toughened glass, but not structural. Its job is to get scratched, scuffed, worn down. When it's too damaged, they just replace it–like a screen protector for a one-tonne glass panel.'

He knelt down, stroking it.

'Below that,' he continued, tapping again more softly, 'you've got five layers of laminated glass. Each one bonded with interlayers–usually PVB or SGP. If one cracks, the rest still hold. That's the muscle of the system. Altogether, it's about fifty millimetres thick. Each pane weighs over a tonne, and they're tested to take more than five tonnes of pressure–so you're safe, even if a bus full of tourists came marching through.'

Still talking, Steele ran a hand along the frame.

'The whole thing's set on steel supports with rubber gaskets. Lets it breathe–heat, cold, vibration, it's built to move just enough. You're not standing on glass, Marlowe. You're standing on engineering pretending to be invisible.'

Standing up, he pointed at the black square.

'But a well-angled charge of C4, however, can take it away in a second. You see, the glass might be tempered and it might be strong, but only the sacrificial sheet is taken and replaced, while the other glass is left. And that glass, over years, will weaken, no matter how strong. We'll find small, infinitesimally tiny cracks that, when struck by significant force, will shatter. Have you ever seen *Squid Game?*'

Marlowe shook his head.

'Is that the cartoon with the kid that looks like a sponge and wears a tie?'

'You're such a philistine,' Steele replied. 'It's a game show of sorts, shall we say. And at one point, they must cross a bridge made of glass, where a random part of the glass bridge will shatter. This is the same–although instead of crossing the bridge, you're trying to kill me on it. Randomly, one of these sections will explode, the glass will fall away onto the road below, and you and I will have less space to fight on. The chances are, we might even be on the glass when it shatters–a sort of Russian roulette, controlled by anyone who still holds

Marlowe Coins. I might as well get some worth from them, after all.'

Marlowe nodded, hefting his knife.

'Good for you,' he said coldly. 'But are we going to talk shit for another half an hour, or are we actually gonna get this done?'

———————

30

SQUID GAME

STEELE LUNGED FORWARD, BATON EXTENDING WITH A METALLIC snap as he swung it towards Marlowe's temple.

Marlowe ducked, his self-defence chain unfurling, and he caught Steele's knife on the chain, metal ringing against metal.

'Been practicing, have we?' Steele asked, launching a combination–baton high, knife low. Marlowe's chain whipped forward, catching Steele's wrist but Steele rolled with it, turning the pulled arm into a spin that brought his baton around faster than expected. The metal connected with Marlowe's shoulder, sending pain through his already battered body.

'A rather recent crash course in combat, thanks to you, actually,' Marlowe hissed through clenched teeth as a low rumble shook the walkway. A lit square of glass flashed red and exploded downward, glass raining down as cold air rushed in through the new void.

'First casualty,' Steele said, unperturbed. 'Let's hope it wasn't anyone's lucky number.'

Marlowe circled away from the hole, chain spinning defensively. He struck out, the links cracking against Steele's forearm.

'Something poetic about this,' Steele said. 'You've spent your career on bridges between worlds. Now you'll die on one.'

Marlowe didn't respond. He'd seen him fight and knew there was every chance that with his years of experience, Steele was the better fighter–moving with the skill of someone whose combat skills hadn't faded behind a desk.

Steele closed the distance. Marlowe flicked the chain again, wrapping it around Steele's baton hand and yanked.

Steele twisted, using the tension to pull Marlowe off-balance.

Idiot. You already tried that and it failed. Think cleverer.

As Marlowe stumbled, Steele's knife slashed across his bicep.

'First blood,' Steele said conversationally. 'The investors will be pleased.'

Another glass panel flashed and exploded. Faint traffic noise from London grew louder through the gaps.

'Running out of real estate,' Steele observed.

Marlowe rushed forward, absorbing a blow from the baton to close distance. He wrapped the chain around his fist and with the makeshift chain knuckleduster connected solidly with Steele's jaw. The one-time spy recovered instantly though, driving his knee into Marlowe's midsection.

The air rushed from Marlowe's lungs as an elbow to his neck sent him to his knees.

He rolled as Steele's baton came down where his head had been.

'Disappointing your audience,' Steele said, spinning the baton.

'Just getting warmed up.' Marlowe got to his feet, sweat mixing with blood.

When Steele attacked again, Marlowe stepped inside the swing, taking a slash across his back but wrapping the chain around Steele's neck. He twisted, pulling it tight.

Steele slammed his elbow repeatedly into Marlowe's ribs. His face reddened, movements becoming desperate–but then suddenly, he went limp and twisted, grabbing Marlowe's wrist and executing a perfect judo throw.

Marlowe landed hard on his back. Before he could recover, the glass panel beneath him flashed red–

'Shit!' Marlowe scrambled to the side as the glass fractured. His lower body fell through empty space, hands catching the edge of the remaining floor.

His legs dangled over the yawning gap, the road far below.

Steele walked over to where Marlowe hung.

'Almost too easy,' he said, raising the blade–

Marlowe swung his body sideways and kicked upwards with both feet, swiping Steele's ankle, sending him backwards momentarily.

Using the moment to gather himself, Marlowe rolled back onto the walkway–as two more panels exploded in quick succession, leaving them on a narrow strip of glass.

The fight was funnelling into a straight line. Marlowe whipped his chain forward, the tip catching Steele across the eye. Blinded momentarily, Steele swung wildly, and Marlowe ducked under the next swing, driving a fist into Steele's solar plexus.

The two men grappled, teetering on the edge of a void. Steele was stronger, but Marlowe fought with desperation.

A flick of the chain wrapped it around Steele's wrist, and Marlowe followed with a vicious yank, sending Steele's knife spinning into the darkness.

Steele head-butted Marlowe, staggering him back. Blood poured from Marlowe's nose, but he maintained the grip on his chain. Steele yanked hard, freeing his arm, and Marlowe countered, using momentum to spin Steele around, disturbing his fighters balance.

The floor beneath them shuddered. The panel under Steele's feet flashed red.

Marlowe saw the realisation in Steele's eyes for a split second before the glass gave way. He lunged forward, chain extended, as Steele began to fall.

With reflexes born of desperation, Steele grabbed the chain, arresting his fall. He hung now, suspended over the street below, his free hand scrabbling for purchase on the jagged edge.

Marlowe stepped back, breathing heavily, blood dripping from multiple wounds. He looked down at Steele, the man who had tried to kill him so many times, now literally hanging by his fingertips.

Another panel exploded behind him. *Soon there would be nowhere left to stand, except the edges.*

Steele's fingers strained against the smooth edge of the glass lip, beginning to slip.

Marlowe stared down at St John Steele as he hung a hundred feet above the unforgiving tarmac and broken glass of Tower Bridge's road. He knew all he had to do was stamp on his fingers and the man would fall to his death–or worse, he would lie there, his body broken and unable to breathe as the blood filled his lungs.

'You can't do this,' Steele said, and the conviction in his tone almost convinced Marlowe he was correct. 'You need me in the same way that I need you.'

'What I need is a goddamn dentist,' Marlowe tapped at his mouth. 'Because the one you hired to stick that tracking beacon in me did such a shit job, I've been in pain for a week. Will you be paying my dental fees?'

'Of course not.' Steele chuckled. 'I could let go right now, and I could fall to the death that you want for me. But you'll live the rest of your life knowing that you didn't cause it.'

'And how do you see that?' Marlowe asked.

'My own explosive gave way.' Steele spat some blood from his mouth, the spittle falling to the street below. 'If I let go, you fail—'

'But you'll still be dead,' Marlowe replied. 'All that work, all that effort for nothing. You failed, Steele. Orchid, *your* Orchid? Dead in the water.'

'It'll live on,' Steele hissed. 'And I'll still have the last word. You won't kill me—'

'Oh, you're right,' Marlowe smiled. 'I won't kill you. You see, I promised somebody I *wouldn't* kill you. Someone else wants that honour. Someone I couldn't say no to. You should go meet him right now.'

Before Steele could reply, Marlowe stamped down with his foot firmly, catching Steele's hand. It was such a shock that Steele instinctively flinched with his other hand as well, and with his eyes wide in realisation, his grip now gone, St John Steele fell from the gantry.

Marlowe didn't see the fall, but he heard the sickening crunch of St John Steele hitting the road below. He straightened, crooked his neck, turned and very carefully made his way back to the doorway, banging his hand on it.

'St John Steele is dead,' he said. 'Let me out.'

'He's still breathing, Mister Marlowe,' a voice said through the door's intercom. 'You will not be allowed out until one of you is dead.'

'Fine,' Marlowe replied. 'I'll wait.'

ON THE ROAD ITSELF, ST JOHN STEELE WAS INDEED STILL ALIVE, but it wasn't a predicament he wanted. His bones were broken, and he could feel that his ribcage had shattered, puncturing his lung, which was now filling with blood. It was a slow, painful death, but St John Steele almost found humour in what had happened.

That was until the shadow crossed in front of his eyes and he stared up at Peter Jericho, The Gravedigger.

'Marlowe promised me I could kill you,' 'The Gravedigger said. 'It looks like he kept his promise.'

Steele said nothing, simply coughing up blood, unable to speak as his lungs filled.

'I could leave you like this right now,' The Gravedigger replied. 'Watch you die—my choice—but I always keep my word.'

Before anything else could be said, or before the guard across the road even raised a rifle to stop him, the Gravedigger raised his own weapon, a Desert Eagle pistol in .50 AE calibre... and shot St John Steele in the head.

With that done, he placed his gun away and pulling up the collar of his jacket, he turned southwards and walked off the bridge, leaving the body of St John Steele on the road.

'Debt paid,' he muttered to himself. 'You owe me a favour now.'

———————

THERE WERE NO POLICE WAITING FOR MARLOWE WHEN HE finally returned down the stairs and back onto the street. The chances were that the C4 explosions, although concerning, had been planned for in the paperwork given–the road had been closed so that any of the essential explosive work that had been prepared wouldn't affect passing traffic.

That didn't necessarily mean that Marlowe could leave unhindered, though. The guard, now unemployed, had no problem letting Marlowe exit the bridge, but as Marlowe walked to the south end he saw the SUVs waiting, black and ominous. He took a deep breath, let it out, and then decided to go towards whatever punishment he was going to gain.

Surprisingly, it was Curtis who met him.

'I thought it'd be McKellen,' Marlowe said, looking around.

'McKellen has his own games to play tonight,' Curtis replied, straight-faced, with no hint of a smile. 'It seems the Minister for Defence has had an accident and needs to make a deal with McKellan to keep his job.'

'What kind of accident?' Marlowe asked.

At the question, Curtis shrugged.

'Whatever McKellan decides is worthwhile,' he said.

Marlowe winced. He never wanted to be on McKellan's bad side as it was. He didn't envy Robertson right now.

'I let him take point on that, on the basis that I got to meet with you,' Curtis said. 'You've caused a lot of shit for us, Marlowe.'

'I think you'll find that *I've* not caused any of the shit,' Marlowe said angrily. 'I didn't book the hitmen. I didn't start the whole coin fiasco.'

'That doesn't mean that you haven't caused us a nightmare. Take a stroll with me.' Curtis started away from the bridge towards Potter's Field Park. 'Just so you know, Trix is safe. She took down Winston.'

'Not bad for someone with no field training,' Marlowe said, not wanting to point out that Ciaran Winston was an unfit hacker who probably wouldn't have put much of a fight up against her if he'd trained.

Ignoring this, Curtis continued.

'Ciaran's in custody; we'll be bouncing him around some black sites for a while. Seems he's been making friends with a lot of billionaires recently, and the crypto funds he stole–as well as the various wallets he'd been using linked to quite a few enemies of the state, which we intend to reverse engineer.

'I thought you couldn't do that with a cold wallet,' Marlowe asked.

'Normally you wouldn't, but Ciaran wanted his own little blackmail box and this opened a load of possibilities,' Curtis smiled. 'So, let's just say there's going to be a lot of warlords pissed at him as well when they realise what has happened.'

'Where's Trix now?'

'In a van over there,' Curtis waved towards the road, where Marlowe could see three grey transit vans. In one of them, Trix was probably sitting on a bench, in handcuffs, making life decisions.

'She's not part of this,' Marlowe said.

'Oh, we knew you'd say that, and I think she did as well.' Curtis smiled for the first time. 'She told us this was all on her, and you were just fighting in self-defence. But we know the truth, Marlowe. We know it was a rogue ex-MI6 operative. Of course, McKellen's pointing out that Steele was also MI5 at one point, so he's trying to convince everyone the blame's on us. As far as anybody outside of Tower Bridge is concerned, we had some emergency roadworks that needed to be done, and the assassins that were trying to kill you will simply melt away into the shadows once more. Or maybe mourn the ones that tried and failed. You did leave a hell of a body count, after all.'

'The Broker?'

'Disappeared, almost as if he was warned,' Curtis replied. 'Gregorovich as well. Seems that somehow there was a confusion in the bureaucratic tape and the Home Office agreed to let him go. As you can imagine, Joanna Karolides is spitting nails right now. If anything, you've made a bigger friend in Charles Baker because you've taken down both Robertson and Karolides in one quick swoop, making them both look foolish. Although Robertson, I think, will have his own concerns right now.'

'And what of us?' Marlowe asked. 'Am I to go in one of these vans?'

'That depends,' Curtis replied. 'We do have a vehicle for you, but it's actually an ambulance. No offence, Marlowe, but you look like shit. We're going to take you to St Thomas's and get you patched up. But after that, I think you need to have a long, hard think about what you want from your life. I know you've got a task you must do, but there's no reason why you can't do it while at Whitehall.'

'Are you offering me my job again?' Marlowe asked with a smile.

'Last time I spoke to you I said I would,' Curtis said, and

there was no hint of sarcasm or amusement in his voice. 'We've got moles, Marlowe, and I need people I can trust, and as much as you go off the rails on a regular basis, you're still one of the most trustworthy people I know. You and Trix together, you could help us clean house.'

'Wintergreen tried that,' Marlowe said. 'She took me in off-books. Karolides tried it too. Both times we got burnt.'

'That's because both times you were off-books,' Curtis said. 'Wintergreen wanted her own little black bag organisation to fulfil her tasks. I'm bringing you in properly, returned to the bosom of His Majesty's government. We'll give you what you need to finish whatever jobs you must do–because let's be honest, Marlowe, you've done everything we've wanted you to do on your own, you might as well get career prospects and a pension.'

Marlowe knew this last line was a joke and nodded.

'I'll have to talk to Trix,' he said.

Curtis looked as if he was going to argue this but then nodded and stepped to the side.

'Monday,' he said. 'Tell us your decision.'

'And if I decide not to come back home?' Marlowe asked. 'Do I get dumped in a black site as well?'

'No,' Curtis shook his head. 'We're not threatening you, Marlowe. We're offering a job. If you don't want to come along, we won't be pissed off. But next time you get into trouble we won't be backing you up.'

Marlowe stretched his side, still feeling the wound bleeding and nodded.

'Nine o'clock Monday.'

'You could always give an answer sooner,' Curtis offered.

'Nah, you can all wait,' Marlowe chuckled as he turned to

walk away, heading towards the vans and Trix. 'I've not slept for a week and I really need a good night's rest.'

EPILOGUE

MARLOWE WASN'T SURE WHAT TO EXPECT WHEN HE ARRIVED AT Thames House on Monday morning at nine o'clock. Part of him had wondered whether he'd be arrested; it wasn't an unnatural thought. What he didn't expect, after moving through the various levels of security at Thames House and being given his visitor's pass, was to be escorted to a small, nondescript boardroom where within sat Joanna Karolides, Curtis, and Emilia Wintergreen.

'This can't be good,' Marlowe said with a smile. It was purely a mask, however, as he observed the people sitting around the table. *This was no smiling matter.*

'Our conversation's expanded slightly,' Curtis remarked calmly. 'I hope you don't mind.'

'Not at all. You've brought my favourite people.' Marlowe sat at the end of the boardroom table, as if trying to keep as far away from everyone there as possible.

'We've some questions about you returning,' Wintergreen cut in, straight to business.

'I'm sure you do,' Marlowe replied. 'And I have some suggestions I'd like to make before we even start.'

'Really?' Wintergreen raised an eyebrow, but Marlowe guessed she wasn't surprised by this. After all, it was Wintergreen who had effectively trained up Marlowe, turning him into the operative he was now.

'I spoke to Trix this weekend and we've had a long conversation,' he said. 'While it's true both of us have had our moments of pissing you all off, I know Trix was on suspension and you've effectively been allowing her to consider returning, while I was always the one that, well, shall we say, caused you problems.'

'You can say that again,' Wintergreen muttered to herself, but loud enough for Marlowe to hear.

He smiled.

'Look,' he continued, 'I'm a good operative and I have been for years. When Rubicon turned up, I took the brunt of it because I wanted to make sure that people who had no interest in this world had a chance to live their lives.'

'And how did that work out for you?' Wintergreen looked up. 'Last I saw her, Tessa Kirk was trying to work for us.'

'That's her choice,' Marlowe replied. 'And I will point out that if I had let her be outed as a Rubicon agent, she would never have *had* that choice.'

He turned back to Karolides.

'I'm sorry if any of my Marlowe Coin fallout landed on your shoulders. It was never meant to.'

Joanna Karolides said nothing, simply watching the scenario while Curtis placed his elbows on the table, pursing his lips.

'So, what's your plan?' he asked.

'First off, give me your offer,' Marlowe replied.

'There is no offer,' Wintergreen snapped. 'We bring you back, you act like a good little boy and maybe in a couple of decades you'll get a nice pension and be sent home to live on a farm.'

She mimicked aiming two bullets at the back of the head.

Marlowe got the message.

'So, we act as if nothing happened,' he said. 'I return, sit in my old role, maybe even go back into the gun cage for a while, yeah?'

'The gun cage was good for you,' Wintergreen replied. 'It was definitely good for me.'

'Doesn't work for me.' Marlowe rose from the chair, nodding to the three people opposite him. 'Thank you for the opportunity.'

'What's your suggestion?' Curtis replied, smiling. 'I mean, you weren't walking in here without one.'

Marlowe paused, still standing.

'Over twenty years ago, my mother created a department in MI5 called Section D,' he said. 'It was an MI5 section that worked off-books, using agents that were primarily disavowed, hence where the D came from.'

He looked over at Wintergreen.

'When my mother died, you gave up your entire life to take it on. And over the decades, you continued with this.'

'Section D doesn't exist any more,' Wintergreen replied. 'It died when I was moved.'

'I know,' Marlowe said. 'You've been promoted out of the role and I know that.'

He looked at Curtis.

'You're under her, but at the same time you're big enough

to run London, so it's not up to you to run it. If I come back, I want to head up a *new* Section D. Autonomous. Answerable only to the three of you. And, no offence, Miss Karolides, by that I mean to anyone who takes your role if you suddenly get fired or if you resign.'

Joanna Karolides nodded.

'No offence taken,' she said. 'I understand that.'

'We also answer to Charles Baker,' Marlowe continued. 'Trix was brought in personally by him. I would expect him to be involved in all meetings as well.'

'Really?' Wintergreen said. And although her voice was cold and dripping with scorn, Marlowe could almost sense that she was smiling inside as she spoke it. 'So you'd like to run this team, would you?'

'I don't see why I shouldn't,' Marlowe replied. 'Look, I didn't come to you asking for a job. You've come to me and pointed out that I'm one of the few people you can probably trust to do things.'

Wintergreen snorted at this and Marlowe spun to face her.

'Tell me a time where I've let you down,' he said angrily. 'And be aware that I'm only accepting times when you *didn't let me down first.*'

Wintergreen had nothing to say, simply folding her arms and leaning back in the chair.

'I come back, Trix comes back,' Marlowe continued. 'Our records are expunged of any black marks and we're left to do our own thing.'

'And by that, you mean?'

'I need to dismantle, or at least transform Orchid,' Marlowe said. 'And before you start complaining, I'm aware that once more, I'm on some damn fool crusade. But it's a dangerous item on your to-do list and we've seen that now. St John Steele wasn't the only person who was doing this, and Robertson wasn't the only politician they've got in their pockets. MI6 doesn't treat it as the threat it really should be, although McKellen might change his mind now. I also work well with McKellen. So does Trix, even if she shot him once. Which makes sense if we're going to be working with him as well as you.'

'Oh, so you're *not* an MI5 operative any more?' Curtis asked.

'I'm whatever it needs to be,' Marlowe replied. 'MI6, MI5, off-books, on-books, I don't care. Section D was known as "section disavowed". I get that. But my Section D will be "*section defended*".'

There was a moment of silence.

'And this team is you and Trix?'

'I want budget for five operatives,' Marlowe continued. 'Myself, Trix Preston, Vic Saeed—'

'No,' Curtis interrupted. 'I am not having that traitorous piece of shit in my office.'

'He won't be in your office,' Marlowe said. 'He'll be wherever you dump us. Probably some supply cabinet in the basement, or a location of my own choosing. I don't care where. The man's made mistakes, but he's proven himself to me. And, more importantly, his balls are held in a box by McKellen, so bringing him in takes Saeed away from MI6.'

Wintergreen nodded.

'I see where you're going with that. Who are the other two?'

'Marshall and Tessa Kirk,' Marlowe continued. 'Marshall

would be brought in as a consultant because of his age. Tessa would be brought in as a field operative.'

The three at the other end of the table looked at each other.

'It's true we're not sure what to do with her,' Curtis said. 'Maybe this could work.'

'I suppose a trial period wouldn't hurt,' Wintergreen muttered.

'You don't understand,' Marlowe said. 'Any trial period isn't for you to decide on us. It's for us to decide on you. We don't need MI5 or MI6. We have the money and the resources to take out Orchid without you. I'm giving you an opportunity to be involved. If we find after a few months that this isn't working, *we'll* walk.'

He smiled.

'Oh, and if I do this, then you help me rebuild my apartment.'

'You're staying in the bloody church?' Wintergreen was surprised by this.

'I no longer own it–or rather the MI5 company I bought it through doesn't,' Marlowe replied. 'It was bought by another company. Nothing to do with me in any way whatsoever. They'll be rebuilding it.'

'Let me guess, if we hunt deep enough, we'll find this linked to some shell company connected to Trix Preston or you.'

'I couldn't possibly comment on that,' Marlowe said. 'What I can say is I want it rebuilt. And if you guys are happy to help me with that ...'

He let the conversation trail off before turning to face Wintergreen directly.

'One other thing,' he said. 'Before I even start this, I want Brad Haynes involved as a US liaison. And I want a word with Sasha Bordeaux.'

'She might not want a word with you.'

'Then I suggest you put your prettiest dress on and find out if that would work,' Marlowe smiled.

'Is that how you think you can talk to someone of my level, Marlowe?' Wintergreen raised an incredibly unimpressed eyebrow.

Marlowe shrugged.

'I think I have exactly five more minutes of this meeting, which means I have exactly five more minutes of being able to speak to you like that. I'm very much aware the moment this is all agreed, I'm back to "yes sir, no sir, yes ma'am, no ma'am". But right now, you need me more than I need you.'

He checked his watch.

'Trix will expect a response, the usual manner, by end of day. You guys have a great time.'

He was surprised as he left the office that no one tried to stop him or ask him any last questions. And as he walked out of Thames House, heading towards *The Morpeth Arms,* where Trix and Marshall Kirk were waiting for him, he wondered whether he had actually made a deal …

Or whether MI5 had played him all along.

THE DECISION, SUCH AS IT WAS, CAME ALMOST A WEEK LATER, on a Friday afternoon. Most of the terms had been agreed; Thomas Marlowe was now the new head of a revised version of Section D, following on in his mother's footsteps. Trix Preston was ops director, effectively the number two, and a rotating group of anonymous operatives would be used—which was a comfortable way of saying they wanted Tessa, Marshall and Vic, but didn't want anybody else in the department to know who was going to be used ... until the day everyone was in the office. This way, people couldn't complain about Russian spies or double agents, which was valid.

The only thing that they did push back on was operational budgets. MI5 had recently become the victim of cutbacks, and so there would be fewer business class flights in Thomas Marlowe's future and more Oyster Cards and Avios upgrades.

Marlowe, however, didn't care about that. He didn't need operational funds from MI5. He had his own war chest that he could use. Trix had destroyed the Marlowe Coin, that was true, but she'd also taken over five million of Ciaran Winston's burned coins and sold them before everything fell down, averaging three to four dollars per coin, which meant that when most people collapsed and had nothing, Trix Preston had made them over *ten million dollars* after fees—ten million dollars that were now fed into a variety of shell companies and high-income accounts, providing Marlowe's original cause with an even healthier bank balance than before.

It wasn't to be used for holidays and fun things, though; Marlowe had already learned first-hand how the latest technology and weaponry would take a severe chunk of that. Identities and legend-creating would take more. And, in the grand scheme of things, their current working war chest of just shy of twenty million pounds, although large, would still not take on even the smallest of organisations they were facing.

After all, many of the people investing in Orchid would call that a weekend flutter.

But with the resources that MI5 and MI6 brought back to the table–and without having to hide any more–Marlowe felt this was a new beginning, especially as the Monday after the agreement was made, workmen arrived at his church in West London once more to rebuild the outside. On examination of the ruins, Marlowe had seen that nobody had yet managed to get into the crypt. It was still unknown and, as far as Marlowe was concerned, still his base.

After all, every super-secret spy needed a super-secret base.

Russell Robertson was honoured for his "quick thinking" in a terrorist attack at his club the day Marlowe and Trix were welcomed back into Thames House. Marlowe assumed McKellen had pressured Robertson enough to turn him, but McKellen didn't tell Marlowe as much because McKellen wasn't talking to Marlowe right now, blaming him for the loss of one of his best double agents. Marlowe had explained that with Robertson now working for the dark side–or, rather, McKellan–Vic's double agent-ness was effectively removed anyway. It was hard to be an agent working behind the scenes on the Minister for Defence's staff when the Minister for Defence he was watching was giving the information personally now.

McKellan hadn't accepted this, so that would be a fun conversation to be had down the line.

The same day that Robertson had received his standing ovation in Parliament for his heroic actions, Marlowe received a message from Max Schen. It seemed Max still had people in Whitehall, and had been informed of Marlowe's impending promotion, congratulating him and reminding

Marlowe that it was Max who had assisted him when he needed him the most.

Marlowe had laughed at that. He had wondered how Max would spin it–that he was an ally rather than an enemy. But then, of course, he *would* do that. He had seen first-hand through a multitude of CCTV cameras, fed to the Marlowe Coin holders, that Marlowe had taken his last enemy and kicked him off a bridge.

The Gravedigger had disappeared, as had The Broker, Volkov and Gregorovich. Marlowe assumed the latter three were all playing happy families somewhere but knew that at some point all of them would return and, with the ways of spy craft as they were, he couldn't be sure if they would be allies or enemies.

There was, however, one loose thread–unfinished business that Marlowe needed to deal with before he could officially sign on the line, and this was provided in the Royal Albert Hall a week on from Robertson's resignation.

MARLOWE DIDN'T KNOW WHO WAS PERFORMING THAT NIGHT; HE needn't have worried. He didn't even reach the auditorium, as at the entrance to one of the bars, a familiar face, Brad Haynes, appeared. He said nothing, simply nodding to Marlowe in a friendly way and then cocking his head towards the bar. There, sitting at a high table on a tall chair, was the woman that Marlowe knew as Sasha Bordeaux. In fact, the only thing he knew for sure about her was that her first name *was* Sasha, something she'd told him a few months earlier. He entered, walked up to the table, and sat opposite her.

'First time we ever met was in a bar,' he said.

Sasha looked up at him.

'I don't like being told what to do,' she said, 'but you seem to do this a lot.'

Marlowe nodded.

'I know,' he replied. 'It's something I need to work on.'

He said it with such seriousness that Sasha Bordeaux couldn't help herself and started snorting with laughter.

'You're a prick, Marlowe,' she said. 'You caused us unending issues in Berlin. You could have destroyed the special relationship our country and yours has.'

Marlowe ignored the comment. He was pretty sure that him being a prick in Berlin would definitely *not* have destroyed hundreds of years of diplomacy.

'You needed to meet with me,' she said, 'before accepting some job, right? I was told by Wintergreen she'd take it as a personal favour if I took this meeting, so whatever you need to pass to me, let me know.'

'I don't have anything to pass to you,' Marlowe replied. 'I just wanted to tell you I was sorry, that I understand what I did was an act that put you into an unfair position. But I wanted you to also know, as we might work together down the line, that I would do it again in a heartbeat if it meant keeping my country safe.'

Sasha considered the line, nodded, and saying nothing held out her hand to be shaken.

Marlowe took it, shaking it.

'I'm guessing I don't get your surname for this, though,' he asked.

'You're lucky you still know my name,' Sasha replied, as she started walking to the exit back into the auditorium. 'Do you want to come and see the show? I do have an extra ticket.'

'As much as I would like to spend time in your company,'

Marlowe replied with a smile on his face, 'I think I'm going to take a rain check.'

'You see, Brad,' Sasha said as he was approaching, 'this is how he treats our special relationship.'

'In fairness,' Brad grinned, 'he'd only go red and say something stupid. It's what happens when you fancy your betters.'

Marlowe ignored the comment, nodding to both.

'See you soon,' he said, leaving the bar.

'Marlowe!' It was Sasha's voice again—not commanding but forceful at the same time. 'You should know, Steele might be gone, but the Orchid he started creating *does* still exist. There are people out there who believed in him enough to keep it going. And they blame you for what happened.'

'Shouldn't they be blaming the Gravedigger?' Marlowe asked, looking round. 'I mean, I was fighting in self-defence and The Gravedigger was the one who shot him in the head.'

'About that,' Sasha replied. 'Peter Jericho happens to be helping us with a problem we needed removed. When asked about this, he pointed out that he was given a dollar bill and a favour from you, which means he took your hit—and therefore *you* were the one who killed Steele.'

Marlowe cocked his head as he thought about this.

'Well, then they'd better come and line up,' he said. 'I'll take on all comers.'

'What was the favour?' Sasha asked.

Marlowe made a pantomime of trying to remember and then shook his head.

'You know, I simply can't remember,' he smiled. 'Enjoy the show.'

WALKING OUT INTO KENSINGTON GARDENS, MARLOWE considered the last time he'd had a secretive meeting at the Royal Albert Hall. He'd met with Wintergreen during the Proms–a performance of *Rachmaninoff's Symphony Number Two,* and then had a nameless assassin try to kill him. It had been mere months earlier, but even now he couldn't remember who the assassin had been. *Was it connected to Kate Maybury?* It felt like it was definitely something sent from Lucien Delacroix, Marlowe remembered, shaking his head.

There had been so many bodies. How was it he couldn't remember the faces any more?

Trix was waiting at the base of the Albert Memorial, rising as she saw him.

'All okay?' she asked.

'All okay,' Marlowe smiled. 'Sasha's on our side, and Brad's agreed to assist us. Well, he will when he's eventually asked.'

They started walking away from the Royal Albert Hall, Trix keeping in step with Marlowe and then sliding her arm through his, linking them. Marlowe was surprised at the overly familiar gesture, but chuckled as she made the skipping motion that the characters did in the movie *The Wizard of Oz.*

'And when do we tell them why we agreed to this?' she asked. 'When do we tell them exactly why we've created Section D once more?'

Marlowe stopped, licking his lips as he thought about the question. This wasn't a quick answer, a glib answer. This had to be a well-thought-out and serious one.

'When we've gone past the point of being closed down,' he said. 'When they realise that what we've done can't be stopped.'

And, with this ominous statement made, Thomas Marlowe and Trix Preston, the new heads of MI5's "Section D", walked off towards Kensington, and whatever trouble was waiting for them.

———

Want the next Tom Marlowe Thriller? CLICK HERE on digital, or turn the page...

Tom Marlowe will return in his next thriller

SENTRY POINT

Order Now at Amazon:

mybook.to/sentrypoint

Released 13th October, 2025

Gain up-to-the-moment information on the release by signing up to the Jack Gatland VIP Reader's Club!

Join at http://bit.ly/jackgatlandVIP

ACKNOWLEDGEMENTS

When you write books, you find that there are a ton of people out there who help you, and so I wanted to say thanks.

There are people I need to thank, and they know who they are, including my brother Chris Lee, Jacqueline Beard MBE, who has copyedited all my books since the very beginning, editor Sian Phillips and weapon specialist Eben Atwater, all of whom have made my books way better than they have every right to be, and my late father-in-law, Alan Farrow, who was an early supporter of these before he passed too soon - and he liked Clive Cussler books, so I had to be doing something right.

Also, I couldn't have done this without my growing army of ARC and beta readers, who not only show me where I falter, but also raise awareness of me in the social media world, ensuring that other people learn of my books.

But mainly, I tip my hat and thank you. *The reader.* Who once took a chance on an unknown author in a pile of Kindle books, and thought you'd give them a go, and who has carried on this far with them, as well as the spin off books I now release.

I write these books for you. And with luck, I'll keep on writing them for a very long time.

Jack Gatland / Tony Lee,
London, May 2025

ABOUT THE AUTHOR

Jack Gatland is the pen name of *#1 New York Times Bestselling Author* Tony Lee, who has been writing in all media for thirty-five years, including comics, graphic novels, middle grade books, audio drama, TV and film for *DC Comics, Marvel, BBC, ITV, Random House, Penguin USA, Hachette* and a ton of other publishers and broadcasters.

These have included licences such as *Doctor Who, Spider Man, X-Men, Star Trek, Battlestar Galactica, MacGyver,* BBC's *Doctors, Wallace and Gromit* and *Shrek*, as well as work created with musicians such as *Ozzy Osbourne, Joe Satriani, Beartooth, Pantera, Megadeth, Iron Maiden* and *Bruce Dickinson.*

As Tony, he's toured the world talking to reluctant readers with his 'Change The Channel' school tours, and lectures on screenwriting, story craft and comic scripting for festivals and conferences such as *Raindance* in London and *Author Nation, The Global Publishing Summit* and *20Books* globally.

A Freeman of the City of London and an introvert West Londoner by heart, he lives with his wife Tracy, just outside London.

Feel free to follow Jack on all his social media by clicking on the links below. Over time these can be places where we can engage, discuss Declan, Ellie, Tom and others, and put the world to rights.

www.jackgatland.com
www.hoodemanmedia.com

Visit Jack's Reader's Group Page
(Mainly for fans to discuss his books):
https://www.facebook.com/groups/jackgatland

Subscribe to Jack's Readers List:
https://bit.ly/jackgatlandVIP

www.facebook.com/jackgatlandbooks
www.twitter.com/jackgatlandbook
ww.instagram.com/jackgatland

Want more books by Jack Gatland? Turn the page...

LETTER FROM THE DEAD

"BY THE TIME YOU READ THIS, I WILL BE DEAD..."

A TWENTY YEAR OLD MURDER...
   A PRIME MINISTER LEADERSHIP BATTLE...
      A PARANOID, HOMELESS EX-MINISTER...
         AN EVANGELICAL PREACHER WITH A SECRET...

DI DECLAN WALSH HAS HAD BETTER FIRST DAYS...

AVAILABLE ON AMAZON / KINDLEUNLIMITED

BURIED SECRETS. HIDDEN GOLD.
UNFINISHED BUSINESS.

LIAM HARPER. EX-UK SPECIAL FORCES,
CAUGHT IN A DEADLY HUNT FOR **LOST GOLD**
IN A SMALL TOWN **FILLED WITH SECRETS...**

FINAL
CLAIM

A **BRAND-NEW** ACTION SERIES CREATED BY **NEW YORK**
TIMES #1 BESTSELLER TONY LEE WRITING AS

JACK GATLAND

ORDER NOW ON AMAZON OR KINDLE UNLIMITED

THE THEFT OF A **PRICELESS** PAINTING...
A GANGSTER WITH A **CRIPPLING DEBT**...
A **BODY COUNT** RISING BY THE HOUR...

AND ELLIE RECKLESS IS CAUGHT IN THE MIDDLE.

JACK GATLAND

PAINT
— THE —
DEAD

A 'COP FOR CRIMINALS' ELLIE RECKLESS NOVEL

A NEW PROCEDURAL CRIME SERIES WITH
A TWIST - FROM THE CREATOR OF THE
BESTSELLING 'DI DECLAN WALSH' SERIES

AVAILABLE ON AMAZON / KINDLE UNLIMITED

JACK GATLAND

THE
LIONHEART
CURSE

HUNT THE GREATEST TREASURES
PAY THE GREATEST PRICE

BOOK 1 IN A NEW SERIES OF ADVENTURES
IN THE STYLE OF 'THE DA VINCI CODE'
FROM THE CREATOR OF DECLAN WALSH

AVAILABLE ON AMAZON / KINDLEUNLIMITED

EIGHT PEOPLE. EIGHT SECRETS.
ONE SNIPER.

THE
BOARD
ROOM

HOW FAR WOULD YOU GO TO GAIN JUSTICE?

NEW YORK TIMES #1 BESTSELLER TONY LEE WRITING AS

JACK GATLAND

A NEW STANDALONE THRILLER WITH
A TWIST - FROM THE CREATOR OF THE
BESTSELLING 'DI DECLAN WALSH' SERIES

AVAILABLE ON AMAZON / KINDLE UNLIMITED

PICK A CARD. PICK A SIDE.

TAROT QUEENS. IMMORTAL ACES.
EXILED JOKERS. FAERIE COURTS.
RYDER WAITES FORGOT THEM ALL.

BUT NOW HE REMEMBERS...

AND NOW... HE WANTS ANSWERS.

NEW YORK TIMES #1 BESTSELLER

TONY LEE

KNAVE
SPADES OF
THE PLAYING CARD WAR 1

THE PLAYING CARD WAR BEGINS JAN 2025
AVAILABLE ON AMAZON / KINDLEUNLIMITED

Made in United States
Orlando, FL
30 December 2025

76042865R00260